D0872743

HEADWATERS DECEPTION

The Art of the Swindle

Patrick J. Hughes

BearLilly Press, Oak Ridge TN

To all of the honest, hardworking farm families out there. You are the most under-appreciated people in America.

CHAPTER 1

Get Bigger or Get Out

L egend has it that James 'Overdrive' Evans has been in a hurry all his life. Growing up on the farm, his Dad used to chastise him for working the draught horses to exhaustion. At puberty, he began eyeing the local girls for a suitable farm wife. The Jap bombing of Pearl Harbor motivated him to propose marriage to the girl he thought most up to the task. When she said yes, he persuaded her to move in at his Dad's farm, so he could enlist and go off to war. Some early tractors had an overly-fast, unsafe road gear called overdrive that he favored, hence the nickname.

It's early afternoon on a school day in the late fall of 1963, and Overdrive was driving around his Sheboygan County, Wisconsin farm in the cow car, a Junker so far gone that further damage from plowed ground, gully washes, or rocks was of little concern. Dairy farmers needed to get bigger or get out of the business. Hoard's Dairyman, Wisconsin Agriculturist, hell all the farm magazines, said so. At age 45, the six-three, slender, and wiry-strong Overdrive sure as hell wasn't getting out, so he was surveying his farm and ruminating over how to expand.

Passersby on the country roads around Overdrive's farm were rare. He always smiled and waved at everybody, hoping that acting neighborly would help keep the peace. The roads near his farm were covered in cow shit from his boys hauling manure for spreading on the fields, and this tended to cause hard feelings.

On this day, Overdrive encountered a fancy black car on Rock Road he'd never seen before, just crawling along, and driven by a fancy woman with dark hair. When no wave was returned, he figured she must be a flatlander. The term flatlander referred to assholes from the metro areas in Southeastern Wisconsin or Chicago way. He thought maybe she'd gotten lost on her way back home from Road America, a popular race track near Elkhart Lake. He smiled at the thought that shit splatter may have caused her to slow down.

Over the years, Overdrive, and his grandfather and father before him, had acquired three small adjacent farms that had failed to successfully transition from old-style subsistence farming, to today's agricultural cash economy. The barns, barnyards, and surrounding pastures on the old Lemke, Adcock, and Ulbricht farms were now part of Overdrive's operation and he used them to raise female calves, or heifers, as replacement milk cows. While reviewing these facilities, Overdrive made some interesting observations, then drove back to the home place, and made some more.

While milking the herd that evening, Overdrive mulled things over and came to some realizations. By the time milking was done, he'd been so excited about his ideas for expanding the farm that he wanted to take his wife, Mary, out to talk it through. Their go-to place for private conversation away from the kids was Harbor Lights, a rustic resort on Lake Ellen about a mile from the farm.

At five-foot seven-inches tall, 130 pounds, and with shoulder length brown hair, the 42-year-old Mary was lean, shapely, and muscle-toned from all the physical labor. She was feisty and spirited, but also loving and caring, and tried to please in her own way. Mary produced babies annually over the first four years of her marriage to Overdrive. After the fast start, the pace moderated somewhat, with the help of the rhythm method. The mushrooming pro bono work force thrilled Overdrive, but Mary decided she'd had enough after six, and volunteered for a hysterectomy. To settle the six kids, ages eight through 17, Mary turned on the TV to McHale's Navy, and asked the girls to make some popcorn. Then they left.

* * *

Overdrive and Mary tapped their bottles of Kingsbury Beer together, and Overdrive launched in, "Everybody's saying dairy farmers need to get bigger or get out of the business. Guess what I want to do?"

Mary mimed deep thought, finger to lip, "Let me guess, get bigger?"

Overdrive nodded, "You know me so well. But seriously, what the hell would I do for a living if we got out of dairy farming now?"

Mary smiled, "Good point, you are sort of a one trick pony, aren't you?"

He gave her the stink eye, "Mary, let's get serious.

We both love this way of life, don't we? Being outside, the fresh air, the independence of it, being our own bosses? The feeling of the entire family working together toward a common goal?"

Mary thought for a moment, then said, "Please don't take this the wrong way, James. But sometimes I think it might be more accurate to say the entire family is working toward YOUR goal."

Overdrive, a trifle surprised, "Well, shit. I'm the head of the household, aren't I? Shouldn't I get to decide how I make a living?"

Mary's eyes narrowed, and she leaned in and said, "Yes, you are, and yes, you should. But don't kid yourself. With all the hard work and uncertainty, we pay a high price for this way of life. I signed up for it when I married you, and I have no regrets. But what about the kids?"

At a loss, Overdrive shrugged, and said, "What about them?"

Mary winced at that, and said, "They're investing the only childhood they'll ever have, working to help pay the price for our lifestyle choice."

The voice of scorn, Overdrive said, "So what? Kids should want to help their parents. We helped ours, didn't we?"

Mary conceded, "Of course, we did."

Overdrive bobbed his head, "You are damned right, we did! I was the oldest son of a dairy farmer, for Christ's sake. Keeping up with the work was a struggle. You helped out on your Dad's fox farm, and your folks rented you out as a washer woman, to help make ends meet. Given the circumstances, we've done pretty well for ourselves, and our kids."

Mary looked disappointed in him, "I never said we hadn't. I'm as proud of us making a go of it, as you are. But don't you see? Times are changing. When we grew up, our friend's lives were just like our own. That's not the case anymore."

Overdrive looked at her, reevaluating, "What're you saying? The lives of our kids are different than the lives of their friends?"

Mary nodded, and said, "Exactly! In summer, every time our kids drive a tractor through Cascade, what do they see? Their friends playing ball at the park, or at the playground by the Mill Pond. When school's going on, afterward, their friends watch TV or go out to play. Our kids do chores before and after school."

Overdrive, voice revving up, "Which explains why this country is going to hell in a handbasket. A whole generation lost. Growing up, and never learning how to work for a living. No wonder ..."

Mary interrupted, "Enough, James. Not tonight, okay? I'm just saying that unlike you, not everybody knows they want to be a dairy farmer, the day they drop out of the womb. This way of life comes with a steep price, and when our kids are old enough to decide, we shouldn't presume they'll choose to pay it."

Overdrive tried to meet Mary half way, if a bit grudgingly, "Okay, I get it, and you may be right. I just have a hard time believing that out of six kids, none of them will choose to farm. And if one does, how'd they ever raise the capital to get started, unless we have a profitable operation for them to work their way into?"

Possibly mollified, Mary said, "Good point. Look, I do the books, I read the magazines, and I agree. We either need to get bigger or get out. If you have ideas for getting bigger, I'm all ears."

Overdrive filled Mary in on his thinking. At the home place, the existing milk-cooling bulk tank, silos, corn crib, and granary have storage capacities that exceed those needed for the current milk herd. Not only that, the barns and pastures at the old Lemke, Adcock, and Ulbricht farms can accommodate more heifers. This means that milk production could be significantly expanded by simply adding on to the barn at the home place, and filling it with more milk cows. The dairy operation would become more efficient overall, through targeted investments that help them make better use of existing assets.

❋ ❋ ❋

The next day, Overdrive and Mary headed to Cascade, about a mile from the farm, for a few grocery items, and to catch up on the village gossip. As they passed the bank, they saw their farm loan officer, Walt Brickner, talking to a striking, well-coiffed dark-haired women, while walking her out to a fancy black car.

Mary, "Well la-di-da, it looks like Walt has his hands full with that one".

Overdrive harrumphed, but kept to himself that the black car is the same one he'd seen on Rock Road yesterday. Walt usually flashed a brilliant smile and gave a full arm wave when he saw Overdrive and Mary, but all they got this time was a straight face and a nod. The woman glanced in their direction, and something about her look and Walt's tepid greeting unsettled Overdrive. Apparently, she hadn't been a lost flatlander after all.

Mary pulled up in front of Reinhold's Grocery, and asked, "After getting the groceries, should I pick you up at Art's?"

Overdrive nodded, and said, "Great idea. You know how Art can talk. I'll need your help getting out of there." Overdrive walked one block along Cascade's main drag, known as Madison Ave. or State Hwy 28, to Art's Service Station.

* * *

Upon entering the service bay, after the niceties, Art gave Overdrive a steady earful of the recent goings on in the vast metropolis of Cascade, population 450. Overdrive listened politely until his patience wore thin, then asked, "Any idea who owns the fancy black car that's out in front of the bank?"

Art's face lit up at the question, and he said, "I don't know the woman. Didn't pay much attention to her. I mean, she's a looker and all, but did you see that car! Wow, that's a 1963 Ford T-Bird Landau, a real beauty! Don't see many of those around Cascade, that's for damn sure. I've seen it a few times now, either parked at the bank, or driving by. Why do you ask?"

Overdrive, nonchalant, "Oh, no reason. I just hadn't seen her or the car around here before. Saw her and Walt out in front of the bank, on the way past."

Art bobbed his head, and said, "Yeah, that car's only been around recently." Then Art changed the topic, "You know, I hate to bring this up AGAIN, but your father is an accident waiting to happen. He still comes shooting out of W. Water St. right onto Hwy 28 without stopping and looking at the stop sign. He did it again this morning. Hell, my business is right on this corner. One of these days, there'll be a wreck that slides into my gas pumps, and the whole village will explode."

Overdrive, hands up a placating gesture, "Okay, Art, I hear you, I hear you. I'll talk to Dad again, I promise." Then Mary pulled in, and he said, "There's Mary. Guess I'd better be going. Say hi to the wife, and thanks for the news."

* * *

Overdrive habitually mulled over whatever was on his mind, while milking the cows. On this particular evening, he'd been worried about two things. First, he couldn't understand why the fancy dark-haired lady he'd seen with Walt had made such an impression on him. Something about the way she stared when they drove by, sent chills up his spine. And what the hell was she doing, crawling along on Rock Road? Was she checking out his land? Why would she? It's not for sale.

Overdrive's other worry was his Dad. Today wasn't the first time that Art had raised concerns over his father's driving, and Art's not the only one. People he hardly knew, in Cascade and around the area, had been dropping hints. He'd already spoken to Dad about this on several occasions, but it hadn't done any good.

Frankly, deep down, Overdrive had bigger worries about his father. He feared his Dad might be losing his mind. He'd been increasingly insistent lately that Overdrive participate with him in a *bridge with the ancestors*, whatever the hell that meant. Dad kept saying he wouldn't be around forever, and needed to teach

Overdrive how to use this family gift while he's still able. Putting it off, had only made his father pushier about it. If he humored his father by participating, at the very least it'd prevent this irrational need from further poisoning their relationship. The crops were all in, and time wasn't as dear right now as it usually was, so that's what Overdrive decided to do.

CHAPTER 2

Head Start

Overdrive hadn't yet worked out all the farm expansion details. But he knew they'd have to pull the trigger on barn addition construction about next March. He wanted to avoid temporarily storing hay elsewhere, and having to double handle it, to fill the storage area, or haymow, in the new addition. Beginning in May, a hay harvest, or cutting, was taken approximately every month. In order to store the August harvest, or fourth-cutting, directly in the new haymow, the addition needed to be substantially completed by then. The March start made that possible.

Spring's work referred to tilling land and planting crops. This extra effort fell on top of the ongoing dairying chores and, in the case of the kids, school. In other words, it made every spring crazy. Overdrive knew that next spring would be even crazier, with farm expansion in the mix. The best way to get a head start, was to finish this fall and winter, all work that could possibly be done before spring.

Milking cows, morning and night, was a routine

activity that Overdrive could do in his sleep. So, he used this time to think and plan. It was late October, 1963, and the poor-yielding alfalfa lands he planned to reseed to corn next year had already been plowed. While ruminating, he came up with three other tasks that could be finished before spring. For plowing the corn ground and cleaning the manure out of the heifer barns, they'd have to hurry because winter was fast approaching. The third task, machinery service and repair, could be strung out between now and next February.

* * *

Overdrive loved plowing corn ground at night on his John Deere 70 two-cylinder diesel tractor. Something about the JD70's sound, which earned it the nickname 'Johnny Popper' throughout the farm belt, drew deer by the dozens out of the Waldo Swamp. They just stood there with their eyes glowing in the tractor lights, staring at him as if he were crazy. He owned a brand new, and more powerful, John Deere 4020 tractor. But this smooth-running six-cylinder diesel didn't attract the deer, and the JD70 handled his four-bottom plow just fine.

Last week the ground had been too wet and smeary to plow, but the cold snap had frozen a thin top layer of soil, wicking moisture from below. The frost layer enabled the soil to support the weight of the equipment, and owing to the wicking action, the drier lower layers were more easily turned over by the plow.

Overdrive desperately wanted to finish plowing all the corn ground before the bitter cold arrived, and drove the frost line so deep that the soil would be locked up until spring. Most days, the thin frost layer wilted in the sun or due to diurnal temperature rise, and the JD70's wheels just spun. But at night, the thin frost layer reappeared, and plowing could continue.

It's well past midnight, and Overdrive was plowing the bottomlands, or lower strip of land along the swamp, enjoying the deer. He heard a honk, and looked up to see the cow car's headlights, at the end of the row. He plowed to the end, idled the diesel, and hopped down off the tractor and into the car.

Perplexed, Overdrive said, "Mary, what the hell are you doing here?"

Mary, sarcastically, "Evidence suggests my pig-headed husband intends to skip sleep for the third night in a row. Apparently, adult supervision is required."

"Well, it's not my fault conditions are only right at night," Overdrive snapped. "You know we've got to finish plowing before the arctic shit storm hits."

Mary, a trifle impatiently, "I know, James. I also know you've got a 17-year-old son who'd run this rig better than you, after a little instruction."

William 'Jumbo Bill' Evans, or more commonly Jumbo, was Overdrive and Mary's 17-year-old son. He was six-four and 240 pounds, making the origin of his nickname self-evident. Jumbo had a strong jaw, chiseled frame, dark brown eyes, and was considered handsome, in spite of wearing his almost black hair in one of Mary's DIY buzz cuts. Athletically, Jumbo's coaches at Plymouth High School described him as a freak of nature. He played both ways in football, and led the conference in pancake blocks and tackles. Last winter in basketball, he led the team in scoring and rebounds. Last spring in track, he set school records in the shot-put and discus throws, and the high-hurdle sprint. He's also quite the social butterfly and a pretty good student, though he doesn't try very hard.

Somewhat dumbfounded, Overdrive said, "Jumbo? You're kidding, right? When the fuck would he plow? He's got chores to do, school, after-school football practice, Friday night games, and when football ends, basketball begins."

Having already thought it through, Mary shot back, "Tomorrow's game, and the next two after that, are all in Plymouth. Jumbo can come home and plow afterward. If he runs the rig Friday and Saturday nights, and you run it on school nights, the plowing will be done in three weeks. Jumbo can even sleep in Saturday and Sunday mornings, if his younger brothers help out with his chores."

Overdrive thought about that, then said, "Huh. Not a bad idea. Okay, tomorrow night Jumbo can ride along with me until he gets the hang of it, and we'll see how it goes."

Then, unexpectedly, Mary added, "Oh, and one more thing. Starting tomorrow you're taking a nap between milkings." Overdrive tried to protest, but she raised her finger and cut him off, "No buts! Without sleep you'll be punch drunk or worse, and won't be able to plan the farm expansion."

Overdrive, too weary to argue, "Okay, we'll do it your way this time."

As he got out of the car, Mary grabbed his arm and softened her voice, "James, you're not alone here, you know. We're all willing to do our part. No bank is going to give us the money for the expansion, if the plan is just in your head. The only way to prove we've thought through the details, is to get them on paper." Then before the door closed, Mary shouted, "Now get back to work, you slacker!"

The following night after the game, Overdrive took Jumbo out on the plow. After 30 minutes of ride-along instruction, he set Jumbo loose on his own, frost plowing for the first time. The next morning, Overdrive inspected the work and Mary had been right. Jumbo's plowing was as good or better than his. Overdrive mused that his oldest son would make a great farmer someday, if only his current obsession with sports didn't lead him astray. When he agreed to plow, Jumbo had made a big deal about having to sacrifice his weekly date night with Lizzie Flint. It hadn't yet occurred to Jumbo that Overdrive viewed Lizzie as a silver lining. She came from a fine farm family.

* * *

When calves are born, Overdrive generally ships the males, or bulls, off to market for cash, but raises the females, or heifers, as replacement milk cows. The heifers are kept at the home place while being weaned from their mother's milk to milk replacer, and then transitioned to a diet of grain and hay. When old enough, they're moved to Lemke's, and then rotated to Adcock's and Ulbricht's as they get older. Finally, they're brought back to the home place when they're about to drop their first calf, and begin to milk. Overdrive runs a mature bull with the herd at Ulbricht's, to avoid the expense of artificially inseminating unproven youngstock.

The ground floors of the barns at Lemke's, Adcock's, and Ulbricht's are used as run-in sheds, to shelter the heifers during foul weather. Manure accumulates, and needs to be cleaned out annually. The job is a bitch, because much of the work must be done manually. These old barns weren't designed with modern shit-cleaning techniques in mind, such as the use of tractor-mounted hydraulically-operated scoops, or pull-behind blades.

Over Saturday morning breakfast, Overdrive took the opportunity to spin up the barn-cleaning task. He cleared his throat to get everybody's attention, and then launched in, "Joe, I need you and your younger brothers to clean the manure out of the three heifer barns before it freezes."

Joe was Overdrive and Mary's second-oldest son, at 16 years of age. He was five-eleven, 180 pounds, and farm-boy strong in an uncoordinated sort of way. He had light brown hair with reddish highlights in a buzz cut, a pointy colicky hairline, a nose that bent slightly to the left, and hazel eyes. Joe was most famous for his smart mouth, which got him in trouble at school, home, and everywhere else. Under certain circumstances, he could be hilarious. Under others, he could make you want to ring his neck. Due to his own poor judgment, the latter was far more common. As if by reflex, Joe said, "Aww, Dad, how come we always get all the shit jobs. What about Jumbo?"

Overdrive stared at Joe, careful to retain his composure, and said, "Jumbo and I are taking turns plowing all night. You know that, and you know why."

Joe rolled his eyes, and said, "Then why not teach

me to plow? It sounds like fun. Shine deer. Bring a shotgun with slugs, bang-bang, fresh venison ..."

Overdrive barked, "ENOUGH! There's more to frost plowing than YOU KNOW. You'll be TAUGHT, when your TIME COMES."

Silence washed over the kitchen table. Mary and Jumbo struggled to fight back smiles, while the faces of the girls and younger boys bleached white. Sensing the need to tack in a different direction, Joe capitulated, and said, "Fine." But unable to stop there, he added, "But John and David are just runts. They can barely lift a fork or shovel, let alone one full of shit." Joe had a point.

Although John was relatively large and strong for his age, he's a pre-pubescent 11-year-old. Heavily freckled, with a sunburn and peal complexion, John had hazel eyes, and his buzz cut was brown with reddish highlights. Standardized tests scored him in the Brainiac range, and he drew family-wide blank stares with his explanations of how the physical world worked.

David was also large and strong for his age, but being an eight-year-old, that's not saying much. He possessed the most beautiful cherubic face, with dark brown eyes, framed by a blondish brown buzz cut. David's siblings considered him spoiled, since he received the lion's share of the contraband candy bars smuggled into the farm by their grandpa, Overdrive's Dad.

Joe continued in a whiney voice, "Can Grandpa help?"

All heads remained immobile, but eyes swiveled toward Overdrive. After a deep breath, and then another, Overdrive managed to say, "As it turns out, I need to see your grandpa this morning on another matter. I'll ask him if he's willing."

Joe took the deal, and said, "Thanks, Dad." As the tension in the room quickly dissipated, Joe motioned to John and David, and said, "Come on runts, we've got a shit job to do." Joe got up from the table and trudged out the back door, with his younger brothers following along behind.

Overdrive wanted to get the barn cleaning task started properly, but couldn't deal with anymore of Joe just now. So, he turned to his oldest son, and said, "Jumbo, take the cow car and drive your dumb-ass brothers over to Lemke's for a look-see. Talk them through how to use the scoop to load the spreader, and tell them which field to spread the shit in. Then bring them back so they can gear up. If the shit's too solid for the scoop attachment, help them replace it with the fork."

Jumbo nodded, "You want me to check in on them after an hour or so?"

Overdrive shook his head, "Don't bother. We'll get an earful over supper."

After telling Mary he needed to speak with his father, and the nap would have to wait, Overdrive pushed his way out the back door. During the drive to Cascade, he reflected on the breakfast conversation and couldn't help but smile. As a young boy, Overdrive's favorite line with his Dad had been *why do I always get all the shit jobs?* Joe was right, cleaning the heifer barns was a shit job.

* * *

Overdrive spotted his father's car parked out front of what the locals referred to as the Old Opera House. Attempts by recent proprietors to rename the tavern after themselves failed to stick, and it appeared the current owner had given up trying. Overdrive parked and headed in, dreading the conversation to come.

Overdrive's father, William 'Old Bill' Evans, was in his late sixties, but was fit for his age and retained a full head of thick, graying hair. He stood erect at just under six-feet tall, and although a little heavyset, still moved fluidly as if he were a younger man. Being an affable Welshman, he enjoyed social interaction, and was willing to tolerate German card games like sheepshead to get it. When Overdrive walked in, he spotted Old Bill playing cards with some of the village elders. Father and son smiled and nodded to each other, and Overdrive took a seat at the end of the bar. Old Bill threw in after the hand ended, and moved to the adjacent stool.

After the niceties, Overdrive started off with, "Word around town is, it's just a matter of time before they have to use the jaws of life to cut you out of a wreck at the corner of W. Lake St. and Hwy 28."

Old Bill recoiled, and shot back, "Word around town, my ass! It's that busy body Art, isn't it! Ever since I skinned him for a hundred bucks playing sheepshead three weeks ago, he's been bad mouthing me behind my back. It's him, isn't it?"

Overdrive tried to hold a straight face, failed, but then recovered to say, "Well, more folks than just Art have suggested you need to abide by the stop sign and look both ways at that intersection."

Old Bill, in an exaggerated low-pitched growl, "I knew it, that sonofabitch! I'll make him beg for mercy the next time we play cards." Then he paused, eyes twinkling, and added, "But you didn't come all the way down here to lecture me about my driving, did you son?"

Overdrive nodded, and said, "Well no, actually. Joe, John, and David need some help cleaning the manure out of the heifer barns before it freezes. I was wondering if you could lend them a hand."

Old Bill paused a beat to let his smile spread, "Sure, but why do I always get all the shit jobs?" They both laughed, and Overdrive slapped his father on the back.

Overdrive offered to buy a round of beers if his father would join him out of earshot, at a table in the far corner. He wanted to get Old Bill's reaction to the idea of expanding the farm, but feared people could overhear unless they moved. With Kingsbury and Hamms Beers in hand, they ambled over to the table together and Overdrive filled Old Bill in on the farm expansion plans, such as they were, and asked what he thought.

Old Bill gathered his thoughts, and said, "Well, everybody's saying get bigger, or get out. Are you and Mary sure you want to get bigger?"

Overdrive nodded, "Absolutely. Been thinking about it for a long time."

Old Bill chewed on his lower lip, then said, "From what you've said, I can tell you're pretty serious. More acres of land. More cows to milk. That's a lot of work. How many hired hands do you figure you'll need?"

Surprised by the question, Overdrive lingered over taking a swig. He decided to play it straight, "We don't plan to have any hired hands."

Old Bill's eyebrows shot up, "I'm sorry, I must be going daft. What?"

Overdrive looked down, and said, "We don't plan to have any hired hands."

Old Bill, flabbergasted, "Son, who's going to do all that work?"

Overdrive leaned closer, "Well, there's me and Mary, of course, and the kids are older now and can do more, and we're hoping you'd want to continue to help. You know, to keep the farm in the family."

Old Bill, in a reassuring voice, "You know I'd give my right arm to keep the farm in the family, son. You don't have to worry about me, I'll do whatever these old bones allow. But have you done some figuring? Is it even possible?"

Overdrive conceded, "Not as much as we need to. But we plan to limit the expansion to what the family, and the machinery we own, can handle."

Old Bill bobbed his head, and said, "Well, you and Mary are both good with figuring, I'll grant you that. It just seems like a big risk, and a boat load of work."

Overdrive nodded, now grim, "It is, but if we pull it off, we'll have a family farm with a future. Otherwise, we'll have to get out of farming sooner or later."

Old Bill exhaled heavily, and said, "You're probably right, and if it's the only way to keep the farm, I guess I should be cheering you on for wanting to try. It's just, ... well, just thinking about it, brings back those old fears. The ones that dogged me during the Great Depression, when I almost lost it all."

Overdrive leaned closer, "I can understand that. But things are different now, Dad. Back then, the whole country was going down the shitter. There was nothing to grasp onto, to break the fall. Today, the economy is booming. The people we do business with can lend us a hand, if we need one."

"Maybe you're right." Then, Old Bill held up a finger, and continued, "Look, I know you hate it when I bring this up, but with something as important as this, we should seek advice from the Welsh ancestors."

Overdrive leaned in and whispered, "Dad, keep your voice down."

Old Bill swiveled his head, saw no eavesdroppers, and lowered his voice, "They started farming in this county in 1848, and farmed in the old country for centuries before that. You'd be surprised how much help they can be."

Overdrive, in a low voice, "Dad, you need to keep that Welsh crazy shit to yourself. Do you hear me! People might take it the wrong way, and try to have you committed. Just because the old County Insane Asylum in Winooski burnt down, doesn't mean they haven't already built someplace else to lock you up."

Old Bill looked disappointed in him, "I hear you, son. But just so you know, without their advice, there wouldn't have been a farm for you to buy. You've always been pigheaded. I hope you outgrow it, before you reach the crossroads."

Overdrive's eyebrows shot up, "Crossroads, what're you talking about?"

Old Bill doubled down, "The crossroads is where, if you choose the wrong turn, you lose it all. Taking the right path, is something your ancestors have done forever. Think about it, of course they'd have valuable experience to share."

They both leaned back and drained their bottles. Then Overdrive, careful to keep his voice calm, said, "Look, we both want the farm kept in the family. We both agree, expanding is the only way. Mary and I want you on board before we move forward. If Mary asks, can you promise to say you're on board?"

Old Bill thought about that, then said in a low voice, "Yes, of course. But on one condition. You participate in a bridge with the ancestors. I know from the outside looking in, it sounds crazy, and you don't believe in it. But that'll change when you experience a bridge for yourself. You'll just have to trust me on that."

Overdrive wasn't surprised by his Dad's condition. He'd already decided to humor him, and participate in a bridge. The excruciatingly long pause was merely for affect. He wanted his Dad to owe him one, by seeing his participation as a huge favor. Finally, Overdrive rolled his eyes, and said, "Fine, Dad, I'll do that."

As a big smile spread across his face, Old Bill said, "Well, I'll be damned. There's still hope for the challenged. Maybe you're not such a dumbass after all."

As the conversation wound down, Overdrive agreed to come over to Old Bill's shack of a house in Cascade, after milking that evening. He'd have to make up some excuse to tell Mary. Maybe tell her he needed to give Old Bill another lecture about his poor driving. He always tried to be honest with Mary, but in this case, saw no alternative to misdirection.

* * *

When Overdrive arrived at Old Bill's shack, he noticed the window shades were down. He knocked, and when beckoned, entered. His Dad asked him to lock the door, and while doing so, noticed that only candles lit the small living area. Old Bill was seated in one of the stuffed chairs, and motioned for Overdrive to take the other. On the small table between the chairs, were two cocktail glasses and a bottle.

With a very serious expression, Old Bill said, "I know you don't believe in what we're about to do. I didn't my first time either. Dad got me over that hump by letting me see for myself. That's my plan tonight, unless you've a better idea."

Overdrive said, "Dad, you're the expert here. I've no idea what's going on."

Old Bill nodded, and said, "Good. I'll walk you through what you need to do to participate, and then we'll bridge. After we're done, I'll explain more about it."

Overdrive bobbed his head, and said, "Fair enough."

Old Bill, in an instructional tone, "I'll do all the talking with the ancestors, in Welsh. Then I'll translate their responses, so you can understand. If they rattle on among themselves, I'll wait, and translate the outcome. Any questions?"

Credulous, Overdrive shrugged and said, "What're we going to talk about?"

Old Bill, thoughtfully, "I figured we'd tell 'em about the farm expansion ideas, and then ask 'em what they think. You'll have to tell me what t'say."

Overdrive nodded, and said, "Okay, sounds like a plan."

Old Bill poured a jigger of dark liquid into each glass, and said, "This is *Drysien Gwyllt*, a Welsh liquor.

It's made with what they call wild brambles, or black-berries, that're fermented and marinated in spirits. Are you with me so far?"

Overdrive, trying hard to hide his amusement, "So far, so good."

Old Bill, once again instructionally, "We alternately sip this, and whisper a Welsh phrase that I'll tell you next. This ritual begins the session with the ancestors. It usually takes a minute or so to get started. Understand?"

Overdrive, with a hint of curiosity, "Yes. But how'll I know it's started?"

Old Bill shook off the question, and said, "Just pay attention, you'll know. Now, the Welsh phrase we say is '*a fo ben, bid bont*'. We'll have to practice its Welsh pronunciation, until you get it right. Got it?"

Overdrive shrugged, "I guess. But what does it mean?"

Old Bill said wisely, "It means *if you want to be a leader, be a bridge.*"

Old Bill had Overdrive whisper '*a fo ben, bid bont*' over and over, correcting him as he went along, until he figured the enunciation was close enough. Then they both began sipping *Drysien Gwyllt* and whispering '*a fo ben, bid bont*', over and over, and within a minute the bridge to their ancestors was opened.

Old Bill began speaking in Welsh, perhaps introducing who's on his end. Overdrive sensed a vague presence and noticed a change in the candles, as if they'd somehow gotten brighter. Then, remarkably, he began hearing voices speaking gibberish, or rather, Welsh. Voices that weren't his Dad's.

After a while, Old Bill asked Overdrive to share

his initial thoughts on how to expand the farm, as simply and concisely as he could. This took some time. They worked out a process where Old Bill would hold up his hand, when he wanted Overdrive to stop. This provided Old Bill time to translate to Welsh, what he'd heard thus far.

When finished, Old Bill started fielding questions from the ancestors. If he didn't know the answer, he'd translate to English, so Overdrive could provide it. Near the end, Old Bill asked the ancestors where they'd be able to help. After the chatter died down, he translated the summary response for Overdrive.

Ending the session was done in the same manner as beginning it. Sip and whisper, over and over, until the room grew quiet, the candles dimmed, and the sense of presence disappeared.

* * *

When it was over, Old Bill and Overdrive both got up to pee, and move around a little to get the circulation going. Then Old Bill popped open two bottles of Hamms Beer, and poured a bag of pretzels into a bowl.

Once settled into their chairs, Old Bill asked, "Well, what'd you think?"

Overdrive bought time by munching pretzels, and washing them down. Then he said, "Some good questions were asked, like how're you going to work all that land, how're you going to milk all those cows, how long will you be in the bank?"

Old Bill, encouragingly, "What else?"

Overdrive took another handful, crunched, sipped his beer, and said, "They seemed to think they could help us pick the best nearby lands to rent, decide what crops to put where, and find the best livestock bloodlines for expanding the herd."

Old Bill, head bobbing, "What else?"

Overdrive ruminated a moment, then asked, "Who was on the other end?"

Old Bill, in a matter of fact manner, "Your Welsh bloodline ancestors. All of them. Your grandfather, great-grandfather, their wives, and so on. The more recent generations tend to talk the most. Their life experiences are more relevant. As you know, some of them farmed in this county, even in this township. My Dad, your Grandpa, spent half his farming years developing what's now your farm."

Overdrive, still skeptical, frowned and said, "What are they, spirits? How'd they know all those things?"

Old Bill, patiently, "They've passed away, so I guess spirits is as good a word as any. What they know is simply their life experiences. For pure blood Welsh descendants like us, communication over the bridge is so clear, it's as if anything learned by our Welsh ancestors is never forgotten."

Overdrive, trying to apply reason with limited success, "Can all Welsh do this? I mean, the Flint's are Welsh. Can they?"

Old Bill said wisely, "To the knowledge of our ancestors, and believe me I've asked, we're the only ones. Only our bloodline can be a bridge, so to speak."

Overdrive had a thought, "If they had this power all along, why weren't they ... you know ... Welsh aristocracy or something?"

Old Bill, as if the question was expected, "They

wanted to be farmers, and used their powers to become very good ones. That's the lifestyle they cherished."

Overdrive, like a dog with a bone, "But why uproot your entire life, and migrate half way around the world to a wilderness? Why settle in Sheboygan County, Wisconsin, of all places? It makes no sense."

Old Bill thought for a moment, "As I understand it, by the 1840's, the English had finally gotten around to enforcing their doctrines everywhere in the conquered kingdoms, including remote and hilly places like Wales. Rather than convert to the Church of England, your ancestors migrated to America."

Overdrive, still unsatisfied, "America sure, but why here?"

Old Bill, wisely, "You're asking the same questions I did, son. They were farmers looking for land. They sent family to each U.S. territory being settled at the time, and compared notes. This part of Wisconsin reminded them most of home, and had fewer deadly epidemics at the time, so they decided to settle here."

Overdrive, unconvinced, "Huh. Well, then you'd think the area would be filthy with Welshmen, right? But it's not."

Old Bill, a trifle impatiently, "Well, you're right about that. There weren't many Welsh settlers right around here. Most were clannish, and stuck together to preserve the language. Wisconsin did have a few large Welsh settlements though, in villages like Rewey, Cambria, and Wales. Our family chose to keep their distance from the large Welsh enclaves."

Overdrive, perplexed, "Huh. Why do you suppose that is?"

To buy time, Old Bill took a handful of pretzels,

crunched them, and drained his bottle. Then, he nodded to himself, flashed a mischievous grin, and said, "Trying to escape the reputation, I guess. You know, claiming to be able to speak with the dead, and all. Back in Wales, they were viewed as batshit crazy."

Overdrive, caught off guard with head back and bottle to lips, got beer down the wrong pipe, and broke into a coughing fit. When it finally subsided, with eyes watering and face red, he managed to croak, "You're shitting me, right? They were known lunatics, even back in Wales?"

Old Bill, eyes twinkling, "I shit you not. It was common knowledge."

Overdrive pulled out his hanky, dried his eyes, and blew his nose. Then he looked at his watch, and said, "Look, it's getting late and I've got to run. This has been... interesting... to say the least."

Old Bill nodded, "It might take a while to wrap your mind around it."

Overdrive, dead serious, "That's the understatement of the century. In the meantime, for Christ's sake keep this Welsh crazy shit to yourself, okay?"

Old Bill gave him the three-fingered Boy Scout salute, and said, "On my honor. With everybody but you, mums the word. With you, however, I reserve the right to continue to point out when a wise son should consult with the ancestors."

As he was leaving, Overdrive said over his shoulder, "Fine, you do that."

* * *

On the drive back to the farm, Overdrive's mind

spun into a state of distraction, and kept spinning well into the night. Now wide awake in bed with Mary sleeping at his side, the questions just kept coming. Were ancestors really speaking through his Dad? Or, had Dad babbled Welsh to himself, and fed Overdrive a line of bullshit in English? But why would Dad purposely deceive him? What possible motivation could he have? And, even if he wanted to, how could Dad do it? Could Dad somehow manipulate him into feeling a presence, seeing candles brighten, and hearing unfamiliar voices? Since when, can Dad do impersonations, and throw his voice? Sonofabitch! Was tonight real?

Perfect, just perfect. Presuming tonight wasn't a hoax, Overdrive came from a long line of known nutjobs. If true, at least they had the good sense to isolate themselves from other Welsh settlers, here in Wisconsin. So long as this dirty little secret remained buried, as Dad believes it is, our lives can go on as usual, right? I mean, we're fifth generation, and so far, so good.

By nature, Overdrive wasn't inclined to worry over things he couldn't control. He'd been exposed to new information tonight, and the only thing he controlled was what he did with it. What the new information was, exactly, was a matter of interpretation. Either his father is a slick-as-shit con man, or he really can bridge to the Welsh ancestors. If the former, how'd Overdrive go forty-five years without noticing before? If the latter, holy shit!

For years, Overdrive's Dad had been telling him that without the ancestors, he'd have lost the farm during the Great Depression. Overdrive had always rejected as nonsense any reference to them, but now he's not so sure. They made some pretty astute observations tonight, didn't they? Maybe he should ask Dad how they helped, and see what he says. If his Dad feeds him a line of bullshit, he'd see the con for sure, now that he's looking for it. Overdrive decided that's what he'd do. He'd ask Dad how they helped, and listen very carefully.

Should he tell Mary? Hmmm ... oh god no. Not yet, anyway. Overdrive figured there's not much upside to telling your wife she married into a family of nutjobs. That conversation could wait until he's sure it's really true. To get to the bottom of it, he'd have his Dad check in with the ancestors now and then, for advice on the farm expansion. Each instance would provide another data point on whether they're real and have value, or just bull. The more data points, the better.

CHAPTER 3

Farm Expansion Plan

Over the next several weeks, Overdrive plowed on school nights until dawn, milked the cows, and took a five-hour nap after morning milking. Then he'd spread out on the kitchen table for several hours each day, to work on the farm expansion plan. Afterward, while milking in the evening, plowing at night, and milking again the next morning, he'd mull over his plans.

As part of this process, Overdrive revisited whether they should stick with dairying. They'd tried raising steers and feeder pigs for meat, chickens for eggs and meat, sheep for wool and meat, and had even dabbled at growing cash crops like field peas and sweet corn. Past experience suggested none of these sidelines had dairying's potential, and new calculations based on current market prices bore that out. He knew the original settlers had first grown wheat, and then hops, but that dairying eventually became the mainstay in this area. He figured there must've been good reasons for that, and decided the expansion would scale dairying.

With 40 cows currently being milked, the fundamental question became how many more to add? To simplify, Overdrive bounded the problem. First, he never wanted to expand again, it being a pain in the ass, and all. Second, the current farm had under-utilized assets, so he wanted to expand just enough to take up the slack.

The farm's existing assets were a hodge-podge, more the result of acquiring adjacent failed farms than any sort of planning. Even at the home place, what was built at any given time was driven by the greatest need, and what could be afforded back then. Hence, when Overdrive calculated how many more milk cows could be supported by fully utilizing the silos, granary, corn crib, haymow, and so on, each asset provided a different answer. Likewise, the Lemke, Adcock, and Ulbricht barns could all accommodate more heifers being raised as replacement milk cows, but the increments varied barn-to-barn.

After much consideration, Overdrive targeted doubling the milk herd to 80. The current age-based heifer allocations to the three heifer barns were arbitrary. Adjusting them to put more heifers where the greatest excess hay storage existed, enabled total heifer count to double across the three barns. At the home place, the existing silos could accommodate a doubled milk herd. The granary and corn crib fell short, so he'd either grow what he could store and buy the rest, or store oats and ear corn at the co-op for a fee. The bulk milk cooler would be too small for daily pickups, but the processor's truck could come after each milking.

Next, Overdrive sketched out the requirements for the barn addition at the home place. 40 more stanchions were required, with half on each side of the center aisle, butt-ends facing center, and head-ends facing mangers, a feed-cart aisle, and the outside wall. A vacuum line to each stanchion's petcock was needed, so the portable milking machines could be plugged in and operated at each location. They'd need four box stalls for calving cows and new born calves, two on either side of the center aisle. Drinking cups were needed at each stanchion and box stall, so the cows could self-water. Above, they needed a storage mow, and so on.

Of all the requirements, Overdrive was most excited about the automatic barn cleaner. In the current barn, shit fell out of the cows onto the center aisle, was manually pitched into a wheel barrow, and walked to the end of the barn, up a ramp, and dumped into the manure spreader. Family legend attributes Jumbo's chiseled frame to this brutish twice-daily task. With a barn cleaner, gutters circle the center aisle and serve to guide chain-driven paddles. Shit either falls directly into the gutter, or can be easily scraped there. Then, twice daily a button is pushed and the paddles automatically slide the shit out of the barn and up a ramp, where it drops into the spreader. Overdrive wanted the barn cleaner installed throughout the entire length of the existing barn and new addition. This would require breaking out the existing barn's center aisle concrete slab, so new concrete could be poured to form continuous gutters and a center aisle throughout.

With double the cows at the home place, and double the heifers across the three youngstock barns, more feed would be required, meaning more land to grow it. To provide all of the straw or oats stalks, oats, ear corn, silage or chopped field corn, and hay required, Overdrive estimated he'd need to rent 250 acres of additional work land next year.

This begged the question of whether Overdrive's existing fleet of tractors and machinery could till, plant, and harvest all that extra acreage. Overdrive had an elaborate methodology, involving functions and objectives, to address this question. For example, putting in the oats, an objective, required three functions, namely tilling, rock-picking, and planting. Other sequential objectives included putting in the field corn, and so on, or harvesting first-cutting hay, oats, and so on. Based on meticulous records kept by Mary, Overdrive knew the tractor-hours per acre required for functions such as tilling, planting, cultivating, hay cutting, baling, corn chopping, and so on.

To apply this information, Overdrive sketched out on a calendar for the coming year, the dates when he believed effort would begin and end, for each objective. He then broke down the time lines for each one, and inserted the functions that'd be performed each week. This told him, week-by-week, what each of his tractors and other pieces of machinery would be doing, and what they must accomplish. This provided the basis for determining whether the machinery he owned could get the job done. After going through this exercise, he concluded that his current machinery could easily handle an additional 250 acres.

After grinding on the plan for a week, with lots of time spent ruminating over it while milking and plowing, Overdrive knew he'd taken it as far as he could, without bouncing it off of Mary. They agreed to head to

Harbor Lights after the evening milking, so Overdrive could share his thinking in private.

* * *

Upon entering Harbor Lights, Mary went to nab a quiet table in the far corner while Overdrive headed to the bar for beer, said hello to the few patrons seated there, and soon joined her. After tapping their bottles of Kingsbury together and taking a sip, Overdrive talked Mary through his farm expansion thinking thus far, and explained how he'd gotten there.

Mary listened intently, and said, "That's pretty impressive for a first go at it, James, it really is. See what wonders a little sleep can bring?"

Overdrive admitted, "You were right about the naps, and putting Jumbo on the plow. It's made a big difference. So, what do you think? If we're going to do this, we've got to start talking to the bank pretty soon."

Mary bobbed her head, and said, "Well, I certainly agree that if we expand, the focus should be on dairying. It's hard work, and has its ups and downs, but those sidelines we tried were even worse."

Overdrive smiled at that, then said, "Excellent, we agree on dairying as the focus, that's good. What else? Any reaction to the rest of it?"

Mary paused to gather her thoughts, and then said, "You know how, when you hear something for the first time, you sometimes have an initial reaction that maybe isn't the right one? When I heard 80 milk cows, I nearly peed my pants."

Overdrive couldn't afford to lose Mary right out of the gate. He said carefully, "So, you figure maybe the initial reaction wasn't the right one?"

Mary smiled, and said, "Being a little devious aren't we, putting words in my mouth? But I liked your explanation of how you got to 80. Making better use of what's already bought and paid for, makes a lot of sense to me."

Seeing an opening, Overdrive pressed on, "80 surprised me too, when I first came up with it. But putting out the effort to expand the farm on top of everything else we do, is a pain in the ass. By going big now, we'd never have to do it again."

Mary paused thoughtfully for a moment, "I can see that. What I'm not yet seeing, is how our family could keep up with all the extra work. How'll we milk 40 more cows twice a day, and work 250 more acres?"

After a moment of empty air, the best Overdrive could come up with was, "Well, the barn cleaner will free Jumbo up for other things. And don't forget my Dad has lots of idle time. Plus, the younger kids are old enough now to do more."

Mary stared at him a moment, then said, "Ah-huh, well, I still don't see it. But you know what? I think the plan's solid enough to have an initial conversation with the bank. My concern is moot, if we can't get the financing to begin with."

Overdrive smiled at that, then said, "Fair enough."

Mary said, "Beer's gone. Morning milking beckons. Time to go home."

They drove in silence back to the farm, each lost in their own thoughts. Overdrive believed he and Mary made a great team. The way she grasped concepts upon first hearing them, only to zoom in on the potential weaknesses, was uncanny. When they arrived home, he asked her to schedule them at the bank.

* * *

Early afternoon on the next day, Overdrive and Mary arrived at Cascade Bank for their appointment with farm loan officer, Walt Brickner. They hoped to verify that the bank intended to provide the usual seasonal financing for spring's work, as it had every year for the past two decades. Based on a verbal description, they also hoped the bank would express strong interest in financing the expansion. They'd never missed a payment, and Walt had been handling their account since the beginning. They believed, based on this track record, that Walt viewed them as honest, hard-working, and skilled farmers. They hoped to leverage that good will.

When they entered his office, Walt flashed a brilliant smile and gave them both vigorous handshakes, like he always did. After exchanging pleasantries, Overdrive reviewed the needs for spring's work, described the farm expansion concept, and asked Walt if they'd be doing business again next year.

Without hesitation, Walt responded, "If it were only up to me, no question we'd be doing business again next year. I'd need more information on the expansion, of course, but there'd be no question on the seasonal financing."

With raised eye brows, Overdrive asked, "But it is up to you, isn't it?"

After an awkward pause, Walt said, "Well, we're a branch of the Fond du Lac regional bank now, and this year they've established a new policy. An HQ rep needs to directly participate in placement of farm loans."

Overdrive was speechless, so Mary broke the dead air, "Walt, did they give you any reason? I mean, we've never missed a payment here in two decades."

Walt exhaled heavily, and said, "The only reason given was that the country's business expansion was in an advanced stage, where farm loans began to carry more risk. It has nothing to do with your past performance."

Somewhat recovered, Overdrive said, "There've been two or three downturns since we've been banking here, and we've made it through every time. Cutting us all off because a few farmers might've screwed up doesn't seem fair."

Walt tried to tap dance, "James, we're not cutting you off. I've no reason to believe that HQ won't endorse my recommendation. Like I say, spring's work is routine. I just think the expansion could be a problem, if not presented properly."

Breathing a little easier, Overdrive asked, "Okay, what do you recommend? We know expanding will make us a better business, but explaining why that is to a bank, isn't something we do every day."

Walt thought a moment, then suggested, "How about you come in and pitch the expansion to me a week in advance of the real meeting? That way you'll have time to make changes, presuming any are needed."

Overdrive nodded, now mollified, "That sounds like a good plan."

Mary smiled, "Thank you Walt, we really appreciate it!"

Walt bobbed his head, and said, "Well, like you say, after two decades of never missing a payment, I owe you that much. Hey, not to change the subject, but has anybody told you that Old Bill's gotten into the habit of rolling right out onto Hwy 28 without stopping and looking … …."

On the way home, Overdrive and Mary shared their concerns about a stranger from Fond du Lac making the call on whether or not the farm expansion gets financed. Mary thought Walt hadn't been completely honest with them, based on the way he'd been squirming in his seat. Overdrive had missed the body language, but agreed that something didn't seem right. Everything he read and heard said the economy was booming, which meant Fond du Lac's reason for the new policy was bullshit. One thing's for sure, before they see Walt again, they've got a lot of work to do.

* * *

The weather held, and Overdrive and Jumbo finished the plowing. Overdrive decided to get Jumbo going on the machinery repair and maintenance task, so progress would be made while he and Mary did their deep dive into the farm expansion plan. Getting him started now meant he'd easily finish by mid-February, and in the meantime could resume his social life with Lizzie Flint.

Overdrive's way of tutoring Jumbo on the task was to walk-and-talk him through a viewing of the machinery, the available shop space for working on it, and the machine shed where finished implements would be stored. Overdrive emphasized the importance of sequencing the work on each piece of equipment, in reverse order to when it'd be needed next year. This way, after being serviced, the last-needed machines could be tucked into the back and corners of the machine shed, furthest from the doors. Conversely, the first-needed machines would end up near the doors, and accessible. There're only a few possible ways to get everything into the shed's cramped space, and from memory, Overdrive shared the best one.

The lone exception to the reverse-order rule, was the tractor-pulled oats combine. Being large and unwieldy, it's best to service and store the combine first, and only park things that'll be used before oats harvest in front of it. To get started, they pulled the combine into the shop area, and Overdrive pointed out what typically needed to be done to this machine. Replace broken blades on the cutter bar, broken blade guards, worn belts, worn shear pins, and so on. Grease all the fittings, start it up, pour old drain oil over all the moving parts, and so on. He instructed Jumbo to identify the needed parts, and have his mother fetch them from the appropriate farm implement dealer.

Overdrive asked for a heads-up whenever Jumbo moved from one machine to the next. This enabled verification of what'd been done to the previous machine, its proper storage in the shed, and reverse-order selection of the next-up machine. It also provided an opportunity to advise Jumbo of the next machine's to-do's.

* * *

For the deep dive on the farm expansion, Overdrive and Mary needed significant blocks of time, without interruption, to make progress. Each school day after morning milking, they spread out on the kitchen table, and worked side-by-side. The goal was a written plan documented well enough to be understood by Walt. Mary knew Overdrive's hen scratching would be incomprehensible to anyone but her, so she volunteered to do the writing. She also wanted to double-check whether the family and existing equipment could handle 250 more acres and 40 more milk cows. Overdrive took on developing realistic cost estimates for building the barn addition, renting the extra land, and purchasing the extra cows. After completing these independent tasks, they'd work together to synthesize income and expenses into a cash flow analysis, beginning next March when the prospective loan period would begin.

Previously, Overdrive had identified the requirements for the barn addition in reasonable detail, but for cost had nothing but a wild ass guess. To remedy this, he studied articles from his farm magazines about adding onto or building new barns, which he'd been saving for years. The level of cost breakdown in these sources varied from total project cost per square foot, to line item costs for each construction material and function. As he went through the information, Overdrive kept track of the year for each source, and escalated past costs to the present, so they'd be comparable. Overdrive's confidence grew, as multiple sources led to similar estimated costs. But to be safe, he also called dealers and contractors he'd done business with in the past, and picked their brains.

Through this process, Overdrive gained an understanding of the styles of barn additions available, and the reasons why an arched roof was best for his application. The existing barn's gambrel roof had four planes, the two top ones along the roof ridge at a slight pitch, and two lower ones set much steeper, and ending at the side walls. Gambrel supplanted the simple two-plane gable-style years ago, because it provided much more hay storage space under the roof, and a person could walk upright anywhere beneath it. But gambrel required large supporting posts and pegged beams internally, which interrupted the storage space. These internal obstacles limited the locations where Overdrive's bale elevator could be placed, increasing the hand work necessary to fill the barn with hay. Nowadays, curved laminated beams enabled arched roof barns, which like gambrels, were fully walkable, but required no internal posts or beams.

Overdrive took the path of least resistance for estimating land rental costs. He spent a few evenings driving around making social calls with owners renting land nearby, and got all the data he needed. Overdrive also took the easy way out when estimating the cost of acquiring 40 milk cows. He knew a cattle trader out of Plymouth, Gib Buyer, that he'd done business with before. Gib had always treated Overdrive and Mary fairly, and when called, provided all the data needed.

Mary was inclined to take Overdrive's labor and machine productivity estimates with a grain of salt, having experienced many times the living hell created when he underestimated. But to her surprise, when she went through the exercise herself, she also became convinced that the existing fleet of tractors and machinery, manned by the family, was easily capable of handling an additional 250 acres of work land.

Mary also investigated the best way to milk 80

rather than 40 cows. With 40, the primary milker, usually Overdrive, ran three portable milking machines. A second person, usually Mary, performed a variety of tasks. She readied the next cows by washing their teats with warm soapy water, helping them to relax and let down their milk. She also carried full milk pails to the milk house, where she climbed a stool, and poured it through a filter into the bulk milk cooler. After exploring several scenarios, she settled on an option that allowed them to milk 80 cows in the same time as 40, while requiring one additional person and six portable milking machines instead of three. The primary milker would man four machines, and the secondary milker would man two, plus be responsible for readying the next cows for all six. The third person would carry the milk and pour it into the cooler.

For the cash flow analysis, Overdrive and Mary laid out expected monthly income and expenses for an entire year, starting next March. They assumed they'd begin paying rent for the additional land in March, the barn addition would be constructed from March to mid-August, and the 40 new milk cows would arrive at the beginning of May, and drop calves uniformly throughout May and June. Income included the milk check, and cash generated by selling bull calves and other livestock, such as poorly performing milk cows. Expenses included costs for ongoing household and farm operations, land rental, spring's work, the purchase of 40 milk cows, and design and construction of the barn addition.

After grinding on the plan for over a week, Overdrive and Mary stepped away from it for a few days to get caught up on other things, and clear their minds.

Then, they spent another evening at Harbor Lights to kick around the plan.

* * *

At Harbor Lights, the crowd was larger than usual, and disentangling from the chit-chat took some effort. But eventually Overdrive and Mary reached their usual table in the quiet corner, with beers in hand. Overdrive leaned in, and whispered, "Don't tell anybody, but I may be crazy. Going through all those farm magazine clippings and costing the barn addition, gave me a stiffy."

Never one to miss an opportunity, Mary whispered back, "I'll pretend I didn't hear that. But FYI, next time you get a stiffy come see me, it's been awhile."

Overdrive snorted, stifled a laugh, and dropped his voice, "Yes mam, I'll do that. But seriously, I really did enjoy costing the barn addition."

Mary, showing a hint of her impish grin, "Yes, you are cause for concern. The more tedious the better, for you."

Overdrive mimed a glower, "Yeah, well look who's talking. I nearly blew a gasket coming up with that objective, function, and tractor run-hour bullshit, and the next thing I know, here you are pointing out my mistakes."

Mary held up her hands in surrender, "I know, I know. There really is something wrong with us, isn't there? I mean, who spends their only slack time all year, making damn sure that next year there'll be none!"

Overdrive checked the room to see if anybody was eavesdropping, and said, "Let's tone it down before we draw a crowd, and get down to business."

"Fair enough." Then, Mary thought a moment, and said, "When I stand back and look at the expansion, the thing that troubles me the most is being into the bank continuously, rather than seasonally. Something about that bothers me."

Overdrive's eyebrows went up, "Mary, what do you mean?"

Mary exhaled heavily, and said, "Well, you know as well as I do. Every March we borrow for spring's work, because there's no way the milk check can cover the extras like fuel, seed, and fertilizer. But in recent years we've always been able to pay that off before the next February rolls around."

Overdrive nodded, "That's right. And we want to keep it that way, right?"

Mildly exasperated, Mary half-snapped, "That's exactly my point! Geez, James, you can be such a dumbass sometimes. We just spent two days wrapping our minds around the expansion. Didn't you even look at the numbers?"

Overdrive winced, held up his hands in a placating gesture, and said, "Yes, of course I did. We'll be able to payoff spring's work, same as always."

Mary pressed her point, "Yeah, but what about the barn addition? The 40 cows? Without other income streams, we'll be paying on those for years."

"Oh shit! Now I see what you're saying." Overdrive thought for a moment, then asked, "How many years are we talking?"

Mary looked disappointed in him, "I don't want to talk about how many years, do you? I want to talk about what else we can do, to generate income, or cut costs. I sleep better starting each March with the previous year's slate clean."

While Mary took a long pull from her bottle, Overdrive gathered his thoughts, and said, "I sleep better that way too. With farming, something's always going wrong – too wet, too dry, milk price tanks, tractor breaks down. The only way to survive is to be flexible, and being into the bank makes that harder."

Mary put down her bottle, and said, "Well put. So, what're we going to do about it? How can we generate more income, or cut costs, or both?"

Overdrive thought about that while he took another sip, then said, "Remember all those sidelines we tried? Pigs, chickens, sheep, cash crops – we know how to do them. Maybe the timing is right for one of those?"

"Bingo, I've looked into them." Mary leaned in, "To bring in the kind of money we'd need, our only shot would be to rent more land and put in cash crops."

While that hung in the air, Overdrive and Mary both finished their beers. Then Overdrive said, "How many more acres are we talking?"

Mary caught his eye, and said, "About 200, give or take, ought to do it. I've already verified that it'd be theoretically possible for the family to handle it with the existing machinery. We'd need reasonable weather, no unusual breakdowns, everything would have to go right."

As the reality sunk in, Overdrive muttered, "And we thought last year's spring's work was crazy. Imagine working 450 more acres."

Mary said solemnly, "I know. But if we're going to do this, we'd better do it now. Old Bill isn't getting any younger, and Jumbo graduates next spring."

Overdrive's eyes widened after having a thought, "Hmmm, that reminds me. We should start inviting Lizzie Flint over once in a while. You know, so she can get to know the rest of the family, and find out how wonderful we all are."

Onto his scheme, Mary said, "Thinking Lizzie might help keep Jumbo around, are we? I must admit, the same thought has crossed my mind. I'll give some thought to getting Lizzie around more, without us appearing too obvious."

* * *

Rental acres had exploded to 450, and Overdrive felt the need to take a pass at applying his normal land management practices to the expanded acreage. For many years, Overdrive had managed his crop rotation and manure spreading strategies to minimize out of pocket costs for fertilizer, while raising feed for his livestock. He and Mary kept field-by-field annual records on crop planted, manure applied, purchased fertilizer applied, and crop yield. Sometimes, to support crop rotation or fertilizing decisions, soil tests were conducted on selected fields and they recorded those results as well.

Overdrive's traditional crop rotation started with corn for a few years, then oats under-seeded with alfalfa, then he'd leave the land in alfalfa for a few years, and finally, he'd rotate back to corn. This made sense because corn was a nitrogen hog, spreading manure for its nitrogen content caused phosphorus and potassium build up, rotating to oats/alfalfa knocked those nutrients back down, and alfalfa rebuilt nitrogen levels, making the lands corn-ready once again. When Overdrive had to rotate corn to oats/alfalfa, he'd generally pick the corn lands with the highest excess phosphorus and potassium. When he had to plow down alfalfa for corn, he'd generally select the poorest stands with lowest yields, so long as they'd been in alfalfa long enough to restore the nitrogen. Years for a full rotation cycle varied, for many reasons.

Overdrive's desired crop outcomes were driven by the needs of his livestock, hay for feed, straw for bedding, oats and ear corn for meal, and field corn for silage. He had storage buffers for all of these, but the wildcard of last year's weather meant he came into each spring with varying amounts of each fodder remaining, or carried over. Next year's plantings were driven by predicted carryover, plus the need to care for double the number of livestock next winter.

Some of Overdrive's land use decisions for next year had already been made. For example, back in early October, he'd plowed down large tracts of aging alfalfa, freeing these owned lands for corn next year. But after running the numbers, corn acreage now far exceeded the additional field and ear corn needed, which meant enough of the old corn ground could be rotated to oats/alfalfa to satisfy the expanded milk herd's straw bedding requirement. These rotations left a huge hay deficit, which they'd have to make up with rented hay lands. Deducting these hay acres from the 450 total acres to be rented, revealed rented acreage remaining for peas and sweet corn.

These mental gymnastics made Overdrive realize that doubling the milk herd created a new problem he'd never dealt with before. The 20-acre Side Hill pasture had been able to keep up with a 40-cow milk herd, but 80 would over-whelm it. Fencing adjacent work land to expand the pasture was an option, but it'd require him to rent more land.

Instead, Overdrive decided to augment the herd's diet every day with fodder using bunk wagons. These topless rectangular boxes mounted on four-wheel wagon racks had sidewall openings at the bottom, where cows reached in and ate. On any given day, Overdrive would use the cheapest bunk wagon fodder available. In season, pea vines and sweet corn waste would be available from the cannery, free for the taking. Once Overdrive's sweet corn was picked, the stalks left standing in the field could be chopped. After those ran out, standing hay could be green-chopped. Once the silos were filled, leftover field corn could be chopped.

CHAPTER 4

The Deal

Overdrive and Mary arrived at Cascade Bank for their dry run with Walt Brickner, feeling as ready as they'd ever be. Walt got right down to business, "The written plan you dropped off yesterday? Frankly, it's a marvel. I've been through it with a fine-tooth comb. Obviously, a lot of thought has gone into it."

Overdrive smiled at that, "Thanks Walt, we appreciate you saying that."

Mary smiled and chimed in, "We really do."

Walt nodded and said, "Filling out a loan application from that'll be a breeze. Under normal circumstances, that's probably what we'd do right now."

Overdrive, "What you're saying is, these aren't normal circumstances."

Walt, now serious, "Exactly. Remember, this whole HQ approval thing is new to me too. So, let's stick to our original plan of having a dry run. What you say at the meeting, may be the most important thing. The HQ rep may be too busy to read the written plan, or even the loan application."

Overdrive spent fifteen minutes pitching the loan. Walt listened intently without interrupting, and then said, "Let me give you an initial reaction, before we get into the details. That wasn't half bad. You exuded confidence and were brief and to the point, which is always best in front of busy people."

Mary inserted herself, "Thanks Walt. But don't hold back, okay? James is a big-boy, he can take it. We don't do this every day, so tell us what's what."

Overdrive, Mary, and Walt went back and forth for almost an hour. Walt knew them, knew their farm, and had read the plan. He was surprised that Overdrive and Mary believed the entire loan could be repaid in one year. He understood their desire to get back to seasonal financing by the following spring, but initially anyway, questioned whether it'd be possible. Once convinced, though, he made suggestions on how to structure the deal to be most practical.

What made most sense to Walt, was to treat the whole thing, spring's work and the farm expansion, like one big construction loan. The bank would approve the maximum amount that could be drawn, meaning the line of credit, and establish a six month draw window from March through August. Overdrive and Mary would decide how much to draw, and when, based on their needs. During the draw window, they'd make end of month interest-only payments on the funds drawn to date. During the September through February repayment period, they'd make end of month principal plus interest payments, with the last one resulting in full payoff.

When reminded that nothing ever goes exactly as

planned on a farm, Walt offered his assurances that the bank would offer flexibility within reason, as it always had been in the past. For example, rather than paying off the principal balance at the end of February, perhaps it could be deferred by two or three months in exchange for them paying more interest overall. Worst case, they'd be able to roll it into next year's seasonal financing if necessary.

Walt believed one key message would sell the loan. By making a few targeted investments, the farm would become a more efficient business through better utilization of existing assets. This message was plain as day in the written plan, but he feared the headquarters rep would never read it. Rather than dance around this point like he'd done today, Walt wanted Overdrive to make it an explicit statement, right at the beginning of his remarks.

As the meeting broke up, the receptionist knocked and entered with a phone message, "Sorry to interrupt, Walt, but you wanted to know as soon as we heard."

Walt's eyebrows went up, but then he smiled, and said, "Yes, thank you, Shirley. No need to apologize." Upon reading the message, Walt fell silent.

Mary noticed, and asked, "Walt, it's really none of our business, but is everything okay? You look like you've seen a ghost."

Walt took a moment to recover, and said, "Actually, it is your business. I'd asked Fond du Lac who their rep at your loan meeting next week would be. They're sending Rachel Wolf."

Overdrive and Mary looked at each other, and shrugged. Overdrive asked, "Should that name mean something to us? It doesn't ring a bell."

Walt nodded, now grim, "Rachel Wolf owns controlling interest in our parent, the Fond du Lac regional bank, and also chairs the Board of Directors."

Overdrive, "Shit, you'd think she'd have something more important to do."

Mary, "What does that mean?"

Walt thought about that, then said, "I'm not sure. All I can say is that Rachel's been here a few times recently. It's my understanding that she's making an effort to get to know her branch banks better. Maybe that's all it means."

On the drive back to the farm, Overdrive and Mary shared their growing concerns. Having a stranger from Fond du Lac give thumbs up or down on their loan was bad enough. Now, come to find out, the stranger owns the bank and chairs the board. Overdrive wasn't sure what to make of it. Mary, based on Walt's stiff smile and facial tick, believed he was holding something back.

After kicking it around during evening milking, Overdrive concluded there's no point in worrying about things he couldn't control. The bank could send whoever they damn well pleased to the loan meeting. On the other hand, he did have control over what he said there. He decided to take Walt's advice to heart, and update what he planned to say. Beyond that, let the chips fall where they may.

❋ ❋ ❋

When they pulled up to Cascade Bank, Overdrive and Mary noticed the black T-Bird Landau parked out front. Upon entering, they're immediately shown into the conference room, right on time. There sat Walt and the car's owner. Overdrive and Mary locked eyes momentarily, realizing for the first time that the mysterious dark-haired woman was Rachel Wolf. Walt and Rachel stood, Walt did introductions, and they all shook hands and took their seats.

Without hesitation, Rachel glanced at her watch and said, "Unfortunately, I only have a half hour, so I'd like us to get started right away. Would it be helpful if I said a few words about the bank's new policy, and why I'm here?"

Overdrive and Mary nodded, so Rachel continued, "The bank is reviewing farm loans for the upcoming year, a little more closely than usual. We're doing this because the country's economy is nearing the end of a business expansion, when farm loans become riskier. Does this make sense?"

Overdrive said, "I guess so. But the economy is still on a roll, based on everything I read and hear."

Rachel stared at him a moment, like a predator eyeing up her next meal, then said, "You're correct, up to a point. But years of rapid expansion, in the judgement of the bank, can't go on forever. Now, the new bank policy calls for including a headquarters rep in meetings like this, to foster more consistency in lending practices across all branches. Don't get me wrong, we still want to make farm loans. The new policy just helps us pick the best ones. Does that make sense?"

Feeling a chill up his spine, Overdrive fought off a shudder, and as evenly as possible, asked, "That means picking the ones most likely to be repaid, correct?"

Rachel smiled for the first time, the kind that

could turn vicious in an instant, and pressed on as planned, "That's a very important part of it, for sure. Now, let's move on to why I'm serving as the HQ rep. This is just to kill two birds, with one stone. I'm getting to know each of the bank's branches this year, and being the rep at this meeting helps me get to know Cascade. Are there any further questions?"

Overdrive and Mary shook their heads, so Rachel continued, "Good. Then let's proceed. Please tell Walt and I why you want to borrow the money, and what sources of funds you expect to have to support repayment." Then, after making a big show of re-checking her watch, "I'm down to 25 minutes."

Overdrive, doing his best to appear relaxed and confident, described the scope and funding requirements for spring's work and the farm expansion. For the latter, it came through loud and clear that a few targeted investments would make the farm a more efficient business overall, with ample revenue for repayment.

Rachel and Walt listened intently. The messaging was crystal clear, and no questions were required. When Overdrive finished, Rachel turned to Walt, and asked, "Walt, what's your recommendation on this?"

Thankful to be asked, and hoping to please, Walt said, "They've written a detailed plan consistent with what James just said. I've been through it several times. Frankly, it's the best one I've ever seen from a family farm. And they've never missed a payment in 20 years, here at the bank. I recommend we fund it."

Rachel thought for a moment, then said, "You know what? My gut, based on what I've heard today, agrees with you. Let's do it." Walt smiled and nodded, and Overdrive and Mary chorused a thank you.

After handing everyone a copy, Rachel flashed a predatory smile, and said nonchalantly, "Here's the bank's new standard agreement for farm loans. Please work with Walt to fill out a loan application, and get this executed."

Feeling a chill but not sure why, Overdrive smiled thinly, and said, "We will. And thank you again, Ms. Wolf."

With a smile failing to reach her eyes, Rachel said, "You're welcome. Walt, please send me that best-ever plan, though. I'd like to read it when I've got the time. James and Mary, it's been a pleasure. I'm sorry, but I've really got to run."

After Rachel left, the three of them sat in silence for a moment, trying to process what'd just happened. Eventually, Walt broke the silence and they discussed next steps. He volunteered to fill in the loan application, since everything needed was already in hand. They all agreed it'd be best to schedule another meeting to sign and notarize documents, after Overdrive and Mary had read the agreement and were ready to move forward.

While driving back to the farm, Overdrive and Mary shared their initial impressions of Wolf, and about what'd just transpired. Overdrive indulged in a full body shudder, and shared that something about that woman sent a chill up his spine. He also revealed to Mary his previous sighting of Wolf in the black car, crawling along on Rock Road. He wondered out loud whether she'd been surveying the farm for some reason, even way back then. In Mary's view, Walt pranced like a little lap dog when Wolf asked for his recommendation, and was visibly relieved when she followed it. She'd also noticed an unwholesome shine in Wolf's eyes, almost feral, which gave her the creeps. They'd gotten what they'd wanted, but both were mystified by the absence of any feeling of elation or jubilation. They decided to head to Harbor Lights after the evening milking, to review and discuss the bank's new agreement language in private.

* * *

Overdrive and Mary brought the new loan agreement and last year's version along to Harbor Lights, so they'd be able to compare language. They spent about 10 minutes chit-chatting with the bartender and other patrons, then headed for the table in their favorite quiet corner, with beers in hand. After silently reading, and rereading, the new and previous-year agreements, Overdrive said, "There's some new language, that's for sure. But we'll be fine if we make all our payments."

Astonished, Mary said, "James, you're shitting me, right? Didn't you notice how the bank's remedies have changed? Last year, all they could do was garnish the milk check. With this new agreement, they'd be able to take the farm."

Sticking to his guns, Overdrive said, "I saw that. But remember the discussion we had with Walt on flexibility? If the weather or something else messes us up, he'll work with us, like he always has."

Mary shook her head, and pressed on, "I heard Walt. But there's nothing in the new agreement about flexibility, and Walt's not calling the shots anymore."

Overdrive, unwavering, "Come on Mary, there's

nothing about flexibility in last year's agreement either. Yet Walt worked with us."

After a moment of empty air, Mary replied, "Yeah, I know. But Wolf gives me the creeps. What if she forces the branches to be less flexible this year?"

Pigheaded as always, Overdrive said, "If that were a possibility, Walt would've said so, instead of saying what he did. Walt's been completely honest with us. Remember the reasons given for the bank's new policy, and for Wolf being at our meeting? What Wolf said today, is exactly what Walt told us before."

Still not completely mollified, Mary said, "Maybe you're right. There's just something off about that woman. She makes me feel uncomfortable."

Overdrive shrugged, and said, "Like I've told you before, something about her sends chills down my spine. But I've been trying to figure out why that might be. Wolf is rich, talks just right, and has a fancy hairdo, cloths, and car. For us, being around her is kind of like being in a fancy restaurant, isn't it? Not really sure what to say or do, too embarrassed to ask. Maybe that's all it is."

Mary, wavering, "Maybe. But shouldn't we have an attorney look at this?"

Overdrive, frugal to a fault, "That'd just be another bill to pay. Like I said to begin with, we'll be fine if we make all our payments. And we always do."

Mary rubbed her face with both hands, "God, I hope you're right, James."

The next day, Overdrive and Mary met again with Walt at the bank, and all the paperwork for the loan was signed and notarized.

* * *

Overdrive has slept poorly since signing the loan agreement, but last night was especially fitful. After yawning his way through Saturday morning milking, he'd been cleaning up when Old Bill walked in, and said, "Son, we've done our best on the barn cleaning. But at the rate we're going, we won't make it. Lemke's is done and Adcock's half done, then comes Ulbricht's. We need help."

Stifling another yawn, Overdrive asked, "What'd you have in mind?"

Old Bill suggested, "You or Jumbo needs to run the scoop. I'm not very handy with it anymore. Joe tries, but he doesn't seem to have the hang of it yet."

Overdrive forced his mind to clear, "Okay, after breakfast Jumbo's updating me on the machinery servicing progress. After that, one of us will head over."

Old Bill smiled at that, "Truth be told, even with one of you on the scoop, the weekends won't be enough. How about you and I hit it during the week?"

Overdrive bobbed his head, and said, "Sure, I can do that. We can't afford to let any barn cleaning slip 'til spring."

"Thanks, I appreciate the help." Old Bill's eyes narrowed, and he said, "You seem a little tired this morning, son. You alright?"

Overdrive sighed, shrugged, and said, "Must admit, I've been better. We're going ahead with the farm expansion. Bundled it with spring's work into one loan and signed it last week. Haven't had a good night's sleep since, and not sure why."

This news got Old Bill's attention. He deliberated for a moment, then pointed his finger at Overdrive, and said, "This is one of those times when a wise son would consult his ancestors. It'd ease your mind, and help you sleep."

Overdrive eyed his father, then said, "Given what's bothering me, I probably need a shrink more than the ancestors. But you bringing them up reminds me. You've said many times that if not for the ancestors, you'd have lost the farm during the Great Depression. I've been meaning to ask how so? How'd they help?"

Caught off guard, but pleased at his son's interest, Old Bill said, "There were a few old codgers from the Town of Mitchell that went out to California and got rich speculating on land, and then came back to live a life of leisure. Their riches went untouched when the stock market crashed, because they kept it in gold coin. They liked to gamble at playing cards down in Cascade. Before they went to California your grandpa, J.B, used to play with them for penny ante stakes. During the depression, I sat in at their table. Turns out their card playing habits hadn't changed a lick. My Dad was able to share with me the tells, so I'd know when they were bluffing. I won enough gold coin off of them to keep the farm afloat."

Overdrive gave his father the stink eye, unsure whether he was joking or not, "You're shitting me, right? Grandpa helped you cheat at cards?"

Proudly shrugging and flashing a big smile, Old Bill said, "I shit you not."

With a faraway look, Overdrive contemplated the possibilities, and said, "Huh. I'll be damned. Maybe these Welsh ancestors aren't useless after all."

* * *

Overdrive spent the time during evening milking and afterwards, deep in thought. His Dad's revelation about card cheating had shaken him to the core. He'd built his entire life around several fundamental beliefs about his father, and now found himself questioning whether he'd been wrong all these years.

Old Bill had always claimed to have kept the farm afloat during the Great Depression by gambling. But Overdrive had long harbored the suspicion that the card playing, rather than to save the farm, had more to do with his Dad's desire to socialize and have fun in Cascade. Driven by this belief, at an early age, Overdrive had become the responsible one who kept things going on the farm. In Overdrive's view, his hard work, more so than his father's card playing, had really saved the farm. Now he wasn't so sure anymore.

Overdrive had also concluded that the best way to secure the future of the farm was to buy it as soon as possible, and run it his way. When still with fuzz on his chin, he'd eyed the local girls for a suitable farm wife, because he knew he'd need a good one. After graduating high school, he'd taken a job at Kohler Co. in addition to helping on the farm, because he knew he'd need the money to buy it. At Kohler, he chose to be paid by the pieces produced, or by *piece work*, rather than by the hour. This way the harder he worked, the more money he made.

When WWII broke out, Overdrive persuaded his fiancé, Mary, to move to the farm with his parents. In exchange for room and board, she helped them keep the farm going while he joined the Army and went off to war. Yes, he'd been a patriot. But more importantly, the Army's pay, though meager, could all be saved because he'd have no opportunity to spend it. What mattered most to Overdrive was amassing the money he'd need to buy his father's farm.

Mary's presence on the farm was a good thing, in more ways than one. Tragically, Overdrive's mother died of a stroke while he'd been away at war. Grieving and otherwise alone, Old Bill never would've been able to keep the farm going without his future daughter-in-law's help. Mary also gained a love and emotional attachment to the farm during those years, which has never wavered since. The savings from Kohler and the Army had been enough for the down payment, and Overdrive and Mary had married and bought the farm after WWII.

If Old Bill truly had saved the farm by gambling, then Overdrive had spent about 30 years harboring an unfairly dim view of his father. Though never openly disrespectful, what Overdrive really thought must've slipped out from time to time over all those years. His Dad's a pretty sharp man, and surely, he'd have picked up on that vibe. After being an asshole for so long, how does a son walk that back?

On the other hand, part of Overdrive still believed he'd been right all along. Dad being able to bridge to his dead ancestors was crazy, right? After thinking on it long and hard, Overdrive decided he wasn't yet ready accept or reject the bridge. He needed more data, and decided to get it by encouraging his father to check in with the ancestors now and then for advice, as he and Mary moved forward with the farm expansion. Each check-in would help judge if the bridge was real or not. Until Overdrive knew for sure, he felt it best to keep Mary in the dark. He'd never kept secrets from Mary before, and didn't cherish it now. But he feared she'd push to have his father evaluated, and if necessary, treated. He'd heard stories about elderly folks being evaluated and then institutionalized. He knew his father would wither in an institution, and was reluctant to open any doors to that possibility. Even if the bridge was fiction, he figured his Dad having odd beliefs didn't make him a danger to himself or others. His driving might, but not his odd beliefs. Overdrive made a mental note to speak to his Dad again about his driving.

CHAPTER 5

Family Matters

Winter was coming. In a last-ditch effort to finish cleaning the heifer barns, Overdrive pulled Jumbo off the machinery servicing task. On weekends, Jumbo ran the scoop tractor with Joe, John and David doing the hand work, and Overdrive emptying the spreader on the fields. During the week, Overdrive ran the scoop, his well-rested father ran the spreader, and they shared the hand work. With all Evans family testosterone focused on barn cleaning, they managed to win the race against Mother Nature, barely. Several cold snaps with heavy snows hit before they finished, requiring use of the tractor-mounted snow blower to clear a path to the fields for the spreader, and multiple tractors to pull it once there.

When the heifer barns were finally cleaned, there'd been no celebration. The scene was more like a chain gang staggering back after toiling in a frozen shit quarry. It'd taken several weeks to restore a sense of normalcy. Everybody just needed to go through the motions of their daily lives for a while, in order to recover. Key to Overdrive's rejuvenation was that he loved being outdoors in winter. There's a freshness about it. Everything's all white and tingly, and silent and pastoral, like a winter wonderland. He enjoyed breathing the crisp air, seeing his breath, and the hearing the crunch of snow under his feet.

What Overdrive loved even more was dairying's ambiance in winter. After all these years, he still enjoyed being slapped in the face by sweet and pungent warmth, every time he stepped out of the bitter cold, and into the barn. Magically, the barn heated itself. Overdrive's bookish son, John, tried to explain it to him once. Apparently, the warmth is attributable to the milk herd's respiration and body heat, plus some bullshit about the thermal mass of the three-foot thick field stone foundation walls. According to John, there's nothing mystical about it. That kid can be such a buzzkill sometimes. Thermal mass, my ass.

Overdrive preferred to keep things simple. In his mind, the farm was like a giant flywheel. Due to the family's efforts during spring, summer, and fall, the flywheel entered winter spinning at top speed. This meant all the forage necessary to tide the milk herd and youngstock over until next spring, had been stored in advance. During winter, the farm's flywheel had enough momentum to self-turn until spring. Every day, the family merely needed to dole out food and water to the livestock, clean up after them, and in the case of the milk herd, milk them twice. That was it. The thought that these simple tasks were sufficient to sustain hundreds of livestock through some of the foulest winter weather on earth, caused a deep feeling of contentment to resonate within Overdrive.

With the plowing done, the heifer barns cleaned, and machinery repair and maintenance progressing as planned, there'd finally be some slack time available to catch a second wind. The way Overdrive looked at it, winter's beauty and slower pace provided all the rejuvenation necessary to prepare for next spring's challenges. While this may be true for Overdrive, Mary doubted the same'd be true for the rest of the family. At her insistence, they agree to head to Harbor Lights after the evening milking, for a private discussion about family-wide rejuvenation.

* * *

Aside from a few strangers at the bar, Harbor Lights was deserted when Overdrive and Mary walked in. After settling at their usual table with beers in tow, Overdrive asked, "What's this all about Mary, why're we here?"

Mary said, "We've an extraordinary challenge coming next spring, right?"

Overdrive bobbed his head, and said, "Absolutely! No doubt about it."

With the tone of a schoolmarm, Mary asked, "So, what's the most important thing we need to accomplish during the slow time over the next few months?"

Wary, for fear it's a trick question, Overdrive rubbed his chin and ventured, "Well, the head start tasks are already done except for the machinery fix-ups, and they're going well. So, next up is hardening the bank draw numbers."

Mary sighed deeply, took a sip, smiled a bit condescendingly, and said, "James, honey, let's try again. What'll you need most by next spring?"

Somewhat defensively, Overdrive unwisely replied, "We have a not-to-exceed draw limit from the bank, and the sooner we draw, the more interest we pay. So, like I say, we need to harden the numbers to defer draws until needed."

Mary leaned in and lowered her voice, "James, you can be such a dumbass sometimes. What you'll need most is a bright eyed, bushy tailed work force. Who do you think's going to do all that work?"

Trying to pushback, Overdrive responded, "What? You mean the kids? It's winter, for Christ sakes. The workload is half, and they're living in a picture postcard. If they'd open their fucking eyes for once, it'd take their breath away."

Mary rubbed her temple, and said, "James, this's the only childhood they'll ever have. They're in school, doing chores, and the boys are still staggering from your head start tasks. They're even joking that it's a head start on a death march."

Overdrive laughed out loud, and Mary couldn't help but join him. Soon they're all teared up, red in the face, and gasping for air. When it subsided, they wiped their eyes and enjoyed a moment of silence. Then Overdrive tried again, "Do you think the kids will ever learn to appreciate this special way of life?"

Mary thought for a moment, then said, "I don't know. Maybe some of them will. It'd be more likely if we can give them some down time over the next few months, to do as they please. We'll need them refreshed by next spring."

Overdrive nodded, "Fair enough."

Overdrive and Mary spent the next hour listing all the wintertime chores they couldn't handle themselves. They organized the tasks, and assigned them among the kids, such that all chores could be completed during the morning and evening milkings. Between milkings there'd be school during the week, of course, but the kids would have free time on weekends and during the long holiday break.

Overdrive and Mary knew their brood would want to visit friends in town, host friends at the farm, play sheepshead or board games, ice fish, hunt, sled and toboggan, attend scout and FFA meetings, and so on, and that some of these activities required transportation. They made a solemn oath that they, or Jumbo, would run the younger kids around and be pleasant about it, so the kids could enjoy their activities without feeling guilty. They also resolved, only half-jokingly, to never stick Jumbo with sibling transport duties on Lizzie Flint date nights.

✳ ✳ ✳

With morning milking and breakfast behind them, the entire Evans family was in the living room enjoying the picture window's view of the winter wonderland outside, in the midst of the most vicious winter storm of the season. About two feet of snow had fallen overnight, covering about three feet already on the ground. Snow drifts were almost up to the farm house's eaves. Though only 20 yards away, the giant maple trees could barely be seen through the gale of wind-blown snow, and continuing snowfall. They're in the midst of a full-blown nor'easter, bringing lake effect snow inland off of Lake Michigan. School was closed, of course, and the kids were in animated discussion about what to do first, out in the snow. The Evans kids were a veritable menagerie of ages, sizes, interests, and inclinations. In comparison to them, even the United Nations stood out as an effective decision-making body.

When it came to fun in the snow, Jumbo, 17 and a junior at Plymouth High School, favored activities designed to terrorize his younger siblings. He had enough self-control to avoid hurting anybody seriously, but he reveled in the fact that only he was really sure about that. Joe, 16 and a sophomore, had endured sibling harassment for years at the hands of Jumbo. From all appearances his major goal in life was to pay that forward to his younger siblings, and he saw playing in the snow as a great opportunity to do so. Kathy, Marie, John and David were aware of these tendencies, and knew they'd better watch out.

At 15, Kathy was a five-eight, 130-pound, toned and shapely freshman at Plymouth High School. She was attractive in her own way, with hazel eyes, and shoulder-length auburn hair. Her habit of blowing stray hanks of hair from her face was either annoying or endearing, depending on your point of view. Though smart, boys were a higher priority than school. The boys showing the most interest thus far, tended to drive cars with jacked-up rear-ends. While growing up, holding her own against her older brothers was aided by her in-your-face personality.

Marie was 14 and an eighth grader at Cascade Elementary School. She was five-six, 110-pounds, and every bit as toned as her sister. Time would tell if she became a beauty, but providing a good start were her lightly freckled nose and cheeks, dark brown eyes, and very dark brunette hair worn in a pageboy. Perhaps discouraged by Kathy's knee-to-groin responses, the older brothers didn't tease, taunt, or harass Marie as much. This allowed a more feminine development path than her older sister's, to the extent possible for a girl growing up on a dairy farm. Marie was a good student with a great sense of humor.

Bringing up the rear were John, 11 and in fifth grade, and David, 8 and in second. As the storm raged on, Overdrive and Mary sat back and enjoyed the din, as their children excitedly chattered about what to do out in the snow.

Jumbo mimed a shudder of anticipation, and said, "I know, let's bury John up to his neck in a snow bank. It'll be an experiment right up the little bookworm's alley. We'll see if he's able to dig himself out before peeing in his snow pants."

John eyed Jumbo, unsure whether he'd been joking or not, and then said, "Well, it'd be a shitty experiment, only having a sample of one. And for the record, I'm 11 and don't wear snow pants anymore."

Jumbo shrugged, "Who cares if it's a shitty experiment?" Then, he counted heads with a devilish grin, and added, "But if you insist, up to five could be buried. You know, for the sake of science."

Head snapping around, Joe tap-danced, and said, "Whoa there, big guy. You don't want to do that. Why don't we just bury John and David? I'll help."

Kathy, facing Joe, fists on hips, "Lay a finger on David, and you'll be coughing up gonads before you know it! I swear!"

John, indignant, "What am I? Chopped liver? Nobody came to my defense."

Marie rolled her eyes, and said, "Oh, shut up you little dweeb. You're the one that brought up sample size. Now we're all in deep shit."

Reevaluating, John turned to Jumbo, and said, "If you bury any, science demands that you bury five."

David, in a high-pitched whine, "I don't want to be buried in a snow bank!"

Overhearing the banter, Overdrive failed miserably at hiding his smirk. But Mary, with eyes narrowed, intervened in a loud steely voice, "CHILDREN! There'll be no snow burials today. DO YOU HEAR ME?"

After a moment of empty air, Marie said, "Why don't we go sledding on the Side Hill? That way everybody can have fun."

The milk herd's pasture is nicknamed the Side Hill. It's a long and narrow twenty-acre parcel, with the narrow dimension steeply sloping between the high ground of the home place, and wetlands below. In winter, the Side Hill is a legendary place to sled and toboggan. There's a stone wall along the base of the hill, separating the pasture and wetlands, which acts as a natural snow fence, causing snow to pile up into drifts on the pasture-side, along the base of the hill.

When conditions are right, the drifts are high and crusted enough to send sleds and toboggans airborne over the stone wall, to a soft feathery landing into the snow-covered cattail marsh. When not, the sleds and toboggans crash, throwing the riders into the rocks. It's been a family tradition for generations to invite friends from Cascade and Plymouth out to the farm for a sledding party, and find out the day's conditions by encouraging the least favorite friend to go first. On crash days, it's important to roll off before you get to the bottom. Marie's suggestion to go sledding triggered a heated discussion. One camp wanted to go sledding today. The other wanted to organize a sledding party for tomorrow, so friends could come after the roads were plowed, and save the virgin snow on the Side Hill for then. The party camp won out because Kathy's suitor had been two-timing her, and Marie promoted sending him down the hill first.

After further negotiation, the kids decided that today they'd start out with a snow ball fight, with Jumbo and the girls challenging Joe, John and David. Wise to what that meant, Mary banned ice balls, made by dipping snowballs into livestock watering troughs and letting them freeze, and told them to stay away from the house and other buildings to avoid breaking windows. However, face plants in the snow, face washes with snow, snow down the neck, and so on were fair game. Uttering *I give* meant you're out, and your side wins when the opposing side is out.

* * *

With the kids outside, Overdrive and Mary finally had some peace and quiet. They enjoyed the cozy feeling that came from sitting in a warm easy chair in the midst of a blizzard, totally isolated from the rest of the world. Other than howling wind and an occasional distant laugh or shriek, there's nothing but total silence.

About 30 minutes in, the cocoon of joy ruptured when the phone rang. Mary answered, and called Overdrive to the phone. Overdrive said gruffly, "Hello?"

"Hey Overdrive, it's Scully." Scully and Overdrive had been friends throughout elementary and high school, and had volunteered together for the Army, when WWII broke out. He's employed by the Sheboygan County Highway Department, and supervised the Town of Lyndon County Shed.

Overdrive smiled, and said, "Scully! I bet you've got your hands full today."

Scully said, "Don't I ever. Look, we've got a problem. Think you can help?"

Eyebrows raised, Overdrive said, "If I can, sure. What's the problem?"

Scully dropped his voice, "One of my snowplows is in the ditch on that big hill by the old Ulbricht farm, on Bates Road. I've got my only other snowplow there now, trying to pull it out, but it's a no-go."

Overdrive snorted, "Holy cow, what the fuck happened? You guys have too much to drink last night, playing cards and waiting for the storm to hit?" Dead silence on the line. Fearing the gale had knocked out the phones, Overdrive said, "Scully, you still there?"

Scully, purposely lingering in silence with a big shit-eating grin on his face, finally said, "Yes, I'm still here. Actually, what happened was, Eddie came up over the blind crest of the hill in the snowplow, and there, stuck in the middle of the road, was Old Bill's car. Eddie had no choice but to take the ditch."

Overdrive dropped into a chair, and said, "You're shitting me, right?"

Grinning even wider, Scully said, "I shit you not."

Overdrive, surprised, "What the fuck was Dad doing out in this blizzard?"

Scully, with a touch of snark, "You tell me, dumbass. He's your father."

With a strain in his voice, Overdrive asked, "Did anybody get hurt?"

Scully, in a reassuring voice, "No, no, there's nothing like that to worry about. Everybody's fine except for bruised egos. The tenants in Ulbricht's old farm house took Old Bill in out of the cold."

Overdrive exhaled heavily, and said, "Thank god for that."

A tad impatient now, Scully said, "Going back to my original question, can you help? Our phones are blowing up. Everybody's snowed in and wondering where the hell the plows are."

Overdrive barked, "Yes, yes, of course I can help. Jumbo and I'll both come. We'll bring both diesel tractors. I've already got the snow blower mounted on one of them. But it'll take us a little time to get the weights and chains on the tractors. Then we'll have to blow ourselves a path down to Ulbricht's."

Enjoying the moment, Scully turned the screw, "I'll tell them to expect you any minute. Better hurry, I'd hate to have to tell all these callers both my plows are dicking around on Bates Road because of Old Bill Evans and his horse's ass of a son. That might mess up your square dance card for a while. I mean, who'd want to be seen with you? Mary might not be happy."

Trying to negotiate, Overdrive said, "You wouldn't dare! Now come on, Scully. You know we'll get there as soon as we can. That's low, Scully, even by your standards. I'm hurrying, already! You're an evil bastard, you know it?"

Having had enough fun for the time being, Scully relented, "Not to worry, Overdrive, I've got your back if you've got mine. Now get my plows back on the road, before the fucking Town of Lyndon board starts chewing my ass!"

* * *

Overdrive filled Mary in on what'd happened, while he struggled into his blizzard gear. Then he tracked down the kids, peeled Jumbo off, and at Mary's suggestion directed the rest of them back to the house for hot chocolate and to choose their next fun-in-the-snow activity.

Overdrive and Jumbo trotted over to the machine shed, and fired up the two big John Deere diesels. While the tractors were idling to warm up their engine blocks and fluids, they worked feverishly to install the weights and tire chains. To be safe, they loaded their three longest and heaviest log chains onto the tractors, and threw cold shut links, a mallet, and a ball peen hammer into the tractor tool boxes, in case field repairs were needed. Within minutes they're ready to go.

The snow blower was back-mounted on the three-point hitch, so Overdrive shoved the JD4020 into reverse, and took off backwards. To clear a path wide enough for the tractors, the blower augured snow to the center where the impeller sucked it up and blew it out the shoot. Overdrive slowly made his way from the machine shed to the driveway, down the drive, and right onto Bates Road toward Ulbricht's. Jumbo followed on the JD70.

By the time Overdrive and Jumbo reached Ulbricht's Hill, the county's functioning snowplow had managed to clear Ulbricht's driveway, and move Old

Bill's car into it and out of the way. It'd also cleared Bates Road for a good distance in either direction from the ditched snowplow.

Overdrive, Jumbo, and the two snowplow drivers introduced themselves and huddled in the cleared roadway to plan the mired snowplow's extraction. The only option was to pull the snowplow back out of the ditch along the same route it'd followed going in. Unfortunately, this meant pulling it up the hill. They decided to use the chains to form a single daisy chain of the four vehicles, because the road was too narrow for anything else.

All four men were experienced. They knew that jerking a loose chain would break it, and backlash from a broken chain could be fatal. With great care they slowly advanced their vehicles, one-by-one starting with the functioning snowplow, until all chains were tight. At the horn honk from the functioning snowplow, all four drivers slowly engaged their clutches and began to pull. When the horn blew again, they all pushed in their clutches and rocked back. Once the rocking cadence was established, the audio que was no longer needed. Eventually, the rocking motion created enough momentum to sustain a steady pull and bring the ditched snowplow back up onto the road.

Then, four grown men hopped down off their rides onto the road, and let out a bone-chilling, red-faced, primal roar. It must be a man thing. After the high fives and back slaps, the chains were unhitched and everybody went their separate ways. One of the county rigs plowed its way back to Cascade, and the other continued down Bates Road toward the farm, with Jumbo following along behind. Overdrive went to fetch his father and thank the tenants for taking him in during the ordeal.

* * *

After saying their goodbyes to the tenants, Overdrive and his father walked in silence to his father's car. When they arrived, Old Bill sheepishly said, "I'm sorry, son. I know better than to be out driving in a blizzard. I just ... I don't know ... I just love seeing the countryside when the weather's like this."

Overdrive raised his hand to indicate no apology necessary, and said, "I know Dad. I love it too."

Old Bill looked around, "Must admit, I didn't realize it was this bad out."

Overdrive bobbed his head, and said, "The storm's a beauty, isn't it?"

Old Bill snuck in a sideways glance, and said, "You're being unusually forgiving, son. You slip on the ice and crack your head, or something?"

Overdrive snorted a quick laugh, and said, "No, no, nothing like that. Just still flying high on adrenalin, I guess. Breaking trail to get here. Yanking a snowplow out of the ditch. Everything all white and tingly. Gives me a stiffy."

Old Bill cracked up, "Oh god help us, you are your father's son, aren't you?"

Overdrive smiled at that, then said, "Yes I am, and proud of it. But I'll give you a rain check for your ass chewing. You know, for when I'm back to normal."

Dad, sagely, "Ass chewing's are given to sons by fathers, not vice versa."

Overdrive narrowed eyes and did a comic head

turn, as if somebody might overhear, "Well, when your father's a total screw up, sometimes roles get reversed." They shared a good belly laugh, and then went their separate ways.

* * *

The next day, Overdrive drove the family car into Cascade for minor repairs at Art's Service Station. Apparently, Old Bill running the snowplow off the road was the talk of the town. The locals had also started calling Art's intersection *Old Bill's Corner*, to remind them to be on the lookout for Old Bill running the stop sign. On the drive back to the farm, Overdrive pondered what to do. His last drive-better conversation with his father had been a total bust. Joshing around with his Dad was okay, but he'd been raised to respect his elders, and lecturing him wasn't.

During evening milking, after Overdrive filled her in, Mary said, "You know, James, I've got the same problem with my parents. Any helpful advice, or even a suggestion is dead on arrival if it comes across as a lecture."

Overdrive removed a milking machine from a spent cow, poured the milk into a pail, and said, *"Don't run stop signs* is bound to sound like a lecture."

Mary thought a moment, then said, "This conversation with your father needs to be handled delicately. We can't afford another blowup between you two."

Overdrive and his father had a familiar pattern. They'd be going along fine, working side-by-side, both engrossed in the ebb and flow of the farm's tempo. Then one or the other would do or say something stupid, they'd fight, and Old Bill would disappear for weeks or months. The baggage between them ran deep.

Overdrive shrugged, and said, "Like I say, that's why I'm talking to you."

Mary looked up, put an index finger to her lips, and said, "I've got an idea. How about I come along and soften your Dad up with his favorite treat, before the talk? Hot apple pie, right out of the oven. That'll make him more approachable."

Overdrive and Mary decided they'd make an unannounced social call at Old Bill's shack that evening. Mary recruited John to wash udders and carry milk pails in her absence, and went to the house to get the pie going.

* * *

Old Bill saw the head lights when Overdrive and Mary pulled in, and opened the door before they could knock. They exchanged pleasantries while enjoying their pie, but afterword the room fell into an awkward silence. Overdrive struggled to find the words to get started, and Mary's tap under the table didn't help.

Sensing his son was tongue-tied, Old Bill guessed they'd come to chastise him about his joyride in the blizzard, and asked, "Is this when I'm supposed to redeem my rain check for the ass chewing? You know, concerning the snowplow."

Uncomfortable with where this was headed, Mary stepped in, and said, "Dad, you know we and your grandkids love you, right?"

Taken by surprise, Old Bill said, "Yes, of course."

Mary held his gaze, "We don't know how we'd manage without you. Your help cleaning the heifer barns is just the latest example. Thank you for that."

Old Bill smiled, "You don't need to thank me. I enjoy helping."

Still holding his gaze, Mary said, "With the farm expansion coming, we'll need you even more. In fact, we're going to need you around for a very long time, and our kids need their grandpa."

Unsure where this was going, Old Bill hesitated, then said, "Okay."

Mary thought for a moment, then said solemnly, "We're here because we need you to promise us something. We're asking you, begging you, to promise us you'll be more mindful of your driving. What if that snowplow driver hadn't seen you in time? You could've been killed!"

Repentant, Old Bill said, "I know, Mary. It was a mistake. I didn't realize how bad the storm was until I was out in it. By then, it was too late."

Mary continued, emotion flowing into her voice, "What if someday, you ran a stop sign into the path of an eighteen-wheeler rolling through Cascade on Hwy 28. You'd be killed, no question!"

Old Bill winced, and said, "I know, Mary."

Near tears now, Mary said softly, "What would we do without you? What would the kids do without their grandpa? Promise us, please, that you'll be more mindful of your driving. Can you do that for us?"

There was a moment of empty air, as the emotion built within Old Bill. With a shine in his eyes, he said, "Yes, of course. I promise."

The mood and conversation lightened immediately. Old Bill enjoyed hearing about today's Side Hill sledding party, and Kathy's two-timing boyfriend's rude introduction to the snow-buried stone wall fence on the first run. They were all laughing and having a good time, when Overdrive and Mary rose to leave. Overdrive and Mary drove back to the farm in silence, lost in their own thoughts. Overdrive mused over how worried he'd been, about what to say to his Dad. Then when the time came, he never had to say a word. Mary's handling of his father had been masterful. Everything she'd said tonight, had come straight from the heart. Overdrive glanced over at is wife, and saw the moist shine of emotion still in her eyes. She was looking out the side window, enjoying the snow-covered landscape scroll by under the light of a full moon. In that moment, his feeling of love for her exceeded all moments that had come before.

CHAPTER 6

Making Deals with Others

With chore assignments re-shuffled and school out over the holidays, the extra free time over the rest of December and January began to pay dividends in terms of the kid's rekindled spirits. For Overdrive and Mary, however, this period was a blur of activity. At the heart of it was the fact that they'd already signed for a loan, which established a maximum draw based on their estimates. The challenge now was to shoe horn into their set budget, the real-world costs for the barn addition, rented lands, and new cattle. Given all the red tape and HQ approvals required, Overdrive didn't see going back to Cascade Bank as a viable option.

Overdrive and Mary attacked the barn addition first, because tying down a contract for that would likely require the most calendar time. Unlike renting land and buying cows, they'd never built a barn before. Even so, they'd have to also move fast on the other two, because they wouldn't feel comfortable finalizing the barn addition contract before the land and cattle deals were nailed down.

Overdrive and Mary both wanted Old Bill to be part of the team, as they worked to finalize the barn, land, and cattle deals. Mary wanted him involved so he'd feel valued. Overdrive's interest was to determine if any valuable advice would be forthcoming from the Welsh ancestors. Presuming it's real, keeping his Dad's unusual talent from Mary would be awkward, but Overdrive remained convinced that doing so was best until he was sure about it himself.

* * *

Overdrive, Mary, and Old Bill met over the kitchen table to discuss how to find a contractor to design and build the barn addition. The plan they came up with called for Overdrive and Old Bill to divide up and visit the diners most frequented by area farmers, and ask around for contractor recommendations. Meanwhile, Mary would spend time at the Plymouth and Sheboygan libraries, searching for contractor ads in the yellow pages, local newspapers, and farm magazines.

Later, when alone with his father, Overdrive said he'd handle the networking himself, if Old Bill thought bridging with the ancestors might bear fruit. Old Bill had no doubt they'd provide names of quality barn-building contractors from back in the day. Less certain, was whether Old Bill would be able to run down a currently-operating contractor descended from these well-regarded forebears, but he thought it'd be worth a try.

About a week later, the three of them met to compare notes. Overdrive and Mary had both identified several possible contractors, and Old Bill had identified one. One name appeared on all three lists, and they decided to start there. Old Bill's wink told his son the name was from ancestral lips. Overdrive called the contractor, and he agreed to come to the farm for a look-see the following Saturday. He said he'd have to call back later to set a time.

The contractor, Fred Reineking, called Saturday morning during breakfast and arrived at the farm right after lunch. Overdrive walked him through the site and provided a general vision of where the barn addition would be built, and the barn style and layout desired. Overdrive and Fred hit it off right away. By the information shared and questions asked, Overdrive could tell Fred knew what he was doing. Overdrive especially liked that Fred was flexible enough to allow the possibility for construction steps to be self-performed, presuming Overdrive's crew was capable and had the time. Fred agreed to come back in two weeks with a well-developed design and a cost estimate broken down by step, so Overdrive could see what taking on a step would save.

* * *

Land rental was the next priority since planning spring's work couldn't be done until the land to be worked was known. They wanted land nearby, to minimize commute time and fuel costs. Overdrive had already figured how many acres of established hay land was needed. For the peas and sweet corn, they'd look for lands already plowed and ready to till.

At another kitchen table meeting, they came up

with a simple search strategy that called for Overdrive and Old Bill to divide up the nearby country roads, and simply drive around the farm in an ever-expanding circle. Whether there's rental signage posted or not, when in doubt, they'd stop and inquire about whether the land could be rented. Meanwhile, Mary would return to the Plymouth and Sheboygan public libraries, searching for land-for-rent ads in the local papers and farm magazines. Again, when alone with his father, Overdrive said he'd handle the drive-around, freeing Old Bill to bridge with the ancestors and follow up on any advice they might provide.

A few days later the three of them met again, to share what they'd learned and agree on next steps. They began by discussing the most important criteria for land selection, and came up with a list that included things like distance from the home place, past fertility, field entrances wide enough for the machinery, and whether hay was already present. If not hay land, additional criteria included whether or not it was already plowed, spring wetness, workability, rockiness, and suitability for peas and sweet corn. Then they used the criteria to evaluated options.

The most attractive lands were owned by the elderly Leidemann brothers. Some of it was literally right across Bates Road from the house. Unfortunately, the Leidemanns weren't interested in renting, even though they rarely got around to planting crops in recent years, and if they did, rarely got around to harvesting them. The next best options were the plowed ground at the old Nutters farm, further down Bates Road on the way to Cascade; the hay lands at the old Courtland farm, over near Lake Ellen; and the old Riley and Dugan farms, which were located off of Hwy 28 on separate country roads, on the far side of Cascade.

Old Bill was adamant they consider plowed lands further east for peas, such as his brother Hank's farm and the adjacent one owned by Van Essen. He argued these lands dry and become workable earlier than most, and an early planting is good for peas since they tolerate frost if the weather reverses later. Being closer to Lake Michigan, these lands also experience frequent morning ground fogs near harvest time, allowing more calendar time to harvest the peas before they over-ripen and harden. Mary initially protested due to distance, but after another wink from his old man, Overdrive supported his father.

For peas, as Old Bill suggested they'd target the lands owned by Overdrive's uncle Hank, and old Mr. Van Essen. For sweet corn, they'd target the Nutters farm. Concerning the Courtland, Riley, and Dugan farms, two out of three would provide enough hay land. Over the next few evenings, Overdrive and Mary visited these six landowners for face-to-face discussions. The conversations were all friendly, and with the exception of Dugan's, they'd left with the impression that the land was theirs if they wanted it. Since the Courtland and Riley farms provided the hay acreage needed anyway, they scratched the Dugan farm from further consideration.

In advance of Reineking's return visit, Overdrive and Mary made the rounds again to the five remaining landowners, and this time talked rental rates. Although the discussions were friendly and social, the landowners got the message that this was best and final offer time. Overdrive and Mary had leverage, because no other farms in the immediate area were looking to expand. In every instance, they left with price-certain gentlemen's agreements for the coming year.

In the case of Hank's, Van Essen's, and Nutters', Overdrive had another loose end to tie up. Cash crops were grown under contracts with processors, so he couldn't ink these land rental deals without first having growing contracts in hand. The nearest processor was Stokely-Van Camp in Waldo, so Overdrive paid their field agent a visit the next day. Getting acres might've been difficult in a normal year, because processors generally remained loyal to previous year growers. But construction was already underway to expand the Waldo plant's processing capacity, and plenty of acres were still available to be contracted.

The field man knew Overdrive by reputation to be a skilled farmer. Nonetheless, in the field man's opinion, he more so than Overdrive, was expert at choosing lands for growing peas and sweet corn. He insisted on surveying the lands with Overdrive, before making a commitment. They hopped into the field man's pickup truck, and Overdrive directed him around to the three farms. By the end of the day, Overdrive had growing contracts ready to sign, for all the pea and sweet corn acres he'd wanted.

* * *

At a third kitchen table meeting, Overdrive, Mary, and Old Bill got the ball rolling on doubling the size of the milk herd. They started by coming to agreement on what the perfect scenario would look like. They wanted 40 milk cows from high-quality bloodlines.

The cows should be delivered in early May, after there's enough grass to pasture the herd between milkings, making the too-small existing barn moot. The cows should be dry, but bred back to calve in late spring or early summer, shortly after they arrive. This way the Evans' would benefit from the high milk production that occurs early in a cow's lactation, and from heifer calves to raise as replacements, and bull calves to ship to market for cash. The cows should be proven but have productive years left, aka carrying their second or third calf.

To find the cattle, they settled on a three-pronged approach. Overdrive would invite Gib Buyer, a local cattle trader they'd used in the past, to the farm. They'd brief him on what they're looking for, and Gib would beat the bushes on their behalf. Separately, Overdrive and Old Bill would divide up the local diners and see if the grape vine uncovered any sources. For her part, Mary would return to the Plymouth and Sheboygan libraries, and search for dairy herd auction ads in the newspapers and dairying magazines. As is becoming the rule, during a private moment with his Dad, Overdrive said he'd handle the grape vine himself so Old Bill could pick the brains of the ancestors and follow up on that.

Gib Buyer had a good nose for opportunity, and when Overdrive called, he promised to be at the farm the very next morning. He and Mary both liked the man, and appreciated his responsiveness. Sure, he'd get his cut on the cattle deals, but that was only fair. They knew some area farmers considered Gib to be a shark, but in the past, he'd always been fair to them. They sensed that Gib tried a little harder for them, and thought it might be because he admired good dairy farmers and good dairy cattle, and enjoyed bringing them together.

The next morning, Gib arrived right on time, and as he entered the kitchen his smile grew even broader as he picked up the aroma of hot apple pie right out of the oven. They got caught up over pie with sharp cheddar cheese and coffee, and then Overdrive and Mary filled Gib in on their herd expansion plans. He listened intently as his excitement grew, whistled when he heard 40 head, and could barely sit still by the time they'd finished. Gib appreciated them networking with area farmers and searching for notices of dairy herd auctions. This meant he could focus on expanding the search geographically. They agreed to meet again in a week.

On the evening prior to Gib's return, Overdrive and Mary drove to Old Bill's shack to compare notes. It took Mary a surprisingly long time to rattle off all the dairy herd auctions she'd found. Overdrive and his father were frankly shocked at the number of farmers getting out of the dairy business. Given the choice of getting bigger or getting out, apparently the majority were getting out. Overdrive's grape vine search came up dry, but Old Bill's sources, wink-wink, knew the best dairy cattle bloodlines in the area, and in years past who owned them. One owner's name matched that of a farmer having an auction, so they'd ask Gib to start there

The next morning, Overdrive, Mary and Gib filled each other in on what they'd learned over the past week. Gib recognized the bloodlines. In fact, he went on and on about them in glowing terms. He attributed

Wisconsin becoming America's Dairyland, to livestock brought by Welsh settlers directly from the old country, or by way of Upstate New York and Ohio. Gib made it his business to keep track of the provenance of the area's milk herds, including cases where herds had passed to daughters, who'd then married and taken their husband's names. After inspecting the auction data, Gib became convinced that not one, but at least three of the auctions involved cattle from the desired bloodlines. He said he'd attempt to negotiate group deals in advance of these auctions, for the cows in the herds that met the Evans' criteria. Gib had a good understanding of the market, and before he left, gave them a solid estimate for what 40 head should cost.

* * *

When Fred Reineking arrived for his return visit, Mary had Apple Coogan and coffee ready, and she and Overdrive used the time enjoying the treat to get to know Fred a little better. Afterward, Fred explained the plans, and answered questions. True to his word, he provided fixed costs by construction step, so Overdrive could see what'd be saved if he took one on. By now Overdrive and Mary had a good idea what the land and cattle would cost, and after seeing Fred's numbers, knew immediately they'd need to negotiate with Fred.

Overdrive and Mary's overriding priority was to retain enough new stanchions in the barn addition to double the size of the milk herd to 80. They gave Fred the total price he needed to be under, and discussed with him some corners they'd be willing to cut such as dropping the addition's stairway to the haymow, fewer trap doors, cheaper glass block windows, and so on. Fred left them a copy of his standard contracting agreement to read, and promised to sharpen his pencil and return the following week with best and final revised plans and prices.

Before Fred returned, Gib had finished negotiating the cattle deals and the land rental deals with the five landowners were finalized. The bottom line was these costs had held fast, so the price Fred needed to be under hadn't changed. On the eve of Fred's return, Overdrive and Mary reread the contractor's agreement. When he arrived the next morning, they got right down to business. Fred presented what he called safe and gambler's options. In both cases, the sum of the by-step prices matched the target budget. The safe option cut all the corners previously discussed, but also dropped six stanchions, while retaining the recommended contingency. The gambler's option cut all the corners, kept all the stanchions, and made up the difference by gutting the size of the contingency.

Fred did his best to convince Overdrive and Mary to play it safe, saying over and over again, that his recommended contingency percentage was very realistic, and based on decades of experience with similar projects in the area. He wanted to make absolutely sure that Overdrive and Mary understood that unforeseen costs came out of contingency until exhausted, and thereafter would be paid by them. In other words, the fixed prices per step were not truly fixed, for any step where unforeseen costs were possible. Mary wavered but Overdrive wanted all his stanchions and wouldn't budge. Although not thrilled that they'd have to pay extra if unforeseen costs exceeded contingency, they picked the skinny-contingency gambler's option anyway, and signed the agreement.

Fred said he could start three weeks from Monday, which fell in the first week of March. But to do so, he'd need the first, or mobilization, payment by a week from Friday. Fred warned he had another job teed up, and if the mobilization payment was late, their start date would slip three-weeks. Overdrive was confident he'd have the money, and promised to call when certain.

* * *

Overdrive and Mary spent the next week, between milkings, hardening their estimated schedule for when borrowed funds would be drawn from the bank. This was important because they wanted to minimize interest paid during the draw period, by delaying draws until actually needed. Doing so avoided interest on funds drawn and parked.

Overdrive and Mary had between now and the end of August to draw all funds up to the approved maximum. But they needed good estimates for the dates and amounts of each draw, in order to estimate the draw-period interest they'd have to pay. It was to their advantage to put off payments to others wherever possible. For the land rentals, the owners were ex-farmers themselves, and delaying rent payments until property taxes were due was fine with them. For the cattle purchases, there's earnest money due up front and cash on delivery for the balance. For the barn addition, they used Fred's best guesses on construction step completion dates leading up to project completion and occupancy by mid-August.

The spring's work numbers were a bit of a hand wave, but they'd have time later to harden them week-by-week using historical records. Since the first draw was as hard as it'd ever be, Overdrive asked Mary to call Cascade Bank, and have Walt Brickner set it up. Then he called Fred, and told him he'd have his mobilization money for the March week-one start.

* * *

It's early February, and after a month and a half of working elbow to elbow with Mary and his father on deal making, Overdrive had a strong need to step back and process what'd gone down. He used his alone time while milking and doing chores to ruminate over what had come to pass.

Not being completely straight with Mary was growing increasingly awkward. After Dad had pulled Fred Reineking's name out of his ass, Mary had been taken aback. Then, when he verbalized solid reasons for looking further east for pea lands to rent, Mary surmised his recent sharpness was related to being told how much the family needed and appreciated him. But Gib Buyer raving on and on about the bloodlines Dad had identified was the coup de gras. Now Mary's convinced there must be a new lady friend, or something, behind Dad's newfound mental acuity and she's determined to nose around Cascade and find out what.

Reineking, the wisdom on peas, the bloodlines – it'd all been from the Welsh ancestors. Where else could it have come from? If true, that's three more data points supporting the theory that Dad talks to dead people. Telling Mary would be tantamount to going on record as a believer. Not telling her might be worse, if she walks in on him doing the spirit-thing. Overdrive pondered this dilemma, and concluded he wasn't yet ready to fess up to Mary, but he'd tell his Dad never to bridge without first checking with him on Mary's whereabouts.

The other issue keeping Overdrive up at night was Fred Reineking's contingency. Overdrive struggled to wrap his mind around the concept. It sounded like a kitty to cover screw ups and acts of god. He hoped Fred wasn't a screw up, he certainly didn't come across like one. But even if he were, why wouldn't he pay for his own mistakes? That's what we dairy farmers do. As for acts of god, things unforeseen or whatever, we pay for them too. We get a milk check, not a milk check plus contingency. It wasn't right.

CHAPTER 7

Committed

It's the second week in February, and Mary's random comment during evening milking about the beautiful full moon out tonight, sparked an idea in Overdrive. Frozen and covered with a thick layer of snow, he knew Lake Ellen under moonlight would be a sight worth seeing. When Overdrive asked if she'd be interested in a trip to Harbor Lights after milking, Mary's smile said it all.

The drive to the lake was awe-inspiring. Overdrive and Mary silently took it in because no words could do it justice. Astonishingly bright, the moon cast the snow-covered countryside with an enchanting glow. Harbor Lights was abuzz, full of people enjoying the rare nighttime brilliance of the lake. Circulating and socializing, Overdrive and Mary's already lofty moods surged even higher. When the table with the best view of the lake opened up, Mary snagged it while Overdrive fetched the beer. In a celebratory mood, Overdrive bought two bottles of Lithia instead of their usual, Kingsbury, and ambled over to the table.

Seeing the change, Mary piped up, "Wow, Lithia! What's the occasion? Or have those West Benders at Gehl been giving their local beer the hard sell?"

Overdrive tapped his temple, "Well, it costs more, so it must be better."

"Such a deep thinker you are." Shaking her head in mock dismay, Mary added, "It's a good thing I keep the check book."

Overdrive smiled at that, then said, "Yes, it is. That way you'll get the writer's cramp, when we start cranking out all those farm expansion checks."

"Always thinking of me, right James?" But then the window captured Mary's attention, and she said, "Wow, will you look at that view. The moon's lit up the entire lake. It's like a giant glowing white table top surrounded by trees."

Overdrive bobbed his head, and said, "Somehow the snow seems to amplify the moonlight. And look at those tree shadows. They're as sharp as midday."

Unexpectedly, Mary put on her impish grin, raised her bottle, and said, "James, how about a toast. To the beauty before us, and to new beginnings!"

Overdrive, after a clink and a drink, "Speaking of new beginnings, the first draw hits our account tomorrow. Should we get some checks in the mail?"

Mary's eyes narrowed, "Before doing anything, I'll call the bank to verify. Last time they screwed up, and we had checks bouncing all over the county."

Overdrive mimed a shudder, and said, "Good point. We don't want that happening again. People thought we were crooks. Some probably still do."

Mary's brow wrinkled, "We better not rely on postal service rural free delivery either. They say village-to-RFD first-class mail takes three to four days longer than village-to-village. The delay for RFD-to-RFD can be double."

Overdrive's eyebrows shot up, "Huh, we've got problems then. There'll be a three-week delay if Reineking's check is late, and Buyer needs earnest money or he'll lose our cows. Hell, even the landowners deserve a little something up front."

They both took sips and contemplated what to do. Finally, Mary said, "Why don't we deliver the first round of checks in person? Less worry that way. Plus, it's the best way to get new relationships off on the right foot. What do you think?"

Overdrive nodded, "Hell, it's February, so we've got the time. Let's do it."

Mary's impish grin returned, "Can you handle one more bright idea?"

Overdrive replied unwisely, "Sure, can't have too many bright ideas."

Mary pounced, "Good. I don't want the kids blind-sided by how their lives will soon change. Same goes for your father. We should have a family meeting."

Overdrive, with dread, "Oh shit, Mary. Really? Whatever happened to the family just doing what they're told, when they're told? That's how we grew up."

Mary looked disappointed in him, "James, we grew up in a Norman Rockwell painting. That world doesn't exist anymore."

Overdrive hedged, "Well, maybe so. But we seem to spend an awful lot of time cajoling over what obviously needs to be done. Time is money, you know."

Mary, fists on hips, "James, you can be such a

dumbass sometimes. Listen to yourself. These're your children we're talking about, not hired hands. With the child labor laws nowadays, they'd probably be able to take us to court, and win."

Overdrive snapped, "Yeah, well, you've got that right. The whole country's going down the shitter. Fuckin' child labor laws. Fuckin' contingencies. Fuckin'..."

"James, put a lid on it. I've already heard your down the shitter, fuckin' this and that spiel, more times than I care to remember." Mary, now in his face, "Are we having a family meeting, or not? THINK this time, before you answer."

Overdrive rolled his eyes, "Yes, fine, we'll do that. Have it your way."

After a moment of empty air, Mary said, "Thank you." Then she regained awareness of the beauty before them, turned, and began silently admiring the view.

Overdrive followed her gaze, and noticed a solitary figure far out on the lake. The sight gave him an idea. He felt badly about the turn in conversation, didn't want the evening to end that way, and started to share his thought, "You know, in a few weeks it'll be ice out. Another scene like this won't be coming around until next year. Would you, I mean, er..." But then fell silent.

Mary did a double-take, "Are you asking if I'd care for a moonlight stroll?"

Overdrive tried to tap dance, "Well, um, I was thinking about it. But then I remembered it might not be safe out on the lake. You know I can't swim."

Mary's smile ramped up to high-beam, "As it turns out, Jumbo took John ice fishing last weekend. There's two feet of ice. I accept your offer." Lost, but tap-dancing like crazy trying to salvage something, Overdrive came back with, "Alright then. Come on, you, bottoms up. Let's do that moonlight stroll." Then he waggled his eyebrows, "I'm sure you'll make it worth my while."

Mary rolled her eyes, and said, "Don't get your hopes up, buster."

Overdrive emitted a low growl, faked left, then circled the table right, and lunged for Mary. But by then she'd managed to get away on the dead run, and let out a shriek as she cleared the door, and ran out onto the lake.

* * *

Before leaving for school the next day, the kids learned there'd be a family meeting Saturday morning, participation mandatory. Their grandpa would join them for breakfast, and stay for the meeting. After breakfast, Mary called the bank to verify they had the money, then made calls to set up the in-person check drops. Over the next few days, Overdrive and Mary dropped off the checks and everybody appreciated the gesture. In general, family farmers surviving this many generations since the original settlers, were still held in high regard in rural Wisconsin. This feeling was even stronger among people in a position to know how large an accomplishment that was. Fred Reineking specialized in constructing agricultural buildings. Gib Buyer was a cattle trader. The landowners were all ex-farmers. They all understood.

The good will was palpable, and Overdrive and Mary could feel it as they made the rounds. The understanding and support made them proud and thankful at the same time. These people were rooting for them to succeed. They'd a keen understanding of the challenge, and great admiration for those still willing to try. It felt personal as if they'd all be embarking on a great adventure together.

Fred Reineking's home and shop were on a country road in the Town of Herman. He'd been thrilled to receive his mobilization money a week earlier than requested. He assured Overdrive and Mary that weather permitting, he'd begin moving dirt at the farm the first Monday in March, as promised. They left with a fresh-baked chocolate torte, compliments of Fred's wife.

Gib Buyer came outside to greet them, when Overdrive and Mary pulled into his Farmer's Market, near Plymouth. He'd already paid the earnest money to lock up the cattle deals, so he'd been covering the float on the basis of goodwill. Being reimbursed so soon, with part of his cut on the deal included, put Gib in a jovial mood. He insisted they accept baseball caps for the boys, and hula hoops for the girls, all emblazoned with Farmer's Market, of course.

Overdrive and Mary's visits to the five landowners felt more social than business. Most of them pushed back gently, saying money could wait until just before tax time. But in the end, all appreciated the gesture of a small amount up front, and insisted on giving a small gift in return. The haul included homemade peanut brittle, chocolate chip cookies, and a loaf of sour dough bread, still warm, as well as a bag of hickory nut meats, and a dozen fresh eggs right out of the henhouse. Goodness, it felt like Christmas.

* * *

Saturday morning came, and Overdrive, Mary, Old Bill, and the kids gathered back around the kitchen table, after it'd been cleared and the breakfast dishes finished. Family meetings were rare, and whether out of dread or anticipation, the kids were dead silent for a change.

Overdrive began by saying the reason for the meeting was to discuss plans for the farm expansion, and spring's work. Instantly, worries vanished that some unthinkable punishment was about to be meted out. The older kids had probably sensed that something was up, but was the first time any of them heard directly about the farm expansion. Overdrive explained why they're doing it, and described the vision, including the barn addition, 40 additional milk cows, and 450 more acres of work land. There'd been many questions, and Overdrive and Mary both participated in answering them.

At first the kids were incredulous, and seemed to think Overdrive and Mary were just pulling their leg. Dirt work on the barn addition would start the first Monday in March? The 40 cows were already purchased and would arrive in early May? The additional land was already rented? At least initially, *you're shitting me* is what they were thinking. But gradually they came to realize, this's no joke.

Overdrive thrived on the action of spring's work, and with this year's farm expansion starting up at the same time, he'd be living the dream. He launched into an inspiring explanation of how they'd go about it.

His enthusiasm was contagious, as he explained all the moving parts of what'd soon unfold. He got onto a roll, and everybody just sat in rapt attention, taking it all in.

By the time Overdrive finished, the kitchen's vibe had changed. Everybody felt it. They'd be embarking on a great adventure together. It wouldn't be easy, but they'd pull through together. After a long cold winter of being cooped up inside, the boys were pumped about getting out on the land after school and on weekends. Even Old Bill couldn't wait for the action to begin. The girls were open to, if not thrilled by, the prospect of shouldering unspecified new duties if needed, in addition to their house and garden chores. The family swelled with a sense of pride, but at the same time felt an undercurrent of trepidation. None of them really knew what they'd be getting into, including Overdrive and Mary.

* * *

The next week, Overdrive and Mary received a letter from Fond du Lac regional bank, which was copied to Walt Brickner, at the bank's branch in Cascade. The letter informed them that the bank had exercised its right under a specific clause of the loan agreement, to assign the loan from the bank to the Headwaters of the Milwaukee River LLC, also known as HMR.

The letter clarified that the negotiated maximum draw still applied, and that the bank would continue to be the source of funds for the duration of the draw window, which ended August 31st. However, HMR would service the repayment side of the agreement. Hence, all future payments should be directed to HMR. This included the end-of-month interest-only payments during the draw window, as well as end-of-month principal-and-interest payments during the September through next February repayment period. Overdrive and Mary had never heard of such a thing. Mary immediately called the bank, and Walt was available to meet later that day. Walt admitted that he'd not been forewarned, and was as surprised by the loan assignment as they were. Regrettably, this meant that some unnamed rep of HMR would now be servicing their loan. When asked whether HMR would work flexibly with them when weather and whatnot went awry, Walt shrugged and said ask HMR.

As they drove back to the farm, Overdrive and Mary were near panic. They debated what to do, and decided to call the number given for HMR right away. Otherwise they'd worry, and perhaps there's nothing to worry about. With the kids at school, they'd be able to have a private phone conversation in the kitchen, and they'd use the extension so both could be on the line. Overdrive would do the talking, but Mary would have paper and pen to suggest things to say.

When Overdrive dialed HMR, a receptionist answered in a pleasant voice. He identified himself, and asked to be transferred to whoever'd be managing his loan. She took down the loan number, put him on hold while she identified the right party, and then returned and asked him to hold while she made the transfer.

The male who answered was jovial and friendly, and after introductions asked what he could do for Overdrive today. As an opener, Overdrive said he wanted to introduce himself to his new farm loan officer. Politely self-effacing, the HMR rep explained that the loan was very straightforward, and his role would be far more trivial than the phrase *farm loan officer* implied. Thinking this was an opportunity to build rapport, Overdrive took exception to the role being trivial, and started ticking off the qualities of a good farm loan officer.

Somewhat less jovial now, the HMR rep interrupted, and explained that he wasn't a farm loan officer, but rather a contract law attorney. His job was simple because everything had been clearly spelled out in the agreement. The payment dates and calculations to determine amounts were provided, as were HMR's remedies if payments were delinquent. The matter-of-fact directness of the man sent a chill up Overdrive's spine.

When the rep asked again, if there's anything specific he could help with today, Overdrive and Mary shook their heads at each other, and Overdrive said there wasn't. Then he half-heartedly expressed how much he looked forward to doing business with HMR, and building a strong working relationship with the rep. When this was greeted with an awkward silence, Overdrive thanked the rep for his time, said goodbye, and hung up.

Overdrive and Mary sat for a moment in stunned silence. Then Mary said, "Oh my god, James, what're we going to do?"

Doing his best to appear nonplussed, Overdrive said in a calm voice, "We'll do what we've always done. Pay our bills on time. If we do that, we'll be fine."

Mary wrung her hands, and said, "But with Walt, when we needed a little wiggle room, he'd give it to us. HMR won't give an inch."

Overdrive nodded, now grim, "I know. We'll just

have to pay more attention. Be more proactive when trouble's ahead. If we do that, we'll be fine."

* * *

Over the next several days, under the false veneer of confidence, Overdrive obsessed over the HMR conversation. He used his milking think-time to recall past instances when Walt had been flexible. He relived those circumstances, searching for what could've been done if Walt hadn't been flexible. For most of the recalled instances, he'd been able to think of actions they could've taken to get by. But for others he couldn't, and some instances were so long ago, it'd been hard to remember enough details to be sure, one way or the other.

Overdrive was not by nature a worrier, but he'd been worried sick since the HMR call. Who are they? Why're they now the holders of our loan? Is something crooked going on behind the scenes? When Mary went to Cascade for groceries one day, Overdrive took the opportunity to pull out the loan agreement and reread HMR's remedies. This'd only made matters worse. Now at night, more often than not, he'd spend hours lying awake, staring into the abyss. He needed to open up to somebody about the depth of his concern. Normally he'd confide in Mary, but this time he feared doing so would freak her out. Instead, he decided to maintain a brave front with Mary, and have a talk with his father.

Overdrive hated going to his father with troubles. Doing so made him feel weak and childlike, instead of strong and independent like he wanted to be. Also, he knew going to Dad carried with it the risk of opening a flood gate of future unsolicited advice. Historically, Old Bill struggled to hold back until asked. He sometimes forgot that Overdrive, not he, now ran the farm. But in this case, going to Old Bill made sense because he and the ancestors had been pretty helpful of late. Though not yet a true believer, recent events had moved Overdrive in that direction. He felt a little foolish hanging his hopes on an old man and his dead relatives, but desperate men pursued desperate measures.

✻ ✻ ✻

After the morning milking and breakfast, Overdrive headed to Cascade and found Old Bill still at his shack. Overdrive filled his father in on the situation, and without hesitation Old Bill suggested engaging an attorney now, so he'd be up to speed if things got ugly with HMR down the road. This sounded like sage advice, but unfortunately, neither of them had ever used an attorney before, except for routine real estate transactions.

When Old Bill suggested they bridge to the ancestors, my how Overdrive's view had changed, because he'd already been leaning that way. There'd been swindlers in Wisconsin preying on honest people since before statehood. The ancestors, or people they knew, had no doubt hired attorneys to defend themselves. Law often became the family business, so if they could score some surnames from the ancestors, namesakes may still be practicing locally today.

Old Bill fetched a bottle of *Drysien Gwyllt* and lit the candles, while Overdrive locked the door and closed the blinds. After the ritual opened the bridge,

Old Bill passed along Overdrive's summary of the situation, which spawned a lively discussion up the ancestral chain. When the chatter died down, Old Bill relayed to Overdrive the surnames of several attorneys from as far back as the 1850's, that'd successfully defended farmers from crooks and cheats.

After closing the bridge, Overdrive and his father chatted hopefully. Surely, at least one descendant would still be practicing law locally. Explaining to Mary the origin of these names was the next problem. After kicking around several tall tales, Overdrive visiting diners and talking to local farmers seemed as good as any. Overdrive wasn't proud of fibbing to Mary and didn't want to make a habit of it, but in this case, he didn't see an alternative.

During evening milking, Overdrive told Mary he'd been thinking it might be a good idea to engage an attorney to help handle HMR, and he'd spent part of the day diner-hopping and had some names. He felt guilty and undeserving when the news earned him a kiss. Mary promised to jump on getting an appointment with one of those attorneys, as soon as possible. The next day, Mary found several currently practicing attorneys with those surnames in the yellow pages. She picked the one in Random Lake, whose ad emphasized a specialty in dairy farming issues. Within an hour, they had an appointment for the following morning.

* * *

The next morning, Overdrive and Mary arrived for their appointment with Ted Ritter, the Random Lake attorney. While exchanging pleasantries, they verified that Ted did indeed descend from a long line of Ritter's practicing law in the area, since Wisconsin became a state in 1848. Overdrive provided a verbal overview of the situation, then Mary gave Ted the loan agreement to read. Ted put on his reading glasses, and meticulously devoured the agreement, taking notes as he went. When finished, he pulled off his glasses, sat back, looked up at the ceiling, took a deep breath, and sighed while mouthing a silent *oh shit*.

When Ted broke the silence, he chastised Overdrive and Mary for not engaging him before signing. Then he went on to share his concerns. He'd been particularly aghast that HMR had as their remedy for violation of any term or condition, the ability to claim the farm real estate and force an eviction. Usually only the personal property, such as cattle and machinery, or the asset being constructed, would serve as collateral in a loan of this nature. He also wasn't pleased they'd agreed to pay back the entire principal balance plus interest in only six months. In his opinion, this schedule was too aggressive at the very least, and probably foolish, especially given HMR's severe remedy in case of delinquency.

Somewhat defensively, Overdrive and Mary said they desired to be out of the bank for the farm expansion, so they could revert to seasonal financing for spring's work the following year. According to their estimates, doubling the milk herd, planting peas and sweet corn as cash crops, and general belt-tightening made it possible. To support their conclusion, they gave Ted a copy of their plan.

As he skimmed the plan, Ted quickly realized that Overdrive and Mary's farm expansion plan was exceptional compared to what he'd seen from other dairying clients in the past. The level of thought, planning, and analytics went well beyond anything he'd seen before. Ted's clients were primarily dairy farmers, so he was well aware of the get bigger or get out conundrum they all faced. As his admiration grew, he came to a snap decision. If any area dairy farmers could succeed at getting bigger, it'd be the ones sitting here in his office.

Ted told Overdrive and Mary that he'd been a good judge of character and farm acumen his entire career. They'd only just met, but based on today's conversation and their plan, he believed in them. Just to be clear, he reiterated that they'd been fools to sign, but he believed even fools could work their way out of a jam with his help. He offered to serve as their attorney, and defer fees until after they're out of the woods. Backhanded compliment or not, Overdrive and Mary stood to shake hands, and Ted officially became part of the team.

When the moment passed, they all sat back down to discuss next steps. Ted admitted he'd never heard of HMR before. He promised to look into them, and try to find out who's behind the organization, and what they're up to. In the meantime, Ted advised that it's absolutely essential that every payment be made as scheduled, without fail. The agreement is ironclad, and HMR's remedy would make them unemployed and homeless. On that sober note, Overdrive and Mary departed.

Although still February for a few more days, Overdrive followed a hunch and swung by uncle Hank's and Van Essen's on the way home, to inspect the soil. To his delight, the lands had thawed, and if the unseasonably warm and sunny weather held, they'd be tillable by Saturday. They decided to have another family meeting tomorrow evening, so everyone knew the fun began on Saturday.

❆ ❆ ❆

During evening milking, Overdrive replayed the day in his mind. Something about Ted Ritter gave him a positive vibe, and he'd been heartened by Ted's offer to represent them. It was the same feeling he'd had the day he and Mary delivered checks to Reineking, Buyer, and the landowners. Overdrive had the sense that like these other people, Ted was rooting for he and Mary, and wanted them to succeed.

This newfound support had snapped Overdrive out of his self-doubting funk, a la HMR call, and back into action where he's best. Most area farmers would've dismissed as a waste of time, inspecting lands in February to see if they're ready to work. But by doing so, Overdrive was rewarded with a familiar head-to-toe trill of excitement. His true self had returned, and he'd be on the land in a matter of days.

Overdrive went to bed that night in a great frame of mind. Spring's work was in his wheelhouse, and it began Saturday. He knew what needed to be done, and how to effectively do it. He'd have Mary call the bank for the next draw, and get the seed, fertilizer, and fuel needed by then. *If we do what we've always done, we'll be fine* became his new mantra. He recited it silently and soon drifted off to sleep. For the first time since the HMR call, Overdrive slept like a log.

CHAPTER 8

Spring's Work

Wednesday evening after milking the family, including Old Bill, gathered around the kitchen table for the family meeting. Mary passed around a plate of homemade chocolate fudge, while Overdrive told them spring's work would start on Saturday at Hank's and Van Essen's. By the time the peas were in other lands would be ready to till, so the push that started Saturday would continue until all the crops were in. The Evans men discussed how to reassign the ongoing farm chores, to accommodate the extra workload. Meanwhile, Mary described her plans for this year's garden and care of the orchard, and the Evans women discussed how to shuffle these activities into the ongoing house work and cooking chores. Everyone seemed in reasonably good spirits when the meeting broke up. Old Bill departed, and Overdrive and Mary monitored the chatter among the kids as they got ready for bed and made their way upstairs.

With a taunting tone, Joe said, "It's about time baby Davey started picking rocks." David gave him the stink eye, so Joe mimed a pacifier with his thumb.

Jumbo intervened, "Actually, baby Davey is younger than baby Joey was, when baby Joey started picking rocks."

Joe shook his head, and said, "No way, big guy! That's a lie and you know it! I was WAAAY younger when I started."

David protested, "I'm not a baby!"

Kathy, fists on hips, "Hey assholes, pick on somebody your own size."

Joe turned on Kathy, "You know what? It's about time the girls pulled their own weight around here, too. No more lolling around the house, eating bonbons."

Marie rolled her eyes, "Oh, here we go again. Give it a rest, Joe."

John took the opportunity to insert himself, "All of you, just shut your traps and listen to me for once. We need to stop bickering and have each other's backs."

Drooling sarcasm, Marie shot back, "Oh god help us. Now Professor Dweeb is popping off. Why in the world should we listen to you?"

John shrugged with palms up, "Hello, earth to siblings. I told you de-shitting the heifer barns was just a head start on a death march. Now you know it's true."

Jumbo's eyebrows went up, "Hey, I remember that."

Followed by Joe, "Yeah, me too."

Kathy blew a stray hank of hair from her face, and said, "Yeah, I remember. But even if true, I figured only you male dirtbags would get caught up in it."

Marie bobbed her head, and said, "That's what I thought. But NOOO, they're throwing us all into the deep shit. Kathy, we're going to get calluses!"

Kathy grimaced, "EEW, I hate calluses. They're like boyfriend repellants!"

Joe to his sisters, "Calluses are the least of your worries, look in the mirror."

The babble among the kids gradually moved out of earshot, and eventually turned to silence. While he and Mary were getting ready for bed, Overdrive said, "It'd taken longer than I'd hoped, but talking our way through everybody's chores was worth it, in my opinion."

Mary bobbed her head, and said, "Oh, I agree. It was an eye opener for the kids, to learn what each other did. Wish we'd thought of doing it sooner."

Overdrive, in a thoughtful tone, "It surprised me, when Dad volunteered for heifer duty. I'd been struggling with how to free up Jumbo. Dad solved it for me."

Mary nodded, "Me too. He hasn't had daily duties in years. Maybe he saw your dilemma, and knew John couldn't handle 100-pound bags of meal alone."

Overdrive yawned, "Could be. After that, the dominoes all fell into place."

Mary, after a moment, "You put a lot on Joe's plate. Hope he can handle it."

Overdrive's brow wrinkled, "He'll have to. When there's daylight, Jumbo will be on a tractor. When it's dark, he'll be servicing machinery for the next day."

Mary smiled, "The girls think callused hands are boyfriend repellants."

Overdrive snorted a laugh, and said, "Well then, it's a good thing you figured a way to get those hands more callused than they already are."

Mary leaned in conspiratorially, and said, "The

boyfriend repellant is just a collateral benefit. Between fresh eats and putting things up, the supersized garden and orchard ought to cut our annual grocery bill in half."

Overdrive rose, took Mary's hand, and pulled her into a hug, "I like the way you think." Mary giggled, and let herself be led into the bedroom.

When under the covers, Overdrive kissed Mary good night. He noticed she made no attempt to roll over and go to sleep, so he raised his hand to her cheek, and kissed her again. While raising his hand, he'd inadvertently brushed across her front, only to discover both girls standing at attention. Sensing the green light, the second kiss turned into a third, and the third kiss deepened. One thing led to another, and before long, they were both in full primal pant. When it was over, they drifted off to sleep, entangled in each other's arms.

* * *

On Saturday, the Evans men and boys headed to Hank's right after breakfast. Overdrive attacked the plowed lands first with the disk, an implement with many angled disks that served to break up large clods. Then came Jumbo with the spring tooth harrow, an implement with many arched teeth that reduced remaining clumps to a finer size. Old Bill and the younger boys followed behind, tossing rocks onto a two-wheeled cart and dumping them on the nearest stone wall fence. The scoop tractor with fork attachment, and Old Bill or Joe at the wheel, was used to dig out partially buried rocks, or lift large ones onto the cart.

Saturday was cold but sunny, and the wind was still. Things went smoothly until mid-afternoon, when Overdrive buried his tractor up to the axel in a wet spot. He waved Jumbo down, and hopped a ride to Hank's yard, where they unhitched the spring tooth from Jumbo's tractor, grabbed the log chains off the truck, and returned to the wet spot.

Jumbo took one look, "Geez Dad, what'd you run into, quick sand?"

Overdrive furrowed his brow, and said, "Fucking spring hole, or something. Uncle Hank never said anything about a fucking spring hole."

Jumbo rubbed his chin, and said, "Should we unhook the disk?"

Overdrive snapped, "Shit no! It's the only thing keeping the tractor up."

Jumbo stepped over to the ooze, and tested it, "Dad, look! It's not a real big soft spot, but even I go down when I step into it."

Overdrive said, "Look out, son, or you'll lose your boot." Then, he lunged forward and reached out, "Here, grab my hand before you sink!"

Pulled free, Jumbo said, "Shit, almost sucked me right in! Never saw anything like that before. Aw crap, I got a soaker."

Overdrive shook his head, "You deserve a soaker. Swing your tractor around front, and back it up. Let's get a chain on mine, and see if we can pull it out."

Jumbo did as he'd been told, and then hopped off his tractor and tussled the chain into place, "Should I loop it around here?"

Overdrive bobbed his head, and said, "Yeah, that'll work. Okay, that's good. Okay, now let's get on our tractors. Slowly take up the slack." After a moment, he shouted, "That's good. It's tight. You in first gear? Great. You ready?"

Jumbo, craned his neck to the rear, "Yup. How're we going to do this?"

Overdrive shouted, "Let's see if we can get a rocking motion started, just riding the clutches. If you start spinning, use the side breaks. If you hear me yell go-go-go, stop rocking and just keep going forward. Got it?"

Jumbo nodded but when they engaged their clutches, nothing budged. Overdrive used his side brakes, but that merely alternated which drive wheel slung the mud. When Jumbo's drive wheels began to excavate holes in solid ground, Overdrive hollered for him to stop. They idled their tractors and stepped down to have a look. After some cussing and tire kicking, Overdrive said, "That went well."

Hand on chin again, Jumbo asked, "What now? Should we wave down grandpa and Joe, and get the scoop tractor and Ferguson over here?"

Overdrive spit, "Shit, no. Those pissants won't make any difference."

They tiptoed around the soft spot, and Overdrive observed, "The hole's just wide enough for both rear wheels, and I hit it dead center. Hmm, I've got an idea."

Overdrive had been in this predicament before, and suddenly remembered how to get out of it. He sent Jumbo to fetch a strong cedar fence post about four feet longer than the rear wheel span, two short log chains, and two planks to span the hole front to back. When Jumbo returned, they centered the post on the ground under the mired tractor, in front of the drive wheels, with about two feet extending over solid ground on either side. Then they chained the post to the metal rims of the drive wheels. With the free tractor pulling the mired one, the drive wheels turned causing the post to grab solid ground and pop the mired tractor up out of the hole. They stopped immediately, laid planks across the hole for the disk's wheels, and then eased the tractors forward until the disk was also clear of the hazard.

Everything went smoothly from there on. After the disk and spring tooth had finished and the rock-picking was done, Overdrive pulled three implements at once over the land, one behind the other, to complete the planting. The fertilizer drill inserted granular fertilizer into the soil, the grain drill inserted either pea seeds or pea and alfalfa seeds, and the roller smoothed and packed the final seed bed. Hank's and Van Essen's lands were all planted in peas by the end of the first week in March. At Hank's, Overdrive had also under-seeded alfalfa.

* * *

The Evans men moved on to planting oats with under-seeded alfalfa in selected fields at the old Lemke, Adcock, and Ulbricht farms. These lands had grown field corn the previous year, and had been plowed last fall. On school days, Overdrive and Old Bill kept up the momentum by themselves, with Overdrive on the disk or spring tooth and his father picking stones. On weekends, Overdrive and Jumbo kept the disk and spring tooth in constant motion, and the younger boys helped Old Bill pick rocks. Machinery was serviced on days of foul weather.

School's spring break was coming soon, and Overdrive's aspirational goal was to finish planting the oats/alfalfa, and have as much as possible of the corn ground worked and rock-free before the kids returned to school. With two weekends plus break week, Overdrive would have his boys for nine straight days, and he aimed to make the most of it.

When spring break finally arrived, Overdrive was locked and loaded. The seed, fertilizer, fuel, and spare parts needed were already on hand. The tractors were fueled, and the machinery repaired and greased. The fertilizer and seed boxes on the drills were filled, and the rest of the bagged fertilizer and seed, needed to finish the job, had been loaded onto the ton truck. All the oat lands, and more of the corn lands than Overdrive had thought possible, had already been disked. Half the oat lands had been spring toothed and rock-picked, and were ready to plant.

Spring break marching orders were delivered over the first Saturday morning's breakfast. Overdrive said, "I'm heading over to Lemke's to plant. Jumbo, you need to spring tooth the rest of the oat lands at Adcock's, and then Ulbricht's. The rig's fueled and greased and in the field, as far as I got yesterday."

Then Overdrive eyed each of his younger boys, and said, "Joe, John, and David, you'll be picking rocks with your grandpa. The scoop and Ferguson tractors are fueled, and they and the rock cart are in the field at Adcock's."

Joe said unwisely, "Aw geez, Dad. Why do I always get all the shit jobs? Why not put me on the disk? Or put Jumbo on that, and me on the spring tooth?"

Overdrive, in a low-pitched growl, "Shut your

mouth, and do what you're told! You don't want to get on the wrong side of me during spring's work!"

Joe raised his hands in a placating gesture, "Okay, geez, I got it."

Overdrive took a moment to simmer down, then continued, "As your grandpa knows, there're a lot of rocks out there, some are heavy, some will need to be dug out. Move along quickly, you've got to stay ahead of the planter."

Listening up to now, John asked, unexpectedly, "What're we going to do for food and water? Even death marches include food and water, right?"

Mary smiled, and shook a finger at him, "Don't you get all smart-mouthed like your brother, Joe. Each crew leaves here with a water jug. I'll be bringing sandwiches and fresh water jugs around to everybody at lunch time."

Overdrive stood and said, "Okay, I think we all know what we're doing."

The Evans men and boys all stood, and walked purposefully out into the back yard. Striding fast and long to the tractor hitched to the drills and roller, Overdrive overheard Joe whine *aw, come on grandpa, do I have to sit in the backseat with the runts?* The thought crossed his mind that it's a god damn miracle anything gets done around here, given the motley crew he'd been dealt.

* * *

At the wheel of the John Deere 520, Overdrive trundled slowly down the road to Lemke's, pulling the threesome of fertilizer drill, grain drill, and roller. The weather was perfect. Cool, crisp, calm and not a cloud in the brilliant blue sky. As he crossed the cattail marsh on Rock Road, the lively chatter of the redwing black-birds could be heard over the whir of the tractor. After the marsh, he passed under several hawks riding the thermals, and spooked a rabbit as he eased his way off the road, and into the first field at Lemke's and began to plant.

When planting Overdrive experienced a feeling that some might call euphoria. Living things would sprout in his wake. Mentally, he cloistered himself into a zone of total concentration as if the world had gone silent and time stood still. Every farmer's furrows were equidistant within a drill swath. But when Overdrive planted, the end of one swath and beginning of the next was undetectable by the naked eye. It looked as though a giant drill had planted the entire field in a single pass.

At lunch time a honk-honk snapped Overdrive out of his planting reverie. He looked up to see the cow car, and Mary waving from Lemke's yard across the field. He waved back, to let her know he'd seen her, but decided to plant his way around to that end of the field, rather than stop and walk back. Upon arrival he shut down, grabbed his empty water cooler, and strode quickly over to Mary.

Mary said, "Hey James! Wow! The planting's going really well, huh?"

Overdrive nodded, smiled sheepishly, and said, "It's going, that's for sure. It's a perfect day to be out here. How're the others doing?"

Mary suggested, "Before we get into that, relax a little and have a sandwich. Hand me that water cooler, will you? Here's your fresh one."

Overdrive rubbed his stomach, "Umm, my favorite. Smoked summer sausage, sharp cheddar cheese, and mayo. So, how're the others doing?"

"Seriously. You can't relax long enough to eat a sandwich?" She mimed holding a card to her forehead, "Carnac the Magnificent sees ulcers in your future."

Overdrive smiled at the reference to his favorite Johnny Carson skit, then said a bit impatiently, "Oh, cut the crap, Mary. You know perfectly well that what gives me ulcers, is not knowing how the others are doing."

Mary held up her hands in a placating gesture, "Okay, you big sourpuss. Jumbo and the spring tooth are in Adcock's last field."

Overdrive fist-pumped, and said, "Yes! That's great news."

Mary smiled at her man-boy's gesture, "You're so easy to please."

Overdrive made a rolling motion with his index finger, "What about Dad and our wayward younger sons? How're they doing with the rock picking?"

Mary grinned at his impatience, and said, "They've finished the first field at Adcock's, and are almost finished with the second. Your father wants to know if they should try to dig out the monster. He said you'd know what he meant."

Overdrive's face darkened instantly, "Damn right I know. That fucking boulder broke a bottom right off my plow last fall! Yeah, have him dig it out!"

Mary's eyebrows went up with concern, "Geez James, calm down will you. You're all red in the face, and everything. It's just a rock, for Christ sakes."

Overdrive looked down, glowered, and said, "Yeah, well, we've been smashing something on that fucking rock every year for as long as I can remember. Thousands of dollars pissed down the drain. It's got to stop."

Mary raised her hands, "Okay, I get it. I'll tell him to dig it out. On another subject, what's the plan for getting everybody back to the farm for dinner?"

Overdrive thought for a moment, and said, "I'll plant here until quitting time and pull the drills into Lemke's old shed, in case it rains. Then I'll head over to Adcock's with the ton truck. Some can ride back with me. Dad can bring the rest."

Back in the car, Mary said, "Supper's on the table at 6:00 PM sharp. Don't be late." Then, as she sped off, she flashed her impish grin and shouted, "One more thing. Joe says spring's work would be done a week earlier with him on the disk!"

At quitting time, Overdrive parked his rig in the shed. As he was pulling out onto Rock Road with the truck, none other than Rachel Wolf crawled by in her black T-Bird Landau. By reflex he waved, but the uppity bitch didn't wave back. He continued on to Adcock's, already on edge from the encounter, and nearly flipped out at the sight that greeted him. Jumbo, on the scoop tractor, was in mortal combat with the boulder, while the others gaped at the drama from a safe distance. The crater he'd dug revealed a boulder about the size of a barn.

In a cloud of dust, Overdrive slid the truck to an abrupt halt, jumped out leaving the door ajar, and yelled, "Jumbo, what the fuck are you doing?"

As Overdrive came abreast, Old Bill sidled over and said, "After I'd spent about an hour getting nowhere, Jumbo came over to give it a try."

Overdrive's colorful entrance caused Jumbo to shut down the tractor, hop off, and meet the others at the crater expecting a powwow. Instead, Overdrive began kicking the enormous boulder with his steel-toed work boots, and launched into a blue streak for the ages. Nary a forbidden profanity went unsaid at least once. Old Bill and the boys all backed off a step, for fear they'd become collateral damage. Even Joe knew enough to keep his mouth shut.

It took a while, but Overdrive eventually regained his composure and managed to ask in a relatively civil voice, "Does the fucker even wiggle?"

Jumbo spoke first, "Well, from up on the tractor, it's kind of hard to tell. If it moved at all, it didn't move much. Grandpa, what'd you see?"

Old Bill shook his head, "It never budged. It's like the tip of an iceberg. I've seen them before. Another giant granite boulder, courtesy of the last glacier."

Already spent, Overdrive merely muttered, "Sure as shit. They're like last year's potatoes, the way they float to the surface around here."

Old Bill, being fatherly, "It is, what it is. No sense throwing a pity party."

Overdrive snapped, "Pity party my ass. Goddammit Dad, when your ancestors arrived from Wales, they could've gone to Iowa where there's eight feet of topsoil. But NOOO, instead they settle right on top of the last Ice Age's shitter!"

Old Bill snapped back, "Hey, watch your tongue! I'm still your father, you know. And they're your ancestors as much as mine. As for boulders, who the fuck knew?" He waved his arm, "This was all thick virgin forest back in 1848."

Overdrive took a moment to get ahold of himself, and relented, "Yeah, yeah, I know. Well, like you say, we've seen these before. If I remember correctly, about the only thing we can do is leave well enough alone, or blast the sonofabitch."

Old Bill nodded, and said, "That's about right. So, what'll it be?"

Overdrive's eyes narrowed, "Blast that fucker to kingdom come. I'm tired of smashing machinery on it. You still have blast supplies back at the shack?"

Old Bill flashed a smile, and said, "Of course I do. Don't feel manly without them. You realize we'll only be blowing the top off, right? I mean, it's enormous."

Overdrive bobbed his head, and said, "Yeah, yeah, that's fine. Just make sure what's left is deeper than we till. We'll bury what's left."

Old Bill rubbed his chin, and said, "When do you want this done?"

Overdrive, eyes narrowed, "Spring break just started, for Christ's sake. So, today before dark. Go back to the shack, have some supper, and come back with your toys. After supper, Jumbo will meet you here. Tell him what tools to bring. You guys be careful, you hear? Be out of harm's way before pushing the plunger."

As the family's blasting guru, Old Bill took offense, "You're in no position to lecture me on explosives, son. Not my first rodeo. You know that."

Overdrive, with an ironic smile, "Yeah, well, last time you blew out your car windows. I'm just saying." Then he looked at his watch, and said, "Listen, we're already late for supper. Better run before Mary has a canary. Good luck tonight."

The next morning the Evans men and boys

gathered around the blast site, to admire a scene reminiscent of WWII's Omaha Beach. They carted the fragments to the nearest stone wall fence, buried the rest, and got back to work. The friendly weather held, and by the end of spring break, all the oats/alfalfa had been planted and all of the corn ground had received once-overs with the disk and spring tooth. The rock picking was far behind, but Overdrive didn't care. It's too early to plant corn anyway, and there'd be plenty of time to catch up.

* * *

Overdrive had three types of corn to plant. Ear corn went in first, because it needed the longest growing season for the ears to mature and kernels to harden into a solid grain. Then came field corn, which needed the next longest season, before the entire plant was mature enough to chop for silage. Sweet corn was last to be planted, because harvest-ready milky kernels were achieved much more quickly.

In some respects, corn took less effort to plant than peas, oats, and alfalfa. Corn pickers or choppers tolerated bumpier surfaces, so corn lands didn't need to be rolled smooth. On the other hand, extra passes over the land were required to broadcast fertilizer and incorporate it into the soil with the spring tooth. Starting with plowed ground, the typical workflow was disk, spring tooth, pick rocks, broadcast fertilizer, spring tooth, and plant. The first two steps had been completed during spring break. With the kids in school, Overdrive and Old Bill kept the momentum going by themselves during the week. Old Bill picked rocks and Overdrive followed behind, broadcasting granular fertilizer and then working it in with a second pass of the spring tooth. On weekends, Overdrive planted, Jumbo spread fertilizer and worked it in, and Old Bill and the younger boys picked rocks.

The last Saturday in April was the kind of spring day that Overdrive lived for. It had a gentle fresh air breeze, crisp and cool, yet topped off with a sunny warmth from the cloudless and vivid blue sky. By now the family was a well-oiled machine. All of the ear corn lands were ready to plant, and Overdrive would begin on one of the strips behind the barn at the home place. Old Bill, Joe, John and David would pick rocks from the field corn lands. Jumbo would help the rock pickers until a field was finished, and then he'd fertilize and working it in. When the field corn lands were ready to plant, they'd move on to the sweet corn lands.

As Overdrive planted, a red-tailed hawk glided along overhead, hoping for a tasty morsel to break cover in front of the advancing tractor. As he rounded the curve of the hill, the farmer's lane at the end of the strip came into view. There sat Mary in the ton truck, so he knew it must be lunch time. He planted his way to her, shut down, grabbed his empty water jug, and met Mary at the front of the truck.

Mary wasn't as bubbly as usual, "Hey James. How's the planting going?"

Overdrive smiled, "It's going great. You came just in time. I'm starved and almost out of fuel and seed."

They hugged, and Mary said half-heartedly, "I always aim to please. Here, let's swap water jugs. Sandwiches are in the bag on the hood."

Overdrive pouted, "Tuna salad. Damn, no summer sausage and cheese?"

Mary exhaled heavily, "Me and the girls have been slaving away in the garden. We're out of summer sausage, and I didn't have time to run to Cascade."

Overdrive shrugged, and said, "That's alright, honey. I was just kidding. I love tuna salad. How're the others doing?"

Mary squinted up into the sky, and said, "Jumbo's still down on the flat. He's finished spreading the fertilizer, but working it in is going slower than expected. He's fussing that the rock pickers did a shitty job. He's broken and replaced a few tooth points, and is down to one spare."

Leaning back against the hood, Overdrive said, "Well, shit. That figures. Did you pass that along to my father and your wayward younger sons?"

Mary nudged him in the ribs with her elbow, and said, "You mean OUR wayward younger sons? Yes, I did. Your father claims Jumbo must have the spring tooth set too deep, otherwise you'd have hit those rocks the first time over."

Overdrive smiled at that, then said, "Finger pointing, eh?"

Mary bobbed her head, "Exactly."

Between chews, Overdrive asked, "How're the rock pickers doing?"

"They've finished the flat, and have moved on to Lemke's." Mary seemed about to tear up, "They've had a bit of an accident."

Overdrive's eyebrows went up, "What?"

Pale faced, Mary explained, "A few heifers broke out. After they got them back in, your Dad had to take the Ferguson to fetch tools and mend the fence. That left the boys with the scoop tractor pulling the cart. Joe had to unhitch the cart, to dig out a big rock. When he dropped it onto the cart, it rolled the wrong way, the cart flipped backwards, and rocks went flying. John got hit by one in the shin."

Brow furrowed, Overdrive asked, "Is he okay?" Then he kicked the dirt, "Goddammit! I warned them to be careful when the cart was unhitched."

"John's fine. He's got a big black and blue welt, but no bleeding or broken bones." Fighting off tears, Mary said, "He could've been hurt bad, James."

Overdrive wrapped her in his arms, and said, "I know. I know. But he wasn't. And now hopefully all of them know enough to keep a safe distance."

Mary steadied herself, and said, "I'm sorry I'm so weepy, James. As if John's accident wasn't enough, Rachel Wolf drove by again today. Why is she hovering around? Why can't she leave us alone?"

Overdrive's jaw tightened, and he said, "Those are really good questions."

The family kept grinding on the corn land without further incident. Within the week, Overdrive finished planting the ear corn. The field corn was planted by the end of April, and the sweet corn went in during the first week in May. It'd been nonstop since late February, but at long last, spring's work was done. Overdrive and Mary were proud of what the family had accomplished. Hundreds more acres had been planted than in previous years. In addition, Mary and the girls had planted their largest garden ever, and every tree in the apple orchard had been pruned and sprayed for the first time in years. The family hadn't buckled, but even Overdrive could see that his father, especially, but also the kids, had been wearing down near the end. Mary, god bless her, seemed as resilient as he was.

* * *

Spring's work made Overdrive feel vital and alive, and most of all, competent. There's a lot to it, and he knew what he was doing. Part of the alure was his ability to lose himself in the swirl of activity, and leave his troubles behind. With the field work on top of the ongoing milking and farm chores, there simply wasn't time to worry about anything else.

But this year had been different. No matter how hard Overdrive worked, worries over the HMR loan remained, and weighed heavily on his mind. When trying to drift off to sleep at night, he still recited the now familiar catch phrase, *if we do what we've always done, we'll be fine.* But as his apprehension grew, he became less confident that this was true. Further, the Rachel Wolf sightings unnerved him, and caused dark thoughts to disturb his sleep.

Overdrive became burdened with second thoughts. He wondered whether they should back away from the farm expansion. True, construction on the barn addition had started. But if promised a re-start next year, Reineking would probably only demand cost plus fee for actual work completed. The cattle hadn't yet been delivered, so they could cancel the deals and forfeit the earnest money. That'd piss Gib Buyer off, but if we promised to re-engage next year, he'd get over it. With the peas and sweet corn already in, there's no backing out of those land rentals. But to reduce hay land, they could drop Courtland's or Riley's. It didn't sit well with Overdrive to leave one of his neighbors in a lurch, but it could be done.

The other option was to keep pushing forward. Yes, the expansion plan was aggressive, but they're still ahead of it thus far. With no major breakdowns, spring's work had gone remarkably well. All the crops went in ahead of schedule. Fertilizer expenses had been under budget. Crop seedlings up thus far, looked great. Yes, something was bound to go awry, but they had ways to compensate. They could self-perform construction tasks to reduce cash outflow. With the alfalfa under the peas and oats planted so early, there's a chance of two hay cuttings on those lands instead of one, which meant excess hay to sell next winter.

The more Overdrive thought about it, the more opportunities he saw. Many pea growers didn't bother to claim their own vines, and the cannery just wanted them gone. Same with the sweet corn husks. Vines and husks made excellent cattle fodder, and the Waldo Cannery was only two miles away. With a little extra work to haul free fodder back to the farm, they'd be able to back off on green-chopping alfalfa, leaving more to be baled and stored and sold next winter. On a roll now, Overdrive's thinking began to cross the line from optimistic to delusional. Maybe they'd hit it big with the peas and sweet corn, and so on. It could happen, right?

It wasn't long before Overdrive talked himself into pushing forward with the expansion. After two-and-a-half-months of hard work, the family had too much skin in the game to quit now, right? What kind of a message would that send the kids? Dad's getting older, and Jumbo may not be around after he graduates high school next year. It's now or never, right? We either get bigger or get out. Once the decision to push forward was made, Overdrive felt embarrassed over his own second thoughts. He resolved to never tell anyone that he'd had them. He couldn't expand the farm without the best efforts of the entire family. Best efforts were most likely if Overdrive led with total confidence, whether he felt that way or not. He'd have to man up, and hold his dark thoughts at bay. About then, it occurred to him that knowing who was behind HMR might help him do just that, which reminded him they hadn't heard from Ted Ritter in over two months. He decided to have Mary set up a meeting with Ted, maybe give Ted an ass chewing.

Overdrive felt better after processing his troubles. Good timing, since the next leg of the death march was about to begin. The pasture grass had gotten tall enough to justify putting the milk herd out on the Side Hill between milkings. This meant the new milk cows could be trucked in by the weekend. Before long they and the raised-replacements would begin drop calves along with the regular milk herd. Haymaking was about to begin, with more acres to harvest than ever before. The addition's foundation would soon be in, and in the near term, they may need to self-perform a construction step. Buckle up, it's going to be a rough ride.

CHAPTER 9

May

Mary was able to get an appointment first thing with Ted Ritter, so Overdrive and Mary hurried through breakfast and headed to Random Lake. After the niceties, Ted asked how they're doing on the farm expansion. After Overdrive filled him in, Ted steepled his fingers, smiled, and said, "That's all great news, James, it really is. So how can I help you today? Why're you here?"

Overdrive made eye contact, and said, "Well, it's been over two months and you promised to look into who's behind HMR. Have you had any luck?"

Ted's eyes sparkled with amusement, and he said, "Right to the point as usual, James, that's one of the things I admire about you."

Ted filled them in on what he'd found out thus far. HMR LLC was a wholly owned subsidiary of Development Partners LLC. Whoever created these shell corporations knew what they're doing, because even this modest nugget had been difficult to find. What HMR and DP were intended to do, and who owned them, remained a mystery. Ted promised to keep digging. He suggested they check in monthly by phone for progress, but he'd call right away with anything major.

Some progress had been made, so Overdrive didn't feel the need to press Ted further, and risk straining the relationship. On the drive home, he and Mary kicked around what they'd learned. Neither knew what to make of it, and both agreed their focus should remain on making the HMR payments on time.

* * *

The Side Hill pasture was essentially waste land, too steep to mechanically till. Old Bill's last act before selling his draught horses was to plant a hardy mixture of forage grasses and it'd been used as pasture ever since. During the first week in May, the family began turning the milk herd out to pasture between milkings. The sight of large, black and white animals galloping in all directions, snorting, and awkwardly kicking up their hind legs always made this annual event entertaining. By the looks of it, you'd think it's a fucking jailbreak. After the adrenalin rush passed, the lathered beasts eventually began to use their outdoor time to munch grass, lounge, roll, and so on, as mature Holsteins should.

On the same day the milk herd tasted its first green grass of the year, the family opened the pasture gates at Lemke's, Adcock's and Ulbricht's for the heifers. Being younger and more athletic, the heifer jailbreaks were nothing short of awe inspiring. The heifer pastures were large, relative to the head of cattle, and able to serve as their major food source until fall. The

Side Hill, on the other hand, would need to be supplemented with bunk wagons filled with pea vines, corn husks, green chopped hay, or whatever happened to be in season.

With the change in the daily routines of the animals, came changes to family member chores. In some ways, having the livestock out on pasture reduced the burden on the family, or perhaps more accurately, freed them for haying and other seasonal tasks. The livestock, in large part, could now feed themselves by grazing. But in other ways, the work load increased. A little-known fact is whenever a cow moves, it takes a shit. In winter, cows greet your entrance to the barn to milk them, by standing up and shitting an easy-to-remove solid clump, which reflected their winter diet of hay, silage, and meal. When on pasture, cows herded into the barn to be milked sprayed a greenish slurry as they went. Then afterward, they'd squirt another on the way out. Cleaning that up took considerably more effort.

The season also brought a few new chores. Someone had to walk to the far end of the Side Hill twice daily, and drive the herd back to the barn to be milked. Salt and mineral blocks for the livestock to lick, needed to be placed in the pastures and monitored. Aggressive weeds all over the farm, such as yellow mustard and blue chicory, needed to be pulled by hand before they proliferated. And so on.

* * *

Reineking needed another payment on the barn addition, and the new cows were soon to arrive, so

Mary requested another draw from the bank. When the cattle trucks hauling the new cows arrived, Overdrive directed them to the Side Hill's gated entrance right off of the road. The drivers pulled into the pasture, stopped, opened the tailgates, lowered the ramps, and cajoled the cattle down the ramps to their new home.

When the trucks arrived, the existing herd had been scattered all over the pasture, heads down and grazing. Gradually it dawned on them that something was up, and they became curious. At first, they stood their ground, heads up and staring. Then they trotted up to form a sloppy semi-circle around the trucks, nostrils wide and snorting. Then for no apparent reason they startled, and took off in all directions, leaving the travel-weary newcomers to do what cows do.

Overdrive was encouraged by the clean and healthy look of the new cattle. His primary concern now was how they'd adjust to their new surroundings, and fit into the pecking order of the herd. He made a mental note to tell the whole family to be on the lookout for signs of beast-on-beast aggression. When the cattle trucks rumbled off, Overdrive turned to wave goodbye. That's when he noticed the black T-Bird slowly drive by, and realized Rachel Wolf had witnessed the delivery. He wasn't sure why this bothered him, but it did.

Overdrive shrugged it off and refocused on how the family's life would change, as a result of the new arrivals. The new cows were all heavy with calf, and many in the original herd were also due to freshen in the spring and early summer. Tomorrow, they'd cut out from the rest of the herd at Ulbricht's, the about-ready-to-calve raised replacements, and drive them down the road to the Side Hill. Overdrive knew that within a week, calves would start dropping left and right.

The mother of every calf born became another cow to milk. Soon the number would exceed the existing barn's stall capacity, and the herd would have to be milked in two shifts. Newly freshened cows would nurse their calves while the colostrum lasted, and then the calves would be weaned. The bull calves would be fed milk replacer for a while, and then shipped off to market for cash. The heifers would continue on milk replacer, transition to meal and hay, and later be hauled to Lemke's to join the youngest cadre of heifers being raised as replacements.

※ ※ ※

Haying in Wisconsin is all about timing. Although generally welcome, rain can destroy hay already cut but still on the ground, because it hadn't been sufficiently dry to bale. Overdrive listened to weather forecasts, but rarely relied exclusively on them. From experience, he had the ability to observe day-to-day progressions of weather, and recall past patterns that were similar, and whether or not they brought rain this time of year. But even with experience, deciding when to cut hay was a bit of a crap shoot.

Overdrive owned an Owatonna for cutting hay. This self-propelled machine cut and organized hay into rows, called windrows, in a single operation. As the machine moved forward, the cutter bar hugged the ground while slicing off hay stalks that're slung to the middle by apron belts, where they're crimped to hasten drying, and spit out the back into windrows to lie fluffily on the stubble to air dry.

Overdrive began taking first cutting alfalfa early, meaning in the late-vegetative to late-bud stage. By the time the last field was reached the plants might be flowering and getting a little woody, but on average the crop was highly digestible fiber, needed for high milk production. Let it go too long, and the nutritional value accessible to livestock lessens. An early start also left more spring moisture in the soil for second-cutting, and kept hopes alive for the holy grail of haying, one cutting each month all summer long.

When it's windy, hot, and sunny, hay may be dry enough to bale two days after the cut. If it's calm, cool, and cloudy, it might take a full three days to dry. Overdrive baled his hay using a tractor-pulled John Deere kickoff baler, trailed by a roofless wagon with high sides except for the half-height front. In one operation the baler inhaled the windrows, packed them into small bales, and threw them into the wagon. He never wanted the baler idle when conditions were right, and sometimes the unloading crew couldn't keep up, so he owned four wagons.

Full wagons were hauled to whichever barn was currently being filled. The back of the wagon opened, so bales could be tossed onto an elevator, which dropped them into the barn's haymow. The elevator was mounted on a frame with wheels, and could be repositioned easily, and cranked up or down. Even so, manpower up in the mow was required to fill a barn to its rafters.

When haying's in full swing, bodies were needed to cut, bale, haul wagons, unload, and when the mow was almost full, play goalie up in the mow. Generally,

Overdrive cut the hay, but Jumbo knew how. Overdrive, Jumbo, and Mary all could bale. All of them plus Old Bill and Joe, could haul wagons. Everybody, including Kathy and Marie in a pinch, could help unload. Making hay had the potential to consume the energies of the entire family.

* * *

The fragrance of freshly cut hay drying in the sun, was something Overdrive never grew tired of. The scent put an extra bounce in his step, and god help us, sometimes even motivated the humming of a tune. He'd cut a lot of hay, gambling the weather would hold until the weekend, when the boys would be home to help get it in before the next rain. After working feverishly all-day Saturday, it's now late-afternoon Sunday, and storm clouds were on the horizon. Overdrive was baling as fast as he dared, when he spotted Mary bouncing across the field in the cow car. He eased his rig to a halt, and left it idling with the baler still churning, as he hopped off and quickly strode over to the open driver's side window.

Mary, anxiously, "Storm will hit soon, James. What's plan B?"

Overdrive, forcefully, "Same as plan A, only faster. We need to get it in."

Mary shook her head, "I knew you'd say that. What do you need?"

"Tell them to unload double time. I need two more wagons after this one."

"Roger that."

"Have them bring the tarps with the wagons. If

the sky opens up, we'll cover them here. If not, we'll haul them to the barn, and back them onto the barn floor."

"What about supper, milking, and chores?"

"Have Dad bring the wagons. Feed the boys and start without me."

"Okay. You'd better get back at it, slacker. Time's a wasting."

Overdrive hopped back on the tractor and started to roll. Once baling at normal speed, he pushed the speed up another notch, and stood to protect his aching back from the jarring. He risked cracking the baler frame or worse, but knew it'd be too wet to cut tomorrow anyway, so he'd have time to fix it.

* * *

Overdrive consistently guessed right on the weather, and the rest of first cutting was successfully harvested by the end of May. Normally, first cutting hay had higher nutritional value and tonnage than subsequent cuttings, and would be stored in the home place barn to be fed to the milk herd. The crop was strong on the lands he owned, and although lighter in yield at the rented Courtland farm, at least it was mostly alfalfa. Hay from these lands went to the home place.

At the rented Riley farm, the hay turned out to be more timothy, red clover, and brome grass than alfalfa. Given its lower quality, Overdrive decided to put it in the barn at the old Ulbricht farm, to feed the oldest of the replacement young stock. Overall, first cutting fell short of Overdrive's plan, both in quality and quantity. He hoped taking the hay early explained the quantity shortfall. If so, the shortfall might possibly be made up later, if the early start enabled an extra cutting of hay.

Overdrive kicked himself for failing to shop last summer, for hay land to rent. Then he could've walked the fields, and seen for himself what's really growing there. Old man Riley had led him to believe that the hay would be mostly alfalfa. Maybe when first planted it was, but it sure as hell wasn't anymore.

※ ※ ※

The construction of the barn addition was in full swing. As of the end of May, the excavation and foundation work were completed, and the concrete block walls begun. Unfortunately, large numbers of huge granite boulders and rocks were encountered during excavation. Fred Reineking classified these subsurface obstacles as *unforeseen*, and the cost to remove them had to be paid out of the contingency. Well, actually, the overrun exceeded the contingency, so some of it had to be paid out of Overdrive's pocket. While delivering the bad news, Fred had been contrite and apologetic, but also firm. They both knew he'd done his best to advocate for a realistic contingency, but Overdrive wouldn't hear of it.

Overdrive managed to hold it together while talking with Fred, but during the evening milking he'd been silently fuming, and Mary noticed. She knew he'd blow unless given a chance to vent, so she suggested they head to Harbor Lights after milking, for some privacy and a cold beer.

Not a word was spoken on the drive to Lake Ellen. When they walked into the bar, Overdrive fetched the beer, and Mary staked out their favorite table in the quiet corner. After joining Mary, Overdrive exhaled heavily, and said, "Granite boulders and rocks. How many more times is that glacier going to fuck us over?" Playing along, Mary said, "I know, James. Really. It's getting old, isn't it?"

"Dad's ancestors could've settled anywhere. But no, they had to come here."

She mimed like-mindedness, "Crazy, right? What were they thinking?"

Overdrive growled, "Unforeseen costs, my ass! Wouldn't it be great to ask for a bigger milk check every time we had an unforeseen cost?"

Mary bobbed her head, "They'd laugh in our faces, wouldn't they?"

Overdrive, after a bottoms-up, "Blew through the entire contingency, and then had the gall to hold out his hand for more money. Can you believe it?"

Sensing the rant had wound down, Mary said softly, "But you know, James, we'd still be well within contingency if only we'd listened to Fred to begin with."

Overdrive drained his bottle, "Well, sure. But then we'd have had to reduce the stall count. You know that."

Mary covered his hand with hers, "I know, James, but that's sort of the point of a realistic contingency, isn't it?"

He looked down, "Maybe so, but it's not right, god-dammit! A farmer has an unforeseen cost, he pays. A farmer hires a contractor who has one, he pays again."

Mary's voice softened some more, "I know, James. It's not fair."

Overdrive, to himself, "Everybody gets to pass the buck, except us farmers."

Mary squeezed his hand, "I know, James. But you knew that when you decided to be a farmer. The question is, what're we going to do about it?"

Overdrive shrugged, "Well, it's too late to back off on the stall count now."

Mary squeezed his hand again, "So, what're we going to do? HMR will take everything if we miss a payment, and we can't let that happen."

Overdrive, in a feral growl, "Fucking HMR! And fucking Rachel Wolf! Why's she still driving by, we've got nothing to do with her bank anymore?"

She eyed him, "I know, I know. But focus, James. What're we going to do?"

His eyes narrowed with thought, "Well, for one, pick a construction task to do ourselves. Beyond that, pray we hit it big with the peas and sweet corn."

CHAPTER 10

June

Mary got Ted Ritter on the phone for their monthly check-in, with Overdrive on the extension. Overdrive filled Ted in on farm expansion progress, and they discussed what that meant, and whether midcourse corrections were needed. Ted seemed satisfied that the new cows were adjusting as hoped, and the lighter than expected first cutting hay would be more than offset by an additional cutting. Although he doubted Overdrive would be able to self-perform a construction task to get the barn addition back on track, he let it pass.

Meanwhile, Ted had learned that HMR and DP were both registered in Wisconsin, but that DP was a wholly owned subsidiary of Limitless Enterprises LLC, which was registered in Delaware. Ted promised to keep digging on what these shell corporations were intended to do, and who owned them. When Overdrive asked if all this rigamarole was worth being concerned about, Ted took his time in answering. The takeaway seemed to be that somebody had gone to a lot of trouble to set all this up, so they must've had a reason. There was a certain stench about it, as if somebody was up to no good.

After the call, Overdrive and Mary got on with their day. While mowing second cutting hay, Overdrive kicked around what Ted had said. After a while he shrugged it off, and turned his mind to things he had some control over. He pondered which construction task to take on, how else to raise cash, and so on.

* * *

About half of the new livestock had calved and were milking when the milk tester made his June monthly visit. Milk is sold based on weight and butter fat content, and Overdrive uses a testing service to determine these quantities for each cow in his herd. Overdrive's herd averages improved every year because he ruthlessly culled underperforming animals. Culled cows were put on a truck and sold at the Milwaukee livestock market for cash. Although the animals were clueless, in reality the competition to stay in Overdrive's herd was fierce.

In round numbers, there've been 40 milk cows in recent years. This meant each year 40 calves were born, roughly 20 of which were heifers to be raised as replacements. Presuming they all survived, every year another 20 replacements had their first calf, and began to milk. The career of a milk cow lasts about five years, so roughly eight of the 40 are culled annually due to production drop off with age, leaving 32 plus 20 replacements, or 52. This meant to sustain the herd at 40, another 12 cows in their prime production years needed to be culled annually.

The testing service provides charts for each cow. Milk production generally starts high with the birth of the calf, peaks 40 to 60 days later, and declines steadily thereafter. Individuals to be kept another year are watched closely to detect when they're in heat, and artificially inseminated. Generally, after milking about ten months, the cows are dried up for two months, before calving again. If all goes well, each cow drops another calf every 12-months, or so.

By studying his charts, Overdrive discovered that milk production by the purchased cows, on average, was running a little lower than his existing herd average for newly freshened cows. Butter fat content was running significantly lower. This information triggered a memory from a Hoard's Dairyman article. The gist was that recently moved cattle often had low production during a transition period, until they adjusted to their new environment. He kicked himself for failing to factor that into his expansion plan.

Overdrive dug out and reread the old magazine article. Apparently, simply the passage of time would help the animals acclimate, but that's only part of it. In addition, unnamed sources claimed that some sellers, once sales contracts were signed, would stop feeding their cows grain altogether, and swap cheaper straw for hay, until the cattle were trucked away. So, for the other part, after putting the cattle back on a proper diet, some transition time would be required before full production returned. The article included some typical transition times.

Based on this new information, Overdrive recalculated his projections for the expanded herd's rising milk check. While doing so, he realized that he'd also originally assumed the new cows to be as good as his existing herd, on average. In hindsight, that might've been overly optimistic as well. He made a mental note to watch carefully for where the production of the new cattle topped out.

* * *

Overdrive had been watching his peas like a hawk, and was surprised he hadn't heard from the Waldo Cannery, concerning when they'd be taken. They looked ready to harvest, and it looked like a bumper crop. The vines were awash with long pods, filled to the ends with plump juicy-looking peas. When Overdrive called, the field man said the second week of June was too early, but he'd drive out for a look anyway. Within an hour, he called back and declared the peas ready to harvest. Overdrive initially considered this to be good news, but the field man was talking hesitantly, as if being careful not to say too much. Soon he knew why.

Under the contract, the processor was responsible for the harvest-date decision. Overdrive had received Waldo's earliest planting date, and his peas would be their first harvest. Unfortunately, instead of getting off his ass to see what's happening in the real world, the field man had been basing his harvest-date estimates on planting-date, heat units, and whatnot. They'd been completely caught off guard by how early Overdrive's peas had matured. Their seasonal labor hadn't been hired, the tractors to run the cutters and loaders hadn't been leased, and so on.

The Welsh ancestors had pointed them to Hank's

and Van Essen's because of the ground fogs, but the wider harvest window hadn't been enough. By the time the harvest was made, the peas were starting to harden and didn't fetch top dollar. Harvested when ready, the peas would've come in paying 20 percent over Overdrive's plan. But because they'd been taken past optimal harvest time, the payout per ton was far lower, and the cash payout fell five percent short.

The field man admitted that the crop in the field had been excellent, perhaps the best he'd ever seen. But during the delay, the weather had turned hot and sunny. Overdrive's pea growing contract was the standard one offered to all Waldo growers, take it or leave it. Overdrive had taken it. Although Waldo was responsible for making the harvest decision, through the use of weasel words in the contract, their only obligation was to provide *best efforts* at an optimal harvest time. Legally, Overdrive had no pot to pee in, and he knew it.

* * *

Halfway through evening milking, Mary hinted she'd like a beer at Harbor Lights afterward. Overdrive surmised that her suggestion may've been related to his behavior. He'd been stomping all over the barn muttering to himself, cursing the animals, kicking over empty milk pails, and for his grand finale, managed to break a grain shovel trying to swat a horse fly. Fucking horse fly.

Later, Mary was first to the car. She drove part way down the driveway and popped the passenger door, as Overdrive asked, "Why're you driving?"

After turning left onto Bates Road and rounding

148 | PATRICK J. HUGHES

the sharp turn, Mary said, "I figured I'd better drive in case, you know, we encounter a horse fly or something."

Overdrive's eyebrows went up, "What?"

Mary snapped, not bothering to hide her anger, "You heard me. Wouldn't want you swatting it into a tree using the car."

Overdrive tried to negotiate, "Oh, come on, Mary. That's not fair. I ..."

Mary cut him off, "Isn't it? That was a $30 shovel, James. What the fuck?"

Overdrive remained silent for the duration of the ride to Harbor Lights, and Mary let him stew. When they arrived, Overdrive grabbed the beer, and Mary claimed the table in the quiet corner. Both smiled and nodded to the people they knew, but neither was interested in any chit-chat tonight.

Overdrive broke the silence, "I'm sorry about the shovel, Mary. I think I can bend the blade back into place, and new handles are pretty cheap."

Mary scowled at him, "James, that's not the point. You can't be throwing a tantrum every time we have a setback. You're a grown man, for god sakes!"

Overdrive held up his hands, "I know. I know. I just ... I don't know."

Mary pleaded, "It scares me when you get all red in the face like that, James. You could blow a gasket. Then where'd I be?"

Overdrive squirmed, "You know I'd never leave you in a lurch like that."

Mary said solemnly, "Maybe you wouldn't choose to, but having a heart attack or stroke isn't something you get to choose. I need you, James!"

Overdrive rubbed his face with both hands, "I

know you do. And I need you to. I just get so ... I don't know ... angry and frustrated, I guess."

Mary put her hand on his, "When that happens, talk to me, okay? You know you can vent with me any-time. I'll listen, and you usually feel better afterwards."

He smiled weakly, "I ALWAYS feel better after-wards. But we can't just drop everything, and run down here every time my steam rises. Sometimes I struggle to hold it together until we can be alone."

Mary squeezed his hand, "We live on a farm, James. It's always a short ride out into a field for priv-acy. We should've done that today."

Coming around, "You're right. Would've saved us a fucking shovel, too."

Mary giggled, "No shit. You can be such a dumbass, sometimes."

Almost his old self, Overdrive said, "I know. It just got the better of me. We'd done everything right with those peas. Right variety, lands, fertilizer. Everything. Only to get fucked by a field man asleep at the wheel."

Mary nodded, "Yes, we did. It's frustrating. So, where's the silver lining?"

He thought for a moment, "Well, the alfalfa com-ing up under the peas at Hank's looks great. With the peas off early, we should get two cuttings."

Mary offered a hint of a smile, "Well, that's some-thing anyway."

He said solemnly, "Hitting it big with the peas would've solved a lot of problems. Would've gotten us out of HMR's crosshairs, at least for a while."

Mary nodded, "I was so hopeful, too. I'm tired of worrying 24/7."

He nodded, now grim, "Oh god, me too. Trust me.

Now, in addition to everything else, we'll for sure have to take on a construction task ourselves."

She shook her head, "Geez, James. Is there no other way? We've been going full throttle since late February. How can we ask more of your Dad and the boys?"

He looked down, "We've no choice." After a moment, "It gets worse."

Mary's eyebrows went up, "What? What do you mean?"

They locked eyes, then he said, "The pea check comes 30 days after they're taken. We can't make the end of June payment without it, and it'll be too late."

Mary put her hand to her mouth, "Oh my god, I'd forgotten about that! What're we going to do?"

Overdrive did his best to sound confident, "We'll go see Walt Brickner at Cascade Bank. I bet he'll give us a separate unsecured loan to bridge us through. The pea money is coming, just not in time."

Mary shivered, "We'd better do it tomorrow. Those things take time."

* * *

Mary was able to get an appointment with Walt right after lunch. Meanwhile, the family continued to grind on second cutting hay. Overdrive spent the morning on the Owatonna, cutting, while Jumbo ran the baler. Joe hauled wagons, and he, Old Bill, John, and David unloaded. At their current pace, they'll have second cutting in by the end of June. There'd been plenty of moisture still in the ground, so the overall tonnage was great. Quality-wise, second cutting was much like the first. They continued to put the high-quality alfalfa in the home place barn, and distributed the rest among the heifer barns. The meeting with Walt didn't go as expected. He was friendly, as always, but leveled with them straight away. He knew their loan's backstory, and sensed something was off, or unusual, about that deal. His management had made it pretty clear he'd better mind his own business, and stay out of it. He felt that giving them a separate unsecured loan would jeopardize his job.

On the drive back to the farm, Overdrive and Mary shared their anxieties and debated what to do next. They'd done nothing wrong, but somehow two decades worth of good will at Cascade Bank had gone up in smoke. As if that weren't bad enough, money wasn't their only problem. The family was weary from slaving away in the heat, day after day. To reinvigorate the kids, they decided to take them down to Lake Ellen after milking for an evening swim. They'd ask Old Bill to meet them there, and pick his brain on where to borrow money.

* * *

It took two vehicles to port the entire family to Lake Ellen, so Jumbo drove the cow car with the rest of the gang. Once there, Overdrive and Mary relaxed with their beers on the Harbor Lights veranda overlooking the lake, and enjoyed the sounds of their kids shrieking and splashing with joy. When Old Bill arrived, Overdrive fetched him a bottle and they got down to business.

Old Bill would've gladly lent them the money, but he didn't have it. He'd been surprised Cascade Bank turned them down after all these years. Especially given the fact that the pea check was a certainty, and the loan would've been risk-free. He also understood the seriousness of his son and daughter-in-law's problem.

Old Bill thought back to his own hard times, and those of his father, and grandfather before him. William Evans, Old Bill's grandfather and Overdrive's great grandfather, was one of the earliest settlers in the Town of Scott, moving into the area in 1848, the year Wisconsin became a state. He and his family spent many years subsistence farming, clearing land, and developing a homestead.

When William got to the point where he needed a bank, he used the one in Adell, because it'd been closest. Old Bill's father, J.B., had leveraged that goodwill and continued to use Adell Bank, even though his first farm, now Hank's, was closer to Waldo. After J.B. bought the farm near Cascade that Old Bill took over, and Overdrive now owns, he used both Adell and Cascade for his banking needs. Old Bill continued that tradition but Overdrive had limited his dealings to Cascade, purely for convenience.

Old Bill suggested that Overdrive and Mary pay a visit to Adell Bank. He was hopeful the bank would view their visit as an opportunity to win back the family's business. Either way, they'd find out in a hurry whether Adell wanted them back, leaving time to try elsewhere if they didn't.

* * *

The next morning, Overdrive and Mary were

pleased to learn that the Evans family was still welcome at Adell Bank. Apparently, their reputation as honest, hardworking, and skilled farmers extended beyond Cascade and the Town of Lyndon, to the surrounding communities and towns. Overdrive and Mary signed for an unsecured farm loan with a balloon payment in 60 days. The funds would enable them to meet the HMR end of June interest-only payment, and with a little luck, skate them through thereafter. There'd be money left over after the pea check retired Adell Bank's note, and the milk check was ramping up.

The family was hard at work when Overdrive and Mary returned from Adell. Jumbo was baling hay, Joe was hauling wagons, and he, Old Bill, and the younger boys were unloading. Kathy and Marie were out weeding in the garden. After a brief hug and kiss, Overdrive drove off in the ton truck to cut more hay, and Mary took off in the cow car to pick up where she left off yesterday, cultivating corn. Just another day on the farm, living the dream.

* * *

Overdrive continued to guess right on the weather, and the entire second cutting of hay was harvested by the end of June. They'd also driven another batch of replacements from Ulbricht's to the home place, where they'd calved and begun to milk. By the end of June, all of the purchased cows had done the same. The larger milk herd meant double-shift milking, which further stressed the family.

Recent events dictated that Overdrive revisit the farm expansion plan. As part of that, he used the twilight after evening milking to survey his crops and pastures, looking for needed mid-course corrections. The field, ear, and sweet corn showed no signs of disease or insect infestation, so Overdrive decided to stick with the no-spray gamble and continue to have Mary cultivate for weed control. The alfalfa at Hank's was coming along fast, now that the peas were gone, making two cuttings more certain. The oats would be ready to combine soon, and due to his sparse oat-seeding strategy, there's excellent alfalfa underneath making two cuttings more than a longshot. The heifer pastures were doing fine, but to augment the Side Hill pasture, they'd need to begin hauling pea vines from the cannery.

❉ ❉ ❉

One night in late June, Overdrive burned the midnight oil reading and re-reading the barn addition contract, trying to decide which construction task to takeover. Fred Reineking had done a nice job of describing the steps of construction, and documenting each step's price. The only step with significant savings Overdrive believed his family capable of doing, was removal of the center aisle slab from the original barn.

As currently planned, Fred's crew would use jackhammers to break up the slab, and then haul it away. Old Bill was still handy with dynamite, and Overdrive believed he could blast the old slab into manageable pieces. Then Overdrive and the boys could use the scoop tractor to load the pieces onto stone boats, and drag them behind the new barn addition, where they'd be buried under the final grading.

The next morning after milking, Overdrive asked

his father to come along for a stroll, ostensibly to survey Fred's progress on the barn addition. Fred's crew had been grinding along steadily. The block walls were up, including the glass block windows. The haymow's end-wall and arched roof, which together enclosed the entire project from weather, had also been completed. Inside, the posts and beams to support the haymow's barn floor were in place, but the floor itself, which also served as the livestock-level ceiling, wasn't yet installed.

Overdrive and his father were standing within the footprint of the new addition, on the dirt floor, looking up through the posts and beams to the underside of the arched roof. After the construction progress chit-chat ended, Overdrive moved the conversation on to his real reason for being there, and said, "Dad, did I ever tell you that the foundation excavation cost overran big time?"

Old Bill twinkled his eyes, and said, "Yes, son, you did. If memory serves, you described it as yet another example of money flushed down the drain because my dumbass ancestors settled on top of the last glacier's shitter."

Overdrive kept a straight face, barely, and said, "Yeah, that sounds like something I might've said. Sorry about that."

Old Bill's eyes narrowed, "Since when is sorry in your vocabulary? What's on your mind, son? What about the overrun?"

Overdrive made eye contact, and said, "Well, the construction contract is fixed price per task, with a self-performance option. If we do a task, there's no need to pay the contractor for it."

Old Bill furrowed his brow, and said, "So let me

guess, you want to self-perform a task and make up for the overrun."

Overdrive bobbed his head, and said, "Exactly. I've been studying the tasks, and I think I've found one you can help me with."

Incredulous, Old Bill said, "Do tell."

"Rather than let Fred's crew jackhammer the old barn's slab, how'd you like to blast it out?" Overdrive studied his father's face for a reaction.

Taken aback, Old Bill at first smiled, but then narrowed his eyes, "You're shitting me, aren't you? Goddammit! Don't go pulling my leg about shit like that. You know just the thought of blowing stuff up gives me a stiffy!"

Holding up his hands, "Whoa, whoa! I'm not shitting you! I'm serious. If you blast the slab, me and the boys can haul it away. Can you do it, or not?"

He eyed his son warily, then said, "Of course I can do it."

Overdrive eyed him, "Are you sure? The wall between the old and new sections is already demolished. That means the new addition's walls and roof will be exposed to the blast."

Old Bill scanned the area, rubbed his hands together, and said, "Well, that'll just make it a little more challenging, is all. Trust me. I've got this, son."

CHAPTER 11

July

After the talk with his Dad, Overdrive called Fred Reineking and told him he wanted to talk through an idea that'd be easiest done in person. Fred agreed to be at the farm right after lunch. When he arrived, Overdrive filled Fred in on his idea to self-perform the slab removal, including how he'd do it. Fred's reaction was classic contractor. He kept a straight face, and said he'd talk with his crew right away about sequence of construction. That way, before Fred left, he and Overdrive could agree on when the slab should be removed.

Fred and Overdrive agreed that the last weekend in July would be a good time to remove the slab. That way Fred's crew could return for the last work week in the month. Toward the end of the conversation, things got a little awkward. Fred expressed safety concerns, made some suggestions, and offered to leave behind hard hats. He intimated that having one of his clients blow himself up might dampen future business prospects, you know, if word got around. Fred also made it clear that using his crew to repair blast damage would be extra.

* * *

The next day, Mary got Ted Ritter on the phone for their monthly check-in. Before the call, she and Overdrive agreed it'd be best not to share with Ted, their saga about borrowing from Peter to pay Paul. They hadn't worked with Ted that long, and didn't know him that well. They needed him, and feared he might be such a straight arrow that he'd drop them like a rock.

Overdrive filled Ted in about the goings on at the farm. Ted empathized with their deep disappointment over the peas, and said a number of his other clients have had similar experiences with the Waldo Canning Factory. They've since switched to the cannery in Random Lake, and have been much happier ever since. Ted wished them well on the slab removal, and left it at that.

Ted's new discovery was that the Delaware-registered LE, was a wholly owned subsidiary of Limitless Enterprises International LLC, which was registered in the Cayman Islands. Being outside the USA, Ted doubted he'd be able to learn anything further about LEI. Instead, he'd look for public documents associated with business transactions conducted by the USA-based HMR, DP, and LE.

* * *

By the time the milk tester returned in July, every newly acquired cow had calved and was milking. According to the tester's results, the new cows had improved on both pounds of milk produced and butter fat content. On average, the new-cow metrics remained a little lower than those of the original herd for newly-freshened milk cows, but Overdrive was heartened that the trends were in the right direction. The passage of time and Overdrive's higher quality feed were having an impact, just as the Hoard's Dairyman article had predicted.

* * *

By July, Mary had delegated full responsibility for the garden and orchard to Kathy and Marie, to free herself to cultivate corn between milkings. For the garden, this meant the girls handled the watering, weeding, and produce picking. This year's garden included green onions, radishes, carrots, green beans, lettuce, tomatoes, peppers, cucumbers, zucchini, squash, and potatoes. Many of these were already being enjoyed at the family's table, and yields had been spectacular.

The family hadn't bothered with the apple orchard in recent years, so the orchard had devolved into a mess of ice-storm damaged branches, worms, and disease. Back in March, Mary had enlisted Jumbo to raise the girls in the bucket of the scoop tractor, so they could prune the storm-damaged limbs. Since then, the girls had sprayed the apple trees for pests and disease at the leaf out, flowering, and fruit formation stages.

When the orchard had been established decades ago, the apple varieties were selected so they could be harvested in stages. Paulared apples were ready to pick in mid-August, Mcintosh in mid-September, Jonathon in early October, and Idared in mid to late-October. Every variety was great for eating and cooking, and Mcintosh and Idared also make great apple sauce. The orchard appeared positioned for bumper crops of the various types of apples.

* * *

While the girls were busy with the house, garden and orchard, the rest of the family focused on milking, taking care of the cattle, cultivating corn, harvesting the crops, and now also the barn-slab removal. There's too much work and too little time, and to get through it, Overdrive had no choice but to crack the whip. The corn needed one last cultivation before it became too tall. Third cutting hay needed to be in sometime during the third week of July, so the oats could be combined before the stalks over-ripening and were flattened by the wind. Somehow, all of this needed to be done while freeing up enough of Old Bill to develop a blast plan, install the charges, and blast out the slab the last weekend of July.

The chores to take care of the cattle could be done simultaneously with milking, so Overdrive focused on how to most-efficiently deploy the family between milkings. To begin the month, the family configuration had Mary cultivate corn, himself cut hay, Jumbo bale, and Joe haul wagons and help Old Bill and the younger boys unload. In-between times or on days of bad weather, he and Jumbo would maintain and repair machinery, Old Bill and the younger boys would fetch pea vines from Waldo, and Mary would get caught up with the books.

This configuration continued on into the second week of July. On pace to finish third-cutting hay when hoped, Overdrive added tasks during the twilight after evening milking, designed to get them ready for the oats harvest. These included prepping the old tractor-drawn combine, setting up the blower at the granary, prepping the ton truck to haul oats, and so on.

Staffing the oats harvest was one of Overdrive's least-favorite duties, especially naming the year's *deflector-man*. As the granary neared full capacity, *deflector-man* needed to crawl up onto a beam high inside, and manually point the blower pipe's deflector to throw oats where it needed to go. This was the crème de la crème of shit jobs on the Evans farm. Oat dust billowed from the deflector as the oats rattled through. Drenched in sweat, *deflector-man* became caked in itchy dust from head to toe, and for days thereafter, blew sticky black goobers from his nose. When John was identified as this year's *deflector-man* selectee over breakfast, everyone looked down solemnly. Except Joe, of course, who shot up out of his seat, pumped his fist, and shouted, "YYYEEESSS! It's about damn time!"

A few days into the third week of July, third-cutting hay was in, and the family began the oats and straw harvest. Under the new lineup, Overdrive had Mary cultivate corn, himself combine oats, Jumbo haul and unload, and John on a shovel to help unload, and at the end serve as *deflector-man*. Old Bill and the other boys would haul vines from Waldo, and get caught up on mending pasture fences.

When combining oats, Overdrive set the cutter bar high enough to skim over the under-seeded alfalfa. The combine separated oat seed from straw, diverted the oats into the hopper, and dropped the straw out the back of the machine into a windrow. The straw was elevated above the alfalfa and ground by oats stubble, and in July's heat dried quickly. Often straw could be baled the same day. When combining, Overdrive always had his baling rig and empty wagons parked nearby. If the combine's hopper filled before Jumbo returned, he'd shut down and bale.

By the fourth week in July, the oats and straw were in and the corn had finally become too tall to cultivate. Mary was cut loose to help the girls with the garden. They were awash with fresh produce that couldn't be eaten fast enough, and Mary needed to mentor the girls in the arts of pickling cucumbers, and putting up frozen vegetables. Overdrive and the boys turned their attention to taking a first cutting of alfalfa off of the pea lands at Hank's. This freed Old Bill to develop his blast plan.

✼ ✼ ✼

Old Bill was skilled in the arts of dynamite blasting. When he owned the farm, he'd spent decades blasting boulders and tree stumps to clear additional land for crops. He'd learned the trade as a boy from his father, J.B., who'd cleared hundreds of acres before him. Old Bill's skills were valued locally, and area farmers routinely engaged him for odd jobs, such as felling old poured-concrete silos and whatnot. As he'd gotten older, a few of these jobs had gone awry but so far nobody had gotten hurt.

With the current project, Old Bill had a challenge and he knew it. The original barn's end walls, at both the livestock and haymow levels, were gone. The barn addition's arched roof and end walls were already in place, as were the posts and beams to support the barn floor. But the heavy plank barn floor that would eventually separate the livestock and haymow levels, wasn't yet installed. On the addition's livestock-level floor, the forms were in place for pouring the aisles, gutters, stalls, and mangers, but all the concrete needed to be poured at once, so nothing could be poured until the existing barn's slab was gone.

Old Bill worried that debris from the blast would find a path to the new addition's walls and roof, and damage them. He stood on the existing barn's center aisle slab, and contemplated the problem. When he looked toward the addition, the rectangular opening where the old barn's wall had once been, provided an unobstructed path into the addition. From the threshold between the old and new barns, almost all of the new addition's roof and wall areas were in the line of fire. But the exposure decreased rapidly, the further one walked back into the old barn. Old Bill believed the new addition's block walls and glass block windows would be fine, but he wasn't so sure about the wooden end wall and the wood, tar paper, and shingle arched roof.

Old Bill also worried about potential damage from blast pressure. He walked along the center line of the new addition, and looked upward through the posts and beams. Again, the arched roof and end wall might be vulnerable. But on the near end, where the old barn's haymow end wall had once been, hay bales piled to the roof were a reassuring sight. In his mind, the addition was a large cavernous area, bounded by an enormous surface area, some of which was a soft wall of bales. He believed the pressure pulse would be diffused enough by the large volume together with the soft wall, to avoid blowing off portions of the roof or end wall.

Walking back into the old barn, Old Bill noted that the foundation walls were three-foot thick mortared field stone. The portion of the floor not being blasted was concrete on a bed of sand over solid ground. The ceiling was a heavy plank hardwood barn floor, mostly piled high from above, with hay or straw. Old Bill believed that neither debris nor pressure would be a problem in the old barn.

Following this line of reasoning, Old Bill concluded that the only real concern was high-energy blast debris finding its way to the barn addition's roof and end wall. Direct line-of-sight debris would mostly encounter durable concrete block at glancing angles, and shouldn't be a problem. But ricochets could find the roof and end wall, and to mitigate this risk, Old Bill would try to use blast pressure to help knock down the debris. He'd sequence his charges so later blasts would face headwind from those previous. He reasoned that setting off the charge closest to the addition first, followed in rapid succession by the next closest and so on, would be the best strategy.

Based on these considerations, Old Bill developed a blast plan that specified the size, location, and timing of each charge. Then he itemized the materials needed, and sent Mary to Sheboygan to buy them. Over the next week, he spent his time between milkings drilling blast holes for seating the charges.

* * *

After milking on the evening before the blast, Old Bill talked Overdrive through his plan. Afterward, they discussed how the entire day should go. Overdrive said, "After morning milking, normally we'd drive the cows out to the Side Hill, clean the barn, and go have breakfast. Does any of that need to change?"

Old Bill said, "The Side Hill's too close. The herd would stampede."

Overdrive's eyebrows went up, "Really? Huh. Okay, how about we drive them down the road, then? Would one of the pastures at Adcock's be far enough?"

Old Bill, hand on chin, "I'd use the pasture on the far side of Adcock's hill."

Overdrive nodded, and asked, "Okay, that's what we'll do. Anything else?"

Old Bill looked at his son, and said, "After breakfast, I'll need some help placing the charges and wiring them up. I'd take me all day if I did it alone."

Overdrive shook his head, "No way. We need the afternoon to clear out the ruble before milking. You need to blast by noon. How many of us do you need?"

Old Bill thought about that, then said, "Hmmm ... there's lots of charges to set, wire to string, sequencers to install. I'll need both you and Jumbo."

Overdrive sighed, and said, "Alright then, we'll suspend haying altogether tomorrow, and both of us will help. Anything else?"

Old Bill, staring at his son, "Yes. Make sure Joe, John and David are out of our hair tomorrow morning. Curious boys and explosives don't mix."

166 | PATRICK J. HUGHES

"Good point." Overdrive thought for a second, "Okay. After breakfast, the three of us will get to work, and Mary and the kids can drive the herd to Adcock's. After that, the boys can unload hay until you're ready to blast. Anything else?"

Old Bill, now grim, "I'll be below grade behind the foundation wall of the garage when I shove in the plunger. You'd better take the family down the road."

Overdrive stared at his Dad incredulously, then said, "Seriously? Okay, I guess we can pile everybody into the two cars, and hang out with the herd."

Eyes twinkling, Old Bill said, "Behind a hill a mile away should be good enough. If not, you'll be right there, you know, if the herd panics and breaks out."

Overdrive pointed a finger at him, "That's not funny, Dad. You'd better know what the fuck you're doing."

CHAPTER 12

Barn Blast

The next morning, everything went as planned. Old Bill, Overdrive, and Jumbo set the charges, and wired them back to the below-grade corner of the garage. After an early lunch, Old Bill watched the rest of the family caravan down the road and over Adcock's hill. He gave them a few minutes to get settled, then strode into the garage and sat on the floor with his back to the wall, and plunger between his knees. After a moment of prayer, he slammed the plunger.

Behind the hill a mile away, the blast sounded like WWIII. The entire milk herd startled instantly, as did everyone in both cars. Cows were running every which way. Overdrive ordered everybody out of the cars, and shouted for them to run along the fence lines with arms waving to help the beasts recognize their boundaries, and to yell *whoa-whoa-whoa* in an attempt to calm them down. By some miracle, cow after cow successfully made the turn as they neared the fences. Some circled the pasture left, some right. Soon, the circle-righters established leadership, and the rest followed suit. Then, the leaders fell out of their gallops to a slower pace, with nostrils wide and snorting, and heads whipping nervously from side to side. As exhaustion set in, they dropped into a fast walk, and finally settled and took a stand in the middle of the pasture, and commenced to shit. Overdrive feared one or more of the heifer herds might still be stampeding, so he barked for Jumbo to round up his siblings and go see to them, and then head home for ruble removal. He and Mary jumped into their car, and sped off to see if Old Bill was alright. When they crested the hill, the barn came into view a mile off, engulfed in a giant cloud of dust, and Overdrive floored it. He barely made the turn at the driveway, and screeched to a halt in the backyard. There stood Old Bill, clearly shaken, but unharmed.

Tentatively, the three of them entered the livestock level of the new addition, futilely trying to clear the air by waving their hands. Gazing up through the posts and beams, they saw sunlight streaming in through dozens of holes in the new arched roof. The wooden end wall fared even worse, with many of the boards blown off altogether. Words failed them, so they gawked in silence for a moment, and then carefully moved on to the original barn.

On the bright side, the center aisle slab had been turned to ruble and the pieces were small enough to move. That was the extent of the bright side. The ceiling, or underside of the haymow's plank floor, looked like a prop in a war movie. All they could do was hope the damage wasn't structural. Water was spraying from broken pipes in a number of places, so Overdrive shutoff the barn's main water supply. They'd have to check later to see if the vacuum lines, needed to run the milking machines, had survived.

Somehow, in a little over five hours, they needed to start milking the herd in this barn. All the things that needed to be done before that could happen flashed through Overdrive's mind, and he made a snap decision. He turned to Mary, and said, "I need you to find the kids and tell them there's been a change in plan."

Mary bobbed her head, and said, "Okay. What's the new plan?"

Brow furrowed, Overdrive said, "We've got to get this barn ready for milking. If any heifers broke out, leave them be for now. Instead, drive the milk herd back to the Side Hill. Then we'll get rolling on putting the barn in order."

As she turned and picked her way briskly through the ruble, Mary yelled over her shoulder, "Got it."

Overdrive turned to his Dad, and said, "Let's take a look upstairs."

Old Bill nodded, and said, "After you."

The stairs took them to a framed walkway that appeared as a tunnel when the mow was full of bales. They walked down it to daylight, and out onto a part of the barn floor where no bales had yet been stored. Sunlight streamed in through the roof in dozens of locations, and Overdrive growled, "You've got to be shitting me! How could debris blow right through the barn floor, and up through the roof?"

Astonished, Old Bill said, "That's impossible. The barn floor is two-inch hardwood plank." Then, after a moment, "But those sunbeams say otherwise."

After a slow left to right roof scan, Overdrive said, "There's no roof damage over parts of the mow with hay or straw already stored."

Old Bill followed his son's line of sight, and said, "That makes sense. No way could something blow through all those bales."

Overdrive looked down, and said, "How did it happen?"

Old Bill got down on one knee, "Well, sonofabitch. Look here. This hole's where a knot used to be. So's this one. Those roof holes aren't from slab debris. The blast pressure blew out knots, and made them into projectiles!"

Overdrive knelt, "Where're you seeing this? Huh, sure as shit!"

Old Bill stood and shook his head, "That's a new one on me. Never heard of blast pressure blowing knots out of planks before."

As reality sank in, Overdrive's mood darkened quickly, and he barked, "Goddam sonofabitch! By the time we pay for all these repairs, removing the slab ourselves probably won't save a dime. All this work for nothing!"

Old Bill conceded, "There's some damage. But how much? I don't know."

Overdrive kicked a straw bale, and sent it sailing. Face now crimson, he snapped, "You don't know! Just like you didn't know knots would shoot holes in the roof. Or, the end wall would blow off. What the fuck do you know, exactly?"

Indignant, Old Bill waved his index finger, and said, "Now just a minute, son. That's no way to talk to your father."

Now lost in rage, Overdrive continued his rant, "Do you know what you've done? You've probably caused us to lose the farm! That's what you've done!"

Standing his ground, Old Bill in a low-pitched growl, "Don't lay that shit on me, boy! You're the dumbass that signed that loan agreement!"

Things went downhill fast from there. At the end of it, Old Bill stomped out of the haymow, down the stairs, got in his car, slammed the door, revved his engine, and squealed out of the yard.

❋ ❋ ❋

Overdrive was standing in the barnyard, staring off into the distance when Mary shimmied through the fence and walked in a large semi-circle to his right. She came to a stop directly in front of him, about twenty feet off.

With a concerned look on her face, Mary asked softly, "Are you done now?"

Overdrive became aware of her presence, blinked, and asked, "What?"

Mary repeated in a soft voice, "Are you done now?"

Overdrive shook his head, looked around, and asked, "Done with what?"

With a weak smile, Mary pointed at a dented metal five-gallon gas can laying in the shit off to his left, and asked, "Any idea how that happened?"

Overdrive's eyebrows shot up when he saw the can, "Why, no, I don't."

Mary exhaled heavily, smiled, and said, "When I pulled into the driveway, you were kicking that can around the back yard. After bouncing it off the barn and the milk house, you sailed it over the fence into the barnyard. And there it lays."

Concerned now, Overdrive protested, "I did no such thing!"

Mary beamed him an impish grin, "Yes, you did. The way you were kicking that can around, I figured there must've been a horse fly on it, or something."

Overdrive snorted a laugh, and said, "No. No horse fly. Not that I recall, anyway. The last thing I remember, I was up in the haymow with Dad."

Mary asked wisely, "You cranked up on your Dad again, didn't you?"

Overdrive shrugged, and admitted, "I'm not sure. I guess I might've. Why?"

Mary smirked, "When he passed me on the road, I noticed a few telltale signs. You know, engine roaring, gravel flying. Oh, and he didn't wave either."

Overdrive shook his head, "Oh god help us. What'd I say this time?"

Mary looked down the road, "Well, look James. This little chat's been fun, but the kids are almost back with the herd, and somehow, we'll need to milk them tonight. You might want to hose the shit off your boots, and get your act together. In about five minutes, either you start barking orders, or I will."

* * *

Overdrive got himself back together. When the kids returned, the family gathered at the kitchen table for their marching orders. As Overdrive laid it out, Mary and the girls served a snack because if things went poorly, there'd be no supper tonight until after milking. The barn was still awash with blast fumes and dust, so Overdrive sent the boys scurrying to open all the windows while he fetched and setup their pole-mounted electric-fans. Clearing the slab debris was the critical path item, so Overdrive got the boys organized on that while Mary checked whether the vacuum system was functional.

For ruble removal, Overdrive owned three tractors slung low enough to drive the center aisle of the original barn. He put Jumbo on the scoop tractor to load slab chunks onto stone boats, and Joe and John on the John Deere 520 and Ferguson to pull the boats. Due to the narrow center aisle, none of the tractors could turn around inside the barn. Even worse, since they drag behind a tractor, the stone boats could only move in one direction and had to be loaded from behind. This meant tractors had to drive in one end of the barn and out the other.

Empty stone boats were dragged into the far end of the old barn, and bounced over the ruble to the near end. The scoop tractor followed the same path, in order to load the boats from behind. Once loaded, the boats were dragged out the near end of the old barn, through the new addition over the dirt floor, and outside. Then, the second boat would follow the same path, and the scoop would circle the outside of the barn, in order to come up behind it, and so on. Once outside, the loaded boats were dragged around to the back of the barn addition, and unloaded with the help of David.

After things were going smoothly with the boys, Overdrive caught up with Mary. She had fired up the Surge vacuum system, and then systematically carried a milking machine around the barn to check vacuum strength. At the petcocks furthest from the vacuum pump, the system was unable to pull a strong enough vacuum to run the milking machine. After commiserating on what to do, Mary ran to the house and put in an emergency service call to the Surge dealer in Plymouth, seven miles away. The dealer would repair the vacuum system, of course, but was also a licensed plumber and could repair the water system.

While Mary was gone, Overdrive began walking the vacuum pipe lines, finding leaks by listening for the sound of sucking air. When Mary returned she jumped in to help, and together they marked each leak with duct tape. Next, they turned the barn's main water supply back on, and marked the gusher locations. About the time they finished, the Surge man arrived. They made the dealer's top priority the repair of the vacuum system, because they couldn't milk the herd without it. Overdrive left Mary to assist, and circled back to the boys.

After checking with Jumbo, Overdrive learned that things were going fine except sometimes, when loading, chunks slid into the stalls where Jumbo couldn't reach them with the scoop. Overdrive told him to forget those for now, and press on. Next, Overdrive jogged around behind the new addition, to see if the younger boys had been dumping the chunks as instructed. Everything appeared to be going as planned back there.

Satisfied with what the boys were doing, Overdrive refocused on what else needed to be done. He knew the cows could only be milked when relaxed enough to let their milk down. They'd be spooked by the blast smell and dust, which still lingered, so he relocated the fans hoping to clear the air faster. He also worried that the potholes and general unevenness of the center aisle sand, exposed as the slab chunks were hauled away, would spook the herd. So, Overdrive grabbed a rake and began smoothing the center aisle sand.

The family continued to work at a feverish pace. Soon, all the chunks reachable with the scoop tractor were gone, so Jumbo and his brothers began to heft the leftover chunks onto boats by hand. Overdrive joined in, after he finished with the raking. When all the chunks were gone, Overdrive and the boys grabbed brooms and swept the trace debris and dirt out of the stalls and mangers. By the time the sweeping was done, the Surge man had finished repairing the vacuum and water systems. At long last, the exhausted family staggered to the house and found dinner on the table, meaning the girls had done their part. Afterword, milking started only about a half hour later than normal.

* * *

After milking, Overdrive and Mary piled the family into the two cars, and headed to Harbor Lights. It'd been a hell of a day. To lighten the somber mood, they stopped for custard ice cream cones on the way. Upon arrival, the kids collapsed onto the pier, and dangled their feet in the water while finishing their cones. Overdrive and Mary sat on the veranda and sipped their beers in silence, eavesdropping on their children's chatter, as a distraction from their troubles.

Jumbo said, "Grandpa really blew the shit out of the barn, didn't he?"

Joe bobbed his head, and said, "It looked like a war

zone in there!"

John asked, "Was he trying to do that? I mean, the roof's got holes everywhere, and most of the end wall blew right off!"

Jumbo shook his head, "No, I don't think so. I think he fucked up."

David risked a peak toward the veranda, "I'll bet Dad's pissed."

Joe, in a low voice, "Glad it wasn't me. I'd be a dead man!"

Jumbo elbowed his brother, and said, "Dead boy, maybe."

Marie, in a change of subject, "Geez, Kathy. Pull up your straps, will you? Can't you see that guy over there, ogling you?"

Kathy blew a stray hank of hair from her face, batted her eyelashes, and said, "Of course I see him. Why do you think I pulled them down?"

Marie frowned, and said, "Well, big sis, aren't you a hell of a role model."

Kathy, dismissively, "Oh, bite me. I say flaunt it while you've got it."

David, confused, "Got what?" This cracked up the rest of the kids, and they all jumped in and began splashing, laughing, and shrieking. Overdrive and Mary's gazes met, both sorry the kid's chatter had ended.

Overdrive exhaled heavily, and said, "Hell of a day, huh."

Mary nodded, "That's an understatement. Just so you know, if you suggest we do another construction task, I'll wring your neck."

Overdrive smiled at that, then said, "No worries,

I'll wring my own neck."

Mary said solemnly, "The herd's production was off tonight."

Overdrive squinted out over the lake, "No surprise there. It was a hell of a day for them, too. While milking, I could tell some weren't able to relax."

Mary chewed on her lower lip, "How long you think they'll be off?"

Overdrive shrugged, "Hard to say. We'll keep running the fans continuously. About the time they get used to the sand, Fred will pour the new slab and gutters, so there'll be another adjustment period. It could go on for a while."

Mary nervously twisted a hank of hair, "It gets worse. This month the processor cut what they're paying for raw milk by five percent."

Overdrive winced, "Well, that figures. Talk about kicking a dog when it's already down. The Surge repairs cost us a pretty penny, and god knows what it'll cost to have Fred repair the rest of the blast damage."

Mary rubbed her face with both hands, "We can skate through July, but we're not going to make it through August, are we."

Overdrive looked down and shook his head, "It doesn't look that way. Plus, who knows, the price of milk might drop again next month."

Mary turned away, looking out over the lake, then turned back, "Ted told us to be absolutely sure, without a doubt, that we make every HMR payment on time. We'll have to borrow more money to get through August, won't we."

Overdrive bobbed his head, "Absolutely. The only questions are where and how much. I'd better get Fred out to give us a price on the repairs, pronto."

Mary stared at him a moment, then said, "Concerning where, I guess we're on our own. You know, since you and your Dad are no longer on speaking terms."

Overdrive recoiled, "Yeah, well, rub it in, why don't you?" He thought for a moment, then said, "Dad's advice would probably be to try to leverage our way into a bank, through the people we do the most business with."

Mary thought about that, then said, "Well, we spend a fortune with the John Deere dealer in Glenbeulah, maybe he'll give us an intro at Glenbeulah Bank."

Overdrive winked, "He'd better, or we'll switch to International Harvester."

Mary put on her impish grin, and said, "You hate International Harvester!"

Overdrive laughed, "Yeah, well, he doesn't know that." Overdrive called the dealer when they got home. The dealer claimed to be the bank's largest client and said he'd be happy to introduce them to his good friend, the bank's president.

❋ ❋ ❋

The next day, Fred Reineking arrived when promised, and Overdrive walked him around to see the blast damage. They started in the original barn on the ground level. After giving Overdrive a wry compliment about the mighty fine job they'd done removing the slab, Fred looked up at the underside of the plank floor and whistled. Overdrive sheepishly filled him in about the blast pressure blowing out knots. After a careful inspection, Fred declared authoritatively that the knots didn't contribute significantly to plank strength. In his opinion, the plank and joist looked like hell, but they're still structurally sound. Where the planks appeared lifted, he told Overdrive to just pound them back down.

When led upstairs, Fred whistled again at the sunbeams streaming in through the roof. There're three repair options, and he discussed them all with Overdrive. The old barn had the same cedar shingle as they'd used on the new addition, so one option was to re-shingle the old barn's entire roof. Then, from the outside, the two roofs would match. Or, they could repair only the holes with new shingles. But this option would leave the few new shingles visually prominent in a sea of originals, darkened with age. The third option was to leave it be, and live with the sunbeams and a little rain intrusion. After hearing the prices, Overdrive decided to leave it be.

Saving the best for last, Overdrive then led Fred back downstairs and over into the livestock level of the new addition. Fred was momentarily stunned silent at the sight of the roof and end wall, but then whistled a third time. Most of the wooden end-wall had blown clear off. But none of the boards had broken, and the repair was simply to nail them back on. Fred quoted a price and Overdrive nodded. The roof was another matter. It was peppered with holes, some large while others were smaller, more along the lines of those in the old barn's roof. Fred quoted separate prices for repair-all and large holes only, and Overdrive chose the latter.

When Fred left, he promised to re-plan the job

that night, and have his crew on site first thing tomorrow to begin the final push to completion. As he watched Fred drive away, Overdrive felt a flicker of hope. He'd made some compromises, but the blast repairs were much less costly than he'd feared. Most of the savings from the DIY slab removal would be preserved.

* * *

The following day, Overdrive and Mary drove to Glenbeulah. After buying the parts they needed at the John Deere dealership, the dealer walked them across the street and introduced them to the bank's president as honest, hardworking, and skilled dairy farmers interested in a loan. The dealer went on to say that they'd bought tractors, plows, balers, and so on from him over the years, and never missed a payment. That's all the president needed to hear. Before they knew it, Overdrive and Mary were seated across a desk from the bank's farm loan officer. In less than an hour, they walked out of the bank with another unsecured loan with a 60-day balloon payment. On the way home, Overdrive and Mary joked that their new roller coaster of a life wasn't so bad after all. The feeling wouldn't last.

CHAPTER 13

Doing without Dad

A few days later, the dopamine was long gone and Overdrive's world no longer appeared so rosy. He was a mess emotionally, and he knew it. For one, he missed his father. He knew from experience that time had to pass before they'd be able to reconcile. It might take weeks, or even a month or two. But more so than previous ones, this estrangement left him feeling vulnerable and isolated. There's just so much going on right now, and he missed being able to confide in the old man, and to seek his advice. Another difference this time, was the newfound appreciation Overdrive had gained for the Welsh ancestors. This separation wasn't only from Old Bill's wisdom, but from theirs as well, and Overdrive felt the loss.

Overdrive was down to one confidant, Mary. But he felt as though he'd soiled that nest as well, by not being completely open and honest with her of late. He'd hidden the ancestors from her for obvious reasons, but worse yet, he'd also gotten into the habit of keeping his self-doubts to himself. After spring's work he'd been too embarrassed to share his own second thoughts on the expansion, and since then he'd continued the façade of total confidence, believing it to be the best way to motivate the family. During this time, they'd doubled the milk herd, harvested a cutting of hay every month, harvested the oats and straw, and removed the slab. He doubted all this could've been accomplished if he'd appeared weak.

Overdrive pondered his situation. He felt physically weary, which was completely new territory for him. His work crew was down a man, which meant everyone else had to work that much harder. During today's check-in with the lawyer, Ted admitted that all his efforts to unravel the shell corporations had reached a dead end. Yesterday the milk tester came, and bottom line, the herd was back to normal after the blast, but new cow production had plateaued and would never catch up to the original herd. Further, the price of raw milk had dropped once, and would likely do so again next month.

Seeing no alternative, Overdrive marshaled his waning energy, and generated a revised monthly milk check projection, which of course was lower. He then noodled ideas, hoping to reduce the drop. His only new idea was to pray for an Indian Summer, meaning clement weather deep into the fall, so they'd be able to delay sheltering the herd 24/7 in the barn, and postpone culling the milk herd to 80 to fit them in. The Glenbeulah Bank loan would get them through August, but Overdrive struggled to see his way through September. After much soul searching, his jumbled thoughts distilled into a few key takeaways. Pray they hit it big with the sweet corn. Pray their good luck with haying held, so they'd have enormous quantities of excess hay to sell next winter. Pray for an Indian Summer.

As a man who believed that the lord helped those who helped themselves, Overdrive took little comfort in the thought that everything was riding on hopes for answered prayers. Emotionally wrung out and physically staggered, Overdrive remained convinced that only a fool would let his weakness show at a time like this. He needed the continued best efforts of his family, so he doubled down and swore to exude nothing but contagious high spirits, energy, and confidence. In other words, he'd continue to paint lipstick on the pig.

* * *

Overdrive was surprised by the family's continuing positive response to his glass half full playacting. It's as though they'd gotten a second wind. Without a disparaging word, the boys closed ranks without their grandpa and moved forward with Overdrive. A few days into August, the first-cutting of hay was in off of Hank's pea lands, and they rolled on to the fourth-cutting hay harvest. Overdrive had to push Fred to hurry up and finish the barn addition's plank floor so hay could be stored there. As the hay harvest progressed, Overdrive's confidence in having excess hay to sell next winter grew. Being able to raise cash by selling excess hay was now almost a certainty.

While Overdrive and the boys were busy haying, Mary and the girls were busy canning, freezing, and pickling produce. The harvest was so abundant, they'd run out of jars and crocks. Mary borrowed a vast supply from old Mrs. Lemke, who was no longer able to use them, in exchange for some of Mary's dill and sweet pickles. She and the girls were on track to put up enough garden and orchard produce to cut cash outlays for foodstuffs in half between now and next spring. The savings were modest compared with effort required, but every little bit helped.

By mid-August, the Paulared apples were ripe, and began to show up in the family's lunch bags, and sliced into salads. For Overdrive, something about the taste and fragrance of homegrown Paulareds' brought back happy childhood memories. He wondered why they'd ever stopped caring for the orchard. Just too busy, he guessed, but what a shame. It amused he and Mary both, that the kids viewed eating apples from the orchard as a novel idea. Apple use previously, aside from the boys hurling them at each other while playing games, had mostly been for feeding treats to Lizzy Flint's horse.

Speaking of Lizzie, over the past six months or so, she'd gotten into the habit of visiting Jumbo two or three evenings weekly when weather permitted. She rode cross-lots between the Flint and Evans farms, on a rolling and sinuous trail through woodlands and brushlands in and around the Waldo swamp. The way Lizzie explained it, these excursions were intended to exercise her horse. But she'd broken the trail herself, which suggested there may've been more to it than that. Overdrive and Mary had grown to enjoy the sound of Lizzie cantering into the yard, and the sight of her wave and smile. Even more so, they enjoyed seeing Jumbo's face light up at the sight of her.

* * *

Overdrive had kept a watchful eye on his sweet corn during the entire growing season. At the seedling stage, there'd been uniform emergence and stalk growth, which foretold uniform maturity of the ears at harvest. At ear emergence, there'd generally been one per stalk, which foretold both uniform ear maturity and size at harvest. Overdrive's no-spray, cultivate-only gamble had paid off. As summer progressed, there'd been no signs of disease or insect infestation, and as a result of Mary's cultivation hardly any weeds were visible between the rows.

To avoid a repeat of the pea harvest debacle, Overdrive became even more attentive as his crop approached full maturity. Deciding when to harvest sweet corn can be a challenge. With very little change in external husk appearance, kernels will pass the period of maximum sweetness and start to dent. This time the cannery's field man rose to the occasion. As maturity drew near, he drove to Overdrive's fields each morning and sampled ears. The very same day brownish and dry silks appeared, with plump, sweet, and milky kernels, the harvest began.

The Waldo Canning Factory sent three tractor-mounted pickers, drive-along trucks for each, and several backup trucks, so no picker would ever stand idle waiting for one. When full, the truck would haul its load to Waldo, and another would pull into its place, to drive alongside the picker. Growers were paid per ton of usable corn in husk. Each truck load was sampled at the cannery, to determine the percentage of ears that could be canned as whole kernel or cream style, versus culled as waste. The payout was higher for whole kernel, but also significant for cream style. From a grower's perspective, the payout was highest doing business with a plant like Waldo, which canned both. Plants only canning whole kernel, culled more of the raw corn as waste.

Sweet corn needed to be processed within a few hours of harvest, or precooled without delay. Otherwise sugar converted to starch, and the corn lost flavor and tenderness. Again, the cannery rose to the occasion, and Overdrive's corn was taken immediately into the processing lines.

Overdrive's sweet corn harvest had been a true bumper crop. The cannery had never seen higher values for tons of raw sweet corn per acre and corn quality score. The lion's share of the raw corn met whole kernel standards, most of the rest for cream style, and hardly any was culled as waste. Unfortunately, the entire region's weather had been corn-friendly, and bumper crops were predicted across the board. Although Overdrive's sweet corn yield was far higher than estimated in the farm expansion plan, the crop's cash payout came in only slightly higher. Processors knew they'd be awash in cases of canned corn, far in excess of demand. The lower prices these cases would fetch, were passed along to growers.

* * *

A few days after the sweet corn harvest, Overdrive was mowing hay in a remote field, and getting angrier by the minute. He'd been obsessing over the lower payout caused by the regional bumper crop. He wanted to scream. Hell, nobody could hear him, so he did scream. He roared a low guttural anguish, long and loud enough to make a dying grizzly bear proud. He roared his way to crimson, with veins popping out of his neck, until he couldn't roar anymore.

With that out of his system, Overdrive's mind cleared. He wished confiding in Mary was an option, but his phonily optimistic front had propelled her and the kids into such a productive roll that he couldn't risk screwing that up. Normally, if Mary wasn't an option, his father would be. But, of course, he'd fucked that up too. Overdrive felt the world closing in, with nowhere to turn. But he managed to suck it up, and keep his mind focused on how to solve his problems, albeit alone.

Overdrive pondered his financial predicament. With the expanded herd, the milk check could cover the HMR payments, if it weren't for the side loan balloon payments. But he knew they'd never get through September now, without taking out another side loan. In fact, they'd probably have to kite side loans every month until midwinter, when the excess hay could be sold at top dollar. If the hay payout wasn't enough to retire the last side loan, they'd a problem. After that, there's nothing left on the horizon. The question became, therefore, what else could they do in the interim to whittle down the size of the side loans month-to-month, to ensure the hay payout would end them once and for all.

They'd already decided not to cull the milk herd to 80 until weather forced sheltering the herd in the barn. But even the longest Indian Summer on record would only help a little. With Dad gone, they couldn't possibly takeover another construction task, so that's out. Overdrive realized that shaving costs with the garden and orchard truly did matter, something he never thought he'd admit. But they're already doing it, so it doesn't really help.

Overdrive racked his brain over what else they could do, but couldn't think of anything beyond excess hay. So, he ruminated over how to end up with as much excess hay as possible. Being extra careful with the weather would help, so cut hay wouldn't be rained on, and rot in the field. Scarfing all available pea vines and sweet corn waste from the cannery would help, by avoiding the need to green chop hay. When the cannery waste petered out, chopping the sweet corn stalks left standing in his fields would help, for the same reason. Hell, when that's gone, they'd chop field corn for cattle fodder, if the haymows weren't filled yet. Hmmm ... there's another idea. Make sure every haymow is filled to the roof.

* * *

Overdrive needed as much excess hay to sell next winter as was humanly possible to store. This required every haymow to be crammed to the roof with hay bales. Packing the mows so full involved extreme manual effort, beyond that previously experienced by the boys. Saving the farm depended on it, but Overdrive couldn't share that minor detail for fear it'd deflate the buoyant morale. Instead, he told them they're about to experience a manly challenge that when accomplished, would provide happiness and fulfillment. In other words, it was a tough sell.

To make his point, Overdrive led his four boys on a climb to the top of the haymow currently being filled. As they sat in a circle near the end of the elevator, Overdrive pointed into the gloomy mow and told them to look. There, visible way down at the far end, was a sliver of the barn's end wall. In addition, between where they sat and the far end, the underside of the roof could still be seen. The haymow couldn't possibly be full, because if it were, you wouldn't be able to see the end wall or underside of the roof. The manly challenge was simple. The boys needed to rectify their previous oversights, and completely fill this haymow, as well as all the others. That's right, five haymows, including the ones at Lemke's, Adcock's, Ulbricht's, and the original and new addition haymows at the home place.

Overdrive walked them through what he believed to be the best approach. They should create a human relay line to move bales from the end of the elevator, across the expanse of existing bales, to the far wall. Then they should keep filling from the far end, and work their way back to the elevator. Overdrive magnanimously offered to unload the first wagon, if the boys wanted to spread out up here in the mow and give it a try. They took the bait.

While unloading, Overdrive sent bales up the elevator at a modest pace. He wanted his boys to be able to keep up, and to realize for themselves that hey, we've got this. Sure, it's a challenge, but we can do it. And being able to, is something to be proud of. When the wagon was empty, Overdrive shutdown the elevator and shouted for the boys to come down for some air. They skittered down out of the haymow and walked outside, one by one.

Overdrive handed them a water jug to pass around, and observed his boys intently. He knew from the looks of them, and from his own experience, what they'd been through. They'd been passing bales from one to another, while half-bent over, or lying on their backs or sides on other hay bales. They'd been crabbing sideways on their bellies, threading themselves into crevices between the roof and hay, dragging the next hay bale along behind. The August day was hot and humid, and they're sweating like pigs, with tee shirts and skin plastered with chaff. They're a little bloodied here and there, from the hay bale stubble. But most importantly, they're swaggering around, sharing the water, brushing chaff off each other, laughing and joking, and proud of what they'd accomplished.

Overdrive got his boys talking about how it went, and then just listened and nodded. After they talked themselves out, he suggested they break and head back home for an early lunch. He planted the seed that while home, perhaps they should address some of the issues they'd just raised, through better provisioning. His boys were suddenly excited about long sleeves, jeans without holes, work boots, gloves, and so on. Had Overdrive started by telling them to dress that way, they'd have laughed at him. But after unloading one wagon, they saw the light.

Henceforth, the boys soldiered on, packing to the roof one haymow after another. Overdrive took over both cutting and baling, so all four boys could work as a team to fill up the haymows. They never complained, but it was physically demanding work, and over time the swagger faded and exhaustion began to set in.

✻ ✻ ✻

About a week later, Overdrive finished cutting the alfalfa strips behind the home place barn, and drove the Owatonna back to the buildings, in order to refuel and grease the machine for the next day. Mary saw him coming from the garden, and met him at the gas pump. She felt they needed to talk privately, plus a cool dip in Lake Ellen would do the kids a world of good. They made plans to pack up the family in both cars and head to Harbor Lights, after the evening milking.

As they'd been cleaning up after milking, Lizzie Flint cantered into the yard. Uncomfortable leaving Jumbo and Lizzie behind unchaperoned, Mary invited Lizzie to come along. When called, Lizzie's mom's only concern was would there be enough daylight for the ride back. All agreed that if it need be, the horse could stay the night in a box stall and Jumbo would drop Lizzie home by car. What to wear was an issue, since Lizzie's sleeveless blouse, riding pants, and knee-high Dehner riding boots clearly wouldn't do. But Kathy solved the problem by offering up one of her swimsuits, and a pair of flip flops.

Overdrive and Mary hopped into the cow car for the ride to the lake, and told Joe, John, and David to ride with them. Through eye contact and a wink, Jumbo let them know he appreciated being able to escort Lizzie and his sisters to the lake in the better car. When they arrived at Harbor Lights, all the kids made a mad dash for the water. Mary snagged a few seats on the veranda overlooking the lake, and after a side trip to the bar, Overdrive joined her. They sat in silence for a moment, sipping their beers, and enjoying the scene.

Jumbo and Lizzie swam out to the raft, where the water was deep enough to dive. Joe, Kathy, and Marie cannon-balled off the pier. John and David waded in the shallows, hunting for clams in the mucky bottom. After a while, Joe, Kathy, and Marie swam out to the raft. For the first time, Overdrive and Mary enjoyed seeing extended interactions between Lizzie and their other children. By all the chatter and laughter, they seemed to be getting on famously.

Mary continued to gaze out at the raft, and said, "Lizzie seems really nice. Joe and our girls can be a little awkward around other people, but not with her."

Following her gaze, Overdrive said, "She is really nice. Not only that, she does a nice job of filling out her riding pants, and that swimsuit."

Mary rolled her eyes, "Leave it to you to point that out. You're right though. She's absolutely gorgeous. She'll have plenty of options down the road."

With pride, Overdrive responded, "Our son has no shortage of positive attributes too, you know. Bright, athletic, strong work ethic."

Mary, also with pride, "I know, I really do. He's all those things, plus has a great sense of humor. He'll have plenty of options down the road, too."

Thoughtfully, Overdrive said, "Well, they're together now. Maybe it'll last. She's been coming around on her horse, more and more lately."

Mary smiled gently, "That she has. And Jumbo's face lights right up every time. There's hope for sure. It could work out. Wouldn't that be something?"

Overdrive nodded, and put on a wistful smile, "Indeed. She's one of the few girls around here Jumbo's age, not clueless about the demands of farming."

Leaning in conspiratorially, Mary whispered, "We should bring Lizzie along to the lake more often."

Overdrive enthusiastically bobbed his head, "Yes, we should."

Overdrive and Mary fell back into silence, sipped their beers, and enjoyed the scene. Out on the raft, a game of king of the hill was in progress, pitting Jumbo against the world. A few shrieks and splashes later, it's apparent Jumbo's winning. With Lizzie being the last to go, Jumbo gave chase around the raft and caught her by the waist. She desperately wrapped her arms around his neck, clinging for dear life and pleading for mercy. But Jumbo's tickle turned her pleads to giggles, and broke her grasp. Lizzie got the heave ho, followed by a big splash.

While another game got started out on the raft, Mary exhaled heavily, and said, "James, I need for us to have a serious conversation."

Overdrive looked at her warily, and said, "Okay, what's up?"

Mary said gently but firmly, "I'll cut right to the chase. The kids are exhausted, and even if they weren't, school starts soon. We need your father back."

After a moment of empty air, Overdrive began to turn crimson, and sputtered, "Over my dead body, that careless sonofa..."

Mary interrupted, "Don't you dare. Not in public. And with Lizzie here? What? Are you crazy? We need to have an adult conversation about this."

Stricken, looking around, Overdrive lowered his voice, "Mary, he almost blew up the entire barn, old and new. I'm just not ready to talk about that yet."

In a cold voice, Mary said, "Listen up, buster. School starts soon. We need your father back, so you're going to have to apologize to him. End of story."

Cornered, but still defiant, Overdrive retorted, "He's the one that almost blew up the barn. He should be apologizing to me."

Mary looked disappointed in him, "James, you asked him to blast out the old slab, and he did his best. You want him to apologize for doing his best?"

Defiance flickering out, Overdrive conceded, "Well, not exactly. Now that you put it that way. But you know how I hate puckering up to the old man. I'm going to have to figure out some way to approach him, so we both can save face."

Mary pressed on, "To hell with you saving face. Pucker, pucker, pucker."

* * *

While milking, mowing, and baling Overdrive had plenty of time for solitary reflection on his state of affairs. Mary wasn't interested in hearing any more of his shit until, in her words, he got off his ass and got his father back. The truth is, nobody wanted Old Bill back more than he, because boy oh boy, he'd love to talk to his Dad about now. But Overdrive knew from experience that both he and his father needed to be fully baked, before they'd be able reconcile. He'd made the mistake in the past, of approaching his father before he'd been ready. It'd been a humiliating disaster, and only served to extend Old Bill's absence.

Meanwhile, Fred's crew was moving along steadily on the barn addition. The plank barn floor was in, and the family was already filling the new haymow. On the livestock level, the new stanchions had been installed, and the concrete poured. Work still in progress included the electrical, plumbing, and installation of the trapdoors, shoots, and automatic barn cleaner. The Surge man was in the process of expanding the vacuum milking lines to the new stanchions. The entire project was on track to be completed by the end of August. Overdrive was still gravely worried over his financial situation. They'd have no problem making the HMR interest-only payment at the end of August. But the disappointing sweet corn check would fall short of kiting them through the third week of September, when Glenbeulah Bank needed to be paid off. Then, at the end of September, the much larger HMR principal-plus-interest payments would begin. Overdrive needed to be 100 percent certain they'd be able to pay HMR.

Overdrive and Mary needed to find another bank to borrow money from. He'd been chatting Mary up on the topic during milking in recent days, and West Bend Bank looked like their best bet. Aside from John Deere, Gehl Brothers in West Bend was their largest supplier. They bought directly from the factory, and also regularly conducted field trials of new designs of manure spreaders, choppers, and whatnot before these products went into production. Overdrive and Mary knew Gehl was a large client of West Bend Bank, and believed they'd provide an introduction. Overdrive placed the call and wasn't disappointed.

CHAPTER 14

Making Amends

T he next morning, Overdrive and Mary were at West Bend Bank with the Gehl rep. Just as had happened in Glenbeulah, their supplier provided a glowing introduction for them, directly with the bank president. The president peppered them with questions, made a snap decision, and instructed his farm loan officer to take care of them.

The loan officer skipped due diligence and got right down to business. The bank and the Evans farm were in different counties, Washington versus Sheboygan. Out-of-county farm loans had an extra hoop to clear, but he assured them it's just a formality. As a branch of a regional bank, they'd have to secure approval from the regional headquarters. He thought he'd have it by the following morning, and promised to call when he did. Then he apologized profusely for having to inconvenience busy farmers like themselves, but they'd have to drive the 40-mile roundtrip again, to sign the paperwork and pick up the cashier's check.

When the loan officer's call came the following morning, the news wasn't as expected. For some reason, regional headquarters had Overdrive and Mary on a high-risk list, and had declined the unsecured loan. Something to do with a large farm expansion loan still outstanding with a third party. Overdrive asked whether a secured loan was a possibility, but apparently, it's against bank policy to make secured farm loans if the bank's position was subordinate to another lender. In this case, the bank would be subordinate to the same third party.

As the discussion wound down, Overdrive and Mary learned a few tidbits they hadn't known before. West Bend Bank had been independent until last year, when Fond du Lac regional bank acquired them. Apparently, Fond du Lac had been expanding aggressively through acquisitions recently, and the loan officer rattled off a number of examples. They'd already known about Cascade Bank, of course, but until this conversation had no idea that Fond du Lac also owned Adell and Glenbeulah. The loan officer was very professional and apologetic, but said neither he nor the bank president could do anything about headquarters policy.

After the call, Overdrive and Mary sat in stunned silence for a moment. They needed to speak in private, but the girls were in the house doing laundry. A silent nod later, they used the old *check on the crops* line, and drove off.

Overdrive snapped, "Well shit, now what the fuck are we going to do?"

Mary gasped, "Fond du Lac put us on a high-risk list? Can they do that?"

Overdrive, even angrier, "Apparently so! They destroyed our fucking credit! It took 20 years of never missing a payment, to build that fucking credit."

Mary seemed about to tear up, "And not just in West Bend, but everywhere! They've bought up banks all around us!"

Overdrive thought about that, then said, "Apparently we'd just been lucky at Adell and Glenbeulah. They happened to be in Sheboygan County."

Mary wiped her tears, and said, "I don't feel lucky."

Overdrive bobbed his head, angrily, "Neither do I."

Mary had a thought, "We need to find a bank not owned by Fond du Lac. Or, if they own it, the bank needs to be in Sheboygan County."

Overdrive nodded, now grim, "I think you're right."

Brow furrowed in worry, Mary asked, "But when's it going to end, James?"

Overdrive pounded a fist on the steering wheel, and said, "It ends mid-winter, when we sell the excess hay. Until then, we keep borrowing from Peter to pay Paul. When we sell the hay, we won't need Peter anymore."

Mary smiled weakly, "I hope you're right, James. God, I hope you're right."

❊ ❊ ❊

Another grueling week passed, putting up hay and produce from the garden. After evening milking, Overdrive and Mary packed the family into two vehicles and headed to Harbor Lights. The kids barely had the energy to walk from the car to the lake, but slowly perked up once in the cool water. Sipping their beer and watching from the raised veranda, Overdrive and Mary both knew the family couldn't carry on like this much longer.

Mary had an uncanny ability while in public, to retain a pleasant smile and tone of voice, as well as discrete volume, while verbally ripping her quarry a new asshole. Overdrive had experienced it many times, and even had a pet name for it. Mary's *smile-un* routine. Not one to beat around the bush, she turned to her husband and began to light him up.

Smile-un, "So, James. After our last little chat out here on the veranda, I thought I'd be seeing your father out at the farm by now. What gives?"

Stricken, "Ahhh... I, ahhh... I haven't had a chance to go see him yet."

Smile-un, "It's been a month since the blast, James. Time's a wasting."

Scrabbling, "But, Mary..."

She cut him off, "Kids are going back to school soon, James. What then?"

Trying to tap dance, "But, Mary..."

She cut him off again, "I've been slaving away to help you fulfill your farm boy fantasies since the day we married. I'm tapped out and can't do anymore."

Feeling unfairly blindsided, tap dancing like crazy, "But, Mary..."

Smile-un, "Your kids have been slaving away since each turned five and old enough to do anything. They're tapped out and can't do anymore."

Tired of tap dancing, getting pissed, "Mary, listen..."

Smile-un, "We can't do anymore, James. We won't do any more. Especially, knowing the only reason we're working so hard is that you're too proud and pigheaded to apologize to your own father."

Starting to turn crimson, "Mary, listen to...."

Smile-un, and cutting him off again, "Listen up, buster. Either you apologize and get him back, or we'll see how well you keep up with the farm all by yourself."

Fire engine red, "Mary, listen to me. He...."

Smile-un, "You're not listening. I said apologize to your father. And for your information, your father's not the only one that deserves an apology. You're looking at another, for putting up with your shit all these years."

About to burst, "Will you let me say..."

Smile-un, "No, I won't. Not one more word until you apologize. We're done here. I'm rounding up the kids to head back home. We'll meet your sorry ass at the car unless you prefer to walk, which would be fine by me."

❊ ❊ ❊

The kids were chattering and refreshed on the way back home, and went off to bed without noticing that their parents weren't speaking. Overdrive and Mary kept their distance. When they retired, they shared the same bed, but ignored each other until sleep came to Mary. Wide awake, Overdrive laid there feeling a strange sense of admiration for what Mary had done to him. He'd set aside his misgivings about not enough passage of time, and try apologizing to his father tomorrow.

Mary's demand for an apology of her own had caught him off guard. *For putting up with my shit all these years*, or something like that. He tried to recall what else she'd said. *She and the kids have been slaving away. We can't do anymore. We won't do any more.* And that last one was a doozie. Something like, *we'll see how well you keep up with the farm all by yourself.* She wouldn't dare, would she? When she gets that way, who knows what she'll do. Just to be safe, he decided to apologize to Mary tomorrow, too. Although for what, he wasn't sure.

Usually after making decisions, sleep came easily to Overdrive. But this time, he'd still been wide awake an hour later. Something's still bothering him, but what? Overdrive tried to step back from the day, and refocus on the bigger picture. There must be something in it, that's keeping him awake. Maybe it's the usual, being on HMR's choke-chain-style short leash. They needed another side loan from somewhere. He decided this'd be the first order of business after making amends with Mary and Dad. Three heads were better than one.

With another decision made, Overdrive felt surely sleep would come now. Instead, another hour passed, and he'd still been wide awake. There must be something else troubling him. It could be not knowing the who and why of the shell corporations, or the unexplained sightings of Rachel Wolf. But he'd been living with these for a while. Why would they keep him awake tonight?

Finally, his mind struck the mother lode. Being estranged from his father and projecting false confidence to Mary and the kids, had been taking its toll. It left him feeling emotionally and physically drained, and wasn't sustainable. For weeks he'd felt alone and isolated because he was. Overdrive missed being able to confide in Mary about everything, and his Dad about almost everything. Hell, now that he believed in them, he even missed bridging to the ancestors. Suddenly, Overdrive realized he needed the support of all three. But the real epiphany came a moment later. To have all three, he'd have to tell Mary about the Welsh ancestors. After he decided to tell her tomorrow, sleep came instantly.

* * *

The next morning, after milking and breakfast, Overdrive told Mary he owed her an apology, and asked if she'd take a ride with him. She gave a curt nod, and he silently led her to the cow car, opened her door, helped her in, closed her door, and drove them behind the barn. At the crest of the hill, Overdrive stopped, and they got out and leaned against the hood of the car. It was high ground with a majestic view of their land, gently sloping off toward the Waldo Swamp.

When it came to the social graces, Overdrive was about as clueless as a man could be. Apologizing wasn't his forte, but he did the best that he could. Mary, of course, knew all of this and politely remained straight-faced and silent while inwardly enjoying the show. She let him awkwardly stumble through to the bitter end, and then graciously accepted his apology. Then she gave him a peck on the cheek, and flashed her impish grin. All was forgiven.

Overdrive said solemnly, "I'll be heading to Cascade as soon as we're finished here, to make things right with Dad."

Mary let out a whoop and jumped into his arms,

"Oh thank you, James!"

Neither wanted to break the embrace. But when they did, Overdrive said, "Just to manage expectations, don't forget that Dad's a proud and stubborn man, and may not instantly return." Mary nodded, "We'll cross that bridge when we get to it." She understood, and told him so by giving him a peck on the cheek, and flashing her grin again.

After they stood their awkwardly, for what seemed like an awfully long time, Mary broke the silence, "There's something else, isn't there?"

Overdrive looked down, and said, "Yes, there is, actually."

Mary made a rolling motion with her index finger, "Well, out with it, James. You've got to go see your Dad, and then get back to haying. Me and the girls are trying to finish the sweet pickle crocks today."

Overdrive smiled weakly, "Well, there's something I've been keeping from you for months. It's been tearing me up inside, and I want to get it off my chest."

Mary's eyes narrowed, "Oooohhhh kkkaaayyy. I'm listening."

Overdrive took a deep breath, and said carefully, "Earlier this year, a couple of times you said my Dad seemed sharper than usual. Remember?"

Mary's eyebrows went up, "Why yes, I remember. What of it?"

Overdrive said, even more carefully, "What he was suggesting was surprisingly helpful, remember?"

A trifle impatiently, Mary responded, "Yes. Yes, it was. So what?"

Overdrive lowered his voice, "Well, not all of that was coming from Dad."

Mary wrinkled her brow, "What? What're you talking about?"

Overdrive looked down again, "Dad's a little different than most people, Mary. He's able to get advice from his Welsh ancestors."

Mary shook her head, "What? They've all passed away, haven't they?"

Overdrive ventured a peak at his wife, and said, "Yes, they're all gone. But he's still able to communicate with them."

Mary's eyes narrowed, "Oh, bullshit, James. Your father can talk to the dead? What's this crap all about?"

Overdrive stared at her a moment, then said, "I know it sounds crazy. That's what I thought at first, too. But I've seen it."

Staring hard back at him, "What? You've seen your father talk to the dead?"

Overdrive nodded, and said, "Yes, I have. Parents, grandparents, the whole ancestral chain. All the way back to the old country."

Mary snapped, "James Evans! You're such a bullshitter!"

Overdrive shook his head, "I'm not kidding, Mary. Why would I? I was there in his shack, while he spoke in Welsh with his ancestors."

Fists on hips, Mary said, "Well, if that's true, he needs his head examined."

He said, "No, Mary. Dad's fine. He's just different than most people."

Concerned, Mary said, "But James. What if your Dad needs help?"

Overdrive took both her hands in his, and said, "Mary, Dad's fine. He's been this way his entire life. Same with his parents, grandparents, and as far back as anybody knows. Hell, they were all known lunatics, even back in Wales."

Mary involuntarily coughed out a laugh, "You're shitting me, right? Known lunatics? You mean, I've married into a long line of known lunatics?"

Overdrive laughed, "Exactly. That's what I've been trying to tell you. And just so you know, the kids are probably fruit cakes, too."

Mary giggled, and said, "This might take some getting used to."

Overdrive flashed her a smile, and said, "Take all the time you need. I did." On the way back to the farm house, he made Mary promise not to spill the beans to anybody. Then, he dropped her off, and headed to Cascade to find Old Bill.

❋ ❋ ❋

Overdrive spotted Old Bill's car out front of the old Cascade Opera House, pulled into a parking space, and headed in. He was greeted by the bartender, who pointed to the end of the bar, where Old Bill sat with a younger guy about a decade older than Overdrive, who looked vaguely familiar. Overdrive ordered a round of beers for them all, and had a seat.

Old Bill, a tad standoffish, "So son, to what do we owe this great honor?"

Overdrive didn't take the bait. Instead, he smiled, and said, "Hi Dad, how about introducing me to your friend?"

Old Bill allowed, "Right you are. Where are my manners? Darkwater Flint, this is my son, James." The men shook hands, then Old Bill said, "You two may remember each other. A band of Potawatomi used to come around to the farm in the spring, to spear spawning northern pike. Darkwater was among them."

Overdrive's eyes widened in recognition, "Why, yes. Yes, I remember you. You tried to teach me how to spearfish in that little creek out in the cattails. The one that crosses both Rock and Bates Roads."

Darkwater nodded and smiled, "Yes, I tried. But as I recall, sleuthing through marshes wasn't your forte, at least as a little kid. With all your thrashing around, we never got within spear chucking distance of anything."

Overdrive smiled and bobbed his head, "Yeah, that sounds about right. I'm afraid my coordination hasn't improved much over the years, either."

The three of them chatted briefly about old times. A small band of Potawatomi Indians used to return each spring to their sacred ancestral lands, which happened to be on the Evans farm. The pilgrimage continued throughout the years that Old Bill's father, J.B., ran the farm, and during the early years of Old Bill's tenure, when Overdrive was a small boy. The band came to honor their ancestors and spearfish the spring spawning run, in the marsh. The Evans' allowed them to camp where they always had, adjacent to the burial mounds on the fringe of the Waldo Swamp. Eventually, the band's elders began to die off, and interest in the annual spring pilgrimage waned.

One of the Flint boys married a Potawatomi and had a son, which they named Darkwater after the tannin-stained creek in the marsh. The marriage didn't work out. In his early teens, Darkwater decided he preferred life with his mom up north with the Potawatomi, to farming with the Flints. The Potawatomi lands eventually became a reservation, in Forest County. Darkwater lives there still, in Wabeno. Today he's a sought-after fishing and hunting guide, booking most of his business through the tourist trade out of Eagle River. Darkwater had always admired Old Bill, for being open and welcoming to his people long after most folks in Sheboygan County had written them off as vagrant itinerant trespassers. Darkwater still came to Sheboygan County several times annually to see his father and the Flint relatives, and always made a point to call on Old Bill in Cascade. During the discussion, Darkwater repeatedly referred to the sacred ancestral lands on the Evans farm as the headwaters of the Milwaukee River. Overdrive kept his surprise to himself, but it made him wonder. Was Darkwater's casual use of this phrase just a coincidence, or did it somehow connect to his nemesis HMR?

When the three-way conversation wound down, Overdrive asked if he could speak with his father in private. Darkwater happily obliged, and went off to join some of Cascade's town fathers in a game of sheepshead. Once alone, Overdrive awkwardly made it right with his father. Old Bill let him dangle awhile, just for the fun of it, but then smiled and slapped his son on the back. Once more, they're father and son. When Overdrive asked if he and Mary could come over to the shack after evening milking for some brainstorming, Old Bill was all in.

* * *

Mary brought an apple cobbler right out of the oven, and vanilla ice cream, along to the shack that night. She was a magician with apples, and she knew anything she did with them ranked among Old Bill's favorite treats. By the time the cobbler and ice cream were gone, they'd been one big happy family again.

Overdrive began the serious conversation by updating Old Bill on what'd happened during his absence. He led off by saying that blasting the slab, net of repair costs, had still saved them most of the value of taking over that task. He then went over the other issues regarding the farm, HMR, the banks, and the sweet corn harvest. The bottom line was they'd make the end of August HMR payment, but would need another side loan to skate through beyond that. They needed to pay-off Glenbeulah Bank the third week in September, and from the end of September onward, the much higher HMR principal and interest payments kicked in.

When Overdrive finished, Old Bill shook his head, and said, "I'm gone one month, and you two turn into Bonnie and Clyde?"

Overdrive held up his hands, "Come on, Dad, what choice did we have?"

Old Bill thought about that, "I see your point. So, what's your next move?"

Overdrive shrugged, "Well, the John Deere dealer and Gehl Brothers gave us intros to bank presidents, because we do a ton of business with them. There's nobody else like that, so we're kind of stumped. We thought about maybe asking Walt at Cascade to recommend another bank."

Old Bill shook his head, "I'd think twice about doing that. You said yourself, Walt's worried about his job. If so, he'll be looking for ways to get back into the good graces of his masters."

Overdrive's eyebrows went up, "Really? Okay, for the sake of argument, say you're right. What could he do? To get back into good graces, I mean."

Old Bill put his hand to his chin, and after a moment said, "Walt doesn't know why, but he either knows or suspects that the lady running Fond du Lac regional bank has it in for you. Wolf, is it? He might figure he'd get back in Wolf's good graces, by telling her you came around looking for leads to more money."

Overdrive tried to protest, but Mary interrupted, "James, your father has a point." Then, she paused, and asked, "If Rachel Wolf knew, what might she do?"

Old Bill tapped his temple, and said, "She'd realize her current policy left you an opening at branches within Sheboygan County. She'd close that opening in a heartbeat. She might even notify non-affiliated banks in the region."

Startled, Overdrive snapped, "What? Could she do that?"

Old Bill said wisely, "Banks did it all the time, during the Great Depression. If you hired a lawyer and called them on it, they'd just offer up their evidence that you're a high risk, and say it's customary as a courtesy to notify colleagues. You know, to help each other avoid placing bad loans."

Overdrive held up his hands in a placating gesture, "Okay, okay. Going to Walt is clearly a dumbass idea, and I should've seen it. Just haven't been thinking clearly, since Darkwater called the farm the headwaters of the Milwaukee River."

Mary gasped, "What? Excuse me, but who's Darkwater, and why did he call the farm the headwaters of the Milwaukee River?"

Old Bill filled Mary in on the background, and said, "The band elders always called that little tinkle running through the cattail marsh the headwaters of the Milwaukee River. Where they camped, down on the flat between the marsh and the burial mounds, they called the little prairie."

Overdrive said, "It struck me as a hell of a coincidence, when that phrase rolled out of Darkwater's mouth."

Mary snapped, "No shit, Dick Tracey! When were you planning to tell me?"

Old Bill intervened, "Mary, there's no need to get all riled up. Darkwater is a very good friend of mine. If he knows anything and can help, he will."

Mary said, "I appreciate that. And I'm sorry for being a little snippy with your communications-challenged son, but he deserves it. It's a long story."

Overdrive moved quickly to change the subject, "I appreciate that too, Dad. Maybe Darkwater can help. But what we need right now is a loan. Any ideas?"

Mary gave Overdrive the stink eye, then said, "Okay. How about this for a plan? I'll find some bank options in the yellow pages, and do enough calling around to weed out any affiliated with Fond du Lac." After a moment of silence she presumed no better ideas were forthcoming, and continued, "So, James. Are you going to address your recent communications shortcomings, or shall I?"

With that deer in the headlights look, Overdrive said, "I ... er ... oh hell. Dad, I've come clean with Mary about the ancestors. She knows all about them."

Startled, Old Bill did a slow head turn toward Mary, and said sheepishly, "You wouldn't turn me in now, would you? Harmless old man like me?"

Mary offered her impish grin, "Oh hell no. If this story ever got out, they'd cart you, hubby, and kids all off in a padded wagon. Then where'd I be?"

Old Bill smiled at that, then said, "Yeah, bringing that up was my next line of defense. You know, after the harmless old man routine. It requires some schtick for us lunatics to hide in plain sight among the general populous."

Mary giggled, "Actually, the whole thing makes me feel kind of special. Not every father-in-law comes complete with his very own spirit world! Hell, if farming doesn't pan out, we can give Ringling Brothers a call. They can put us all in a cage, and sell tickets"

Overdrive deadpanned, "If there's three squares a day and no shit jobs, count me in."

CHAPTER 15

Rude Awakening

The rhythms of the farm quickly adjusted to having Old Bill back in the mix. His return lifted the kid's spirits, and none too soon. On the day he returned, the men and boys plunged into a last-ditch effort to finish harvesting fourth-cutting hay before school started. During this stretch, Mary and the girls mounted their own final push, to finish canning, freezing, and pickling garden produce.

A few days later, with the remaining fourth-cutting hay already down on the ground and drying in windrows, Overdrive had driven over to Hank's pea lands, to see if the alfalfa's second crop was far enough along to cut. When he returned, Mary unexpectedly ran out of the house toward the car. The look on her face said something was seriously wrong, and she began to tear up as she jumped into the cow car and said they needed to talk. Without a word, Overdrive drove behind the barn to the crest of the hill. A dark sense of foreboding washed over him as he rolled to a stop. He'd never seen Mary so worked up before.

Mary handed Overdrive a letter just received from HMR by certified mail. After reading, Overdrive sat silently and stared out over their lands for a very long time. The letter stated that a term of the loan agreement disallowed additional borrowing from the originating bank's branches, in order to satisfy payment obligations under the loan. The letter cited a violation at Adell Bank in June, and another at Glenbeulah Bank in July. As a result, HMR was exercising its right to demand payment in full, within 30 days of receipt of this letter. Should on-time payment not be received, HMR will immediately exercise its march in rights to possess the farm real estate. Personal property remaining on the premises upon march-in, will be forfeited to HMR.

Eventually, Overdrive reached out for Mary's hand, and said calmly, "Well, there's no time for a pity party. We'll have to fight it. Use Ritter. Go to the courts. We can't just drop everything and clear out in 30 days. And we sure as hell aren't forfeiting our livestock, machinery, crops, and everything else."

Mary said grimly, "We could probably get into see him this afternoon."

Overdrive nodded, "Let's do that." Then after a moment, he said, "I keep thinking about what Darkwater said. It can't be a coincidence. There must be some connection between the Potawatomi and HMR, and maybe even Rachel Wolf."

Mary bobbed her head, and said, "I agree. There's got to be some connection. Maybe telling Ritter would help somehow."

Overdrive nodded, "Wouldn't hurt, let's do that, too." Then his eyes narrowed, and he said, "You know, the Potawatomi came every spring back when J.B. ran the farm. I wonder if he knows something Dad and Darkwater don't."

Mary's eyebrows went up, "You mean bridge with the ancestors?"

Overdrive shrugged, and said, "It wouldn't hurt. Maybe they'd have some ideas on what the connections might be. The agreement is so black and white, I fear Ritter can't win in court if that's all he's got. He needs to know who we're up against and what their motive is, and he hasn't been able to find out himself."

Mary thought about that, then said, "Sounds like ancestors first, and Ritter second, might make sense."

Overdrive nodded and said solemnly, "That's what I'm thinking. We'll go to Dad's shack tonight, and then see Ritter in the morning."

Mary looked at her watch, "Let's head back. You talk to your Dad, and I'll call Ritter's office."

✳ ✳ ✳

After evening milking, Overdrive and Mary told the kids they're going to Cascade to see an old friend of grandpa's from long ago. They asked Jumbo to drive his siblings to Lake Ellen for a swim, and gave him enough money to buy each a soda at Harbor Lights.

Overdrive and Mary arrived at the shack, and were welcomed inside by Old Bill. After Mary and Darkwater were introduced, and the small talk ended, Overdrive shared the bad news with his Dad and friend. Old Bill was visibly shaken, and remained silent. But Darkwater was full of questions, so Overdrive gave him a brief overview of the original Cascade Bank loan, assignment to HMR, and so on. By the time Darkwater was up to speed, Old Bill had recovered. Red-faced and fists clenched, Old Bill said, "Those fuckers! My Dad spent most of his life clearing and developing that farm, and I did my best to finish what he'd started before passing it on to you. This is personal! I'm glad you came, son, because the ancestors are going to want to help."

Overdrive's voice cracked, as he said, "I appreciate you saying that Dad, I really do. I ...we ...Mary and I ... we know we've got to fight it. We're just not sure how. We're seeing Ritter in the morning, and need all the help we can get."

Determined to push on, Old Bill said, "Mary and Darkwater, would you mind waiting out in the car, so we can get started?"

Overdrive saw discomfort in Mary's face, and said, "Actually Dad, I was hoping Mary could stay. We've no secrets, and we're in this fight together."

Old Bill rubbed his chin, "You know, son, your late mother and you are the only ones among the living I've ever included in a bridge. And in both cases, I asked them first. You want me to ask?"

Overdrive, without hesitation, "Absolutely. And what about Darkwater? Headwaters of the Milwaukee River can't be a coincidence, and the ancestors might ask things only he knows the answers to."

Old Bill nodded, "I can see that. Mary and Darkwater, please wait outside."

After they left, Old Bill and Overdrive locked the door, closed the window shades, and used the ritual to open the bridge. After a brief conversation in Welsh, Old Bill nodded to himself, and translated for Overdrive. Given the topic and stakes, and after being re-assured that Mary and Darkwater were as loyal and emotionally-invested in the farm as they were, the ancestors had given their consent. Overdrive waved them in, and closed and locked the door behind them.

After Mary and Darkwater were seated, Old Bill explained the ground rules. Mary and Darkwater would be living-side monitors of the bridge, which meant they'd only hear the living-side voices. Also, to preserve the secrecy of the ritual, they couldn't be present when it's opened or closed. When they nodded their understanding, Old Bill asked Overdrive to begin feeding him narrative about the farm loan. He wanted to start at the beginning, and explain to the ancestors the whole sordid tale. The mere mention of the name Wolf raised a hornet's nest of chatter among the ancestors. Old Bill raised his hand for Overdrive to stop, and strained to catch it all. He interrupted in Welsh, here and there, as the chatter went on and on. Eventually the buzz died down, and Old Bill translated a summary.

Dating back before statehood, there was a legendary family of swindlers operating in Wisconsin by the name of Wolf. The ancestors had many anecdotes to share. Back in 1836, the Wolfs had used phony pamphlets to sell outrageously-priced lots in Sheboygan to immigrants arriving in Buffalo on the Erie Canal. The pamphlets suggested a developed harbor, docks, streets, warehoused supplies, and so on. Having only recently crossed the Atlantic to New York City, and ferried up the Hudson River to Albany, the immigrants didn't know any better. They found out the truth when the schooner from Buffalo dropped them off on a rock at the mouth of the Sheboygan River, with all their worldly possessions. By then the ship had set sail, with the Wolfs waving goodbye and having pocketed payment-in-full.

The ancestors knew of the scam because Old Bill's great-grandfather, William, had heard firsthand accounts from surviving 1836ers. Aside from dense virgin forest, in 1836 there'd been nothing for 40 miles in any direction from Sheboygan, except an abandoned sawmill up the Sheboygan River at the falls. The only means to communicate with the outside world was by Indian Trail. Then winter came. Welcome to America.

Land speculation became a Wolf family specialty. They'd missed out when the stage coach road went in through Greenbush on the bee-line from Sheboygan to Fond du Lac. But a few years later in 1856, when the railroad was being planned, they managed to buy up all the land around an isolated mill site called Glenbeulah, two miles east of Greenbush, for next to nothing. After plotting a townsite at the new location, the Wolfs bribed the contractor building the railroad to divert the tracks from Greenbush to Glenbeulah, by signing over a few lots for free. Once the railroad came to town, the Wolfs made a killing on the rest of the lots. Again, Old Bill's great-grandfather, William, had heard firsthand accounts from ex-Greenbush residents that fled when the town imploded.

Later, the Wolfs got into banking back when anyone in Wisconsin could establish a bank by common right without restriction. In other words, the only qualification required to be a bank was to call yourself one. Early on, they made a bundle issuing worthless bank currency in exchange for bartered goods, and then skipping town to resell the goods elsewhere. As time went on, the Wolfs moved on to more sophisticated schemes, which involved the operation of banks and multiple other businesses, simultaneously.

One of their favorite swindles was to form a bank capitalized by nothing but a promissory note from another business. Then they'd raise cash from depositors at the bank and creditors at the business, and skip town with the loot in the form of personal assets, leaving the depositors and creditors to fight it out. This scam joined ancestral lore because Old Bill's grandfather, also William, played cards with a businessman that'd capitalized a Wolf-controlled start-up in exchange for 49 percent interest, only to lose all his money, plus be liable to the depositors of a failed bank whose connection to the start-up had been unknown to him.

Wisconsin's Banking Law of 1903 outlawed the most obvious scams, but by then the Wolfs had already amassed enough wealth and expertise to keep right on swindling, albeit in manners increasingly more sophisticated. They began using as tools, banking corporations properly organized in accordance with the laws of the state, in conjunction with impenetrable shell corporations. The ancestors knew because Old Bill's father, J.B., had taken on as a hired-hand, a farmer that'd lost his farm by getting tangled up with a Wolf controlled state-chartered bank. Since this latter example bore remarkable similarities to the Evans' current predicament, the ancestors believed the Wolf family crime spree lived on through Rachel.

Upon hearing all this from the dead, the living sat in stunned silence. Then Overdrive lost it, and launched into a diatribe of self-loathing, "Goddamn sonofabitch! I'm a fucking idiot! Why didn't I have Dad tell them about Rachel Wolf back in February? Here we are, six months later, and we're just learning ..."

Mary interrupted, "James, honey. You didn't know."

Overdrive, in a low-pitched growl, "That's just the point! I should've known she's after us! How else could 20 years of bank goodwill evaporate overnight?"

In a calm, fatherly tone, Old Bill said, "Come on, son. Mary's right. You couldn't have known. Besides, beating yourself up isn't going to help."

Darkwater waved his hands to get their attention, and said, "Look, I'm new to all this. So, maybe what I'm about to say is really stupid. But saying *Rachel Wolf* to the ancestors was like hitting the jackpot, right? I mean, wow! Maybe we can hit another jackpot by saying *Headwaters of the Milwaukee River*."

Old Bill bobbed his head, and said, "Darkwater, that's an excellent idea."

Old Bill asked Darkwater to put himself in the ancestor's shoes, start at the beginning, keep it simple, and feed him what to say. Darkwater started out by explaining that he descended from a band of Potawatomi, which considered the Evans farm to be sacred land. Until the 1920s, the band made annual spring pilgrimages there, to honor their ancestors at the burial mounds, and spearfish the spring spawning run. The band referred to this destination as the Headwaters of the Milwaukee River, which coincidentally, is the namesake of the entity that called the loan on the Evans farm today. Ancestral chatter exploded at the news.

When the rumble died down, Old Bill looked Darkwater in the eye and shared that the ancestors had great respect for the Potawatomi, and felt the government had treated them poorly. Further, his father, J.B., had many fine memories of the spring pilgrimages by his band. At Old Bill's urging, Darkwater continued, and unexpectedly, the rest of his story was new information for everyone, living or dead.

Darkwater lived on the reservation in Wabeno, and when not otherwise engaged as a fishing or hunting guide, made a point to attend tribal council meetings. Currently, siting a new reservation to host a casino, was the hot topic at council. Financially, the existing casino on the Forest County reservation was a bust. Due to location and poor roads, it attracted mostly hardscrabble locals rather than deep-pocket gamblers from the region's metro areas. The tribe was poor and desperately seeking a better revenue stream. Darkwater knew that many locations were actively under consideration for the new casino, but he'd missed some meetings and couldn't verify whether HMR was among them. In the future, he promised to schedule his guide work so all council meetings could be attended.

These revelations set off another chatter storm among the ancestors. After it died down, Old Bill summarized what he'd heard. The ancestors believed Rachel Wolf was using a page from her family's crime playbook. A state-chartered bank in Fond du Lac is being used to self-deal with a separate shell corporation, HMR, also controlled by her. If the Potawatomi were serious about developing a casino, they'd need money. A big regional bank out of Fond du Lac would probably be one of their first stops. If true, this would explain how the tribe and she met.

Once Wolf saw the opportunity, there's probably

no better platform than a regional bank when hunting for land. In this case they needed land with a tribal history strong enough to cajole governmental approvals for creation of a new reservation. Once the land and approvals were secured, by hook or by crook if necessary, Wolf would be in a position to develop and operate a casino with the tribe, and make a killing. Money would provide a hell of a motive.

The living participants in the bridge were speechless once more. After an interval of dead air, at Overdrive's urging Old Bill thanked the ancestors profusely for the thoughts they'd shared. It's only speculation, and as of yet there's no proof, but how well it all hung together was frightening. The session over, Mary and Darkwater were shooed outside. Then, Old Bill and Overdrive used the ritual to close the bridge, and joined the others for some fresh air.

Everyone stood in a circle in front of the shack, to say their good-byes. Darkwater planned to drive back up north to Wabeno, the following day. He made a solemn promise to attend the next tribal council meeting two nights hence, as well as every future meeting for as long as they needed him to. He also promised to reach out to his closest tribal friends, to see if they knew any more than he did.

* * *

That night in bed, sleep came quickly to Mary, but Overdrive laid awake for hours with his mind racing. He'd been blown away by the theory put forth by the ancestors, and couldn't stop thinking about it. There's no proof, of course, but it all made sense. Compared to

Forest County, the farm would be a great place for a casino. Driving on good roads, it's only about an hour from Milwaukee and Green Bay, one-and-a-half hours from Madison, and a little over two hours from Chicago.

If it's true, if Rachel Wolf was behind HMR, this whole thing had been a swindle right from the start. The new headquarters approval process for farm loans. The new standard loan agreement. Rachel serving as the headquarters rep. Assignment of the loan to HMR after the first draw. The sole purpose all along had been to force them off the farm, have the land declared a reservation, and develop and operate a casino.

Eventually, Overdrive began to doze off. He dreamed of a barker, like one of those on the midway at a county fair. He couldn't make out what the barker's shouting, so he read his lips. *Come on in and try your luck at the Headwaters of the Milwaukee River Casino. Everybody's a winner, at the ...* Sonofabitzz .. zz .. zz.

CHAPTER 16

Fight for Survival

T he next morning on their way to Random Lake, Overdrive and Mary discussed how to handle things with Ted Ritter. They'd have to give Ted the HMR letter, which meant they'd have to come clean about borrowing from Peter to pay Paul. The best way to reveal the Wolf-HMR-Potawatomi-casino theory was less obvious. This speculative bomb needed to be dropped delicately because, like any good attorney, Ted would be curious about how they came by it. They decided to fib a little. They'd say Darkwater heard at tribal council, a discussion of possible locations for a new reservation and casino, and that HMR was among them.

Upon arrival, Ted's legal secretary seated them in the conference room and brought fresh coffee. Shortly, Ted walked in and gave them a hearty greeting. After exchanging pleasantries, Ted asked how they're doing versus the farm expansion plan, like he always did. Anticipating the question, Overdrive responded by handing Ted HMR's letter and saying there's more urgent business to attend to. Ted calmly put the letter down and asked to be told what's so urgent, saying he'd read the letter after hearing the explanation.

The way Overdrive spun it to Ted, they'd basically been following Ted's advice to be absolutely certain every HMR obligation could be paid on time. Things were tight, so to create a financial buffer they took out a series of unsecured loans on the side, with 60-day balloon payments. Their plan was to sustain the buffer by always taking out a new 60-day loan in advance of the previous loan's balloon payment. This would continue until mid to late winter, when they'd sell their excess hay for top dollar. The hay revenue would retire the last side loan, plus adequately buffer the remaining HMR payments.

According to Overdrive's glowing description, the side-loan plan had been working to perfection until a snag occurred in August. West Bend Bank's parent required headquarters approval for out-of-county farm loans. As it turned out, the parent was Fond du Lac, they'd placed Overdrive and Mary on a high-risk list, and had rejected the loan. A few days later HMR's letter arrived.

With that, Ted held up his hand to pause Overdrive's monologue, and read the letter. After finishing, he pulled the HMR loan agreement out of his file folder, and re-read it as well. Then he looked up at the ceiling, shook his head, let out a big sigh, and said, "You should've consulted with your attorney, presumably me, before taking a side loan at a branch of the Fond du Lac regional bank."

Contrite, Overdrive said, "We realize that now, Ted. We really do."

Ted locked eyes with one, and then the other, and said, "After the fact is too late. Look, this's your farm at stake here, not mine. Am I your attorney, or not?"

Startled, Overdrive blurted, "Yes. Yes, of course you are!"

Ted, in a frosty voice, "Then start consulting with me, before going off half-cocked. HMR has you in a dangerous position. Didn't I make that clear?"

Overdrive tried to tap dance, "Yes, you did. That's why we buffered with side loans. They've gotten every cent on time. Why do they care where it's from?"

Ted shook his head in disbelief, "HMR doesn't care. Don't you get it? The agreement says they can help themselves to your farm, if you violate any term. They know the farm value far exceeds what you owe. They'd been hoping you'd give them a legal reason to take your farm, and you did."

Overdrive winced, "We gave them a legal reason to take our farm?"

Ted nodded, "Says right here in the agreement that additional borrowing from the originating bank's branches is not allowed. Fond du Lac originated the loan, so branches are off limits. You gave them a legal reason not once, but twice."

Overdrive, not bothering to hide his anger, "Well, shit! It's not right, and we want to fight it! We think the controlling owner of Fond du Lac regional bank has been trying to force us off our farm since day one. She wants to have it declared a Potawatomi Indian reservation, in order to develop a casino there."

Ted's eyebrows and hands shot up, and he blurted, "What?"

Overdrive launched into an impassioned disclosure of what'd been learned from Old Bill's friend, Dark-water. The version of reality shared, however, was the one cooked up by he and Mary on the drive over.

Ted listened intently, took notes, and then said, "Well, first off, what you just said doesn't make any sense. The Potawatomi are a federally recognized tribe. Their reservations are federal. To my knowledge, the last major tribal legislation by Congress was in the early 1950s, and it directed the Bureau of Indian Affairs to terminate existing rural reservations, and move their populations to urban areas for assimilation. It caused a stink, and the last I heard, things were at an impasse."

Overdrive's eyebrows went up, "What? Are you sure? Darkwater's been a good friend of my Dad for decades. It's hard to believe he'd lie to us."

Ted thought about that, then said, "Well, like I say, the last I heard. Even so, I doubt the Bureau of Indian Affairs is now all of a sudden in the business of creating new reservations to host casinos. As far as I know, they don't even allow gaming on existing reservations."

Unable to listen any longer, Mary said, "Ted, something's not right. I was there and heard the same thing James did. Darkwater even mentioned something about the existing casino on the Forest County reserva-tion being a financial bust."

Ted frowned, and said, "Huh. Well, look, I don't do much tribal work in my practice. It's certainly possible that something's changed. I'll look into it, okay?"

Overdrive nodded, and said solemnly, "Please do, Ted. We'd appreciate it. Darkwater wouldn't lie to us about what's being discussed at tribal council. And if a casino in a better location were impossible, why would the tribe talk about it?"

After more discussion, Ted had to admit that something must've changed recently. The Headwaters of the Milwaukee River, or HMR, was a pretty unusual phrase to be suddenly popping up independently all over the place. As a simple matter of geography, the creek originating on the Evans Farm was indeed part of the HMR. There had to be a connection between some or all of these HMRs.

Ted was less clear on why Overdrive and Mary felt this had anything to do with the controlling owner of Fond du Lac regional bank. But as Overdrive recited the facts one more time, it began to make sense. He looked up at the ceiling for a moment, then said, "Hmm, well, that does all seem to hold together. It's plausible but circumstantial. So, who is the controlling owner? Did you get a name?"

Overdrive said, "Rachel Wolf."

Ted leaned back and looked up at the ceiling again, frowned, and said, "Wolf. That rings a bell. Why does that name sound so familiar?" Then he gasped, and jerked upright, "Oh shit! That can't be. Can it? Sonofabitch! What if it is?"

Overdrive leaned forward, and asked, "What if it is, what?"

Ted chose his words carefully, and said, "Lawyering in this area has been my family's business for five generations. Years back there'd been a family of swindlers by the name of Wolf. Various run-ins with the Wolfs were legend in my family. I'd assumed they'd all died out, but what if they haven't?"

Overdrive nodded, now grim, "Bingo. That's what we think. And another thing, we've seen her multiple

228 | PATRICK J. HUGHES

times slowly driving by the farm after the loan had been assigned to HMR. Why would she be monitoring our operations, if she didn't still have a financial interest in the farm?"

Instantly, Ted got to his feet, began to pace, and became more animated than they'd ever seen him before. His words came rapid-fire. If she's one of THE Wolfs the legal remedies would be limited. They'd been very good at identifying legal escapes, and blocking them in advance. They'd stop at nothing. Outright cash bribes, offering up shares of the deal, blackmail, you name it. If need be, they'd target and compromise every judge, town board member, planning commissioner, and so on, needed to close a deal. It came second nature to them.

Ted grabbed the HMR loan agreement off the table, reread it again, and then tossed it back down in disgust. He laid out for Overdrive and Mary a preliminary survival strategy. Their best chance would be to find alternative financing, and payoff HMR in full within 30 days. If this could be done, HMR would have no grounds to march in. Even then, HMR might sue over the branch bank violations. But if so, Ted felt he'd win in court because all financial claims by HMR and the branch banks had been satisfied on time. If the local courts had already been bought off, Ted felt the appeals process would reach beyond her circle of corruption. If not, they'd threaten to go to the newspapers and other media, and expose the entire swindle. Wolf would cut and run, rather than risk ruining her regional bank and losing any chance of developing a Potawatomi casino elsewhere.

Overdrive and Mary were shocked and dismayed

at Ted's stark assessment. But at the same time, they'd been amazed at how rapidly he'd grasped the severity of their situation, and identified a potential escape route. With their confidence in Ted growing, the discussion moved on to sources of alternative financing. Ted suggested one of his clients, Oostburg Bank, might take this on. This independent bank had recently fought off a hostile takeover attempt by the Fond du Lac regional bank, and Ted was in a position to introduce them to the bank's president.

Defending against takeovers wasn't in Ted's wheelhouse, so he hadn't been directly involved. But as a result of that fight, he figured Oostburg Bank already knew that Rachel Wolf controlled the Fond du Lac regional bank. Whether it'd occurred to them that she might be a descendant of the legendary crime family, he wasn't sure. Presuming she is, Ted was certain that enlightening the bank about that connection would motivate them to step in with the money, and solve Overdrive and Mary's problem. The families behind Oostburg Bank had been fighting corruption in the region's banking industry for decades. He knew this because the corruption had been largely inspired by the Wolf family, and the bank had hired Ted's great-grandfather, grandfather, and father to fight it.

Ted offered to take on their case on a fee for service basis, with all fees deferred until the HMR debt was retired with alternative financing. This way, Ted's fees could be paid out of the financing he'd help them arrange. When Overdrive and Mary agreed, Ted said he'd push Oostburg Bank for a meeting tomorrow, if at all possible.

The conversation shifted to what to say to the

bank. All agreed that it'd be best for Ted to do most of the talking, since he knew the people. Somehow, they needed to get the bank to see this as an opportunity for them. The initial idea was to tout Overdrive and Mary's operation as one of the county's most successful dairy farms. A proven operation like this provided a great financing opportunity, with low risk. But after kicking that around, the three of them concluded this strategy alone wouldn't carry the day. Overdrive and Mary were essentially strangers walking into the bank, asking for a lot of money in a hurry. Even with Ted doing the talking, it sounded more like a stickup than an opportunity.

Given the bad blood between the Oostburg and Fond du Lac banks, the next idea was to emphasize the opportunity for Oostburg to swipe one of Fond du Lac's clients. But this idea fizzled since technically, with the loan assigned to HMR, Fond du Lac wouldn't lose anything. Another thought was to suggest that the same person that attempted a hostile takeover of their bank, is now attempting to force Overdrive and Mary off their farm, and hope they'd have proof later if needed.

By the time the meeting ended, they'd decided that Ted would provide the introductions, vouch for the quality of Overdrive and Mary's farm expansion plan, and then connect the dots leading to Rachel Wolf. He'd make it clear that the loan was being sought to prevent Wolf's takeover of Overdrive and Mary's farm. They weren't sure which direction the bank would take the conversation thereafter, but just in case, Overdrive would be prepared to explain actual performance of the expanded farm, versus plan. After the bank meeting, they'd reconvene at Ted's office to discuss next steps and action items.

Later that day, after the evening milking, Overdrive and Mary received a call from Ted. Oostburg Bank's farm loan officer agreed to clear his morning schedule, and wanted to know how early they could be there. As Ted had hoped, the bank president would make himself available for the start of the meeting. For the first time since the arrival of HMR's letter, Overdrive slept well that night.

* * *

The next morning, Overdrive and Mary entered the lobby of the Oostburg Bank five minutes prior to the arranged time. Ted Ritter rose from his seat and gave them a hearty welcome. Soon after, the bank president's personal secretary walked up and introduced herself, and asked that they follow her into a conference room. After asking everyone's preferences, she said she'd return with coffee momentarily, and that the president would be into see them shortly.

Before the coffee arrived, the bank's president, Peter Nyenhuis, and his farm loan officer walked in. Ted led the introductions, and Peter joked that he hoped they didn't mind him crashing the party. About then the coffee arrived. There was a prepared cup for everyone, and a pot and fixings in case anyone wanted more. The secretary left, and everyone took a seat.

Ted Ritter spoke first, following the script from the previous day's meeting with Overdrive and Mary. He started off by explaining why they came, touting James and Mary's operation, and then led Peter and his loan officer through the whole sordid tale of the original loan, its unusual circumstances, Rachel Wolf's personal involvement, the assignment to HMR, shell corporations and where they were registered, side loans, HMR's march-in letter, and so on.

Near the end, Ted boldly stated that he'd be able to prove that Rachel Wolf was behind HMR shortly. In his closing remarks, Ted emphasized that in spite of it all, James and Mary had doubled the size of their barn, doubled their milk production, and grown and harvested a cornucopia of excess hay to sell next winter, all since last spring. Then, he circled back around to the need for a loan to payoff HMR within 28 days. Ted forcefully asserted that James and Mary were good for the loan. He claimed them to be exceptionally skilled farmers, and anyone who carefully examined what they'd done with their farm over the last two decades, would come to the same conclusion.

When Ted finished, the room fell silent. The Peter and loan officer had been mesmerized by what they'd heard. Eventually, Peter recovered enough to ask, "Ted, how is it that HMR had march in rights against the farm? Normally, for a loan of that nature, the collateral would be something like the livestock bought with the money borrowed, or at the very most, the personal property in general."

Ted nodded, and said, "That's exactly right, sir. Collateral would normally be what's acquired with the funds, and if part of that were too illiquid, personal property in general. Using the farm real estate is highly unusual. But that's what's in Wolf's so-called new standard farm loan agreement."

Peter exhaled heavily, and said, "Ted, is it really true that there's 30 days to pay in full, and the personal property is supposed to be removed over that same 30 days? I mean, it'd be physically impossible for a farm family to clear out all their worldly possessions within 30 days of receiving a letter out of the blue."

Ted bobbed his head, and said, "You're exactly right again, sir. Normally, as a practical matter, the evicted party would have 60 days after defaulting on the payoff to remove personal property. Real estate would transfer after the premises were vacated. Again, what's in Wolf's agreement is highly unusual."

Peter leaned forward, frowned, and said, "Ted, as a banker, I'm having a hard time understanding why a bank would include a clause in a loan agreement, which forbids further borrowing from themselves. With the weather and markets as they are, farming seldom goes as planned. If more money were needed, why wouldn't they want to lend it to a reliable borrower?"

Ted held up an index finger, and said, "You make an excellent point, sir. I can't be certain yet, but I have a theory. I believe Rachel Wolf has a more lucrative use in mind for this property than farming, and plans to pursue this alternate use as soon as the farm falls into HMR's hands. Forbidding further borrowing from her own regional bank furthers this goal. With few exceptions, your bank being one, Fond du Lac owns every bank in the region."

Peter stared at him a moment, then said, "Ted, I mean no disrespect. But how is it that you allowed James and Mary to sign that agreement?"

Ted smiled, and said, "No offense taken, sir, it's a fair question. I wasn't engaged by James and Mary prior to execution. But this doesn't reflect poorly on them either. Put yourself in their shoes. They'd been banking in Cascade for 20 years, had always made their payments, and had always been treated fairly. They'd no reason to believe their own bank would try to force them off their farm."

Peter narrowed his eyes, and said, "Ted, I'm old enough to remember the Wolf crime family, and so are many of the folks on our board. And that Fond du Lac hussy's attempt to take us over still burns bright in all our minds. But until now we, or at least I, hadn't considered that the two might possibly be connected. That is interesting."

Peter spent the next 10 minutes peppering James and Mary with questions, and afterward the loan officer carried on for another 15 or so. By the time they'd finished, both had concluded that James and Mary were exactly what they appeared to be. Honest, hardworking, and highly competent dairy farmers, who operated on the misplaced faith that the nation's banks were also what they appeared to be. If only it were true.

Peter was nothing if not decisive. On the spot, he made James and Mary's case his farm loan officer's top priority. The size of the loan would require board approval and the next regularly scheduled meeting would be too late, so Peter said he'd call an off-cycle meeting specifically to consider their application. Moving forward with the process, of course, was contingent on Overdrive and Mary providing the latest farm expansion plan, status versus plan, last five years of state and federal income tax returns, tour of farm, and so on. The loan officer agreed to be at the farm for his tour the following morning.

As the meeting broke up, Peter reminded them that he couldn't guarantee loan approval. Bankers were conservative by nature, and when borrowers were in a hurry, usually even more so. He emphasized to Ted the importance of having proof that Rachel Wolf was behind HMR. On that note, everyone stood, shook hands, and said their good-byes. As the three of them walked outside, Ted observed that it's lunchtime and suggested they reconvene at his favorite diner.

* * *

Ted, Overdrive, and Mary settled into the diner's most private booth, ordered lunch, and dove into a hushed discussion over coffee. All felt the bank meeting had gone splendidly. Overdrive and Mary had taken Peter's no-guarantee warning as ominous, and floated the idea of pursuing loans at multiple independent banks. But in Ted's mind, Peter had merely been encouraging them to take the process seriously. He reasoned that walking into other banks cold, without president-level access, was a longshot. Overdrive and Mary had a farm to run, and Ted's time was better spent proving Rachel Wolf to be behind HMR.

The discussion turned to how to find the proof. They brainstormed, winnowed the list, and then Ted assigned action items. Overdrive and Mary would get word to Darkwater that he should specifically pursue whether the tribe had already partnered with HMR, or was considering doing so. Ted's office would pursue the Wolf-to-HMR connection, including finding out current federal policy toward new reservation creation and gaming. They'd also pull records and maps from the Sheboygan County Register of Deeds Office, and identify all lands that could legitimately be considered part of the headwaters of the Milwaukee River. As the meeting broke up, Ted suggested daily telephone calls until further notice, with the Evans' calling Ted's office after evening milking. Tribal council met that night, so Overdrive and Mary told Ted they'd call Darkwater after he returned from that. If anything useful was learned, they'd buzz Ted right after.

On the drive back home, Overdrive and Mary planned the rest of their day. Overdrive needed to bale hay at Hank's, and Mary was up to her eyeballs in Mcintosh apples, putting up sauce. Since Old Bill had the relationship with Darkwater, they wanted him on that call. To keep him at the farm that late, they decided to invite him to stay for supper, and help the boys unload hay until the call.

When invited, Old Bill said wryly, "That's mighty big of you, son. Feeding me, and all. Considering, I'll have put in 12 hours for free on your farm by then."

Overdrive winked and slapped his father on the back, "No need to thank me, Dad. Learned everything I know from the master. What's that you always used to say? When it comes to draught horses and family, feed's cheaper than wages?"

❋ ❋ ❋

That evening after milking, the family cleaned up as always. Then, Mary shooed the kids out of the kitchen, using popcorn as the bribe. Overdrive closed the door behind them, and Mary dialed Darkwater. As the line rang, Mary handed the receiver to Old Bill. Shortly, Darkwater picked up, and Overdrive and Mary could hear one side of the conversation as the old friends exchanged pleasantries. Then Old Bill told Darkwater to hang on for his son, and handed Overdrive the receiver. All business, Overdrive said, "Hi Darkwater, James here. A couple of things. We've met with our attorney, Ted Ritter, and he provided an introduction to the Oostburg Bank. Things went well, and there's a chance they'll lend us the money."

Jubilant, Darkwater said, "That's wonderful news, James! Congratulations!"

Measured, Overdrive said, "Let's not get ahead of ourselves, it's not a done deal yet. But, if you can believe this, Oostburg Bank recently fought off a hostile takeover attempt by Rachel Wolf's regional bank. Ritter thinks they'd make the loan for sure, if they knew the same person was trying to force us off the farm."

Darkwater didn't know exactly what to think about that, "Okay. But we know that, right? Can't you just tell them?"

Overdrive shook his head, "We think we know. But we can't tell anybody how we think we know. If we did, they'd drag us off to the funny farm. We can't even tell Ritter. But look, with a little help from you, Ritter thinks he can prove it."

Darkwater said, "Okay, what's he need? You know I'll do anything I can."

Overdrive said solemnly, "Ritter wants you to find out if the tribe is already partnered with HMR, or is thinking about it."

Darkwater, in an upbeat voice, "Huh. Sure, I can do that." Then, unexpectedly, "Does he care if they've partnered with anybody else? Tonight's big news was they've just partnered with an outfit called Development Partners."

Overdrive blurted, "What? Are you serious? HMR is a wholly owned subsidiary of Development Partners."

Darkwater went on to fill them in on what else he'd learned. DP's charge was to find an appropriate location for the reservation and casino, acquire the land, have it legally converted to a reservation, and develop the casino. Although the tribe's ancestral lands extend all over the upper Midwest, only Wisconsin sites were being considered. When asked why, the DP rep said the wheels had already been greased in Wisconsin, for gaming and rapid land conversion to a reservation. Multiple locations were under consideration, including the headwaters of the Milwaukee River. In addition to the size of the pool of nearby gamblers, ease and cost of land acquisition would strongly influence the final location selection.

✳ ✳ ✳

After Old Bill left and the kids were in bed, Mary dialed Ted, and he picked up on the first ring. Overdrive, in a hyped-up voice, "Ted, this is James and Mary. Sorry for calling so late. But there's important news from Darkwater."

That got Ted's full attention, and he said, "No problem, James. Tell me."

Overdrive, still hyped, "The Potawatomi are partnered with Development Partners to find a location for a new reservation and casino."

Ted gasped, "Sonofabitch! Did Darkwater hear this first hand?"

Overdrive, voice in transition, "Yes, at tribal

council."

Ted, hyped himself, "Any mention of HMR?"

Overdrive, in a nearly normal voice, "None. But DP said the search is limited to Wisconsin because the wheels are already greased there."

Ted gasped again, "DP actually said that publicly? Darkwater heard them?"

Overdrive said, "That's what he told us. He also said multiple Wisconsin locations were under consideration, including HMR."

Mary added, "Darkwater said ease and cost of land acquisition would strongly influence final location selection."

Ted exhaled heavily, and said, "Well, that figures. Shit, I'm afraid I've got some bad news on that front."

Ted filled Overdrive and Mary in on what his paralegal had learned from today's visit to the register of deeds office. Within the last few months, HMR had acquired the Lage, Salveson, and Nitsch farms at below-market prices. The Evans farm was the last domino yet to fall. According to the maps, these four farms made up the headwaters of the Milwaukee River. Ted wanted to know if these other farmers were forced out, or simply didn't know the value of their land. Overdrive volunteered to find out, since he and his father knew all three farmers personally.

Ted's other news was that he'd worked through Wisconsin's Congressional Delegation, and had successfully scheduled a call with the Bureau of Indian Affairs for tomorrow morning. He'd be speaking with the BIA rep whose purview included the Wisconsin tribes. Hopefully he'd learn what'd changed recently to make it easy to create new reservations in Wisconsin, where gaming was legal.

CHAPTER 17

Due Diligence

The next morning, Oostburg Bank's farm loan officer arrived just as Overdrive and Mary were finishing breakfast. Overdrive went outside to greet him, while Mary cleaned up. Fresh cups of coffee were waiting on the table when the men returned, and they all took a seat. After the niceties, the loan officer suggested a time-saving idea that involved him site auditing their records, rather than dragging originals to Oostburg to copy. Mary volunteered to pull out and organize the records, while Overdrive led the loan officer on a tour of the farm.

Overdrive had envisioned a quick walk-through of the farm buildings and drive-through of the lands at the homeplace, Lemke's, Adcock's, and Ulbricht's, following by an even quicker driving tour of the rented lands. Rain was coming and he was itching to wrap-up the tour in an hour or two, to get over to Hank's and bale hay. He knew by heart the dimensions, sizes, capacities, acres, and so on, of everything he owned and rented, and presumed these would just be scribbled down by the loan officer as he rattled them off. He presumed wrong.

The loan officer's style was methodical, and involved a clip board, the taking of copious notes, and independent verification of everything. Overdrive told him the number of stanchions in the barn, but he counted them anyway. Told the size of the electrical service, he nonetheless opened the box and tallied the amperes himself. Told the height of the silos, he actually climbed to the top, clamped a weight to the end of his tape measure, and dropped it to the ground. And so on.

Finally, after what seemed to Overdrive like an eternity, the pace began to move along more quickly. Whether this'd been due to Overdrive being accurate 100 percent of the time, or lunchtime rapidly approaching, Overdrive wasn't sure and didn't care. It'd been 1:30 PM, by the time he'd unloaded the loan officer onto Mary, and raced to Hank's to start baling.

With the storm looming and four empty wagons to fill, Overdrive let it rip. To be saved, the hay would have to not only be baled but also unloaded, because the tarps had shredded during the previous storm, and the haymows were all too full to allow wagons to be backed in for shelter. Old Bill hauled the first wagon home and unloaded as quickly as he could alone, but when the boys got home from school, the family really started to kickass. At milking time, Jumbo took over on the baler so Overdrive could join Mary and milk the herd.

By the time the baling was done and last wagon emptied, it'd been after dark and Overdrive had been helping for an hour after finishing with the herd. Everyone was beyond exhausted. As they staggered around the barn toward the house, it began to sprinkle. The boys raced ahead and only got half-soaked, but Overdrive stuck to a pace that his Dad could sustain, and the two of them arrived drenched. In the mudroom, men and boys silently struggled out of wet work boots and clothes, toweled off, and pulled on whatever was handy so long as it was clean and dry. As the aroma of hot apple pie seeped in from the kitchen, you could literally hear their spirits rise by the telltale chatter. When the kitchen door was opened, a boisterous din erupted. Before them sat helpings of pie and ice cream on the table, with Mary and the girls smiling in the background. Overdrive and Mary locked eyes across the room, smiled, nodded, and enjoyed the scene.

✳ ✳ ✳

Alone at last after saying their good-byes to Old Bill and shooing the kids out of the kitchen, Mary dialed Ted. Just like the previous night, Ted picked up on the first ring. Overdrive unloaded about having to waste time handholding the nitpicky farm loan officer, which snowballed into the entire family having to work late to get the hay in before the storm. Concerning the time spent, Ted offered an alternate interpretation. To him, the loan officer's thoroughness was good news. It proved that Oostburg Bank was looking very seriously into the opportunity of doing business with them. After some back and forth, Overdrive calmed and Ted shared what he'd learned from the Bureau of Indian Affairs.

244 | PATRICK J. HUGHES

In a nutshell, the BIA told Ted that no new federal Indian reservations were being created anywhere in the country. Official BIA policy was still driven by House Concurrent Resolution 108, enacted in 1953, which created goals for terminating reservations and relocating populations to urban areas. Relocations were supposed to include job training and housing assistance, but Congress never funded those. Wisconsin tribal members who opted for this only received one-way bus tickets to Chicago, Milwaukee, or St. Paul. Needless to say, losing tribal status and lands in exchange for bus tickets didn't go over well. 50 tribes nationally lost federal recognition, the Menominee in Wisconsin among them.

Apparently, the bruhaha convinced the tribes they needed effective political advocacy at the national level. They began joining the sleepy National Congress of American Indians, formed in 1944, in droves. All of a sudden, the NCAI wasn't sleepy any more. They pressured the government to halt the termination process, and by about 1960 it ended, at least unofficially. Many of the tribes are now fighting to have their federal status reinstated.

Ted joked that once the BIA rep got rolling, it was hard to shut him up. In his view, the 1953 law had over reached, and caused a backlash. Younger American Indians began branding their elders as sellouts, and calling for greater militancy to regain full treaty, hunting, and fishing rights. These youngsters, mostly college kids or recent grads, formed the National Indian Youth Council in 1961. Since then the world has been going to hell in a handbasket, with fish-ins and protest marches springing up all over the place.

Meanwhile, tribal elders continued to push their political agenda on Capitol Hill. In the view of the tribes, working their way out of poverty would require retained or restored federal tribal recognition and reservations, and the right to form tribal governments, draft constitutions, reassert their sovereign rights, and develop enterprises to sustain themselves. In other words, roll back federal policy set in 1953 to what it'd been under the Indian Reorganization Act of 1934.

The tribes scored a success by qualifying for assistance under the Economic Opportunity Act, better known as LBJ's War on Poverty, which just became effective in August. Now they're eligible for youth programs, community action programs, small business loan programs, and whatnot. According to the BIA rep, the Act gives the Office of Economic Opportunity or OEO, the right to stick their noses into BIA business. He described OEO as a bunch of commies, so apparently there's no love lost between OEO and BIA.

Gaming continues to be illegal on federal Indian reservations, at least as far as the BIA was concerned. But Congress never funded anti-gaming enforcement, per se, so it's likely that some is going on. The legalization of gaming is known to be a top priority of the NCAI, but no such legislation has gotten out of Congress yet. Just last month an NCAI delegation had come to BIA, and advocated that BIA sponsor the legislation, but BIA had refused. He doubted the War on Poverty had authorized the OEO to allow gaming on reservations, but BIA being out of that loop, and OEO being a bunch of commies, he wasn't entirely sure.

While venting, the BIA rep happened to mention state-authorized reservations, so Ted had peppered him with questions to learn more. Apparently, state-authorized reservations are lands held in trust by the states for American Indian tribes. With state trust lands, title is held by the state on behalf of the tribe, and generally the lands are subject to state law but not subject to local property taxes. The federal government and the BIA have no say over what's done on state-authorized reservations.

What Ted had learned left him with two urgent priorities. First, find out whether the newly-minted Economic Opportunity Act somehow enabled OEO to foster gaming on federal Indian reservations. Second, find out whether Wisconsin-authorized Indian reservations existed, and if so, whether state law allowed gaming on them. He figured these efforts may take a few days to a week. In the meantime, he urged Overdrive to speak with Lage, Salveson, and Nitsch and get the stories behind them selling out to HMR, and defer the next call until after he'd done so.

* * *

The next morning during milking, Overdrive and Mary discussed options for getting the rest of the crops in. They'd never run this much land before, and with only them and Old Bill around five days a week, the way forward was unclear. Mary wanted to be left out of the remaining field work, to keep up with the orchard and garden. This narrowed Overdrive's options, and he reluctantly settled on letting his Dad green chop fifth-cutting hay for the milk herd, now that the cannery's husk waste had run out, and the sweet corn stalks had all been chopped.

Letting his father green chop freed Overdrive to cut with the Owatonna, so the hay harvest could be finished over the weekend when the boys were home. All the haymows in all the barns were already packed to the roof, except the one in the new barn addition. After last night's unloading frenzy, there's still some room in the mow, but it's getting near the top. From now on, unloading wagons will require a relay line of boys up in the mow. If all went well, chopping field corn to silage, and blowing it into the silos could start next week. With the self-unloading wagons, Overdrive and his Dad could move the silage harvest along at a nice pace during the week, and they'd kickass on the weekends. For the ear corn harvest, they'd better get on the schedule of one of the custom corn pickers that served the area now, because those boys booked up fast.

When milking was done, Mary went to the house to fix breakfast, and Overdrive reviewed his harvest thinking while cleaning the milking machines. They'd invited Old Bill for breakfast to discuss workload, and as Overdrive was walking from the barn to the house, Old Bill drove into the yard. They greeted each other, and walked in together. Over breakfast, the three of them got on the same page about how the rest of the crops would be harvested. Then Mary got busy with her apples, and Overdrive and Old Bill ruminated over how to approach Lage, Salveson, and Nitsch about their HMR buyouts. Calling another farmer in advance to schedule a chat would raise suspicions, so they decided to just drop in on them in the evenings after milking. The farmers wouldn't necessarily be home or available, but that's a chance they'd have to take.

* * *

A week had passed before Overdrive and Old Bill successfully completed conversations with Lage, Salveson, and Nitsch. Visiting these farmers was an unusual occurrence, but not unheard of. To allay suspicions, they said they're using the short breather between haying and silo filling to see how the farming business was going for others in the area. They knew farmers were generally flattered when approached by peers for advice and wisdom.

Overdrive and Old Bill had known these farmers for decades, and the conversations came easily. Lage had taken a part-time job with the county highway department a few years back. He continued a scaled back dairy operation until about three months ago, when he used Gib Buyer to broker the sale of his remaining livestock. About a month later, he sold all the land except for one acre where the house, barn, and out-buildings are located. Now he's working for the county full time. His advice was to get out of farming to enjoy life while you can.

Lage kept one tractor and a few implements for gardening, mowing, and puttering around on his one acre. Everything else still serviceable had been sold to local farm implement dealers. Since he'd stopped updating his machinery over a decade ago, most of it was junk, and still sat in the shed. But Lage claimed great success in selling it, piece by piece, to flatlanders moving into the area and buying up old farm houses. Apparently, they use that shit for lawn ornaments.

Salveson said he sold his farm, house and buildings included, about three months ago. The deal allowed him to continue farm operations until the first of November, for an orderly exit. He didn't need to vacate until the end of December. He bred back his best livestock and Gib Buyer is in the process of negotiating their sale. The rest he'll sell by the pound down at the Milwaukee livestock market.

Salveson's advice was to sell out and move north. He and his wife had always joked about how this part of Wisconsin was too hot and humid. They planned to retire and flee the heat. They're looking forward to living in a cabin on a lake near the border with Upper Michigan, where snow, ice, blizzards, frost bite, and whatnot can be enjoyed more months of the year. After hearing the tale, Overdrive and Old Bill eyed each other and backed out quickly, for fear the delirium was contagious. Fucking Norwegians.

Nitsch also sold out about three months ago. He kept several acres including the house, farm buildings, and an area with limestone springs where he'd developed a few trout ponds. Nitsch's livestock were long gone. He already worked fulltime for a farm implement dealer, and planned to do so until retirement. As a side business and hobby, he planned to open the ponds to the public, making them a place where parents could bring their kids to fish. His advice was there's more to life than working on a dairy farm 24/7.

Lage, Salveson, and Nitsch had all been thinking about getting out of dairy farming. In every case, their kids had finished high school and decided to move on with their lives, to something else. None of them had been in any particular hurry to sell their lands, but they all seized the opportunities when a man from HMR came around with unsolicited offers. In every case, accepting was an easy means to an end, which probably explained why none of them bothered to dicker on price. To hear them tell it, they knew what they wanted to do with the rest of their lives, and what was offered was enough to make that happen. As innocently as possible, Overdrive had asked all three farmers if they'd ever seen a fancy dark late-model car in the area, driven by a women way overdressed for farming. Sure enough, they'd all seen the car and noticed the women, about a month or so prior to HMR showing up on their doorsteps. When asked, the farmers didn't really know or care what HMR's plans were, and only Lage would hazard a guess. He thought maybe they planned to establish some kind of private trout fishing and pheasant hunting preserve. The tillable land was interspersed with wetlands and the channel of Nichols Creek, which sprung from multiple limestone springs, including Nitsch's. The segment of the creek that meandered through these farms was loaded with native brook trout, and the adjacent wetlands were filthy with pheasants.

* * *

It's Monday morning, haying for the year was finally over except for green chopping, and Overdrive was pumped about today's start of silo filling. But as Overdrive and Mary were finishing breakfast, they got a surprise call from Peter Nyenhuis, the President of Oostburg Bank. Peter was gracious to a fault and apologized profusely for the short notice, but he wondered if it'd be too much trouble to give him a tour of the

farm today. While touring, he'd like his farm loan officer to spend a little more time looking over the books.
Being their last hope and all, Overdrive wasn't really in
a position to say no.

A half-hour later, the bankers drove in while Overdrive was greasing the corn chopper. Mary waved them
into the house, and fresh coffee was waiting on the
kitchen table. After exchanging pleasantries, Peter got
right to the point. He'd checked with Ted, and was
aware that Rachel Wolf's involvement in HMR couldn't
yet be proven. He also knew his board members, and
understood how conservative they were. After con-
ducting his own detailed review of the draft loan application, Peter believed he'd have to personally advocate
for the loan, for it to have any chance of approval. This
he couldn't do in good conscience, without seeing the
farm firsthand and having his loan officer take another
look at the books. He hoped no offense would be taken,
but it is what it is.

Peter wanted to personally verify the answers to
a list of questions, and rattled them off in case knowing them influenced where they went on the tour. Was
the barn addition completed and fully functional? Was
the milk herd large enough to fill the newly expanded
barn? Was the bulk milk cooler large enough to accommodate the expanded herd? Were the haymows
in the original barn and barn addition full? Were the
haymows in the heifer barns full? And so on. When
the questions ended, Overdrive and Mary caught each
other's eye and heaved a big sigh of relief. They knew
the answer to every question was yes.

Overdrive and Peter rose and headed outside for
the tour, while Mary stayed behind and worked with

the loan officer. Reading people wasn't Overdrive's forte, but even he noticed that Peter became more relaxed as he was taken around the farm. Part way through the tour, he literally began to gush with enthusiasm. ... *Without seeing for myself, I never would've believed there'd be so much excess hay to sell.* ... *Wow, you'll have to cull almost 20 cows to squeeze the herd into the expanded barn.* ... And so on.

Mary caught Overdrive's eye as he and Peter came back into the kitchen, laughing and joking. Overdrive winked to let her know that all was well. As they had a seat at the table, the loan officer indicated that he'd seen everything he needed to see. The last milk check, the check book log, the most recent milk tester report, and so on, were all consistent with what he'd been told previously, and everything seemed to be in order.

It was lunch time, so Mary served up more fresh coffee, tuna fish sandwiches, and apple kuchen for dessert. As lunch wrapped up, Peter again apologized for the unusual scrutiny. He said they'd earned his vote and in 10 days when the board met, he'd fight as hard as he could to get their loan approved. As everyone said their good-byes, Overdrive and Mary could tell Peter wished he could promise that the board would decide in their favor, but he just couldn't. He clearly still wasn't sure how it would go, without proof that Rachel Wolf was behind HMR.

CHAPTER 18

The Swindle Revealed

L ater, on the day of Peter's visit, Ted Ritter's office phoned to say that Ted was out of town for several days, so he'd need to initiate the next call. His office promised to give them a heads-up in the afternoon, on the day Ted would call in the evening. Overdrive and Mary were aghast that Ted would travel during their time of greatest need. During the days they fought off the worry by working harder, but at night sleep was becoming more and more difficult.

Two days later Ted's office called, and that evening after milking Mary made the kids a pan of fudge to enjoy while watching TV or doing homework, and Overdrive shooed them out of the kitchen and closed the door. A few moments later the phone rang, and Overdrive and Mary picked up simultaneously on the first ring. After hurriedly exchanging pleasantries, Ted spent a moment assuaging his client's anxieties by reassuring them that the need to travel was driven solely by their case. Before getting into how that was so, Ted wanted to know if anything interesting had been learned from Lage, Salveson, and Nitsch. After Overdrive filled him in, Ted didn't try to hide his disappointment. He'd hoped that HMR had somehow wronged these additional parties, which would've made Overdrive and Mary's case stronger in the event they ended up in court. That they all saw Rachel Wolf's distinctive car in the area shortly before HMR came calling was interesting, but not exactly incriminating.

Overdrive also told Ted about the Peter Nyenhuis surprise visit. Ted felt Peter's desire to see the farm firsthand was reasonable, and him caring enough to bother was good news. No surprise either, was Peter's continued uncertainty over loan outcome, without proof connecting Rachel Wolf to HMR. In case the proof angle failed, they all promised to think on how else to buck up the loan application.

When his turn came, Ted opened a firehose of new information onto Overdrive and Mary. The federal Office of Economic Opportunity or OEO, was still in the throes of establishing itself, and hadn't done anything to foster gaming on federal Indian reservations. In fact, there'd been no discussion on the topic whatsoever. The head of OEO didn't want to dismiss the possibility in the future, but it currently wasn't a priority. In other words, OEO was a dead end.

Next, Ted had called his local state rep, who happened to be a good friend. When he asked about Wisconsin-authorized Indian reservations, Ted expected a referral to some seldom seen bureaucrat relegated to a dank and moldy corner of the state's oldest office building. Instead, as a member of the Appropriations Committee in the Wisconsin State Legislature, his friend knew all about it.

Wisconsin's fiscal year runs July through the following June. The appropriations bill to fund the state for the current year was signed into law by the Governor in June, and became effective the first of July. It included an amendment sponsored by the State of Wisconsin's Conservation Commission, which authorized the State to accept donated lands and hold them in trust as reservations for American Indian tribes dwelling in Wisconsin. The amendment also made gaming operations on these state-authorized reservations legal.

Ted had been shocked by this news, and the quickest way to get his hands on a copy of the statute was to drive to Madison, so that's what he did. Since arriving, Ted had read the statute, and has been using his friend, the state rep, to understand the context of how such a thing came to be, and meet the people involved. As it turned out, the Conservation Commission directs the Wisconsin Conservation Department. Every year an event known as the Conservation Convention was held, to gather public input on how best to run the Department. In recent years, citizens had been complaining about the deleterious effect the tribes were having on the state's game and fisheries. The Commission wasn't eager to take on the tribes, but had no choice as the agitation grew more visible in the media, and politically embarrassing. In 1963 they formed a committee to look into the matter.

The committee found that the tribes freely admitted to poaching outside their reservations, and ignoring state fish and game laws while doing so. The tribes were destitute due to federal mismanagement, and claimed their actions were required for survival, and would continue until other means of sustenance were secured. They were unanimous in their belief that gaming on their reservations would enable them to live within the cash economy, and stop poaching. Apparently, the committee agreed. Their recommendation, draft legislation and narrative rationale in report-form, was delivered to the Commission in March. Only today had Ted succeeded in securing a copy, which he'd skimmed but planned to thoroughly study later in his hotel room. According to Ted's friend, the Commission had been overjoyed with the recommendation, which was viewed as win-win for conservationists, the tribes, businessmen, and other stakeholders. They went straight to the Governor, and on his authority, the legislative language was lifted from the report and inserted verbatim into the must-pass appropriations bill. As of the first of July, it's the law of the land in Wisconsin.

Ted did his best to summarize for Overdrive and Mary, what it all meant in plain English. Article IV, Section 24 of the Wisconsin Constitution stipulates that "the legislature shall never authorize any lottery..." The Wisconsin Supreme Court had always interpreted this to mean that all forms of gambling were illegal in Wisconsin. The new law declared that the Constitution was never intended to, and does not now, exclude all gambling. Specifically, it does not exclude gaming on Wisconsin-authorized Indian reservations, defined as lands held in trust by the State of Wisconsin as reservations for tribes dwelling in the state.

The Wisconsin Conservation Department's existing statutory authority to acquire lands and establish refuges was expanded under the new law, to include acquisition of lands to be held in trust by the state as reservations, provided that certain conditions were met. First, the lands acquired must be donated to the state. Second, the donor may designate the tribe for whom the lands will be held in trust, however, only federally-recognized tribes currently dwelling in Wisconsin qualify. Third, the tribe must make an annual payment in lieu of real estate taxes, so local taxing authorities maintain property tax revenue neutrality.

Ted found it interesting that the new law even directed how gaming on state-authorized reservations would be regulated. It granted new authority to the Wisconsin Department of Administration, to protect the integrity of gaming on Wisconsin-authorized Indian reservations. The law stipulated a number of regulatory requirements. First, the Department shall negotiate and sign a gaming compact with each tribe before they commence gaming operations, to set forth the rules, regulations and conditions for gaming. Second, the Department shall establish an Office of Gaming Compliance to ensure effective concurrent regulation by both the state and the tribes of the gaming operations. Third, gaming compliance oversight shall ensure Wisconsin citizen clients of, or vendors to, the tribal gaming operations are fairly treated.

Ted's friend helped him schedule several morning and early afternoon meetings tomorrow, where he'll learn more about how the new law came into being and status of implementation. Among them is a meeting with the member of the Conservation Commission, who'd served as chair of the committee that drafted the legislation and report. Another meeting is with the head of the Conservation Department's Real Estate Program, which is now responsible for acquiring donated lands to hold in trust for reservations. The third meeting is with the head of the Department of Administration's newly formed Office of Gaming Compliance, which is responsible for regulating tribal gaming operations. As the phone call wrapped up, Ted said he'd be driving back to Random Lake late tomorrow afternoon. By then, Ted felt he'd have a wealth of new information that would be difficult to explain over the phone. So, they made plans to meet in person at his office tomorrow evening, after milking. Ted asked Overdrive and Mary to call Darkwater beforehand, and find out who authorized the current gambling on the Forest County reservation, and the dates of any tribal council meetings over the next ten days before the bank board met.

* * *

When Overdrive and Mary arrived at his office the following evening, Ted gave them a warm welcome but the strain was beginning to show on all their faces. Ted had fresh coffee waiting on the conference room table, along with a plate of coconut chocolate chip bars from his wife. After taking their seats, Ted asked what they'd learned from Darkwater.

Overdrive relayed that the current Potawatomi gambling wasn't authorized by anyone. It's a federal reservation, which keeps the state and local authorities at bay. Although the Bureau of Indian Affairs could shut them down, the tribe had stoolies at BIA for advance warning of any raids, and a plan in the event of one. Basically, they'd shoo their clientele away, shutdown the operation, and hide the gear. It'd only happened twice, and they'd never been caught. As for tribal council, they'd meet once more before the bank board met. Three days prior.

When Overdrive finished, Ted opened up another firehose of new information. The Conservation Commission's committee had been comprised of one commissioner, four academics from the University of Wisconsin-Madison, and one rep each from the business, banking, agriculture, and conservationist communities. The committee's makeup was a pretty good example of the Wisconsin Idea, a term used to describe the participation of academics in the state's policymaking process. The notion was to bring the knowledge and inspiration of the university more fully into the service of the citizens of the state, by appointing professorial subject matter experts to committees such as this one.

The committee interviewed reps from every federally-recognized tribe in the state, and every reservation was visited. This led to additional interviews with reps of the BIA and several tribes in adjacent states. The academics on the committee followed that up with historical research, which led to the committee's final report including an excellent summary of federal mismanagement of the tribes since the late 1800s. Ted hit the highlights to help Overdrive and Mary understand why the new law happened so quickly.

In 1887, Congress passed the Dawes Act, which changed the ownership of tribal lands to individual ownership of eighty-acre parcels. In Wisconsin, the net result was a giant land grab. After each tribal member received their parcel of worthless rocky soil, the extra land was sold to whites for hunting lodges and fishing camps. As an example, the Ojibwe or Chippewa of Wisconsin, lost more than 40 percent of their reservation lands. Over the next four decades, federal policy regarding the tribes was one of assimilation. The federal government created schools that attempted to rid tribal peoples of their cultural traditions and ways of life, by breaking tribal ties and molding them into the image of white settlers. In Wisconsin, such schools were established at Keshena, Oneida, Lac du Flambeau, Tomah, and elsewhere.

After assimilation failed, Congress passed the Indian Reorganization Act in 1934. This essentially reversed the Dawes Act, and encouraged tribes to form tribal governments, draft constitutions, and reassert their sovereign rights. The change of heart didn't last long. As the Great Depression lingered, advocates for dismantling the reservation system and freeing the federal government from the cost of protecting the tribes and their property gained ground.

Finally, in 1953, Congress passed House Concurrent Resolution 108, which created goals of "termination and relocation." Ted noted that the report dovetails with what he'd been told previously by BIA. The law was supposed to move tribal populations from rural reservations to urban areas through job training programs and housing assistance. But Congress never funded it and one-way bus tickets failed to pass the laugh test with most tribe members.

The committee's field trips to the reservations

revealed abject poverty everywhere, making it understandable why abiding by Wisconsin fish and game laws wasn't a high priority. The tribes believed that gaming on their reservations would enable them to work their way out of poverty. Given the context, and unable to come up with any better ideas, the committee conducted a deep dive study on the gaming suggestion and it proved to be solid.

Ted was impressed by the strength of the narrative arguments in support of the draft legislation. The Professor of Economics estimated substantial net economic benefits to Wisconsin for providing in-state gambling alternatives, which would reverse the state's current large net outflow of gambling dollars, and raise in-state tribal standards of living. The Professor of American Indian Studies documented the current socioeconomic plight of the state's tribes, and outside of gaming, the dearth of opportunities for improvement. The Professor of Zoology and Limnology explained the catastrophic impact of over-harvesting fish on the state's fisheries, and identified the many areas around the state where tribal pressure was exacerbating the problem. Likewise, the Professor of Wildlife Ecology painted a dire future for bear, deer, pheasant, rabbit, squirrel, and other game populations, unless tribal hunting pressures could be relieved.

For their part, the leaders of every tribe signed a letter appended to the report, declaring that once gaming operations enabled sustenance within the cash economy, their members would thereafter abide by the state's fish and game laws whenever they ventured outside of their reservations.

When his monologue was finished, Ted paused to

give Overdrive and Mary a chance to take it all in. Then, Overdrive said, "This isn't going away, is it?"

Ted shook his head, "No, James. I don't think so."

Mary said, "But gambling has always been illegal in Wisconsin, hasn't it it?"

Ted nodded, and said, "Yes, up to now the Wisconsin Supreme Court has always interpreted the Wisconsin Constitution to mean no gambling, period. But in this new law, the legislature declares otherwise."

In a meek and wavering voice, Mary said, "But isn't it possible that this'll be overturned? I mean, doesn't the Supreme Court have the final say?"

Ted tilted his head from side to side, and said, "Yes and no. Theoretically they do. I asked my state rep friend the same question. He said during floor debate, some concerns were raised over whether the law would be upheld in the courts, if challenged. But these concerns were dismissed."

Downtrodden, Mary said, "But why?"

Ted pursed his lips, and said, "Well, no member could think of a harmed party that'd be motivated enough to finance a court challenge. The conservationist, business, banking, and ag communities were all for it. Even the Catholics saw it as a way to finally get bingo and raffles."

Overdrive, in a voice of scorn, "Well, shit. Where're all those busy bodies when you need them."

Ted nodded, and said, "I hear you, James. The state's more prudish constituents might put up a fuss, but on what grounds? The law doesn't require them to go to a reservation and gamble. And they don't have the political swing they used to. Most folks just wish they'd mind their own business."

Overdrive, solemnly, "Okay, it isn't going away. Where does that leave us?"

Ted took a deep breath and shook his head, "Well, the head of the Real Estate Program at the Conservation Department told me that he'd already been called on by the Potawatomi and Development Partners. The head of the Office of Gaming Compliance at the Department of Administration told me the same thing."

Mary snapped, "W-w-what?"

Overdrive, in a low-pitched growl, "You have got to be shitting me!"

Ted hunched his shoulders and leaned into the table, "Both were told that the Potawatomi and DP would be coming back in October, with lands ready to donate, and draft language for a gaming compact."

Mary closed her eyes, put her hands together, and said, "Oh, god help us!"

Overdrive winced, and spat out, "Those fuckers!"

Ted rolled his shoulders back, and said, "I also spoke with the member of the Conservation Commission, who'd served as chair of the committee. He told me the rep for the banking community had been Rachel Wolf."

Mary gasped, and Overdrive beat the table with his fist, and said, "That's not funny, Ted! Is this some kind of a sick joke?"

Ted stared at him a moment, then said, "I wish it were, James, but it isn't."

Mary, in panic mode, "What're we going to do?"

Ted eyed them both, and said in a calm voice, "We secure a loan from Oostburg Bank and payoff HMR."

A heated discussion followed. Overdrive and Mary couldn't understand why, out of all the bankers in the State of Wisconsin, Rachel Wolf had been named to the committee. Why her? Ted had asked the committee Chair the same question. He said she was a logical choice. She's politically-connected, and in control of a large regional bank whose service area overlaps some of the tribal lands. She'd been invited to participate, and was happy to serve. He'd no way of knowing about Rachel, and the family she came from, and still doesn't. But inadvertently or not, he put a fox in the henhouse. Had she not been named to the committee, none of this would've happened. It's unfortunate, but it is what it is.

The new information helped connect some of the dots, but Ted still couldn't prove that Rachel Wolf was behind HMR. She hadn't been the DP rep that accompanied the Potawatomi on their visits to the two state agencies. She hadn't been the HMR rep that bought the Lage, Salveson, and Nitsch farms. Rachel had been very clever, pulling all the strings from behind the scenes. Ted could tell the bank a few new things. For instance, the more profitable use of the farm that HMR had in mind, was a casino. Also, having traced the shell corporations and by monitoring tribal council, he could now positively connect the Potawatomi to DP and HMR. But he still couldn't connect Rachel Wolf to any of them.

The discussion turned to what else, if anything, could be done before the bank board met in seven days. Ted took out a notepad and sketched a timeline. Four days out, tribal council. Seven days out, bank board meeting. 12 days out, earliest they'd have an Oostburg Bank cashier's check if the loan's approved, due to bank processing time and the weekend. 14 days out, earliest HMR could be paid off with certainty by use of a courier service with guarantee. 17 days out, if not paid off by then, the farm transfers to HMR. 18 days out, the first day of October. 34 days out, the first tribal council meeting after HMR has the farm. 48 days out, the last day of October.

After kicking these dates around, something occurred to Ted. The Potawatomi and DP reps had told the state agencies they'd be back in October, which is 18 to 48 days out. But the earliest opportunity to secure tribal council approval of the HMR location, would be 34 days out. Presuming both agencies could be scheduled on the last day of October, this left at most 14 calendar days to complete all the legal work to donate the land, develop gaming compact language, develop presentations, travel to Madison, and so on. This'd be almost impossible.

Ted concentrated, and tried to put himself into DP's shoes. The agency deals would require trail-breaking thought. By comparison, the tribal approval was easy. You'd want more prep time for the agency deals, surely. Without a doubt, DP would much prefer to secure tribal council approval at the next meeting, which is four days out, to buy more time for agency deal prep. But there's a problem. The earliest that HMR can seize the farm is 17 days out.

You wouldn't want to seek tribal approval for the HMR location, before controlling all the HMR lands, would you? Wait a minute, why not? If the tribe approved and then the deal fell through, so what? It happens all the time. Getting that approval is a small investment. But if you're very confident that you'll own all the land by the time it's needed, why not get that approval out of the way? If you did, it'd create more calendar time to prep for the all-important agency meetings. Prepping for the agency meetings is a BIG investment. So big that you'd want tribal approval in the bag before pulling that trigger.

Next, Ted thought about what it'd be like to be in the Potawatomi's shoes. They'd met Rachel Wolf because she'd participated in the committee's fact-finding tours. She'd have established personal relationships with the elders. The elders may even attribute the passage of the new law to her, in some way. The point is, there'd be no need for Rachel Wolf to hide her identity from them. If you're a tribe being peppered with inquiries from unsavory types about teaming to establish a casino, wouldn't you rather team with someone you already know?

Ted followed this line of reasoning to its natural conclusion. When DP seeks tribal approval, there's a chance they'd drop Rachel's name to help seal the deal, or maybe even have her there in person. But even if they didn't, at the very least DP would feel comfortable talking openly about her. If Darkwater asked enough leading questions, there's a good chance he'd get Rachel's name mentioned publicly in association with DP and HMR, and that's all they'd need. Somehow motivating DP to seek tribal approval in four days, might be the best and last hope of exposing Rachel Wolf as the brains behind HMR, before the bank board meets.

After this epiphany, the discussion turned to what, if anything, could be done to motivate DP. In a short while, Ted had a plan that the three of them felt good about. Using blank stationary rather than letterhead, Ted typed out a letter from Overdrive and Mary to HMR, and had them sign it. Paraphrasing, the letter said full payoff by the deadline was impossible, but if HMR waived its march-in rights and allowed Overdrive and Mary to continue to operate the farm, they'd negotiate in good faith and arrive at an additional amount of compensation for HMR. If DP hadn't already been planning to seek tribal approval in four days, broadcasting the default should push them over the edge to do so. Ted would arrange to have the letter delivered by courier tomorrow.

With that done, the discussion turned to the instructions Darkwater would need in advance of tribal council. Presuming they showed up, Ted figured DP would circulate a document, called a prospectus, describing the HMR lands before and after casino development. They'd also likely make a presentation highlighting the benefits to the tribe, hand out hardcopies, and field questions. If Darkwater sat near the front, he'd be in a good position to nab the paper before it ran out, tape record the meeting, and snap pictures. They'd need photos of the DP reps together with tribal elders, and if they were lucky, Rachel Wolf would be among them.

If Rachel Wolf wasn't present or mentioned, Darkwater's job became much more difficult. He'd need to ask questions, in an effort to motivate either the DP reps or tribal elders to publicly reveal Rachel Wolf's involvement and get that on tape. Ted promised to put some thought into it, and gin up some questions that'd come across innocently, yet tease out what they wanted to hear.

With Darkwater's tasks resolved, discussion turned to the next challenge, which was how to get the materials gathered in Wabeno to Ted in time for the bank board meeting. The U.S. Postal Service maybe would work, but to be safe they decided to hire a courier service. The roundtrip from Random Lake and back was approximately an eight-hour drive, so the courier would have plenty of time. Even so, breakdowns and accidents do happen, and the farm was on the line. Ted pushed for paying extra for the courier service's guarantee, which they backed with their own statewide road service network, and Overdrive and Mary agreed.

After everything was thought through, Ted dialed Darkwater with Overdrive and Mary on the line. Ted filled him in on what they hoped would happen at tribal council, and what they needed him to do. Darkwater assured them he'd be up to the task, and said he owned a reliable Polaroid camera for taking snapshots of his client's trophies, but not a tape recorder. To solve that problem, Ted promised to have his office call tomorrow with the details on what recorder to buy, and where to find one nearby. They'd reimburse Darkwater later.

The way it was left, no matter what happened at tribal council, Darkwater would call Ted's office, collect, immediately following the meeting. The courier service would be standing by, and if it's a go, they'd retrieve the materials from Darkwater and have them back to Ted's office the following day. For the rendezvous point, Darkwater proposed a public and easily found location in Wabeno, and Ted jotted it down. At the end of the call, Overdrive and Mary heaped their heart-felt appreciation onto Darkwater for going to all this trouble on their behalf, Darkwater joked he'd dream up a suitable quid pro quo, and Ted chimed in that the courier would bring cash for the tape recorder.

* * *

When they hit the sack that night, Overdrive's mind was churning at warp speed. Sleep came quickly to Mary, and he was thankful for that. As he watched her, tears welled up in his eyes as he thought of how hard she'd fought to save the farm, how hard the entire family had fought. He was proud of them all. He wondered how a righteous god could possibly let them fail, after all they'd done and been through. They'd done everything they possibly could've thus far. But unfortunately, Overdrive still had the sinking feeling that it wasn't enough. With 13 days gone since the HMR letter arrived, only 17 remained before either the Oostburg Bank loan came through or they're left homeless. It seemed so unreal.

The thought that his worries would be over, if only they could prove Rachel Wolf was behind HMR, gave Overdrive little comfort. He didn't doubt that Ted had left no stone unturned, but after months of digging he'd gotten nowhere while she'd run wild with political connections, committee appointments, tribal elder relationships, shell corporations, self-serving new legislation, and whatnot. Now, in the 11th hour, they had one last chance. But it's in the hands of Ted and Darkwater, and beyond his control. Overdrive felt powerless and resented that the things he could control, didn't seem to matter anymore. Here he was, on the brink of his own life's most defining moment, and what he did between now and then didn't matter. That's not right. There must be something he could do. Overdrive pondered Lage, Salveson, and Nitsch for a moment. Good grief, he and Mary used to square dance and play sheepshead with these people. HMR had come into his own back yard and vacuumed them up, and he hadn't even known about it. At first, he'd written them off as fools for accepting below-market prices for their farms. But who's the fool now? If we're forced off the farm in 17 days, we'll get nothing plus lose all our personal property if it isn't cleared out by then. The thought sickened Overdrive with disgust and anger.

Overdrive went around and around like this for most of the night. He hadn't a clue why beating himself up made him feel better, but it did. Overdrive accepted that he may go down, but if so, he planned to go down fighting. All of this was way beyond his experience and, yes, working harder wouldn't save his farm. But there'd be no harm in it either, so that's what he planned to do. Over the next 17 days, goddammit, he's got a farm to run.

Overdrive also decided to enlist his Dad, and bring the ancestors into the fight one last time. There must be some other way to leverage the assets of the farm and raise cash, and the ancestors might help him see it. With another source of cash, the farm may be attractive enough for Oostburg Bank to step in, whether or not there's proof for the bank of a revenge play against Rachel Wolf.

CHAPTER 19

Last Gasp Maneuvers

Overdrive threw himself into silo filling. Between milking's, weather permitting, the spent his time on the John Deere 4020, pulling the two-row chopper as it spewed chopped field corn, stalks and ears and all, into a self-unloading wagon. He pushed his machinery to the limit, using the chopper's sound to tell whether it could handle greater throughput or was about to clog, and tapping the tractor's speed-control lever up or down a notch, accordingly.

The job of hauling and unloading the wagons fell to Old Bill during the week, and Jumbo or Joe on the weekends. It didn't matter who did the unloading, they couldn't keep up with Overdrive. When he broke for supper and milking, all the wagons were generally full and needed to be unloaded during milking, to be ready for the next day. Every night after milking, Overdrive put a newly sharpened cutter bar into the chopper, and readied the one he'd just pulled out for future use.

In a normal year, silo filling was among Overdrive's greatest joys. When the sky was blue and the day bright and sunny, the fall colors literally leapt from the maple trees into your eyes. The air was always fresh and crisp. He found the pungent smell of chopped field corn pleasing. He enjoyed watching the pheasants, rabbits, and deer flee his corn as the whine of the chopper neared. But this wasn't a normal year. In 16 days, HMR would force Overdrive and his family off their farm unless the loan came through. The tribal council meeting, the last hope of connecting Rachel Wolf to HMR, was three days out. The bank board meeting that'd decide whether they're still farmers or homeless vagrants, was six days out.

Rather than enjoying the fall, Overdrive used his chopping time in a desperate mental search for another way to raise cash from the farm. When weather forced them to shelter the herd in the barn for winter, he'd have excess milk cows to sell. There'd be large quantities of excess hay to sell, hopefully in late winter at peak price. What else? Overdrive's mental gymnastics came up empty, but tonight was the bridge with the Welsh ancestors, and his hopes rode on them.

* * *

That evening Overdrive and Mary arrived at Old Bill's shack, both weary of the burden they shared, and struggling to keep a flicker of hope alive. The ancestor-bridge ground rules had remained the same, living-side monitors weren't allowed to observe the ritual, so Mary waited outside until Overdrive waved her in.

After the bridge was open and everyone was settled, Old Bill asked Overdrive to begin feeding him concise narrative to update the ancestors on the farm loan situation. Revelation after revelation whipped the ancestors into a louder and louder frenzy. The HMR letter, the new state law, the Potawatomi connection, HMR's land grab for the reservation, and so on. Then they explained to the ancestors the reason for tonight's bridge. They needed ideas on other ways to raise cash from the farm. If efforts to prove Rachel Wolf is behind HMR fail, all hope rested on making the farm attractive enough to finance on its own merits. The milk check and selling excess cattle and hay may not be enough.

This question raised a holy hornet's nest of ancestral chatter that Old Bill had trouble keeping up with. He translated to English a series of possibilities suggested by the ancestors. But the initial ideas, such as to sell the replacement youngstock, and so on, would cripple the dairy operation and make the farm less attractive to finance not more so. Overdrive interrupted and had his father clarify this, which prompted an explosion of chatter to new heights. When it finally petered out, Old Bill's face lit up like a Christmas tree.

Old Bill smiled wryly, tapped a stubby index finger to his temple, and said, "Son, your grandpa, J.B., suggests you have a logging company appraise the standing timber on that 50-acre island of high woods in the Waldo Swamp."

Overdrive's mouth dropped open and eyebrows shot up, "Sonofabitch! Now that's an idea. Why didn't I think of that?"

Mary gasped, "What island of high woods?"

Too excited to sit, Overdrive sprung out of his chair and began to pace, "There's a high-woods out in the Waldo Swamp that's part of the farm. It's 50 acres of virgin timber. It's never been touched. Ever!"

Mary stood, and started to tear up, "Oh my god, James. Are you serious?"

Overdrive stepped over, pulled her into his arms, and nodded gently with his chin on top of her head, "Yes, Mary. It's ours and it's got to be worth a fortune. Grandpa, Dad, me. We'd all just sort of written it off. Its surrounded by marsh, and getting logs out of there may not even be possible."

Old Bill began speaking in Welsh, paused for chatter, spoke and paused again. When the chatter died down, his Welshman's wry smile returned, and Old Bill said, "Pain in the ass maybe, but the logs can be gotten out. Wait until hard freeze, harness up a good team of horses, and pull the logs over the ice and out onto your bottom lands. Any logging company can load and haul them from there."

Overdrive laughed, gave his wife a squeeze, and said, "Hey, I know how to drive a team. Never in a million years would I've guessed I'd do that again."

Old Bill slapped his son's back, "Don't forget my brother Hank still has his Percherons. The old softy couldn't bare parting with them when he quit farming, so he's been keeping them as pets ever since. About time they earned their keep."

Suddenly Overdrive felt overcome with gratitude. His eyes moistened and voice cracked, "You know, this might just do it. Might just be enough for the bank. I'd ... almost lost hope. Please thank Grandpa for us, Dad. Please thank them all."

Mary broke down and sobbed uncontrollably, and Overdrive pulled her in even tighter. Tears began flowing down his cheeks as well. Old Bill put an arm around each of them. From the chatter, Overdrive guessed that maybe the ancestors considered it their pleasure to do what they could, from wherever they are.

* * *

Energized by hope, the next morning while milking the cows, Overdrive's mind was racing. He mulled over the various ways of generating a credible timber estimate, eliminating methods that couldn't possibly be completed before the bank board met, five days out. As the milking activity progressed down the barn's aisle, Overdrive bounced his ideas off of Mary. By the time milking was finished, they had a plan that both were confident in. Fortunately, it's the weekend, and Jumbo's available. Right after breakfast, Overdrive and he would head to the Waldo Swamp, and Mary would begin scouring the yellow pages for logging outfits.

After learning the plan over breakfast, Jumbo changed into appropriate clothes, grabbed his chest waders, and met Overdrive at the cow car. By then, Overdrive had already loaded a spool of baling twine, three orange hunting vests, a sack of staple nails, bow saw, machete, and two hammers into the trunk. Both always carried jack knives, and today Overdrive also brought his compass.

With Overdrive at the wheel, the cow car headed around the barn and down the lane toward the swamp. While bouncing along, they discussed the need to find a path from the high woods to Overdrive's bottomlands, or strip of work land adjacent to the swamp. They needed a route shallow enough to wade.

Overdrive rolled to a stop as the lane crested the hill behind the barn. From this high vantage point, they could see the Waldo Swamp and the island of high woods within it. Unlike Overdrive, who considered hunting a frivolous use of time, Jumbo was an avid enthusiast. He knew the nearby wetlands and woods like the back of his hand because during fall, he spent every spare hour between Lizzie, school, football, chores, and harvests trudging around in them. Jumbo pointed out a landmark at the edge of the bottomlands for Overdrive to aim for. Entering the swamp there provided the shortest hike to the marsh.

When they arrived, both men hopped out and geared up. Jumbo wiggled into his waders. They both dropped hammers into the tool loops on their pants, and scooped handfuls of staple nails into accessible pockets. Jumbo led the way into the swamp, carrying the bow saw and machete. Overdrive pulled on all three hunting vests, one over the other, and carried the spool of twine.

There'd been a hard frost, so the mosquitoes and black flies were down for the year. But most of the leaves were still up on the trees and underbrush, and once inside the swamp, visibility was poor in every direction. Getting lost in the Waldo Swamp wasn't something to take lightly. Since the arrival of the original settlers, over a dozen people had lost their way in the Waldo Swamp and died because of it. The most recent was a deer hunter only five years ago.

Though Jumbo was confident he knew his way, Overdrive insisted they put an orange vest on a tree at the entry point, tie an end of the baling twine to the tree, carry the spool, dole out twine as they went, and use staple nails to tack the twine to trees here and there. Jumbo might be in school when the timber appraiser arrived, and relying on his own memory to get to the high woods wasn't an option.

The going was slow, as Jumbo and Overdrive meandered their way into the swamp. At the beginning, they encountered woods with clumps of thick underbrush they'd weave around. But after about 75 yards, the underbrush became ubiquitous, and Jumbo had to hack his way through it while Overdrive strung the twine. After another 75 yards, they reached the edge of the wetlands. Jumbo walked the edge until he found the landmark for what he considered the best marsh crossing. This location was a pinch point where the wetlands narrowed to only 50 yards or so. Overdrive strapped an orange vest onto the largest nearby tree.

With the exception of a few stunted willows and other scrub growth, the marsh was treeless and the high woods clearly visible on the other side. There's some open water between where they stood and the high woods, but also many clumps of cattails and other types of bulrushes. Jumbo knew that this marsh crossing had a firm bottom, and sinking into the muck wasn't a concern.

Overdrive and Jumbo spent a few minutes discussing how to proceed. They decided to suspend the twine between the large tree with the vest on it, and another enormous tree on the far side of the marsh, 50 or so yards away. This way the twine could ride above the clumps of growth in the wetlands, over the entire span of the marsh. To get started, Jumbo climbed the vested tree where they stood, and secured the twine onto the main tree trunk about 30 feet up. When he got to the far side, he'd do the same using the tree they'd already targeted.

Overdrive and Jumbo wanted the twine spanning the marsh to survive a high wind. They knew that choosing thick-trunked trees on either side of the marsh, which swayed only modestly in the highest of winds, would help. But the possibility that the two trees could sway in opposite directions still had them worried. To compensate, they decided to leave some droop or slack in the twine. The 30-foot high tie-offs were intended to keep the twine above the marsh vegetation throughout the entire span, even with the slack.

Jumbo put on the last orange vest, picked up the spool of twine, and began to wade across the marsh. As he went, he doled out twine with his hand held high over his head. Wading was easiest in open water, so Jumbo weaved around the clumps of growth as best he could. When he got to the far side of a clump, he'd flip-up and jerk the twine until it went up and over, and then pull the twine into a tight line back to the tree where Overdrive stood. Circumventing the clumps, and maneuvering the twine in this manner, Jumbo slowly made his way forward. At the deepest spot, Jumbo's waders still had about a foot to spare.

When he got to the high woods, Jumbo strapped the last vest to the giant tree they'd previously targeted, and climbed into it with the spool of twine. He and Overdrive yelled back and forth until they agreed on the amount of slack to leave, and then Jumbo tied off the twine about 30 feet up. While Jumbo waded back across the marsh with the spool, it occurred to Overdrive that squirrels, deer, or other varmints might have a taste for baling twine. He kicked that around, and concluded electric fence wire might've been a better choice, but it's too late now.

By the time they got back to the house, Mary had already found a logging contractor who could have an appraiser at the farm by early afternoon. Overdrive immediately made the call to try to lock that in. After introductions, Overdrive filled the logger in about the 50-acre high woods, the need to wade 50 yards to reach it, and so on. They went back and forth, with the contractor questioning the wisdom of wasting appraiser time if harvesting the timber was impossible.

Overdrive did some fast talking not to lose him, including walking him through a feasible scenario for harvesting the timber. The chain saws and other gear needed to down the trees and trim them to logs could be brought in easily enough, either by pulling a dingy through the marsh or over the ice if they waited for winter. No question, they'd have to wait for the thickest ice to pull the logs out.

Even before Overdrive could finish, the logger started sputtering a litany horror stories about past marsh crossings in winter. Among the horrors mentioned were thin ice due to springs and currents, unsupported ice shelves caused by changing water levels, and so on. When the rant ended, Overdrive calmly declared there'd be no need for the logger to worry because he'd pull out the logs himself.

To Overdrive's surprise, rather than assuage the logger's concerns, the offer stoked his fury. He started sputtering about his labor and saw fuel investment, needed to down and trim the trees, going down the shitter. No fucking way would he put that money at risk on the faint hope that the logs could be pulled out by some naive farmer, who obviously had no idea how hard that'd be.

This verbal volley caught Overdrive off guard. After hearing the logger's horror stories, doubts about the draft horse idea had already begun to creep in. Mind racing, Overdrive paused briefly, unsure what to say. Should he plunge on? Offer to pay for the appraisal? Or what? Goddammit, he needed that appraisal!

Overdrive took a deep breath, and with as confident a tone as he could muster, plunged on. He told the logger he'd wait for the winter's thickest ice, and use draught horses to pull the logs across the marsh, out of the swamp, and onto his bottomlands. From there, trucking the logs to the sawmill would be a piece of cake. They'd be able to use Overdrive's well-developed farm lane, and bring in trucks, a lifter, and anything else they needed.

On a roll and desperate to seal the deal, Overdrive began making things up as he went along. He told the logger he'd used draught horses to pull logs across marshes in winter many times. For a dash of credibility, he added that springs and varying water levels may rule out using the natural ice. Taking his bluff to new heights, Overdrive went on to say that these issues could be overcome by breaking the natural ice, laying in tree branches and limbs, and hauling in and packing down snow. The snow bridge created would freeze solid right down to the trimmings and water, and in his experience, would easily support the weight of a horse team.

Overdrive continued to layer in more lies, hoping they'd form a web and support each other. He said he'd built snow bridges before, and owned everything needed to do it again. He had a truck with a large box for hauling snow, and a hoist for dumping it where needed.

He had a scoop tractor for spreading it out and packing it down. He owned an eight-foot wide snow blower perfect for harvesting snow and throwing it into the truck box. For labor, in addition to himself, he had his Dad, an uncle, the uncle's horse team, and four boys, all antsy in winter without enough to do. Eventually, the logger interrupted the line of bullshit to say he's in.

The logger said he sometimes did his own appraisals, but being short and unable to swim, couldn't safely do this one. When he'd told Mary earlier that someone could be at the farm this afternoon, he'd been thinking of himself. Overdrive countered that he needed the appraisal in three days or less, due to its connection with other business matters. The logger said that'd be no problem, he'd just send an affiliated appraiser. In fact, he's got one in mind that'd be perfect. The guy is of Dutch descent, and has that long and lean look about him. Hell, this guy even hunts wood ducks and fishes for trout, so he's got his own pair of chest waders. The logger promised to check his availability, and call right back.

A half hour later, the logger called to say the Dutchman would be at the farm in an hour, waders and all. Overdrive couldn't help but think what a great country this was. People motivated by money got off their asses when you needed them to. He was still smiling inwardly, when the Dutchman drove in. Overdrive and Jumbo fast-walked outside to meet him, discussing their plan as they went.

After introductions, Overdrive filled the Dutchman in. Jumbo grabbed his waders, hopped into the cow car, and led the Dutchman in his pickup truck down to the swamp. Then, after parking and donning their waders, Jumbo led the Dutchman along the twine-marked path to the marsh and high woods.

The Dutchman needed to inventory the various types of trees, measure their girths at ground level, and estimate the number and length of logs that each tree would yield. After quickly walking the 50-acre tract with Jumbo, he said he'd be able to finish his task by spending the rest of the day, all day tomorrow, and probably some of the following day. He told Jumbo to assure his Dad that having a written quote in three days wouldn't be a problem. Jumbo left him there to get started, knowing he'd be able to come and go as he pleased.

CHAPTER 20

No Contingency Plan

After Jumbo and the Dutchman left for the swamp, Overdrive threw himself back into silo filling for the rest of the afternoon. The first silo was nearly filled, and today's wagon-loads would probably take it to the top. Then he'd let it settle overnight, climb to the top in the morning, and estimate by eyeball the number of wagon-loads needed to refill it tomorrow. After repeating this a few times, the settling would be done and the silo would be full.

When Overdrive came into the house for supper, Mary handed him HMR's response to their letter, delivered by courier that afternoon. It'd been unopened, and Overdrive decided to leave it that way. They'd planned to call Ted Ritter after milking anyway, so might as well wait and read it to Ted over the phone. Why spoil your day sooner, when it can wait until later?

Conversation over supper turned to the Dutchman. Nobody'd seen him drive out from behind the barn to leave. After supper, everybody'd be out in the barn milking or doing chores, except Kathy and Marie, who'd be cleaning up the dishes and picking and washing apples. They'd be in the best position to notice the Dutchman leave, so Overdrive asked the girls to keep an eye out for him. If he hadn't returned by end of milking, Jumbo would have to go looking for him.

During milking, Overdrive mulled over where things stood. He felt conflicted. On the one hand, the stress and worry of the HMR situation was wearing him down. On the other hand, he knew in his heart they'd done everything they could've, and felt good about that. In fact, getting an appraiser into the high woods the day after the idea hatched was a feat to be proud of.

About then, Old Bill fast-walked into the barn, arms a waving, and Overdrive snapped out of his reverie to attend to his Dad. By the expression and gestures alone, he diagnosed the problem before his father even spat it out. The fill pipes had clogged, the blower had sheared a pin, and his father needed help. Overdrive got the attention of Jumbo, who'd just finished pushing the meal cart around the aisles to feed the grain, and gestured him to go with his grandpa.

As Overdrive walked to the house after milking, the Dutchman drove through from behind the barn and waved. His eyes followed the pickup down the driveway, only to see brake lights. There, slow-walking across the driveway was Kathy, in short-shorts and bare-bellied with her sleeveless blouse untucked and tied up tight under her boobs. With waggling hips and a seductive come-hither smile, Kathy was obviously displaying her wares. On the far side of the driveway stood Marie, gaping with horror, in a look that mirrored his own.

As Overdrive pulled off his boots in the mud room, Kathy sauntered over to inform him that the Dutchman had left, then giggled as she turned on her heal, and walked away. Oh well, at least she'd re-buttoned her blouse and tucked it in. While the barn crew cleaned up, Mary had the girls make popcorn. Then she used it to lure the kids out of the kitchen, shut the door behind them, and dialed Ted.

Their attorney picked up on the first ring. After exchanging pleasantries, Overdrive read the HMR letter aloud. As expected, HMR declined to waive their march-in privileges. The letter went on to repeat the timetable for removal of the Evans family personal property, to avoid forfeiture. Next, Overdrive filled Ted in on the 50-acre high woods, and the timber quote they'd have in advance of the bank's board meeting. This was news to Ted and, if anything, he was overly generous in his praise of their quick thinking and action. Soon they knew why.

Although still investigating the paper trails of the shell corporations and making inquiries regarding any public filings they may've made, Ted had nothing new to report. He'd also been checking in daily with the two state agencies, to see if the Potawatomi or DP had made any further contact. There'd been none, but both agencies still expected a call soon, to schedule their October meetings.

With the bank meeting rapidly approaching, Ted suggested they review the timing of events, to make sure nothing had been missed. One day out, tribal council meets in the evening, Darkwater calls Ted afterword, and Ted calls Overdrive and Mary. Two days out, presuming there's something useful to fetch, Ted's courier takes an early morning handoff from Dark-water in Wabeno, and drives the materials to Ted's office by early afternoon. Also, two days out, the logger delivers the standing timber quote by late afternoon. That evening, they all meet at Ted's office, to share the materials received and make last minute plans. If all goes well, three days out will be a full uninterrupted day to prepare for the bank's board meeting, which starts first thing in the morning, four days out. After checking it twice, the three of them were confident that they'd captured the key events. Overdrive and Mary had a farm to run and questioned the need for their participation on prep day, three days out. Ted pushed back, so they decided to defer that decision until the meeting at Ted's office the night before.

As the call ended, Ted tried to send Overdrive and Mary off on a positive note, "You know, the quick turnaround on HMR's response sends the message that they've taken the bait. When Darkwater calls tomorrow night, there's a damn good chance we'll have the proof we need that Rachel Wolf is behind HMR."

Mary sucked in a quick breath, and gushed, "God, I hope you're right, Ted. Wouldn't that be wonderful?"

Overdrive, in a skeptical voice, said, "I'll believe it when I see it."

Ted ruminated a moment, then choose to respond to Mary's more upbeat remark, "Yes, it sure would be. I'm just saying. There's a really good chance."

Mary, hopeful, "I'll keep my fingers crossed, Ted. Maybe we all should."

The three of them left that hang in the air for a moment. Then jokingly, Ted said, "I'd like to offer a friendly amendment, change *fingers* to *fingers and toes*."

This triggered a nervous laugh from everyone, followed by dead air.

Overdrive broke the silence, "Ted, hypothetically speaking, say Darkwater learns nothing at tribal council. Would it then be time for Mary and I to start hustling to find an auctioneer to organize a fire sale of our personal property?"

After a thoughtful silence, Ted said, "I think that'd be jumping the gun, James. Let's see what happens at the bank first. It's only four days out. If that fails, I can go to court on your behalf, and force HMR to a more reasonable schedule."

Overdrive, now dead serious, "But what if you can't? If the bank turns us down, 10 days later, we'd lose everything still on the premises."

Ted said firmly, "You'll just have to trust me on that, James. No court in Wisconsin is going to let those assholes force you off your dairy farm in 10 days."

Overdrive tried to sound convinced, and wished he were, as he said, "Okay, Ted, I believe you. Sorry I even brought it up. Just feeling the pressure, I guess."

Calm, professional, "There's no need to apologize, James, really. It's a valid concern. If it makes you feel any better, I've already drafted the motions and scheduled a court appearance. If the bank turns us down, we'll go straight from the bank to court. I'll kick HMR's ass on a reasonable schedule. I wish I could say the same on the whole thing, but unfortunately they haven't done anything illegal."

* * *

By call end, Overdrive and Mary were beat. Together they herded the stragglers among the kids upstairs to bed, and then silently went about their own bedtime routines. Once under the covers, they shared a long embrace, kissed, and reassured each other that everything would work out. Then they each turned onto their favorite sides for sleeping, and sleep came quickly for Mary.

Wide awake and mind racing, Overdrive remained motionless until Mary's breathing told him she's asleep. Then, he carefully changed position to be more comfortable for contemplation. He couldn't get over how Ted had already drafted the motions for court and scheduled an appearance. Was this a good lawyer planning ahead to move fast under any eventuality, or a sign Ted already knew they're totally fucked? Surely, he'd tell us if he already knew, wouldn't he?

Overdrive ruminated over how to spend the next few days. Should he just have faith that the bank loan would come through, and throw himself into his work? Or, would it be more prudent to spend this time developing a contingency plan, and implementing it to the extent possible? If the bank stays on the sidelines, it'd be handy to have a plan for clearing out as much of the personal property as possible before it's no longer theirs, wouldn't it?

Ted seemed confident that no court in America's Dairyland would allow a dairy farmer who just lost his farm, to lose everything else to boot, owing to an impossibly-short vacate period. But up until a few days ago, Ted had also been confident that gaming wasn't allowed on Indian reservations in Wisconsin. What if he's wrong, again? What if Wisconsin's current movers and shakers, Rachel Wolf among them, are about to roll out

America's Gamingland as the new state slogan.

Thinking more deeply, Overdrive realized that he wasn't sure what he'd do, exactly, if he refocused on contingency planning. It's just so overwhelming. For livestock, he's got the milk herd and three cohorts of replacement heifers at different ages. Who'd buy them going into winter? No farmer's going to have enough excess feed to bring in all those extra cattle and be able to tide them over until spring. And even if he did, what're the odds that he'd also have enough empty stanchions, and run-in sheds or barns, to shelter the cattle?

Overdrive dismissed that possibility and tried thinking through some other angles. Maybe there's a farmer out there who'd buy all the cattle and feed as a package deal. Who'd do that? It'd have to be somebody with facilities equivalent to his own, but sitting empty. But what're the odds that somebody like that exists? And even if they do, would moving all of that in 10 days be feasible? Maybe on a court-ordered schedule, but no way in 10 days.

It appeared too complicated, so Overdrive pondered the angle of simplifying the problem by carving it up into pieces. Okay, let's put the blinders on and just think about the livestock. He involuntarily shuddered when it crossed his mind that the only realistic option for disposing of the livestock, might be to ship them to slaughter. Gib Buyer was an excellent cattle trader, but brokering deals for this many cattle would be impossible in 10 days, and might take more time than any court would grant. If they had an auction, farmers with empty stanchions or looking to upgrade their herds might go for the milk cows, and others with under-used

290 | PATRICK J. HUGHES

run-in sheds or barns might go for the heifers. But at the fire sale prices they'd likely bring, and after paying the auctioneer and for advertising, an auction may not raise any more cash than the slaughterhouse. What about the feed and bedding? Hmmm ... if the court granted enough time, they might be able to sell the hay and straw at an auction, and have the buyers haul it away before the deadline. It'd be grunt work, but they might also be able to empty the oats out of the granary. They'd have to hand-shovel it into the gravity chute to the basement, and flow it into gunny sacks. Then muscle the 100-pound sacks onto the ton truck, and haul them to the Cascade Feed Mill.

What about the silage and ear corn? Hmmm ... the silage would probably have to be abandoned in place. Using the unloader was the only way to get it out of the silos, and all the unloader did was blow it into the chute, where it dropped into a cart. What then? Who'd buy it? How'd it be hauled away and re-stored? As for the ear corn, if the court granted enough time, maybe a custom picker could come in and not only pick the corn, but also haul it away to a buyer.

Then there's the truck, tractors, and machinery. It's all in good working order. If the court granted enough time, they might be able to sell it at auction. Or, maybe one or more farm implement dealers could be cajoled into buying the items, to resell as used on their lots. Either way, they'd only fetch pennies on the dollar.

After contemplating this dismal landscape for several hours, Overdrive came to the same conclusion as Ted. He might as well just keep the faith, and merrily fill his silos over the next few days. If the worst happened, Ted would buy him some time in court. What's HMR's hurry anyway? They can't build a casino overnight. Plans will need to be developed, approvals granted, and whatnot. The Salvesons have until the end of December to get out. Even with world-class gaslighting by HMR, it's hard to believe evicting us in advance of the Salvesons could be justified in court. On that pleasant note, Overdrive finally succumbed to sleep.

CHAPTER 21

Manic Swings

A lthough he'd only slept a few hours, Overdrive felt oddly energized the next morning. After milking and breakfast, he climbed the filled silo himself to see how far down the silage had settled. He estimated that three more wagon-loads, at most, would fit. Then, Overdrive took a moment to enjoy the view from his silo's catwalk perch, still hopeful that he'd be enjoying it for many years to come.

Overdrive's anticipation was growing by the minute. That evening Ted would call to tell them what Darkwater had learned at tribal council. Overdrive tried not to let his emotions get ahead of events, for fear of a letdown later. But it wasn't easy, and he imagined Mary was engaged in a similar battle. He chopped three loads of silage, let Old Bill unload the first two, and saved the last one for when Jumbo returned from football practice. The Dutchman put in a long day in the high woods, and was seen leaving about dusk.

Evening milking proceeded uneventfully. When

done, Mary asked Overdrive to clean up the milking machines by himself, so she could go to the house and put an apple strudel into the oven. He nodded, understanding that strudel was tonight's means to lure the kids out of the kitchen before Ted called. Overdrive sensed that Mary might be letting her hopeful side get the best of her, but even he couldn't help but hope.

As time passed, Overdrive and Mary grew more and more worried, waiting for the call. The kids had long since departed the kitchen, with the door closed behind them. The main phone on the wall was within reach of Mary, and the extension sat on the table in front of Overdrive. They're literally shaking with anticipation. Fascination with pushing strudel crumbs around their plates had waned long ago, replaced by impatient frustration.

Finally, the phone rang. Overdrive and Mary locked eyes, took deep breaths, and picked up at the same time. Ted was so excited he didn't even bother with the niceties. Instead, he gushed, "James! Mary! Tribal council approved HMR as the casino location! Better yet, Rachel Wolf made the pitch in person!"

Already choking with emotion, Mary's voice cracked as she said, "Oh my god! Really? Oh, thank you, thank you, thank you, lord!"

Overdrive held back, and asked, "Did Darkwater get pictures and audio?"

Ted, in a jubilant voice, "Yes, yes, he's gotten everything we asked for! He's got Polaroids of Wolf with the tribal elders. He's got audio of the entire meeting from the second row. He's got copies of the prospectus and presentation."

Overdrive was speechless. Tearing up, he set his

receiver on the table and walked over to Mary, who stood as he pulled her into his arms. Mary, receiver still in hand, put her arms around his neck and released herself into him. She sobbed openly, trying to muffle the sound in his chest, to avoid alarming the kids in the next room. Time passed, then her receiver began crackling, louder and louder, until Mary recovered enough to put it back to her ear.

Ted shouted, "Hello? Is anybody there? HELLO? IS ANYBODY THERE?"

Mary tried to respond, but nothing came out. Trying again, she managed to croak, "Yes, Ted. We're still here. We're sorry, we just needed a moment."

Overdrive wiped his eyes as he stepped back to the table, picked up the extension, and said in a raspy voice, "Hello, Ted. I'm back."

Ted laughed, and said, "No problem. I understand completely. Trust me. I'd needed a moment of my own, when Darkwater gave me the good news."

Overdrive asked, "Have you called the courier service, yet?"

In an assuring voice, Ted said, "Not yet. But as soon as we hang up, I will. I talked to them earlier today, and they're standing by. They'll be leaving in the wee hours, to be at the rendezvous point first thing tomorrow."

When the call ended, Overdrive and Mary just sat there together in silence, enjoying the moment and drying their eyes with napkins. They called Darkwater to thank him, but received no answer and thought nothing of it. Then they called Old Bill, and shared the good news with him. Eventually, Mary looked at the clock, and realized it's past bed time for a school night.

She dashed to the bathroom mirror to see what could be done to keep up appearances, and then busied herself rousting the kids upstairs to bed.

Overdrive stepped into the living room, had a seat in his favorite stuffed chair, and picked up the latest Hoard's Dairyman magazine. Although totally spent and unable to focus on anything, he'd had enough presence of mind to do what he'd normally do and avoid spooking the kids. After the kids were upstairs, Mary lightly touched Overdrive's cheek, and reminded him he'd barely slept the night before. They went through their bedtime routines, climbed into bed, and were out by the time they hit the mattress.

*　*　*

The next morning during milking, the Dutchman came into the barn briefly before heading back to the high woods. He told Overdrive that he'd be done with his field work by noon, and that the logging contractor himself would be back by supper time, to hand deliver the quote. The Dutchman joked that if the logs were to be extracted in this lifetime, Overdrive had better have access to dozens of horse teams, not just one. Apparently, went it rains it pours.

After milking and breakfast, Overdrive climbed the chute of the silo again, 75 feet to the top. He'd had a little extra bounce in his step all morning, and could've kept climbing forever. It's a perfect fall day in Sheboygan County, Wisconsin and the view from the top was spectacular. But unlike yesterday, he no longer hoped he'd see it again, now he's sure of it. Only one more wagon-load would fit into this silo, and after that they'd move the fill pipes to the other one.

Overdrive was pulling out of the yard with the chopper and an empty wagon, when Mary ran out of the house and flagged him down. Flushed, Mary shouted over the tractor noise, "Ted's on the phone. He says it can't wait."

Mary ran back into the house, and Overdrive shut down his rig and followed. Entering the kitchen, he saw the extension on the table waiting for him, and Mary on the wall phone. So, he sat down, picked up, and said, "Hello?"

Ted, in a calm and professional voice, "James, I'm sorry to interrupt your work. But I thought you should know something right away."

Overdrive's eyebrows went up, and he asked warily, "Know what?"

Ted said, "Darkwater didn't show up at the rendezvous point this morning."

Mary snapped, "What? What do you mean …"

Overdrive interrupted, "You're shitting me, right?"

Ted, in a neutral voice, "When Darkwater didn't show up, the courier waited and gave him another hour. Then he found a pay phone and called my office."

Overdrive frowned, and said, "That doesn't sound like Darkwater."

Ted agreed, "I know." Then, after a moment, "Are you both sitting down?"

Mary, in a concerned voice, "Yes, why? What's happened?"

After a moment, Ted said, "I'm not entirely sure yet. When the courier called the first time, I gave him Darkwater's address and told him to go there. I thought maybe he'd overslept or something."

Now also concerned, Overdrive growled, "First time? You mean he's called twice? Was Darkwater there?"

Choosing his words carefully, Ted said, "Yes, the courier called me back. When I tell you this, don't go jumping to any conclusions. All we know for sure is that Darkwater's house and car were burned to the ground last night."

Overdrive snapped, "What?"

Mary gasped, "Oh my god!!! Are you serious? Is he okay?"

Ted, voice still neutral, "When the courier arrived, both county and tribal police were guarding the site, and the county Fire Marshall was on his way. The police had no comment."

Overdrive dropped his voice, "Oh my god!!! You mean he could be dead?"

Ted, struggling to keep his voice steady, "Some of the volunteer firemen were still around, packing up, when the courier arrived. He got a little information from them. Apparently, the house and car were both infernos before they arrived. All they could do was prevent it from spreading. They hadn't seen a body, but it wasn't their job to look."

Mary retreated into shocked silence. All Overdrive could muster was, "Sonofabitch!!! What've we done? We've gotten him ..."

Ted interrupted, "Don't go there, James. You haven't done anything. If there's any blame here, it's with me. I'm your attorney. I apologize, but it never occurred to me that any of this had the potential to put Darkwater in harm's way. And just to be clear, we don't know that it has. We just don't know."

Overdrive, sounding defeated, "What're we going to do?"

Ted, now more upbeat, "I've an idea, but I need your permission. I'd like to pull back the courier, and put a private investigator on this. There'd be a cost, of course. But it's the only way to find out in a hurry what's really happened."

Overdrive exploded, "Fuck the cost! Of course, send in the PI! We're talking about Darkwater, here. He only got involved as a favor to my Dad."

Ted, relieved and determined at the same time, "I'm glad you agree. I know a top-notch PI. We've already spoken. He'll be on it immediately, the moment I ask. I'm going to run now, and make that call. I'll keep you posted."

❋ ❋ ❋

After Ted hung up, Overdrive and Mary sat in silence for a long moment. Overdrive suggested they keep this news from his father, until there's something definitive to say, and Mary agreed. They prayed that Darkwater wasn't home at the time, and was unharmed. Each shared their hope that the fire was just an unrelated accident. But deep in his heart, Overdrive knew better. In spite of what Ted had said, he felt responsible. Hell, he was responsible. Had he not talked Mary into signing that agreement, none of this ever would've happened.

With heavy heart, Overdrive trudged back out to his rig. Rather than wallow in self-pity, he drew a deep breath, hopped on, and drove off to chop one more wagon load of silage. Mary was still up to her eyeballs in Mcintosh apples, and got back to work on them. She spent the rest of the morning pealing, coring, slicing, cooking slices into sauce, and canning the sauce. Just before noon, she noticed the Dutchman drive out of the driveway. It reminded her to have a sandwich ready, for when James came in for lunch.

Not long after, Overdrive drove into the yard hauling a self-unloading wagon filled with silage. He parked, blocked a tire, and headed into the house. Lunch was a solemn affair. Overdrive nodded when Mary told him the Dutchman had gone. Mary nodded when Overdrive told her they'd move the fill pipes and blower to the second silo, once that last wagon was unloaded.

After lunch, Overdrive set about greasing the chopper and refurbishing all his cutter bars. He'd just finished his third and final cutter bar, when the logging contractor drove in. After exchanging pleasantries, the logger handed Overdrive the quote. Overdrive tried his best to keep a straight face, but the value of the standing timber was truly eyepopping. He'd pulled a few logs out of his other woodlands before, but hadn't done it enough to know what to expect. The logger said that for big jobs, he liked to have a quick look-see for himself, and that's why he'd come early. Overdrive got the hint, and agreed to lead him to the high woods.

They rode in the logger's pickup, around the barn, and along the farm lane toward the Waldo Swamp. When they got to the crest of the hill, Overdrive asked him to stop for a moment. They took in the view from this high vantage point, and Overdrive pointed out the high woods, clearly visible from here. The logger whistled, which gave Overdrive the impression he might be impressed.

After bouncing the rest of the way down the lane to the bottomlands, Overdrive pointed to the orange-vested tree far off in the distance, where they eventually rolled to a stop. The twine had survived, so they followed it through the swamp to the marsh. From this vantage point, only 50 yards away across the marsh, the logger gained a true appreciation for the magnitude of those trees. After a moment, he whistled again. Oh, he was impressed alright.

The logger used the ride back to the farm buildings, to chat Overdrive up about commitments and timetables. As incredible as it may seem, this gave Overdrive the impression that the eyepopping quote might actually have been lowballed. The logger shifted gears into a full-blown sales pitch, dropping carrots here and there. He offered to do Overdrive a huge favor, his words, only possible because the Dutchman had told him the marsh bottom was firm. He could, you know, bring in his big equipment to bridge the marsh with a logging road. That way Overdrive wouldn't have to run all over kingdom come recruiting a bunch of Amishmen and their draught horses. High speed, you know, for a draught horse is a slow trot. Those Amishmen, you know, don't believe in trucks and horse trailers. Hell, it'd take them most of the winter just to get here.

Overdrive played along, said he'd think about it and get back to him. He left out the part about, you know, if the farm's still his he'd get back to him. When they got back, Overdrive asked the logger to head down the driveway and roll to a stop beside the house.

This way the pickup would be pointed out toward the road, and hopefully he'd get the hint. When the pickup stopped, Overdrive thanked him for sending the Dutchman out right away, shook his hand, and said he'd get back to him. Then he said it's milking time and without further explanation, stepped out, shut the door, and turned and walked into the house.

For a dairy farmer, saying it's milking time is like a fighter pilot ejecting his seat before the crash. It works almost every time. Overdrive desperately wanted to get out of that pickup before being asked WHEN he'd get back to him, and he'd succeeded. Once inside the house, he stole a peak out the window, and smiled broadly when he saw the pickup turning onto Bates Road. It wasn't really milking time yet, supper came first. But there'd been a grain of truth to it, anyway.

* * *

Overdrive and Mary busied themselves with milking the cows. The familiar routine was comforting. They'd hoped to get an update from Ted around supper time, but the phone remained silent. Surely, he'd call this evening. Waiting was the worst part. They wanted, no, they needed to know what'd happened to Darkwater.

Overdrive pondered his situation as he milked. He knew he needed to work like a madman over the next few days, to keep his mind out of the darkest places. About then, Jumbo came by with an update. He'd recruited Joe to help with the silo filling, and together they'd managed to squeeze in the entire last wagon-load. Overdrive told him to round up his grandpa, Joe, and John and start moving the filler pipes to the next silo. He'd join them after he finished milking. With the pipes on an empty silo, he'd be able to throw himself into his work until all the cards were out on the table, good or bad. If the worst happened, they'd abandon two full silos instead of one, but at this point, he didn't give a shit anymore.

Later, though it's dark and getting late on a school night, Overdrive and the crew struggled on, trying to finish the filler pipe move. When David arrived to fetch him for a phone call, Overdrive told the crew to break for the night after completing a few must-finish tasks. Then he jogged down to the house.

After kicking off his filthy boots on the back stoop, Overdrive entered the mud room and glanced into the kitchen. Mary was there alone, the door to the living room closed for privacy, with the phone extension waiting for him on the table. Mary's facial expression told him a full clean-up would have to wait. He stepped out of his coveralls, washed his hands, and took his seat.

Overdrive established eye contact with Mary, spent a moment to catch his breath, picked up the receiver, and said, "Hello?"

Ted said, "Hello, James. Working late tonight I see. I'm sorry to interrupt."

Breathing heavily, Overdrive said, "Yes, first silo's full. We're moving the fill pipes to the second one. But we're done for the night anyway, so no problem."

Ted, all business, "That's great progress, James. You're well ahead of the other farmers in the area. Listen, I've got an update and thought it'd be best to tell you both at the same time."

Breathing almost normally, Overdrive said, "I appreciate that, Ted. Tell us, please. Mary and I've been anxious to hear from you all day."

Ted, in a neutral voice, "Well, the good news is, they've finished searching what little remains of Darkwater's house and car, and there's no body."

Mary gasped, "Oh thank god! That's wonderful news!"

Overdrive asked, "What's the bad news?"

Ted exhaled heavily, and said, "The PI hasn't located Darkwater."

Overdrive's eyebrows went up, "What? Well, why the hell not? He couldn't have gone far without a car."

Ted, in a calm voice, "The PI canvassed some neighbors milling around the scene. They saw Darkwater being picked up by his lady friend in her car, about half an hour after he arrived back home from tribal council. The neighbors said they'd waved and appeared in good spirits."

Overdrive said, "Let me get this straight. Darkwater called you right after he got home. Then shortly after, left home in his lady friend's car?"

Ted, in a professional voice, "That's what I think, yes."

Mary said, "Ted, we called Darkwater last night to thank him, right after you gave us the good news. There was no answer. That might explain why."

Ted nodded to himself, and said, "Interesting. Yes, it might."

Overdrive asked, "Did the PI find the lady friend?"

Ted said, "Yes, he did. The neighbors provided descriptions of her and her car. They knew she lived in Laona, but didn't recall her name. The PI thought they might've ended up at her house last night, so he drove up there." After a chuckle, Ted said, "Laona is so small, the PI just drove around until he spotted her car, and knocked on the door. Her name is Robin Thunder."

Mary asked, "He found Robin but not Darkwater? How can that be?"

Choosing his words carefully, Ted said, "Well, Mary, the gist of it's that Darkwater spent last night there with Robin, and then disappeared this morning."

Mary gasped, "Disappeared? What does that ..."

Overdrive interrupted, "But surely Robin knew where he went, right?"

Ted, in a slow and deliberate voice, "No, she didn't, but let me back up a little. Robin was reluctant to cooperate at first, so the PI called me collect on her phone. I put it to her this way. A long-time friend of Darkwater learned of the fire, feared for his safety, and hired us to find him. She didn't believe me at first, but when I mentioned Old Bill Evans, she knew all about him. After that she gladly told us what little she knew. She's worried sick over Darkwater. She expressed relief that somebody was looking for him that he'd actually want to be found by."

Mary gasped again, "You mean others are looking for him?"

Ted said calmly, "Yes, but let me explain. They'd gone out to celebrate last night, and ended up at Robin's place. This morning, Darkwater was eating breakfast and watching the local TV news, when she went into the shower. When she came out, he's gone and somebody's pounding on the front door."

Overdrive snapped, "Who's at the door?"

Ted, still calm, "Robin yelled for Darkwater to

answer the door. When he didn't respond, she walked over in her robe and peaked out the window. On the stoop were two tough-looking strangers, with two more at the street by their car. She didn't recognize any of them, and refused to open the door. That caused the two strangers at the street to drive off, and one of the others to jog around to the back of the house. Shortly after, the two strangers returned with a tribal police car right behind. She did recognize the police, and felt safe enough to let them in."

Mary exhaled, and said, "That poor women!"

Overdrive stared at the fridge a moment, then asked, "What'd they want?"

In a matter of fact voice, Ted said, "They told Robin they're looking for Darkwater, but wouldn't say why. She let them search the house. The TV was still on, his coffee cup half empty, and his eggs and toast half eaten. On the table was a scribbled note saying *thanks for last night*. Based on what they found, they apparently believed her that Darkwater had vanished while she'd been showering. They took off in a hurry, probably to give chase."

Overdrive, in a puzzled voice, "I don't understand, why would the tribal police and these other guys be after Darkwater?"

Ted thought a moment, then said, "They wouldn't say and Robin didn't know. She didn't even know that Darkwater's house and car had been destroyed by fire. All she knew was that they'd celebrated the tribal good fortune last night, along with a lot of other people, and this morning he's gone."

Overdrive, "Are the tribal police and those other guys working together?"

Ted lowered his voice, "That's what I think, yes. When Robin wouldn't let them in, they fetched the tribal police rather than break the door down."

Overdrive frowned, and said, "Huh. Do you think Darkwater still has the photos and whatnot with him?"

Ted, upbeat, "It's a possibility, yes. Robin said he had a backpack with him last night, and it's nowhere to be found now. He must've taken it with him."

Overdrive asked, "Well, what now?"

Ted, in a neutral voice, "Robin's house had a back door, and the PI checked out back. Darkwater clearly ran into the woods on foot, and one or more of the police or tough guys followed. The PI is trying to track him now."

Overdrive asked, "Who are those other guys? Any idea?"

Ted thought a moment, then said, "Robin doesn't know. She said they had a look about them that made her feel unsafe. The PI has no clue either, but he's pretty sure he'd better find Darkwater before they do."

Mary, in a hopeful voice, "So, Darkwater's still okay, as far as we know."

Ted said wisely, "Yes, Mary, I believe he is. But to be clear, all we know for sure is that he was alive and running on foot at about eight o'clock this morning."

Overdrive stared at the ceiling, and said, "Well, that's something anyway. Any theories about what's going on? I mean, what the fuck!"

Ted sucked in a deep breath, and said, "James, Mary, just to be clear, everything I say from here on is pure speculation. Darkwater was sitting in the second row at tribal council. He'd surely been seen snapping photos. Maybe even the tape recorder had been seen. This may've raised suspicions among the wrong people. Robin knew of Old Bill Evans, so it's probably no secret among the tribe that Darkwater had a friend in a family that partly owned the headwaters of the Milwaukee River. If DP found out, they'd want to make damn sure no photos or audio tapes made it back to Cascade before HMR had control of the farm."

Mary gasped, "Oh my god! Darkwater really is in danger!"

Ted paused to choose his words carefully, then said, "Hold on, now. Like I said, this is all speculation. All we know for sure is that the tribal police and some other unknown people are looking for Darkwater. We don't know for a fact that the other people are from DP, and mean to do him harm. But for Darkwater's sake, we shouldn't rule that out either. The PI has a sense about these things, and like I say, he's pretty sure he'd better find Darkwater before they do."

As the discussion wound down, they all agreed that given the circumstances, there's no point in getting together in person. Tomorrow was prep day for the board meeting, but Ted said he'd make do with the information he had, and told Overdrive and Mary to spend the time running their farm. Overdrive shared the standing timber quote verbally, which triggered a whistle and a welcomed, but brief, feel-good chat. Ted promised to call if he heard more from the PI, otherwise they'd just meet at the bank the following morning.

CHAPTER 22

Darkwater Goes Missing

It's 6:10 PM on September 17th, 1964 at Potawatomi Tribal Council Hall in Wabeno, Forest County, Wisconsin. Darkwater had arrived early for the 6:30 PM council meeting, hoping to snag two seats in the second row. He wanted to be right up front to capture the best audio recording possible, and felt the second row would be less conspicuous. As tribal members filed in, several asked if the adjacent seat was taken, but Darkwater told them he's saving it for his lady friend, Robin Thunder. He knew full well that Robin wouldn't be coming, but he needed the seat for his backpack. He wanted the tape recorder hidden but sitting up high for better audio pickup, and putting it in the top compartment of the pack with the pack on a chair was his solution. He'd leave the compartment flap open, and when he wanted to record, he'd reach in and push the button.

Darkwater felt relief when the lights were alternately dimmed and raised, indicating that tribal council was about to start. Now people would settle elsewhere, and stop asking about the seat. But he sensed that fending off interest in the seat had drawn attention, and for some reason, this made him feel exposed and vulnerable. He scanned the venue repeatedly, and paid close attention to the sounds around him. There appeared to be a buzz of anticipation in the air. The council began by dispensing with routine matters. After those were finished, Darkwater experienced a feeling of pins and needles as the lead elder of council launched into an overview of the tribe's history with Development Partners LLC, and the purpose of that partnership. Darkwater's heart thrummed at the news that DP was here tonight, seeking approval for a specific location for the new reservation and casino. The thrum escalated to a full heart-pounding adrenaline rush, when Rachel Wolf was introduced to make the pitch and answer questions. When she identified the Headwaters of the Milwaukee River as the ideal location, Darkwater almost peed in his pants.

Wolf gave an overview while her assistants passed out copies of her presentation and the HMR prospectus, and then launched into the most eloquent and compelling sales pitch Darkwater had ever experienced. He did his best to remain discrete, nonchalantly slipping his hand in and out of the pack's compartment to tap the record button. When the hardcopies came around, he slipped two of each into his pack. Wolf was very relaxed, roaming around the dais with her microphone, and Darkwater busied himself snapping photos of her with the tribal elders in the background.

But the whole time, Darkwater still had that feeling of being exposed and vulnerable. He kept his senses on high alert, and noticed about a dozen tough-looking guys scattered around the venue, which he'd never seen before. Then, in spite of his best efforts to remain invisible, he noticed one of the toughs and a tribal policeman conversing, while looking and pointing in his direction. This made Darkwater feel extremely uncomfortable. In his gut he knew that the growing curiosity in him, must be related to his photo shooting and taping.

Darkwater spent the latter part of the meeting closely monitoring the sights and sounds around the venue, and ruminating over who the tough-looking strangers might be. He thought he saw eye contact and slight nods between Rachel Wolf on the dais, and the strangers in various locations. This led him to believe they might be associated with DP. By meeting end, he knew for a fact that all of the tough guys were paying special attention to him.

After Wolf finished, tribal members were given the opportunity to ask questions and voice their yeah or nay positions. Only council members had actual votes, but the elders wanted to know where the tribe in general stood, before casting their ballots. The overwhelming sentiment among the crowd was to move forward, but to Darkwater's surprise, several members of his own band voiced opposition. They felt building a casino on sacred lands with burial mounds would dishonor their ancestors. Darkwater agreed, of course, but given the circumstances remained silent. After everyone said their peace, council voted to approve, with Darkwater's band's elder casting the lone dissenting vote.

When the meeting adjourned, Darkwater did his best to use the jovial crowd headed to the exits for cover. Many tribal members were making plans to celebrate the tribal good fortune, and a few invited him to join. When Darkwater smiled noncommittally, and said he'd have to check with the boss, they understood him to mean Robin Thunder. Darkwater's true concern was whether the tough guys had other plans for him. He half expected to be cornered before getting out of the hall, or worse, out in the parking lot.

To his great relief, Darkwater made it out of the venue, into his car, and out of the parking lot. Still worried, he used a few rudimentary driving maneuvers to determine if he'd been tailed. He didn't appear to be, and began to wonder if he'd just been stupid all evening. By the time he got home, Darkwater had convinced himself there'd been nothing to worry about. He actually was in the mood to celebrate, so he called Robin. Generally, she's always up for a party, and he wasn't disappointed. However, her yes was conditional on her picking him up, because she hated being seen in public in Darkwater's Junker-of-a-car.

With the party plans set, Darkwater called Ted Ritter and shared the good news. Then he washed up, changed his clothes, and deliberated what else to throw into his pack. He figured he might get lucky and end up at Robin's house, so he crammed in a change of clothes for tomorrow, along-side the photos, tape, and paper from tribal council. If at Robin's place in the morning, he'd get to the rendezvous with the courier by borrowing her car. He'd done it before, and knew it wouldn't be a problem. About then Robin pulled up out front and honked.

❋ ❋ ❋

Darkwater and Robin had a great time, one thing led to another, and he ended up spending the night at her place. The next morning, they had coffee, toast, and eggs while watching TV. Robin finished first, and rose to go take her shower. Before she sauntered off, Darkwater caught her arm, and asked her to switch channels to the local morning news.

The lead story was the Wabeno fire. Right off, Darkwater recognized his house and car, or rather what little was left of them. His mind began to race, and his thoughts immediately jumped back to that dark place from the night before. The tough-looking guys were probably associated with DP. They'd seen him snapping photos, and maybe even running the audio recorder. Okay, but so what? They wouldn't destroy his house and car over that, would they?

Now worried, Darkwater's mind sped through the possibilities. What if DP found out his name from someone in the tribe, and that he's friends with the Evans family? It's no secret among his own band, or even the tribe in general. His band had voiced opposition, publicly, over the use of sacred lands for a casino. But maybe DP jumped to the conclusion that the plight of the Evans farm was the real reason. Plus, DP knew for sure that he'd taken snapshots and hardcopies of the prospectus and presentation, and perhaps knew of the tape. He had the goods, and DP wouldn't want them getting back to Cascade before HMR had the farm. Hmmm ... maybe they'd burnt him out to destroy the goods.

As the puzzle pieces came together, Darkwater broke into a full panic. His car had been there, so they might've assumed he'd been in the house. But when a body wasn't found, they'd know him to be alive, creating the possibility that the goods were with him and hadn't burned. They'd have no choice but to come looking for him. Much of the tribe saw him with Robin last night, so it's only a matter of time before they come here.

Mind now at warp speed, Darkwater considered his options. Of utmost importance, he couldn't be found with the goods. Handing them off at the rendezvous would be great, but he feared Wabeno would be crawling with DP guys, and discarded the idea of going back there. What if he hid the goods, then said they went up in smoke when they found him? Mentally, he put himself in DP's shoes and didn't like what he saw. Rather than take his word for it, they'd likely beat the shit out of him to make sure. Whether he told them or not, he'd be a loose end and might end up dead.

Darkwater was coming around to *keep the goods and avoid being caught* as a better course of action, when his prey-anxiety kicked in and nape-hairs rose. By instinct he walked to the front of the house, and peaked through the window curtains. Just then a car pulled up, and four of those tough-looking guys piled out. Thinking on the fly, he scribbled *thanks for last night* on a napkin, grabbed his backpack, and took off out the back door and into the woods on foot.

To create separation from his pursuers, Darkwater sprinted as fast as he could. He knew they'd try to track him, and he'd have to create diversions to throw them off. Backtracking from false-path diversions took time, and he needed significant separation to avoid being seen. He had a pretty good sense of the lay of the land around Robin's house. She lived near the edge of town, two road crossings from Chequamegon-Nicolet National Forest, an enormous wilderness area. He needed to escape into that wilderness area.

Out Robin's back door, Darkwater encountered gently rolling woods with light ground cover. On the far side of a knoll he came upon dense ground cover, and used the natural screen of the hill to hide himself, as he created a diversion path going right of the cover, and continuing in that direction until he reached a small stream. Then he backtracked up the stream 50 yards, pushing as quickly as possible through the tangle of vegetation overhanging the water. He stepped out of the water when he saw a deer trail, and set off in the direction of the national forest. Once on the deer trail, he broke into another sprint.

Darkwater approached the first road with great caution. He picked a crossing point where the dense cover on both sides came right up to the road. He rose to peak over the brush and scan the area, noting a house in either direction, but significant distances off. Shit, a car! He ducked back down, flattened, and remained motionless. The car motored along very slowly. When it neared, he could make out through the brush, a toughguy at the wheel and a tribal policeman in the passenger seat, scanning left and right. Lying there in the brambles, Darkwater couldn't believe how stupid he'd been not to realize it sooner. The tribal police and DP were working together.

Darkwater waited for the car to pass, and then inched toward the road slowly to retain a visual on the car as it crept away. When the car was out of sight, he darted across the road, picked up the deer trail, and sprinted as fast as he could. He had no idea how close behind his pursuers were, and he needed separation to set up another diversion. With cover and a downslope shielding him from the road, he worked his way cross lots toward the second road. Where running was possible, he ran hard. But even where the underbrush was dense, he pushed through with haste.

Concentrating intensely to avoid a fall, Darkwater was also scanning for vegetation, topography, and other features to assist with his next diversion. About a mile beyond the first road, he found the perfect spot. The deer trail took a steep downslope to a stream that cut into the bank of the hill. The trail continued across the stream, and was wide and worn enough that the passing of another human would leave no sign. His other options were to go up or downstream, and in either case, the hill provided a visual shield from the rear. He doubted the pursuers had enough manpower to cover all three options, so they'd have to guess. Upstream was closer to the general direction Darkwater needed to go, so he set off that way.

After what Darkwater judged to be about a half mile, another wide and well-worn deer trail crossed the stream and he took it. He wasn't as young as he used to be, so rather than sprint, he set a sustainable long-distance pace. By late morning, Darkwater had crossed the second road, confident in not being detected. He was now inside the national forest. He moved off into the wilderness a safe distance, and set up another diversion. Then he continued on for about a mile and settled in to rest along a small babbling brook.

* * *

Darkwater crawled to the edge of the brook,

drank until sated, and sat back in a comfortable but invisible position, to rest and ponder his situation and options. Now, in addition to DP, the Potawatomi Tribal Police were after him. In hindsight, it made sense. Once DP and the tribe had gotten into bed together, the tribe had as much to lose as DP if the goods reached Cascade. Darkwater turned over in his mind what this new reality meant. He knew DP had a dozen or so guys, because he'd seen that many at tribal council. The tribal police also had about a dozen guys, but unfortunately, five or six of them were outstanding trackers, and they had dogs.

Darkwater knew dogs couldn't follow a scent if they didn't know what it was. But if the trackers had his scent, their dogs would be a problem. Diversions or not, they'd eventually pick up his trail again. He thought about where they might find his scent. It's possible they wouldn't, because aside from the cloths he wore and the backpack he carried, all his other possessions had gone up in smoke. Their best bet would be to find something at Robin's house. He supposed the pillow cases or sheets might give him away. Darkwater knew Robin liked to wash the bedding after he stayed over, but the trackers might get it first. Sonofabitch!

Still hyped, Darkwater pondered his options. He felt bad about leaving Robin to deal with his mess. But he couldn't think of anything that'd be accomplished by going back, and doing so would certainly put him at risk. Robin knew how to take care of herself, and he believed she'd be okay. He'd purposely kept her in the dark about everything. She didn't know about HMR, the goods he carried, why he'd asked to borrow her car, why he'd left on foot instead, or where he'd gone. She didn't know anything.

Darkwater had already missed the rendezvous with the courier. Mind racing, he contemplated trying to get to a phone. If he could talk to Ted, maybe another rendezvous could be arranged. But being from Wabeno, he wasn't entirely sure where to find a pay phone in Laona. There might be one at the gas station or grocery store, but he wasn't certain. Even if there were, with his pursuers everywhere, he doubted he'd go unnoticed getting change and using a phone. For all he knew, the phones were under surveillance.

Darkwater considered going up to a house, and asking to use their phone. People around Laona were so poor that many didn't have one, but perhaps he'd be able to tell if they did, from the lines coming in from the road. Of course, places that had past service before being disconnected would still have lines. Shit, even if he found a house with a live phone, they'd never let him in. Couldn't blame them either. A stranger comes to the door and asks to use the phone, with face and hands bleeding from briar scratches, soaked head to foot, and covered in detritus. Rather than let him in, they'd likely call tribal police. He couldn't risk it. At least right now, nobody knew where he was, and he needed to keep it that way.

Darkwater inventoried his possessions to help him realistically assess his options for where to go and what to do. He had his wallet with 37 dollars in cash, his BankAmericard, and his driver's license. He always carried a jackknife and butane lighter. He didn't smoke, but the lighter was handy in his guide business, for lighting fires. His backpack was still dry, and had one change of clothes, his overnight kit, his jacket, and the goods from tribal council. On his feet were the loafers he'd worn last night.

Darkwater was anxious to get moving again, because he wasn't sure how far behind his trackers were, and whether they had his scent and dogs. The nearest towns to Laona, were Wabeno, over nine miles due south, and Crandon, over twelve miles due west. He'd be a fool to go back to Wabeno. With his home and possessions destroyed, there'd be nowhere to go, plus the place would be crawling with tribal police and DP guys. Crandon seemed to be the better bet. It's the county seat of Forest County, has pay phones, and is home to the nearest car rental. It might even be far enough away that his pursuers would dismiss it, in their search.

Crandon was due west on US HWY 8, and Darkwater mulled the best way to get there. He quickly discarded as too risky the idea of hitchhiking, but gave more thought to walking along the highway. There's a fair amount of traffic, and he'd have to duck for cover every time a vehicle approached. There're a few areas where getting to cover in time might be a problem. It'd be pretty risky. The better alternative, Darkwater thought, would be to hike the little-used back-country trail in the national forest. It'd add some distance, maybe four to five miles, making the overall hike 16 to 17 miles long. But Darkwater lived an active life as a guide, was fit, and knew he'd make it. Of greater concern was how long it might take.

Somehow Darkwater needed to get the goods to Ted before the board meeting at Oostburg Bank, which was the day after tomorrow. He knew it was about noon now, and as a worst case, he assumed the board would meet first thing in the morning. That left the rest of today and tomorrow to tackle the hike, presuming getting to Crandon the night before the board meeting solved the problem. He'd have to move along at a pretty good clip, but he could do it.

Next, Darkwater thought about what he'd have to do once he reached Crandon. It might be late tomorrow night before he got to a pay phone and called Ted. Would that leave Ted enough time to get a courier to Crandon and back to Oostburg by 8:00 AM the following morning? The roundtrip drive would take about nine hours, if the courier originated down by Ted. It'd be theoretically possible, but it'd be really close. He'd be more confident if the courier service ran 24/7 and was responsive as hell, but he wasn't sure about either of those.

Darkwater's other option was to push himself really hard, and hope to reach Crandon early enough tomorrow to rent a car. If he'd a car, there'd be plenty of time to drive to Oostburg. But a car rental place would only be open to 6:00 PM at best, or 5:00 PM more likely. Time was wasting, so Darkwater came to a decision. He'd take the hiking trail to Crandon, and move along at the fastest pace he could sustain. If he got there early enough to rent a car, wonderful. If not, he'd call Ted and hope the courier service could get the goods to him on time.

* * *

With a new sense of urgency, Darkwater picked up his pack and set off. He'd a general idea where the trail was, and began bushwhacking in that direction. The going was slow, but fortunately the trail wasn't far.

Once on it, Darkwater tried several strides and paces, until he found a combination that moved him down the trail at the fastest speed he could sustain. While moving along, he kept his senses on high alert, and pondered what to do if he encountered another hiker. He probably couldn't avoid being seen, but he'd be able to tell the difference between a real hiker and somebody just there looking for him. In case he had to run, he wanted instant recognition and as much head start as possible.

After several miles with no encounters, Darkwater relaxed somewhat as he moved along swiftly. He turned his thoughts to practical matters. The trail roughly paralleled a stream and he'd been crossing small feeders regularly, so water wasn't a problem. But all he'd eaten this day was a half a piece of toast, and a few bites of scrambled eggs.

Also weighing on Darkwater's mind was whether he should press on throughout the night, or stop and rest. Physically, he'd probably be able to press on, but he wasn't convinced doing so was the smart move. The trail was reasonably well developed, but there'd also been plenty of roots, rocks and washout gullies. These're easily avoided in daylight, but not after dark. Loafers provided no support and if he sprained an ankle, he'd never make it in time.

Darkwater hiked throughout the afternoon, and on into dusk. He'd only encountered one hiker, a real one, who'd just nodded and passed him by. He'd deferred the decision on whether to press-on or rest, until the falling darkness revealed what kind of visibility he'd have in the moonlight. As dusk began to fade into darkness, the cloud cover thickened and he knew he'd have to stop.

Darkwater was still concerned that the tribal police were tracking him. Even more worrisome, they might have his scent and dogs. As he crossed a deer trail, an idea for another diversion occurred to him. He hoped the next stream crossing wasn't too far ahead, and he wasn't disappointed. About a half mile along he came upon one, and studied carefully the upstream and downstream directions. He decided he'd overnight downstream, in the direction of giant fir and pine trees and a sweeping bend around the back of a hill. He knew that water was the best bet for camouflaging his scent, and the trees and hill would help visually screen him and his campfire later on.

Darkwater waded downstream 20 yards, stepped out, and hid his backpack. Then he took off his sweaty shirt and black T-shirt, and put the shirt back on. To set up the diversion, he grabbed the T-shirt, waded back to the trail, and jogged down the trail in the direction he'd come from until he reached the deer trail a half mile back. There, he ripped the T-shirt into pieces, hid one shred at trailside where the deer trail crossed, and deposited the rest at intervals along the deer trail going uphill. If trackers with dogs came, the dogs would follow the deer trail and the sound of their baying would easily carry to his real campsite.

When finished, Darkwater jogged back up the trail, waded the 20 yards to retrieve his backpack, and then continued wading downstream. He waded around the bend, where the hill separated him from the trail, and began looking for a place to camp. Stumbling along in almost total darkness at a slow pace, Darkwater came upon a place with soft ground streamside on the right, and wetlands to the left. An old campfire circle, scuffed dirt, trimmed underbrush and other telltale signs told him others had overnighted here before. He dropped his pack and got to work. Darkwater would need a fire to see what he's doing, dry his clothes, and later for warmth. So, he gathered firewood and kindling first. While doing so, he noticed the edge of the marsh was lousy with nice-sized frogs. This solved the problem of what to eat, since frog legs were among his favorites. He used his butane lighter to start a fire, and set about catching frogs in the campfire light. Working quickly, he put them out of their misery with his knife, and impaled them onto a stick for ease of carry.

When enough frogs had been gathered for supper and breakfast, Darkwater used his knife to make skewers from underbrush branches. Then, he washed and cleaned the frogs stream-side, and skewered the legs for cooking over the fire. By the time he'd finished, there'd been plenty of coals for cooking. Once sated with frog legs and water from the stream, he carefully stored in his pack for morning, the rest of the frogs. Then, he rebuilt the fire for enough light to cut more underbrush and lay it across the top of two boulders, forming a primitive shelter.

Darkwater gathered dry windfall pine boughs. The fullest ones, he set aside to pull over himself as blankets. The scraggly ones, he stripped of their needles inside the shelter, forming a sleeping surface somewhat insulated from, and more comfortable than, the cold hard ground. Next, he stripped his wet clothes to dry by the fire, and pulled on his second set. When his original clothes were dry, he pulled them on too, enjoying the warmth. Then he warmed himself at the campfire one last time, doused the fire, put on his jacket, and settled into his shelter under a layer of thick pine boughs to sleep.

Darkwater awoke in the pre-dawn to the sound of tracker hounds, baying in the distance. Sonofabitch, they'd found the deer trail! He jumped up, stripped to one layer of clothes, packed, and sprinted by land back to the trail. He wanted the route to be obvious, to draw the tracker hounds to his campsite and delay them further. Once at the trail, he waded into the creek going in the opposite direction from the campsite, confident the dogs would be drawn in the wrong direction. Fortunately, the stream curved toward Crandon, parallel to the trail. After about 100 yards, he bushwhacked back to the trail. He'd have a head start, but he wasn't sure it'd be enough to beat his pursuers to Crandon.

※ ※ ※

Heading down the trail at his fastest sustainable pace, Darkwater rolled over in his mind the layout of the streets in Crandon. He recalled the car rental location, which thankfully was on the east or near-side of town. But he wasn't exactly sure where the hiking trail came out. He pulled up his memories of Crandon, so landmarks such as distinctive buildings would be fresh in his mind. He hoped these'd help him find his way to the car rental, once he emerged from the trail.

Darkwater kept up his pace all morning, pausing only to take in water at convenient trailside locations, and grab another frog leg to nibble. Physically, he's fine, but his worries over being caught from behind were growing. As the hours scrolled into the afternoon, another concern arose. Trail signs had been down at a few intersections along the way, so he'd stayed on what looked like the main trail. By mid-afternoon, he'd begun to panic over whether he'd taken a wrong turn. Rounding a bend, Darkwater spotted a trail junction off in the distance. As it grew nearer, he'd been heartened somewhat by the sight of a trail sign. But apprehension grew, as he covered the ground to the sign. Come on, come on, Crandon's nearby, right? YES! Crandon ahead, one mile and still no sound of baying hounds from behind. He kept marching without breaking stride, and thought about the dangers ahead. The dog trackers behind him likely had police radios, and by now pursuers everywhere knew he'd taken the trail to Crandon.

Sure enough, as he carefully approached the trail head, he saw a tribal police cruiser parked in the gravel lot. But he also saw familiar buildings across the street, and instantly knew exactly where he was, and what direction he needed to go. He back tracked a safe distance, and bush whacked parallel to the street in that direction. When he emerged onto the street, he guessed the car rental agency was about four blocks away. Without breaking stride, he crossed the street and headed in that direction. Motivated by a glance at his watch, he kicked up into the fastest jog he could muster. If closing time was five o'clock, even jogging may not get him there in time.

Settling to a walk just shy of the car rental place, Darkwater labored to even his breath. The sign in the window said hours were 9:00 AM to 5:00 PM, and it was 5:05. But the agent was busy with another customer at the counter, and the door was still open. Darkwater spent a moment to settle his breathing, and as nonchalantly as possible, walked in and got in line. A few minutes later the other customer stepped away, and the agent asked Darkwater for his driver's license and method of payment. Darkwater handed them over, and the agent initiated some small talk and went to work. Sonofabitch! He'd made it!

After being handed the contract and keys, Darkwater asked for two dimes, a nickel, and three quarters in exchange for a dollar bill. While the agent was making change, Darkwater asked directions to the nearest pay phone. With a smile on his face, the agent stepped over to the window and pointed at an intersection down the street. He instructed Darkwater to turn left there, and go two blocks to a filling station on the right, with a pay phone out front.

Peering over the agent's shoulder, Darkwater voiced his understanding and then froze, as a tribal police cruiser drove past. The agent went on to explain where out back, his car could be found. Darkwater thanked the agent, stepped to the window, looked both ways, eased out the door, and slipped around to the back lot.

Still on high alert, Darkwater decided to do a drive-by of the gas station. Sure enough, on a bench with a nice view of the phone, sat a man that had that DP-enforcer look about him. Sonofabitch, they're surveilling Crandon, too! Shortly after, he spotted another tribal police cruiser crossing the street up ahead. Fuck, fuck, FUCK! DP and the tribal police were all over the place!

What now? Think! Darkwater knew his pursuers

would recognize him. Hell, they probably had every pay phone in Crandon staked out, and god knows how many vehicles cruising the streets looking for him. But they didn't know he had a car, or the make and model. As he drove along, looking both ways down the cross streets, he spotted another cruiser a block over. If he kept driving around, they'd catch him for sure. He needed to go to ground, and thought about where in Crandon, would be the best place to do so. He recalled a parking lot that served a super market, general store, and restaurants and bars. By Crandon standards, the area generally drew a crowd. He decided to pull into the parking lot and lay low.

The last row of the parking lot backed up to a fence. Darkwater liked the idea of not having to worry about what was behind him, so he backed into the last row between two other vehicles. From this vantage point, he had a clear view of the busy lot and the commercial areas it served on either side of the street. He scanned the people and vehicles in view and passing by. Convinced he hadn't been discovered, he relaxed somewhat and thought about what to do next.

Darkwater wondered if it's possible to simply drive right out of town without being recognized. He decided to pay close attention to the direction and frequency with which tribal police cruisers and DP vehicles passed. Perhaps he'd be able to pull out a few vehicles behind one of them, and head to State HWY 55 and turn south. HWY 55 wasn't the fastest route south and east to Oostburg, but the only other way went back through Laona and Wabeno.

What Darkwater observed caused him to rethink his plan. The first cruiser and DP vehicle he'd seen had both passed right to left. He'd hoped they all would, as if circling in a regular pattern. Instead, they came from either direction at unpredictable intervals. If he pulled out behind one of them, another pursuer in oncoming traffic would have a clear and close-up view of his face. Watching all the people coming and going gave him an idea. Everybody wore hoodies and ball caps, with the green and gold of the Green Bay Packers most common. The majority of people also sported sunglasses. So, he risked a quick trip to the general store, and returned as just another Packer fan wearing sunglasses.

Once back in the car, Darkwater closely monitored the traffic. He waited for the next pursuer heading right to left in the direction of HWY 55, and eased out into traffic two cars behind. Sure enough, a few minutes later a vehicle driven by a big guy with that DP-look came along in the oncoming lane, nodded to the cruiser, and stared impolitely as he drove by. After he passed, Darkwater checked his rearview, and the DP vehicle kept right on going.

The cruiser turned off shy of HWY 55 but Darkwater kept going straight, and turned south when he reached the highway. He looked ahead, left, right, and in the rearview and all was clear. But a minute later, he came upon a string of tail lights. Darkwater pulled to a stop at the end of the long line, popped his door, and stepped out for a better look. Up ahead was a road block with two cruisers, one a County Mounty and the other tribal police. Forest County had joined the hunt!

CHAPTER 23

Photo Finish

O verdrive had slept surprisingly well the previous night. The last thing he remembered was
lying in bed praying for Darkwater's safety.
He awoke this morning with the sense that his father
deserved to know that his old friend was missing. Mary
agreed that the facts should be shared, but not the
speculations.

After the kids were off to school and milking was
done, Overdrive and Mary were just finishing breakfast when Old Bill drove into the yard. Overdrive rose
from the table, gave his wife a peck on the cheek, and
pushed out through the back door to meet him. He'd
given some thought to how to break the news, and had
decided to wait until after the filler pipes and blower
were fully installed on the second silo. This way, if his
father needed to take the day off, Mary could step in
and haul and unload wagons.

After finishing the job of moving the fill pipes, and
setting and connecting the blower, Overdrive broached
the subject while he and his father were enjoying the

afterglow of a job well done. Overdrive said, "Dad, we've learned some things from Ted Ritter that you should know about."

Old Bill grasped the straps of his coveralls with both hands, leaned back and looked his son in the eye, and said, "Okay, I'm listening. What's up?"

Overdrive exhaled heavily, and said, "Darkwater was supposed to rendezvous with Ted's courier in Wabeno yesterday morning, you know, to hand off the photos and whatnot from tribal council. But he never showed up."

Old Bill's eyebrows went up, "What? That doesn't sound like Darkwater. He knew how important that stuff was. Did Ted's guy call him, or stop by his house?"

Overdrive looked down at his shoes for a moment, "He stopped by. That's when he found out Darkwater's house and car had been destroyed by fire."

Old Bill jerked his hands off the straps, and into fists, "Is Darkwater okay?"

Overdrive, in a reassuring tone, "Yes, yes, at least as far as we know. No body's been found at the scene of the fire. And we know his lady friend picked him up, and they spent the night at her place, in Laona. But he's gone missing."

Visibly shaken, Old Bill put a hand on the blower for support, and said, "Missing? As in Ted's guy can't find him in Laona, either?"

Overdrive nodded, "That's right. Actually, Ted has a PI looking for him now. The morning after, while his lady was showering, Darkwater left a note and took off. The note just said *thanks for last night*. Nobody's seen him since."

Old Bill sat down on the blower's hopper, "What,

he stole her car?"

Overdrive shook his head, "No, no, nothing like that. As far as she knows, he left on foot. That's all we know at this point."

Old Bill propped his elbows on his knees, and held his head in his hands. After a moment, he said, "That makes no sense whatsoever. The bank meeting's first thing tomorrow morning, right? What're you going to do?"

Overdrive shrugged, "Well, Ted's PI is still looking for him. But we'll probably have to do our best at the bank without Darkwater's proof."

Overdrive kept the conversation going, hoping to at least get his father back on his feet. It'd been a big blow, and Old Bill was clearly reeling from the news. Overdrive tried several angles, but the most effective was sharing the timber quote, followed by a bald-face lie about how that'd surely put the farm over the top, and secure the loan. The rest of the day was spent filling silo. Not another word passed between them, but Overdrive had a suspicion that his father's need to stay busy, given the circumstances, was every bit as strong as his own.

✳ ✳ ✳

Overdrive was in a reflective mood as he milked the cows that evening. On the one hand, it'd been a highly productive day of silo filling. On the other, he might've just spent the day creating fodder that no beast would ever eat. If the farm fell to HMR, they'd probably blast down both silos and haul the rubble and silage away to the landfill. The entire day had gone by, and he and Mary hadn't heard a peep from Ted. This surprised them, and their anxiety grew by the minute. Losing the farm would be a sad state of affairs, for sure. But if Darkwater was also lost, they'd never forgive themselves and his father would be inconsolable.

After milking, Mary had the girls make popcorn while the rest of the family cleaned up. Overdrive took a seat at the kitchen table, and silently observed the familiar rhythms of the family around him. Marie popped corn while John tutored her on the underlying physics, as if she gave a shit. Kathy set out the bowls, while Joe teased her mercilessly about the Dutchman. Jumbo rubbed red hot on his sore football muscles. David shouted from the living room that McHale's Navy was about to begin. Overdrive had been born in this house. Hell, his father had been born in this house. The thought of losing it ... was just unthinkable.

Once the kids were out of the kitchen, Mary set the extension phone handset on the table in front of Overdrive, and took a seat near the wall phone. Their eyes met, Overdrive nodded, and Mary called Ted. Ted answered on the first ring, and after the niceties took a deep breath, and said, "I just got off the phone with the PI. The most interesting piece of news ... at about 5:30 PM Darkwater's Bank-Americard was used to rent a car in Crandon, 12 miles due west of Laona."

Surprised, Overdrive said, "Really! Does that mean Darkwater's okay?"

Ted thought about that, then said, "It could mean that, yes. That's certainly my sincere hope. But just to be clear, all we know for sure is the credit card was used. By the time the PI found out, the rental agency was closed for the day. He'll be there when it opens, tomorrow. The PI has a photo of Darkwater, and he hopes the same agent will be in, and able to provide a positive ID."

Mary, in a quizzical voice, "If Darkwater's okay, why hasn't he called?"

Staying neutral, Ted said, "Excellent question, Mary, I've been wondering the same thing. I don't have a good answer. He's got all our numbers, and even in a remote area like Forest County, there must be a few pay phones."

Overdrive interrupted, "Well, shit. Maybe he's headed in our direction. It's only what, a five-hour drive?"

Staying measured, Ted said, "That'd be wonderful if he was, James. It's just hard to understand why he wouldn't call ahead."

Overdrive conceded, "Yeah, I see your point. Is there any other news?"

Ted said, "Well, the PI checked back in with the authorities. Sure enough, the fire's been ruled arson. He also found out the guys working with the tribal police are from a private security outfit hired by DP."

Overdrive muttered, "Well, that figures. Sonofabitch!"

More upbeat, Ted said, "There's more. The PI checked back in with Robin Thunder. On the morning Darkwater disappeared, he'd been planning to borrow her car. For what, she didn't know. But say it was for the rendezvous. That'd mean he's still got the goods with him."

Mary, in a hopeful tone, "That's good, right? I mean, when we find Darkwater, he'll still have the proof that Rachel Wolf's behind HMR."

In a neutral voice, Ted said, "Yes and no. It's good in the sense you mention. But it also explains why DP and the tribal police are so keen to find Darkwater. They've got Robin's house under 24/7 surveillance. They may even be surveilling the few pay phones in the area. That'd explain why Darkwater hasn't called."

The conversation moved on to Oostburg Bank, and the meeting there the following morning. Ted did his best to convey a sense of confidence. After prepping, he felt there'd be a good chance the bank would move forward on the merits of the farm alone. Overdrive and Mary played along, but deep down they knew he'd just been trying to keep their spirits up. As the conversation wound down, they agreed to meet in the lobby of the bank.

Overdrive and Mary caught each other's eye when the call ended, and smiled weakly but in silence. Everything that needed to be said, already had been. Ready or not, tomorrow's the big day. Both were deep in their own thoughts, processing what they'd learned on the call. Mary was also monitoring the clock, as she always did on school nights. When the time came, she rose and began herding the kids into the bathroom and upstairs. Overdrive rose, grabbed the latest issue of Farm Journal, and settled into his stuffed chair in the living room as the kids would expect him to do. Their world may shatter tomorrow, but he figured he'd give them one more evening of normalcy.

* * *

After the kids were down for the night, Over-drive and Mary soon followed. They continued to respect each other's space, as they silently went about their bedtime routines. After crawling into bed and turning out the lights, they kissed and cuddled briefly, reassured each other, and said goodnight. Then Mary rolled over into her favorite position, and mercifully fell asleep.

Overdrive wasn't expecting sleep to come quickly, and it didn't. His mind filled with dark thoughts over the fate of Darkwater. Was it he that had rented the car? If so, where the hell had he gone? Why hadn't he called? Overdrive did his best to fight off even darker thoughts, but they broke through anyway. What if someone had taken the BankAmericard off of Darkwater's dead body?

Overdrive's sense of guilt was palpable. As recent days had unfolded, all the danger signs were there for him to see. Why hadn't he seen them? The Potawatomi were destitute. Gaming was their way out. Suddenly it's legal and a person in the know, Rachel Wolf, had volunteered to make it easy for them. Wolf wanted to move fast for the big money. The tribe wanted to move fast out of need.

For someone like Rachel Wolf, setting up shell corporations and greasing the skids for state agency approvals was just another day at the office. Land was needed for a reservation, so Wolf methodically began vacuuming up parcels of the headwaters of the Milwaukee River. She and the tribe were on a roll, seemingly everything was going their way. Then some guy shows up at tribal council with a camera and a tape recorder, and turns out to be tight with the family being forced off the last parcel. From Wolf's point of view, just another problem to solve.

How could Overdrive not have seen that coming? What'd he been thinking? Of course, Wolf and the tribe would act to shut that down. He'd put Darkwater in harm's way. If anything happened to Darkwater, it'd be on him. Not only was he a fool, but if the worst happened, he'd be the murderer of a close family friend. Even if by some miracle Darkwater showed up safe and sound, he'd already paid a terrible price by losing his house and car and probably his standing within the tribe.

Eventually, Overdrive tired of beating himself up. Instead, he ruminated over what could be done about any of this now. Tomorrow's the big day. Losing the farm meant it'd all been for nothing. Overdrive just couldn't let that happen. His mind ground on, and on, searching for something more he could do before tomorrow. Fatigue and exhaustion began to set in, and the ideas became fewer and further between. But among them was one worthwhile thought.

Overdrive had a firm written quote for the value of the standing timber. But for the excess cattle and hay, he'd reasoned what the values should be but had never actually done the calculations and written down his assumptions. He crept out of bed, careful not to disturb Mary, and silently left the bedroom.

Overdrive felt oddly refreshed, as though catching a second wind. With purpose, he assembled the latest farm magazines, along with a pen and pad of paper. He carried these to the kitchen table, sat down, and got to work. Within an hour, he'd developed solid estimates for the excess cattle and hay. With his mind finally at ease, Overdrive crept back into bed and instantly fell asleep.

* * *

Overdrive awoke with an uneasy feeling in the pit of his stomach. Morning milking had just begun when he caught sight of his father walking into the barn. It's highly unusual for Old Bill to arrive so early, and he guessed this's Dad's way of showing his support on the big day, coming out to help with the chores. The thought touched him, and he'd started to tear up, but caught it just in time.

After milking was done, Overdrive and Mary went into the house to clean up, change cloths, and attempt to calm down over breakfast. The kids had already gone off to school, and Dad had declined to join them for breakfast, saying he had plans in Cascade with some of the town fathers. Overdrive struggled mightily to pull himself together. He knew his 'A' game would be required at the bank.

Overdrive and Mary finished breakfast, cleaned up the dishes and table, brushed their teeth, and headed out the back door. Old Bill had hung around in the back yard to wish them luck on their way out. They appreciated the gesture, and that the elephant in the room hadn't been mentioned. It didn't need to be said. They all knew that either the bank loan would be approved today, or this multi-generational family farm would be lost forever.

Overdrive and Mary used the drive to Oostburg as an opportunity to tune themselves up, and get into the right frame of mind for what lay ahead. Mary began peppering Overdrive with the most pointed questions she could think of. Overdrive fielded them, and then they'd discuss what might've been a better response. Can you read? Did you read the Cascade Bank loan agreement? Then you realized your entire farm's real estate was collateral, and yet you signed anyway. Why is that? Are you aware that it's customary to engage a lawyer to review such agreements before signing? Then why didn't you? How long have you been borrowing from Peter to pay Paul? Are your farming decisions as reckless as your banking decisions? And so on.

By the time they got to the bank, Overdrive's version of dead man walking was long gone. His fight was back, and mind fully engaged. As they pulled into a parking space, a big grin spread across his face. When Mary asked why, he just shook his head. He'd been thinking his wife sure knew how to push his buttons.

Ted met them in the bank lobby, and used the moment to give them a quick update from the PI. The car rental agent provided positive ID that Darkwater had rented the car. Interestingly, Darkwater had also asked directions to the nearest pay phone, and broken a bill to get change to use one. Why no call had been received, remained a mystery.

Shortly, the three of them were led back to the office of the president, Peter Nyenhuis, for a last-minute chat. As events had unfolded, Ted had kept Peter apprised of the progress made connecting Rachel Wolf to HMR. Now, he and Peter worked together to winnow all that information down to the key points, which Ted would have time to cover in front of the board of directors.

Concerning the farm loan, Peter said that it's customary for the bank's own loan officer to present the loan application to the board. Overdrive and Mary were there to help answer questions that may come up. Since Peter had personally toured the farm, he'd also be able to weigh in when appropriate.

When Overdrive handed Peter the quotes for the timber and excess cattle and hay, he looked them over quickly, whistled, and called his assistant to make copies for the board. While waiting for her to return, he thumbed through his folder and confirmed Overdrive's cattle and hay estimates to be in the ballpark with those the bank had done. The documentation of income streams beyond the milk check, in his opinion, could only help.

Next, Peter briefed them, or rather Overdrive and Mary, on how to deport themselves in a board room. His advice was to sit up straight in one of the chairs around the outside wall, maintain a pleasant facial expression, and pay close attention. When asked, speak confidently and with authority at a volume loud enough for all board members to hear, and address them as sir.

Peter then reviewed the agenda. First up, would be the bank's loan officer to present the loan application. Peter said there'd likely be questions that'd fall to Overdrive and Mary. Mary should participate in answers where appropriate. Active participation of the wife in a family farm is viewed positively because it enhances the chances of success, and you want them to know Mary is actively involved.

Usually the room is cleared after the loan presentation and Q&A, so the board can deliberate and come to a decision. But in this case, Peter said he'd stand up to declare there's another essential factor to consider, and introduce Ted to explain. After Ted reviews what's known so far about Rachel Wolf's involvement in the events leading up to today, and the Q&A about that is finished, Peter will excuse the three of them to return to Peter's office, so the board can get to work. With the prelims completed, Peter stepped away to see if the board was ready to see them. Overdrive appreciated Ted's efforts to keep them calm and distracted with small talk while they waited. Having to sprint to the restroom and hurl, probably wouldn't enhance their chances of securing the loan.

* * *

A short while later, Peter stuck his head in the room, smiled, said they're ready, and Mary, Overdrive, and Ted fell into line behind him down the corridor. When they entered the room, the farm loan officer was already standing upfront, and the board members were seated around the table. Peter led introductions, the parties nodded or waved acknowledgement, and Peter directed Overdrive, Mary, and Ted to adjacent chairs along the outside wall. When everyone was settled, Peter asked the loan officer to begin.

Overdrive was impressed with the loan officer's command of his subject. He'd obviously studied their books and prepared for this day. Overdrive noticed that each board member had copies of the HMR nee Cascade Bank loan agreement, the Oostburg Bank loan application, another document summarizing the details of their farm, and the three quotes or value estimates he'd hand-carried to the bank. The board members were listening intently, paging through their materials to follow along, and taking notes.

After the loan officer finished speaking, the early questions were softballs that he could handle, but soon he began nodding them over to Overdrive and Mary. What motivated the farm expansion? With no hired help, how'd you manage to keep up with 40 more cows and 450 more acres? Walk us through how you estimated the amount of excess hay? What's the basis for the hay price you think you'll get? That's a lot of timber, why hadn't you harvested any before? As instructed, Mary actively participated in the back and forth. When each question was asked, Overdrive and Mary would lock eyes and decide who'd go first. Often the other would provide follow up to the same question. They both came across as knowing what's what, which was the god's honest truth.

Then, the tough questions came. A member of the board, "If you read the Cascade Bank agreement, why'd you sign it?"

Overdrive, "We'd worked with that loan officer for 20 years. He knew us to be reliable, and he knew farming. He knew that when weather or something else went awry, farmers needed flexibility and he granted it. We asked him point blank if that'd continue, he said yes, and we believed him."

Mary, "Then right after we took the first draw, Fond du Lac assigned our loan to HMR, and the customary flexibility evaporated."

Another member of the board, "You read the agreement, so why'd you violate it by taking those side loans at branch banks?"

Mary, "We'd met with people who called themselves bank presidents, and just assumed they'd both been independent banks. Had they introduced themselves as branch managers, we would've known to ask which bank they're a branch of."

Overdrive, "It was an honest mistake. Adell Bank had been independent back when my father and grandfather used them. Our John Deere dealer introduced us to the president of Glenbeulah Bank, and we never thought twice about it."

A third board member, "I mean no disrespect, because you seem like nice people. But has your farm been a Ponzi scheme all along, borrowing from Peter to pay Paul, or has it been a profitable business?"

Overdrive, "Never once had we taken a side loan, until HMR came along. With the farm real estate at risk, we needed a financial buffer so the HMR payments could be made with absolute certainty."

Mary, "We've been running that farm profitably for 20 years. We'd be happy to share our tax returns for as far back as you want them."

The pointed questioning went on and on, but Overdrive and Mary held their own. When finished, Peter stood up, set the room abuzz by dropping Rachel Wolf's name, and introduced Ted to explain. As Ted walked to the front, the room quieted, giving him their full attention. Without skipping a beat, Ted led the board through the entire sordid tale, from sportsmen's complaints, committee formation, recommendation, the new law, and so on. As the story progressed, Ted highlighted Rachel Wolf's hand in it at every step. Using her political connections to be named to the committee, building relationships with tribal leaders, deftly guiding the parties to an opportune outcome, lobbying for the legislation, and so on.

Ted layered into the story, Wolf's preparations to

position herself to quickly reap windfall profits from the new opportunity. The shell corporations, partnering with the Potawatomi, targeting the headwaters of the Milwaukee River or HMR site, and buying three of the four HMR parcels. For the fourth, the Evans Farm, she issued a loan based on an agreement customized by her, which in her view would inevitably lead to default and parcel seizure, once the loan was assigned from her state-chartered bank to her shell corporation known as HMR. The Potawatomi and DP, owner of HMR and another shell corporation, have already met with the two state agencies responsible for implementing the new law, and are expected to return with a firm proposal for a new reservation and casino sometime in October.

Ted wrapped up by saying that three nights ago, the Potawatomi Tribal Council gave its final approval of a joint venture with Wolf's shell corporations for establishment of a new reservation and casino at the HMR location. Rachel Wolf was there in person and gave the pitch that sealed the deal. Ted expected to receive photos of Wolf with tribal elders, an audio tape of the proceedings, and copies of Wolf's presentation and the HMR prospectus any day now.

During Ted's entire monologue, aside from his words and the sound of breathing, the room had been dead silent. When he finished, the room exploded with questions. Can't the Lyndon Town Board stop this? No, the lands will be held in trust by the state for the Potawatomi, and outside their jurisdiction. Can't Sheboygan County stop this? No, for the same reason. Isn't gambling illegal in Wisconsin? Not since July 1st, when the new law came into effect. And so on.

It went on like this for an extended period, and

Ted had an authoritative answer to every question except one. Do you have any proof in hand, right now today, that Rachel Wolf was behind HMR? The best Ted could do was swear that in a phone conversation, he'd personally been told by his envoy at tribal council, that photos, audio tape, presentation, and prospectus were in hand, and he could expect to receive them in a day or so. After the last question, Peter thanked Overdrive, Mary, and Ted for their time and excused them from the room.

* * *

After about 30 minutes, Peter ducked his head into the room and asked Ted to join him to answer a few more questions. According to Overdrive's watch only 15 minutes had passed before Ted returned, but in his mind, it'd felt like forever. Before Ted even had a chance to settle back into his seat, Overdrive and Mary were all over him, trying to find out what'd happened.

Ted explained that some of the board members were concerned that if they approved the loan, Oostburg Bank might be drawn into a lengthy and expensive legal battle with HMR, DP, and god knows who else. He reassured the them that HMR's only remedy, should any term or condition of the agreement be violated, was to demand payment in full within 30 days. Should full payment not be received, their only remedy was to march-in and take the farm and seize any personal property left behind. If the bank approved the loan and HMR was paid off before the deadline, HMR had no further remedy and the agreement was concluded. In this circumstance, there'd be no basis for HMR to go after

Oostburg Bank. Some board members still had concerns, so Ted asked them all to pick up their copies of the agreement, and he walked them through, line-by-line.

The board also put Ted on the spot about another issue. If tribal council met three nights ago and proof of Rachel Wolf's involvement was obtained, why wasn't it here in this room today? Ted tap-danced by saying he'd made a mistake and should've hired a courier rather than rely on the postal service. He feared that telling the truth about the fire and whatnot might backfire, and do more harm than good. Ted sensed that some had bought it, but he wasn't sure they all had.

Overdrive nodded his understanding to Ted, and reluctantly returned to the waiting game. On many occasions he'd heard people say waiting was the worst part, and now he knew why. He fidgeted in his seat. He stood up, and paced around the office. He sat back down, and fidgeted some more. Mary made funny faces at him to see if that'd help, but it didn't.

* * *

Finally, Peter came back into his office and had a seat at the conference table. Overdrive, Mary, and Ted all leaned forward in anticipation of the news. Peter, with a weary look about him, tented his fingers, and said, "The good news is, the loan hasn't been rejected. The bad news is, they're still at an impasse."

Just then Peter's phone buzzed, and he picked up, "Why yes, they're all still here in my office. Is that so. Well, who is it? Who?" He put his hand over the mouthpiece, "Does the name Darkwater ring a bell with anybody?"

Overdrive, Mary and Ted all gasped, then Ted recovered and said, "Yes."

Peter, "He wants to see you. Should I have my assistant bring him back?"

Overdrive, in a hopeful voice, "What? You mean he's here?"

Peter, "That's what I've been told. Do you want to see him or not?"

Mary seemed about to tear up, "Of course, we do!"

Peter, into the phone, "Hello? Yes, I'm back. Yes, please show him in."

Overdrive, Mary, and Ted formed an impromptu reception line by the door, while Peter remained seated, looking perplexed. The door opened, and in walked Peter's assistant followed by a living and breathing Darkwater, who'd been smiling until he got mobbed. All three wanted their arms around him, as if to make sure he wasn't some aberration. Mary began sobbing uncontrollably, and although Overdrive and Ted tried hard to fight it off, tears of joy began flowing down their cheeks as well. Slowly, the group hysteria untangled to more of a disheveled group hug, and they began speaking softly among themselves.

Peter stood, but respectfully gave them all the time and space they needed. He sent his assistant for fresh coffee, water, and lots and lots of napkins. When the group's chatter and breathing slowed to near normal, Peter asked, "Would anyone mind telling me what's going on here?"

More cognizant than the rest, Ted said, "Sir, that envoy we had at tribal council? It was Darkwater. We're … er … very glad to see him."

A new realization visibly washed over Peter's face, and he whispered, "Does he have the goods?"

Ted bobbed his head enthusiastically, and said, "Yes, he's got it all. Photos, audio tape, you name it. Right here in his backpack." When the assistant returned, they all sat down at the conference table. While the assistant poured coffee, everyone but Peter grabbed napkins and tried to make themselves look presentable again. Once all had gotten themselves back together, Ted led the introductions. Peter suggested that if there's additional information for the board to consider, it'd be best to get it to them as soon as possible. Darkwater dug the materials out of his backpack, and slid them across the table. Peter scooped up the photos and paperwork, and directed his assistant to make copies and distribute them to the board. Then, he pulled a tape player out of his desk drawer, popped in the tape, and told everyone to follow him.

❋ ❋ ❋

Unaccustomed to being interrupted during deliberations, when Peter knocked, opened the door, and led his minions into the room, the board's reception was cordial at best. Sensing the mood, Peter set the room abuzz when he said, "I apologize for the interruption, but as it turns out, proof of Rachel Wolf's involvement has just arrived."

The buzz in the room grew louder, as Peter set up the tape recorder on the table, his assistant distributed copies, and they began to page through the prospectus and presentation. Meanwhile, Peter directed Overdrive, Mary, Darkwater, and Ted into adjacent chairs along the outside wall, and had a whispered conversation with Ted. After allowing enough time for the board to skim the materials, Peter said, "I expect you may have questions. You know everyone here already, except for one. Please allow me to introduce Darkwater Flint. He's a member of the Potawatomi tribe, and served as the envoy at tribal council that Ted referred to earlier."

A member of the board, "Mr. Flint, these photos show Rachel Wolf with a microphone, standing in various locations on a stage, with some gentlemen in the background. What is she doing, and who are the men in the background?"

Darkwater, "The photos show Rachel Wolf pitching the selection of the headwaters of the Milwaukee River location, for the tribe's new reservation and casino. I believe you have a hardcopy of her presentation. The men in the background are elders from the various bands of the Potawatomi tribe. Together they make up tribal council, which is the governing body for the tribe."

Another board member, "How was Wolf's sales pitch received?"

Darkwater, "All elders but one voted in favor, and approval was granted."

A third board member, "I'm confused. The prospectus implies that DP's subsidiary HMR already owns all the lands called the headwaters of the Milwaukee River. If that's true, why're we here today?"

Ted interrupted, "Sir, you just hit the nail on the head. The HMR lands described in the prospectus aggregate four previously-existing parcels. As of today, HMR

LLC owns three of them, and Overdrive and Mary here, own the fourth. These materials were developed assuming Overdrive and Mary would default."

A fourth member asked, "Why'd they jump the gun?"

Ted said, "The short answer is greed and arrogance. The long answer, Wolf felt the default was in the bag, and wanted more time to prep for the state-agency meetings. They're on the hook to finish the legal work to donate the land to the state, draft language for the gaming compact between the tribe and state, develop presentations, get to Madison, and deliver the pitches, all by the end of October."

The room erupted in discussion. Any remaining disbelief that innocent people were being forced off their farm to build a casino quickly evaporated, and the loan was unanimously approved. After the handshakes, hugs, and backslaps, Peter asked Overdrive, Mary, Darkwater, and Ted to return to his office so the board and bankers could finish the formalities. A short while later the loan officer arrived with documents for Overdrive and Mary to sign, and then ran off to get the loan execution process into gear. Shortly thereafter, Peter arrived to let them know everything was set, and to escort them to the lobby and say good-bye.

After Peter left, Ted sprung the news that he'd anticipated a celebration might be in order, and had taken the liberty to reserve a private room at Four Pillars, his favorite restaurant. He suggested Darkwater likely had a tale to tell, and Old Bill should be there to hear it. Overdrive called his Dad from the receptionist's desk, and then they hit the street. Ted said he'd lead the way to Four Pillars, followed by Mary driving the Evans car, and Darkwater at the wheel of the rental with Over-drive riding shotgun to make sure he didn't get lost.

CHAPTER 24

Darkwater's Tale

The three-car caravan with Ted, Mary, and Dark-water behind the wheels had just parked, when Old Bill pulled into the Four Pillars lot. Old Bill and Darkwater slapped each other's backs, and then fell in behind the others. Once inside, the maître de led them to their private room, and everyone settled in comfortably. Beer orders were placed, and everyone perused the menu and ordered lunch when the beers arrived. Mary suggested they nurse their beers until lunch arrived, empty stomach and all, but everybody else just waved that off and went bottoms up.

Everybody was anxious to hear from Darkwater, but Ted decided to review the facts already known first, so he'd know where to start. Darkwater was impressed with what they already knew, and surprised a PI had been hired. He hadn't been aware that the fires were now officially ruled as arson, but he'd figured as much. He looked around the table to verify that everyone was ready to listen, and then described what happened at tribal council and afterword. By the time lunch arrived, he'd gotten as far as the following morning, when he saw the burnt remnants of his house and car on the local TV news.

Darkwater paused as the waitress set their lunches on the table, and took their order for another round. Then, everyone dug in and Darkwater continued to talk while he ate. With the only interruptions being potty breaks and more beer, he led his spellbound audience through the arrival of DP thugs at Robin's, fleeing on foot, setting diversions to misdirect trackers, discovering tribal police had joined the hunt, abandoning the idea of getting to a phone, and so on, right up to the road block on HWY 55 where he learned that Forest County had also joined the hunt.

* * *

At the road block, several cars up ahead made y-turns and went back north, which provided cover for Darkwater to do the same. He fled back to the hidey hole parking lot, to think. He knew of a large area with gravel pits and limestone quarries at the southern edge of Crandon, because he'd once investigated an abandoned flooded quarry there, as a potential fishing destination for his guide business. This parcel had access from Crandon and from HWY 55, south of the road block. The two access points were connected internally by a private road. Getting onto that private road, was a way to get out of Dodge.

Darkwater tried to recall the details of that parcel. It'd been years, maybe a decade, since he'd been there. He remembered that the private road was gated on both ends. The gates were open and manned during the work week, when the giant dump trucks rolled through. To get permission to enter, he'd had to call ahead and speak with the site superintendent. Even then, he couldn't see the quarry without an escort. It'd been such a pain in the ass, he'd never taken fishermen there.

In his mind's eye, Darkwater could see the gates. If they hadn't changed, they're nothing special. Just steel framing and wire mesh, with a chain and padlock. He formulated a plan, bought the largest bolt nippers the hardware store had, ate at the restaurant a few doors down, and returned to his car to wait for dark. While waiting, he observed his pursuers as they drove by in either direction. When darkness came, he pulled out behind one heading in the direction he needed to go, and went to the rock quarry's Crandon gate. The bolt nippers worked like a charm, and he was down the private road, and onto HWY 55 heading south in no time.

Starting out, every ten miles or so Darkwater executed a maneuver designed to detect whether he'd been tailed. After three of these, he'd been confident enough to just drive on. As the need for vigilance waned, so did the adrenalin that fueled it. The road was winding and full of potholes, it was pitch black, and after a while weariness began to set in. Rather than run off the road asleep at the wheel, he decided to get a room at a cheap motel near Shawano. He could've called Ted then, but didn't because it's the middle of the night. He figured he'd call in the morning.

Darkwater had intended to get up at the crack of dawn, and make Oostburg Bank by 8:00 AM. He usually rose naturally by dawn, but just to be safe, he also set the alarm. The alarm clock didn't work, and as it turned out, neither did nature. He'd been so exhausted from the previous day's hike, and the hours of hyper-vigilance, that he'd overslept by several hours.

Frantic to get on the road, Darkwater took a quick shower, dressed, packed, hopped in the car, and took off. He'd completely forgotten about calling ahead until out on the highway, and decided not to delay him-self further, by stopping to make a call. Getting from Shawano to Oostburg hadn't been a problem, but once there, he'd had to stop and ask directions and didn't get to the bank until 10:30.

When Darkwater finished his tale, his audience sat in silence for a moment, each lost in their own thoughts. With so much to process, words were hard to come by. Overdrive was literally stunned with admir-ation for the resourcefulness and stamina that Dark-water had demonstrated. One by one they stood and stretched. Mary walked over and gave Darkwater a big, long hug. The men just slapped him on the back and shook their heads. They all ambled to the restrooms, trying to wrap their minds around what Darkwater had gone through as they went.

* * *

Everyone returned from break with a boat load of questions for Darkwater. A bit cheekily, Ted said, "Darkwater, the bank board's at an impasse, we're all sitting in Peter's office one heart-beat away from car-diac arrest, and in you walk. What part of *call me* don't you understand?"

Darkwater, with a mischievous grin, "Just being unselfish, you know, sharing the drama. Hey, I picked on-time arrival over calling, and it turned out."

Old Bill, "Old friend, you've lost everything. What're you going to do?"

Darkwater shrugged, "To tell you the truth, getting out of Dodge alive required my full attention. I haven't even thought about it. I guess I'd better figure something out pretty quick, though, because I'm supposed to guide some fishing clients up in Eagle River next week."

Brow furrowed, Overdrive said, "Do you have what you need? I mean, was your guide business gear lost in the fire?"

Darkwater shook his head, "No, thank god. I work out of a resort in Eagle River, and store things there. I'm still good to go for earning a living, at least."

Ted, in a professional tone, "The house and car were insured, right?"

Darkwater nodded, "They'd been insured, but being arson, I'm not sure what that means. Hell, for all I know, they'll try to finger me as the firebug and not pay."

Ted shook his head, and said, "That's not going to happen. I won't let it. After all you've done, it'd be my pleasure to represent you in the matter, at no cost. We can easily prove your whereabouts, and that DP and the tribe had motive."

Darkwater sighed with relief, "I'd like to take you up on that offer. Any idea how long it might take to get a payout? I'll need a car, place to stay, and clothes."

Ted thought about that, then said, "Well, that's a very good question. I'm not sure, but I promise to get the wheels turning first thing in the morning."

Darkwater, "Thanks. I know I'm in good hands,

I've seen you in action."

Overdrive and Mary had been whispering back and forth while listening. Overdrive said, "Darkwater, Mary and I'd like to front you the money for a car. You can pay us back when the insurance money comes in. We're out from under HMR now, and there's leftover financial buffer no longer needed for that fight."

Darkwater, breath hitching in surprise, "You've no idea how much that means to me, thanks. When I say self-employed to a bank, they hear unemployed, and borrowing isn't easy. It's humiliating, and never ends well. Thank you both."

Mary put on her impish grin, and said, "There's no need to thank us, Darkwater. If not for you, we'd be homeless vagrants in ten days."

Darkwater mimed a bright idea with a temple tap, "Good point, one good deed deserves another. You know, I've had my eye on Corvettes for a while, and Ford just came out with something called a Mustang. Is this a blank check?"

Fists on hips, Mary shot back, "Ha, don't push your luck! How about picking something Robin would consent to be seen in publicly, but nothing more."

Overdrive mimed call me, "The leftovers are meager, call before you sign."

Darkwater, hands up, "Okay, okay, I hear you. Just good enough for Robin."

Old Bill asked, "You need a place to stay before going north?"

Darkwater's eyes narrowed, "Tonight would be great, but I'd better head back tomorrow. I've got a lot to do. See Robin, hopefully get her to pick me up when I drop the rental ... find a car and a place to live ... buy some clothes."

Ted said wisely, "I highly recommend you come to my office first thing tomorrow. We need to call your insurance company together. After you introduce me as your legal counsel, I'll find out their initial thoughts on hurdles to clear before they pay. If they're inclined to consider you a suspect in the arson, we'll engage the authorities and start the process of getting you cleared. If need be, I'll keep my PI up there until this is cleared up, or drive up myself."

Darkwater, "I can do that. It sounds like you think I've got a problem."

Ted nodded, now grim, "If you're an insurance company, arson is code for no need to pay. We need to nip that in the bud right away. We do that by pointing the finger at those with motive. I'm thinking we leave the tribe out of it, and just finger Rachel Wolf. We've got plenty to back that up. She'll settle with the insurance company to keep this quiet, keeping them whole when they pay you."

Darkwater said, "Wow, Perry Mason in my corner. Wouldn't have guessed it in a million years. James and Mary picked a good one, when they picked you."

Ted, dead serious, "Actually, Darkwater, I appreciate the opportunity. For generations now, it's been personal between the Wolfs and Ritters."

As before, Overdrive and Mary had been whispering back and forth while listening. Overdrive broke into the conversation, "Darkwater, while listening Mary and I realized that you're going to need cash right away. We'd been planning to cut a cashier's check tomorrow morning at Cascade Bank, anyway, to transfer all of our account balances to Oostburg. Now we're thinking we'll cut two cashier's checks, the second one being to you. An when you pay us back, deduct all those run-for-your-life expenses like the car rental and hotel. Those're on us."

Darkwater sat back, astonished, "I'm speechless. I really am."

Old Bill had been silently ruminating on his old friend's situation, and said, "Old friend, this may be a stupid question. But are you sure it's safe to stay among the tribe? I mean, there's bound to be hard feelings, isn't there?"

Darkwater eyed Old Bill, and nodded, "You're right. That might be a problem, at least for a while. There're others in my band that still remember the spring pilgrimage, and the warm welcome received from your family. Once they hear the underhanded way Wolf tried to steal the farm, they'll understand why I did what I did. But the tribe in general? There'll be hard feelings, for sure. Then there's the fact that I'm half white, which doesn't help either."

Brow furrowed in worry, Old Bill asked, "So, what're you going to do?"

Darkwater shrugged, and said, "Well, like I say, I haven't had a chance to think about a lot of this. The resort up in Eagle River that I work out of? Well, the owner likes me. He knows I bring in a lot of his repeat business. He's made me a standing offer to rent one of his cabins to live in. Maybe it's time to do so."

Old Bill bobbed his head, and said, "You should do that."

Ted, in a serious tone, "The fewer people that know which cabin you live in, the better. Ask the owner to keep it on the down low, and only tell people you trust. It'd also be a good idea to have your mail forwarded to a P.O. Box."

Brow furrowed, Mary asked, "What about Robin? Is it safe for her?"

Darkwater shrugged, and said, "That's a really good question, Mary. I don't know. Things have happened in the last few days that I never would've thought possible. Before all this happened, Robin and I were close to taking the next step. And some of those resort cabins are big enough for two."

Mary said wisely, "You two need to talk. Even if Robin isn't ready to move in, she may need to get out of where she's at. If anything happened to her, you'd never forgive yourself."

Darkwater smiled, winked, and said, "We'll have that talk. I'm pretty sure Robin's ready to move in. She likes excitement, and who better to provide it, right? Hell, I'll be damn near irresistible once I own a car she'll be seen in!"

CHAPTER 25

The Dream Lives On

With the fear of losing the farm lifted, life returned to normal for the Evans family. Overdrive and Mary milked the herd morning and evening, and between times pressed forward with the seasonal work with the help of Old Bill. The kids did their chores during milking times, went off to school on weekdays, and helped with the seasonal work on weekends. The second silo was filled. The daily bunk wagons to the Side Hill pasture transitioned from fifth-cutting hay to leftover field corn. The weather held nicely, and the ear corn was picked before the stalks began to break down. The Mcintosh apples were followed by Jonathons and Idareds in early and late October. Garden and orchard produce had filled the freezer and every jar, crock, and bushel basket, with squash yet to pick and potatoes yet to dig.

Overdrive felt as though he'd learned a thing or two living through the ordeal. He was more resilient. He used to have a reasonably long fuse, but then explode in anger. Now he had a longer fuse without the boom at the end. Oddly, things that used to set him off, he now felt grateful for. The weekly blather about Old Bill's driving heard at Art's Service Station or Reinhold's Grocery, he now interpreted as genuine concern for the well-being of his father. Mary stepping into the breach when needed, being resourceful, and always seeming to call the right shots, he now saw as a major reason why the farm was successful. Joe's whining about always getting the shit jobs still irked him, but hell, nobody's perfect.

It'd been an incredibly difficult and stressful year for the entire family. Being prey to an unknown predator was bad enough. Discovering the predator had been their bank, made it that much worse. Almost losing Darkwater, literally, had pushed them to the edge. Through it all, Overdrive and Mary had done their best to shield the kids from the gravity of the situation. But even so, with the possible exception of little David, they'd sensed that something was terribly wrong. Maybe the experience will make them all more resilient, who knows.

When he thought of the kids, Overdrive couldn't help but shake his head and smile. Sure, he and Mary were proud that the kids were all growing up responsibly, doing well enough in school, and developing strong work ethics. But a more diverse and dissimilar cast of characters, would be hard to imagine. Jumbo the athlete and heartthrob. Joe the Eddie Haskell of the clan. Kathy being literally jail bait, and recently showing a knack for its promotion. Marie seemed to sense that her milieu wasn't normal, and tried to cope with humor. John either knew entirely too much about the underlying physics of everything, or he's one hell of a bullshitter. David had a sixth sense for being present when his grandpa carried a candy bar. Somehow, Mary and he'd been able to expand the farm with only the help of this motley crew plus Old Bill. Incredible, when you think about it.

Overdrive still had worries, of course. Would Jumbo and Lizzie Flint work out? Would Jumbo choose to go farming? How would he bridge to the ancestors after his father passed away? Would it be creepy having Dad on the other side? Then there's Rachel Wolf. Should they let it be, or try for some sort of justice for what she'd put them through? Wolf still owned three of the four headwaters of the Milwaukee River parcels. Would she try again to force them off the farm? If they sought justice, would she be more likely to try again? Or, is she the type to just relentlessly keep trying no matter what, until stopped once and for all? These're all worries, but not urgent ones. Overdrive had time to manage them. At least he thought he did.

THE END

ACKNOWLEDGEMENT

I'd like to acknowledge the contributions of my late parents, Warren and Adeline, for bringing me into this world and into a special way of life experienced by few then, and even fewer now. In a similar vein, my late grandfather, Marvin, late siblings, Jim, Tom and Nancy, and surviving siblings, Sue and Dan, deserve mention. My life experiences on a family dairy farm were enriched by them all, and led to the authentic feel of my fictitious setting, characters, and family dynamics.

Having avid fiction readers to serve as reviewers is essential for first-time authors like me. According to one of mine, treading water with a 35-pound kettlebell chained to a leg would've been less strenuous than reading my first draft. Several revisions later, I hope you enjoy the final product. Many thanks to Paula, Zach, and Jared Hughes, Tim and Liz Vane, and Whitie and Ricci Knutson for helping me polish the manuscript. Special thanks to Tim, for delivering the toughest love with great humor.

ABOUT THE AUTHOR

Patrick J. Hughes

The author was raised on a dairy farm in Sheboygan County, WI. He went on to become the first member of his family to graduate from college, earning two engineering degrees from the University of Wisconsin-Madison and another from Stanford. Novel writing is his second act following a long career fighting climate change while employed at a major research university, large and small consulting firms, and a leading national laboratory. Although his research career led to over 130 publications, when it comes to writing novels, he's a first-time author. He currently resides in Oak Ridge, TN, with his wife, Paula, and together they have two grown sons, Jared and Zach.

Made in the USA
Middletown, DE
23 June 2021